THE NATURE OF A WOMAN

THROUGH THE EYES OF A MAN...

Also by Sylvester Stephens
The Office Girls
Our Time Has Come

THE
NATURE *OfA*
WOMAN

THROUGH THE EYES OF A MAN...

SYLVESTER STEPHENS

SBI

STREBOR BOOKS

NEW YORK LONDON TORONTO SYDNEY

Strebor Books
P.O. Box 6505
Largo, MD 20792
http://www.streborbooks.com

ISBN-13   978-1-59309-233-7
ISBN-10   1-59309-233-4
LCCN 2008943280

First Strebor Books trade paperback edition March 2009

Cover design: www.mariondesigns.com
Cover photograph: © Keith Saunders/Marion Designs

10 9 8 7 6 5 4 3 2 1

Manufactured in the United States of America

For information regarding special discounts for bulk purchases,
please contact Simon & Schuster Special Sales at 1-800-456-6798
or business@simonandschuster.com

DEDICATION

To my Masonic Family,
"Free & Accepted Masons Prince Hall Affiliated,
The Order of Eastern Stars, The Heroines of Jericho"

INTRO

I t is said that the admission of ignorance is the beginning of wisdom. Over the past couple of years my life has been turned inside out and so has my soul. It began on a night when my wife, Alicia, was hosting a poker party with a group of friends. They called themselves "The Office Girls."

I was supposed to be securely tucked away in my sanctuary, the basement as it is more commonly called, while the office girls had their gala upstairs. Unbeknownst to my wife, the ventilating system in our home also served as a hidden microphone. As long as they were in the den I could hear practically everything that they said. I could also sneak out of the basement and walk in the backyard and see what they were doing as well. I know what I was doing was deceptive but I wanted to understand the behavior of women when they were not in the company of men. I convinced myself that it was all for the benefit of science.

The office girls arrived and they were in rare form. They pulled out the cigars, the beer, the liquor; the whole nine yards. Alicia had a huge round table delivered. I don't know how they got that big thing through the doors, but they did.

I gave them an hour or so to settle in and then I snuck in the backyard and hid behind a tall bush. The bush was in front of a long picture window that was almost from the floor to the ceiling. My eyes became crossed as I tried to peek through the window with one eye. I thought hearing them would be a problem because I was outside but they were so loud I could hear them clearly.

They sat in a circle from left to right; Alicia, Wanda, Lisa, Susan, Pam, Darsha, Cynthia, Valerie, Tina, and Tazzy. It didn't take long before they were drunk or at least acting drunk. I must admit, I don't think Alicia was acting. I think she was completely and absolutely, drunk!

"All right! All right!" Alicia said. "It's time for everybody to tell a secret they've never told anybody else."

"Not tonight, Alicia," Valerie said while shaking her head.

"Can we just play cards?" Darsha asked.

"You already know everything about me," Susan added.

"Well, you already know everything you're going to know about me, so don't even turn your discussion this way," Cynthia said.

"Me too!" Tina shouted.

"Me three!" Darsha followed.

"This is what tonight is supposed to be about, we, as women, sharing our secrets. I'll start it off and I hope the rest of you follow suit."

"No it ain't, Alicia," Valerie said, "tonight is supposed to be about getting paid!"

"Anyway, I'll go first and somebody better go next," Lisa said.

"Go 'head, girl," Wanda urged.

"Lately I've been finding good men but they can't seem to match where I am economically."

"Economically?" Wanda asked. "Just go on and say they broke."

"I won't say broke, but they can't bring what I can to the table."

"But what if they love you, or treat you the way you want to be treated?"

"If they can't match what I bring to the table there's no way they can treat me the way I want to be treated, Cynthia."

"Come on, y'all, don't turn this wonderful night into a female pity party!" Valerie whined.

"I'm serious," Lisa said. "If I bring the biscuit he better at least bring the butter."

"Good point," Valerie said. "Now let's get back to the game."

"No, my turn," Alicia sighed. "I love my husband, but I'm scared to death my marriage is not going to work."

"Dayum!" Valerie snapped.

I was stunned. I thought our marriage was perfect. I think even the office girls were surprised by Alicia's little secret. The room was quiet and all attention was on her.

"Why would you think that, Alicia?" Cynthia asked.

"I don't know," Alicia said while playing with her chips. "I just never had a healthy relationship with a man and I'm not sure if the problem is me or them. I'm just afraid."

"Wow!" Pam looked concerned. "But you can have any man you want."

"That's not my problem. My problem is what I want from a man and what that man wants from me are two different things. I mean my own father didn't want me."

"Damn!" Darsha said. "I didn't see that coming."

I didn't see it coming either. I was numb from head to toe. I had never heard anything negative about her father or our marriage. If anyone should have picked up on those signs it should have been me. But I didn't.

"I'll be fine though, if it doesn't work, then it's nothing new," Alicia said discouragingly. "I'm preparing for the worst."

"Where is this coming from?" Cynthia asked.

"From my heart," Alicia spoke softly.

"Girl, Johnny loves you and that's all that matters." Cynthia hugged Alicia.

"You gon' be okay?" Valerie said as she picked up the deck of cards.

"I'll be fine."

"Then let's get back to the game!"

The card game resumed and I was about to go back to my sanctuary when Pam mumbled something that momentarily interrupted their game and my return to the basement.

"I wanna say something," Pam whispered.

"You?" Alicia sounded surprised that Pam wanted to be open with the group.

"Yeah, me," Pam said. "But once I get this out I don't ever want this to be brought up again!"

"Go 'head on, my niggah," Wanda said as she blew circles of smoke from the tip of her cigar.

"Just say it!" Darsha said anxiously.

"Come on now, y'all, I'm winning." Valerie was becoming very annoyed. "Are we here to play cards or have an open mike session on our broken hearts?"

"You're so insensitive," Susan said.

"*You're so insensitive*," Valerie sarcastically mocked Susan.

"Go 'head, Pam, I want to hear this." Tina turned her chair in Pam's direction.

"Well, I can't tell you everything but there's something I've been wanting to share ever since we became close, but I can't."

"Oh yes you can! You done already interrupted our poker game now!" Valerie said.

"Anyway, I, uh, when I was young, before I had my son, I had a little girl and I gave her up for adoption."

"DAYUM!" Darsha shouted.

"DAMN!" Wanda screamed.

"Are you serious?" Cynthia asked.

"Let me finish, y'all!" Pam interrupted. "This ain't easy for me."

"We're listening," Tazzy assured Pam. "Continue."

"The main reason why I'm having a hard time forgiving my mother about giving me up for adoption is because I did the same thing to my child. It eats me up inside. My child's father and I fought during my pregnancy and I didn't think he wanted the child. I didn't want to raise a child alone so eventually I had to give her up for adoption. He wasn't there for me! My father wasn't there! No man has ever been there for me. And I'm pissed off to this day because of it!"

Pam slammed her fists on the table making the poker chips fly in the air.

"Calm the hell down, Pam! That ain't gon' help nobody!" Valerie shouted while grabbing her poker chips.

"Get that girl a valium." Wanda laughed.

"You okay, Pam?" Cynthia asked.

"I feel better. Much better." Pam smiled.

"You okay for real, Pam?" Valerie asked.

"I'm good."

"Okay, back to the game."

Pam sat out the rest of the game and watched as the other office girls continued to play competitively. They had different poker chips worth ten cents, twenty-five cents and one dollar. They started off playing for fun, but the longer they played, the more serious the game became and Alicia was the biggest loser. Wanda had taken over as the biggest winner and she was ready to close out in style.

"Whose turn is it to deal?" Tina asked.

"Mine!" Wanda shouted.

"You just dealt, Wanda!" Darsha shouted back.

"I got to make this money!" Wanda shouted.

"I need this money more than you, Wanda," Alicia said.

"No the hell you don't! I got to feed those big-mouth kids of mine. Yo' skinny ass don't even eat!"

"Here we go." Alicia laughed.

"I'm serious, y'all," Wanda said as she shuffled her cards in her hands. "Them dam' kids will eat hell off the cross and reach back for the crown!"

"I have no idea what that means, Wanda." Susan chuckled.

"You ain't suppose to know, Snow White."

"I got kids." Tina tried to take some of Wanda's poker chips. "Let me win."

"Niggah, I'll cut that hand off!" Wanda grabbed Tina's hand. "You got kids, but you got good kids. Kids that won't rob you in yo' sleep if they need lunch money. My kids are bad! When I whoop their asses, they try to whoop mine back. That's why I keep my taser handy and when them little son-of-a-bitches get outta line I tase them!"

"Wanda, stop lying!" Valerie said.

"Y'all heffas gon' start believin' what I tell you, when I tell you!" Wanda went into her purse and pulled out a taser gun.

"Girl, you know that's not real," Lisa said.

Wanda held the taser in the air and cut it on. "Now! Who want to be the first to get they ass stung to see if it's real or not?"

Wanda stood up from the table and started to chase the office girls around the room. She pinned Susan in a corner and pointed the taser gun at her.

"You better quit playing, Wanda!" Susan held her hands in front of her, keeping Wanda at a distance.

"Come on, Snow White."

Tazzy walked behind Wanda and tried to knock the taser out of her hand.

"Put that thing down before you hurt somebody, girl!" Tazzy laughed.

When Tazzy didn't knock the gun out of Wanda's hand, Wanda turned toward her and pointed the gun in her direction.

"Oh, I see," Wanda walked closer to Tazzy, "you gon' turn your back on a sister for Snow White."

"You better stop, Wanda." Tazzy backed up and stood behind Valerie. "Get that fool, Val."

"Don't be standing behind me, Tazzy!" Valerie pushed Tazzy away and ran in the opposite direction.

Everybody scattered in different directions, running away from Wanda. Tina was still sitting her seat, laughing hysterically. Tazzy ran behind Tina's chair, separating herself from Wanda.

"Y'all get away from me!" Tina shouted.

"Wanda, stop it!" Tazzy laughed.

"Too late now! You tried to go against the people! Once you go white, you know you ain't right!" Wanda kept pointing the taser closer and closer to Tazzy.

Tina jumped out of her chair and ran past Wanda, leaving Tazzy with just the chair between her and the taser.

"Okay, Wanda," Tazzy said, breathing hard. "What do you want, ol' crazy girl?"

"Now we talking," Wanda said, "I want your chips! Poker and potato! And, um, I want your jacket."

"Wanda, your big ass can't fit that girl's jacket!" Valerie said.

"Again, with the insults." Wanda turned toward Valerie and ran in her direction.

"I ain't runnin' from your big ass!"

Valerie stepped to the side and pushed Wanda on the couch. Wanda fell on the taser, accidentally firing it into her side.

"AAAAAH, SHIT!" Wanda screamed. "OH LAWD HAVE MERCY!"

Wanda collapsed on the couch and her body started to convulse. Her eyes went back into her head, and she kept moaning. I wanted to run into the house to her aid but I didn't want Alicia to know I had been spying on them. She didn't seemed to be injured so I stayed outside. And to be frankly honest, it was funny as hell.

"Oh my God!" Tazzy said while running to Wanda's side. "What did you do, Val?"

"I ain't do nothin'." Valerie kneeled beside Wanda and held her hand. "Wanda, you all right?"

"Give her some room to breathe," Lisa said while putting a cool paper towel on Wanda's forehead. "She'll be okay, just give her some room to breathe."

Tazzy and Valerie backed away as Lisa continued to talk to Wanda.

"Wanda?" Lisa rubbed her arm. "Wanda, you okay, baby?"

"Aw," Wanda moaned over and over. "What happened?"

"Sit up, baby." Lisa helped Wanda sit up.

"When I find out which one of you bitches shot me with that thang I'm gon' kick yo' ass!" Wanda said as she rubbed her side.

"That's what y'all get for always playing so much!" Cynthia sat on the other side of Wanda and held her hand.

"That's what I get?" Wanda asked Cynthia. "I almost died!"

"You didn't almost die, Wanda," Darsha said. "You just got shocked."

"Just got shocked?" Wanda asked Darsha. "I just went beyond and back. I saw the bright light and everythang!"

"If you don't shut the hell up I'm gon' tase your ass again!" Valerie said.

"Yes sir!" Wanda said.

"Yo' fried ass layin' up here still talkin' shit!"

"Leave me alone, Cleo," Wanda joked as she put her taser back in her purse.

"Who the hell is Cleo?" Valerie asked.

"Ha! Ha! Ha!" Darsha laughed. "That's Queen Latifah in *Set It Off*!"

"Give me that dam' taser!" Valerie tried to snatch the taser out of Wanda's purse.

"Get this man off of me!" Wanda screamed.

The office girls continued to babble as I walked back to my basement and sat in deep thought. Shortly thereafter, I heard Alicia coming down the stairs.

"You okay down here, baby?" Alicia asked.

I wanted to say hell no, but I pretended everything was fine.

"Yeah, sweetheart, I'm fine."

"Okay." Alicia smiled. "I was just checking on you."

She started to run back up the stairs and then I called her back.

"Alicia!" I yelled.

"Yeah, baby." Alicia peeked her head around the banister.

"Are you happy?" I said. "I mean, are you happy with our marriage?"

"I couldn't be happier."

She looked me right in my face and lied. If she could open up and be honest with her friends, why couldn't she be honest with me? Women always complain about opening up and being honest but I guess that means they want men to open up to them. Alicia went back upstairs excited and happy while I sat in my basement, confused and bewildered. I thought I understood the nature of a woman. The way they thought. The way they behaved. The way they reacted. Apparently, I didn't know shit.

There are over six billion people in the world and we are separated by only a mere six degrees. In the grander scheme of life, six degrees out of three hundred and sixty degrees can be construed as minuscule. But each journey begins with a solitary degree, or a solitary step. It all depends on those whom you meet along the way. Each person that you meet connects the three hundred and sixty-degree circle from your origination to your destination. Case in point, the journey to find one's self can be a pilgrimage around the world or a walk from the backyard to the basement.

CHAPTER ONE

My name is Johnson Forrester. I am a former National Football League player. Today, I have a bachelor's degree in business management, a master's degree in sociology, and a doctorate degree in psychology. As a psychologist, I specialize in the emotional, behavioral and mental processes of the human psyche. Until recently, I had been a mental health clinician for the prison system. I have analyzed hundreds of men, both during their incarceration and their transition from prisoner to citizen.

Having achieved a respectful career in my field, I was encouraged by my mentor, Dr. Warren Glover, to start my private practice. He had recently retired and wanted to leave the mental health care of his newest patients in the hands of someone he trusted. Building a trusting relationship with new patients in the field of psychology is very important to the growth of their willingness to communicate. Dr. Glover thought I would be a perfect fit.

Taking Dr. Glover's advice, I started my own private practice in the city of Atlanta, Georgia. Atlanta wasn't far from the prison I was working for, and I needed to branch off and expand my career. Not to mention, I also had family in the area.

I was initially apprehensive because I wasn't just opening a new office, I was beginning a new type of practice altogether. Assuming responsibility for Dr. Glover's old patients meant that my new patients would be women and women only. Having never had female patients on a consistent basis, my familiarity with the female psyche was undetermined. I contemplated the probability of being unsuccessful but failure was not an option for me. Failure could mean losing my professional reputation, God forbid, wiping out my life's savings.

Getting my practice up and running was more challenging than I had anticipated but where there's a will, there's a way. My wife and friends helped where they could and, before I knew it, I was standing in my office staring at my degrees on the wall.

I reminisced over the years it had taken me to arrive at this point, the disappointments, the extremely hard work, and then I smiled. Because in the end, the final step of your journey is what it's all about. It's not about the road you've traveled, because life doesn't allow you to turn around and go back. It's about your final destination. It's about where your life ends up.

Ironically, my journey to becoming a psychologist began on the couch and not in the classroom. Earlier in my life, I was diagnosed and treated for erotomania. It is more commonly known as nymphomania. Erotomania is a psychological disorder marked by the delusional belief that one is the object of another person's love or sexual desire.

Looking back on my youth, my behavior had all the signs of being emotionally disturbed. Not insane, but disturbed. I had an unusual desire to be accepted and loved by other people. That need for someone else's approval made me lack confidence throughout my life.

My first experience with confidence came when I was fifteen years old and I had my first sexual encounter. I was a sophomore playing football on the varsity team. I didn't get a lot of playing time, but to be the only player who was not a junior or senior brought me a lot of attention.

One day after practice, my girlfriend Regina and I were walking home. She was a junior, so I was quite proud to be dating an older woman, so to speak. We went over to her house to hang out. Her parents worked in the plant so they were never home until the late evening. We listened to music and then wrestled, but nothing serious.

That particular afternoon, we went further than usual. We were lying on Regina's bed and started to kiss. She was using a lot of tongue, something I wasn't used to doing. It felt good, so I thought what the hell? During our friendly wrestling match, I positioned myself between her legs and we started to grind. Regina closed her eyes and began to moan rather loudly. She slid her hand between my legs and squeezed my manhood.

"Take it out," Regina said.

"Take what out?" I said.

"Your thang, I wanna see it."

"Huh?"

"Take your thang out, I wanna see it."

"You take it out," I replied.

"Okay."

Regina had always told me she was a virgin. The football team always told me she wasn't. Some admitted that it was hearsay; others claimed it was firsthand experience. Judging by my experience with her, she was not a virgin but an expert.

"Take your clothes off, Johnny," Regina said.

"Why?"

"Just take your clothes off!"

"Hold on," I said, standing to remove my clothes.

After I kicked off my shoes and pulled off my shirt, Regina unbuckled my pants and snatched them to the floor. She had already stripped herself of her clothing and was waiting for me to join her in the bed.

"Come on," Regina said, pushing her linen to the side and opening her legs. "I'm ready, come on."

That was not the fantasy I had envisioned, but I couldn't afford to let this opportunity to lose my virginity get away. I thought that it would be my passage to manhood.

"Don't I need a rubber or something?" I asked.

"Naw, boy, if you pull it out I can't get pregnant."

"You sure?" I asked.

"Yeah, come on. Put it in."

"Okay," I said, grabbing my manhood and then trying to push it in. "Ouch!"

"What happened?"

"It hurts! It won't go in."

"That's my thigh!" Regina said. "Move your hand, let me do it."

Regina grabbed my manhood and guided it in.

"Ah," Regina said, grabbing my ass.

She kept moaning and talking incoherently. I didn't say a word because it felt kind of weird. It didn't feel the way I had imagined. I was expecting a euphoric sensation but it was wet and uncomfortable. However, it must have felt pretty darn good to Regina because she seemed to enjoy herself.

She kept moving her hips and moaning, and I kept pumping. Her moans became louder and my pumping became faster. I assumed she reached her orgasm because she started to scream and her body began to jerk. She pulled my face to hers and rammed her tongue down my throat. I thought to myself, *DAMN! This is a grown-ass woman!*

"Keep going! Keep going!" Regina said.

Following Regina's instruction, I kept going. The feeling was okay, but nothing that made me want to moan. And then all of a sudden, I felt this sensation at the base of my manhood. My arms started to shake. My eyes rolled back in my head. And like a volcano, that unbelievable sensation shot up my manhood and out through its head.

"OH!" I shouted, collapsing on top of Regina.

"See!" Regina said, trying to squeeze out every drop of juice that I had. "This feels good, huh?"

I heard Regina asking me a question, but I couldn't answer. My orgasm felt even better in real life than it had in my dreams. When I could finally answer, all I could say was, "I love you."

"I love you, too," Regina said.

Of course we didn't love each other, but it felt great to say it to one another. Regina and I had sex a few more times over the next year or so, and each time we said to the other, "I love you." I guess I knew she didn't love me, but at least I was getting the attention I wanted.

I coined that terminology as my own and that became my method of operation. I would make love, and when I had my orgasm, tell each woman I loved her. If she said it back, fine, if she didn't, fine. Actually, my avowal of affection was always reciprocated. Even with my one-night-stands.

As I got older, my sexual desire became stronger and I experimented more. Traditional sex became boring to me. I didn't want to be in a monogamous relationship so I dated married women or women who were in other relationships. I fulfilled the desires their husbands and boyfriends did not. I became their fantasies, telling them I loved them and giving them the attention they wanted and needed. I was attentive and sensitive.

One married woman finally decided to leave her husband after we had been seeing each other for years. I didn't break up her marriage. She was seeing another guy at work and her husband found out. She told me she had feelings for her lover, but she thought I would try to compete with him for her affections. I told her that if she cared for her lover, he should be her choice.

Her pride wouldn't allow her to say it, but she was disappointed that I wasn't ready to fight for her. She tried to insult me by saying I was happy with always being the *"other man."* I let her know that I wasn't the *"other man;"* I was actually *"the man."* I was having sex with her without having to deal with her annoying spoiled rants. As far as I was concerned, once she became available, her value to me diminished.

After I became bored with attached women, I decided to delve into one-night-stands. The thrill of telling a woman I loved her on the first night we met was a turn-on. And hearing her tell me she loved me back, even though I knew it was bullshit, intensified my orgasms.

Which brings me to Yvonne. I met Yvonne one night when I was on a date with another woman. Yvonne had a light complexion, very smooth with no blemishes. Her hair was long and curly. She had a thin shape, not much hips. Her eyes were big and she had long eyelashes that accentuated them.

As I was dancing with my date, Yvonne waved at me. Her friends pointed to her and then me while I was on the dance floor, making Yvonne's intention obvious. When I sat down, she wrote her telephone number on a piece of paper and passed it around five tables to get to me. My date never had a clue.

Eventually, I called her and we hit it off. We didn't live in the same city so it took a while before we had our first date. One week, her job sent her to town for training. We made plans to meet on her last night. We went out to eat and then back to her hotel room. It was late so we didn't pretend that we were not going to make love.

We kissed for a while and then took off all of our clothes. We kissed and then Yvonne rolled on her back. I was a passionate lover and I was expecting Yvonne to be passionate. She was, but she didn't want a lot of foreplay. We had sex in the missionary position only, but that was all we needed. It lasted for a long time and, if I must say so myself, pound-for-pound, I would rank her as one of my best sexual experiences.

I enjoyed myself so much that I went against my one-night-stand rule. The next day, I packed an overnight bag and drove an hour and a half to her house to spend the night. I was going to make love to her all night, get up the next morning two hours earlier than usual, and go directly to work.

When I arrived at her house, she told me to place my bag in her bedroom. As I was changing from my work attire to my casual gear, Yvonne received a telephone call. I couldn't hear the conversation, but I assumed it was private when she stepped outside to her porch. Giving her privacy, I stayed in her bedroom until I heard her come back in the house.

"Did you get settled in?" Yvonne asked.

"Oh, yeah," I said.

"Oh," Yvonne said, "one of my friends is going to be stopping by."

I remembered her friends from the nightclub, and from my recollection, they were fine as hell. I began to fantasize about having Yvonne and one of her friends at the same time. That would have certainly made the drive down worthwhile.

Yvonne paced back and forth from the living room where I was sitting to her front door. Finally, her friend pulled into the driveway. Yvonne stood at the door and waited for her to get out. I peeked out of the window to see which one it was, but I closed the curtain when I realized she would see me looking out.

All of a sudden, Yvonne walked into the living room and said nervously, "If my friend asks who you are, tell him you my cousin, Johnny, from New Jersey, okay?"

"What?"

"Just say you my cousin!" Yvonne demanded.

Yvonne walked to the door and opened it. A tall older gentleman walked in and kissed her. I didn't know what type of freaky shit Yvonne had in mind, but I was not going to be a part of it.

"Hey, Alton," Yvonne said, pointing to me. "This is my cousin, Johnny from New Jersey."

"Hey, Johnny," Alton said, looking at me suspiciously.

"Johnny," Yvonne said, "This is my friend, Alton."

"Your friend?" Alton asked.

"What's up, man?" I said.

"Can I talk to you for a second, Yvonne?" Alton asked.

"Yeah, let's go back here." Yvonne walked toward the bedroom.

They went into Yvonne's bedroom and started to scream at the top of their lungs. Alton did most of the screaming. They became quiet and then walked out as if nothing had happened.

"Well, Alton's getting ready to go," Yvonne said, walking him to the door.

"I ain't going nowhere," Alton said.

"Yes you are!" Yvonne said.

"Watch and see."

"Alton! Would you leave?"

"You want me to leave, huh?"

"Please," Yvonne said. "I will call you later."

"I'll leave, but I want to talk to you first."

"Okay, Alton. I'll be right back, Johnny. I'm going to walk him to the car."

They walked outside and I sat in the living room. It was taking a while for Yvonne to walk back into the house so I peeked outside the window to see what was going on. Alton was yelling and going into his trunk. I didn't know what he was going in his trunk to get, but I'd be damned if I sat around and waited. I calmly went into the bedroom and got my bag and then walked outside to my car. Yvonne left Alton and ran over to my car.

"Don't leave, Johnny!" Yvonne said.

"I think it would be better if I left."

"He's getting ready to leave."

"I ain't goin' no dam' where!" Alton shouted.

"I think you need to talk to your friend over there," I said.

"Let me get you something to drink before you leave."

"Okay," I said, sitting in my truck.

"I'll be right back," Yvonne said, running into her house.

When Yvonne slammed her door behind her, Alton started to walk toward me. I didn't know what he wanted so I got out of my car.

"What's up, man?" I said.

"Hey, bro," Alton said. "I don't know you and you don't know me. I ain't tryin' to start no shit wit' you, man, I just want the truth. That's all I want! Yvonne ain't yo' cousin, is she?"

"You have to ask her that, man."

"Come on, man," Alton said, looking as if he was about to cry. "I love that woman, bro! Do you?"

"Again," I replied. "You need to talk to her, man."

"Bro!" Alton said, looking very angry. "This is killin' me! Just tell me the truth! Please!"

I was saved by the bell when Yvonne walked out with a can of Sprite in her hand.

"Here you go!" Yvonne handed me the can.

"Thanks!" I said, climbing back into my truck.

"You don't have to leave, Johnny. He's getting ready to go."

"Yes, I do," I said. "You two need to talk, Yvonne. Obviously, there's a big misunderstanding."

"It ain't no misunderstanding. Alton needs to go!"

"I told you, I ain't goin' nowhere," Alton said.

"Well, I am," I said. "I'll talk to you later, Yvonne."

"Okay, but I really wish you would stay."

"Take care," I said.

I drove the hour and a half back home prepared to take a cold shower. When I checked my voicemail I had three frantic messages from Yvonne. From what I could decipher, someone had been shot and she was at the hospital. She called the next day and explained what had happened.

"Hey, Johnny," Yvonne said.

"What were those voicemails all about?"

"Oh my God!" Yvonne said. "After you left, Alton pulled his gun out of his trunk and put it to my head!"

"What?" I asked. "Are you serious?"

"Yeah! He told me he couldn't live without me and if he couldn't have me, nobody could!"

"What happened?"

"He said he couldn't hurt me, so he pointed the gun at his chest and then pulled the trigger!"

"He shot himself?"

"Yeah! Right there in my front yard!"

"Is he okay?"

"He's on life support right now!" Yvonne said. "They don't think he gon' make it!"

"Wow!"

"I went to the hospital with him and then I had to leave before his wife got there. But the last thing I heard, he wasn't doing too well."

"His wife?" I asked.

"Yeah, he's married."

"Hold on," I said. "That man tried to kill himself because he didn't want his mistress to be with anyone else?"

"I guess."

"He's a fool!"

"Johnny," Yvonne said, "I need you to come down here and be with me."

"You can't be serious?"

"I need you."

"You could have gotten me killed!"

"He wasn't going to hurt you, Johnny," Yvonne said. "He never tried to hurt me or the guy, it's always him."

"Bye!"

"Johnny, please don't hang up!" Yvonne said. "You said you loved me!"

"Bye, Yvonne!"

"I love you, Johnny!"

"BYE!" I shouted.

I hung up the phone and decided that one-night-stands were no longer my cup of tea. After that, I thought I would try the monogamy thing for a while. I tried desperately to maintain a monogamous relationship, but whenever I met a woman, we would have sex immediately. The thrill of monogamy would be gone and I would move to my next monogamous relationship. During the course of one week, I had five monogamous relationships, and all were sexual. My last go at monogamy was with a young lady named Ariana.

She was born in Brazil but raised in the United States. She was about five feet four inches tall with long, jet-black hair. She had beautiful, brown skin, toned legs and a nice round ass like a black woman.

Ariana spoke Portuguese and English fluently. I spoke Spanish a little, but not Portuguese. I really didn't care if I knew what she was saying or not—just to hear her speak a foreign language in the midst of hot sex was a turn-on.

We talked on the telephone every day for a month. I convinced her that we had known each other long enough to commit to one another. She agreed and we decided to meet at an international nightclub.

Ariana and I had a ball bumping and grinding against each other. We danced practically all night long. After we left the club, I asked Ariana to come back to my house. She thought I was being presumptuous and rejected my offer. Not wanting the night to end, I suggested a five-star hotel. I don't know if making love in a hotel was more virtuous than making love in my house, but she agreed.

I left my car at the nightclub and rode with Ariana. When we got to the hotel we took our clothes off and stepped into the shower. I lathered Ariana's body from head to toe and then she turned around and lathered me. My manhood was standing at full attention, sticking out like a shotgun. Ariana took her time and massaged it from the head to the base. Her hands felt so soft as she squeezed it lightly from top to bottom.

I sucked her hard nipples, which protruded from her breasts. The steam from the shower filled the bathroom with seductive smoke that increased the sexual tension between us. Our bodies fell against the wall of the shower as our cleanliness turned to nastiness. We kissed and fondled until we couldn't take it anymore.

"Come on," Ariana said, taking me by the hand.

We fell on the bed, wet and sudsy. Our bodies were slippery as we rubbed against each other. Ariana opened her legs and grabbed my manhood.

"Oh, *Papi*, it's so big!" Ariana said.

"You like that?"

"Oh, *si*," Ariana said. "But I don't know if I can take it all."

"I'll be gentle," I said, assuming that being gentle meant going slowly.

Ariana and I had wild and crazy sex that night. When the sun was coming up, we were still having sex. That hot Latina kept me up all night. I mean that literally and figuratively. But all good things must come to an end. I had an unwritten rule that daylight would greet me alone. Spending the night with a woman was fine, but waking up with a woman was against the rules.

Even though Ariana and I didn't go to sleep, the rule still applied. I had to hurry and have my orgasm and get the hell out of that hotel room before the sun turned me into a pile of dust.

"I'm about to blow, baby!" I shouted.

"Oh, *si!*" Ariana shouted, moving her sweaty legs up and down the back of my legs like a frog. "Oh, *si!* Oh, *si!*"

"Oh shit!"

"Oh, *si, Papi!*" Ariana shouted. "Shit!"

Ariana's Spanglish was turning me on. I was stroking so deep it felt like I was inside of her stomach. I twirled her hair in my fingers and pulled her head backward to look her in the eyes.

"You like that?" I said, stroking even deeper.

"*Mucho gusto!*" Ariana screamed. "*Mucho gusto!*"

"Oh shit, I'm coming!" I shouted. "Oh God, I love you, baby!"

"I love you, too, *Papi!*" Ariana screamed in my ear.

I reached beneath Ariana and palmed her ass in my hands. I lifted her off the bed, she wrapped her legs around my waist and I pounded her until I was completely spent.

"Oh, *Papi!*" Ariana said, breathing very hard.

I turned on my back and tried to catch my breath. Ariana climbed on top of me and kissed my chest and neck.

"Oh, Johnny!" Ariana said. "I love you so much!"

"Okay."

"Okay?" Ariana lifted her head and looked at me in the face. "What does that mean, okay?"

"You said you loved me and I said okay."

"Okay! Now I got it!" Ariana jumped off the bed and started putting on her clothes. "When you were between my legs you were in love with me, but now that you got what you wanted, you don't love me no more, huh?"

"Calm down, Ariana."

"You men are all alike!" Ariana walked into the bathroom and slammed the door behind her.

Ariana stayed in the bathroom a while and when she finally stormed out she was fully dressed and headed straight for the door. I thought to myself, if she had her clothes on, then whose clothes did she have in her hands?

I rolled over to the other side of the bed to look on the floor for my clothes, and they were gone. Ariana sped up her trot and ran out of the door before I could catch her. I wrapped the comforter around my waist and stood in the doorway screaming for her to come back.

"ARIANA!" I yelled. "Bring my damn clothes back!"

I stood there waiting, but she didn't return. My first thought was to sneak to my car and get out of there, but I didn't have my car. Not only that, I didn't have my keys or my wallet.

"Damn!" I said, slamming the door and sitting on the bed.

I was forced to call one of my college buddies and have him bring me some clothes. Of course, he brought along more of the guys and they ragged me all the way home.

I called Ariana all day long and she refused to answer. I didn't know where she lived or where she worked. My only means of contact was her telephone number. Oh, I begged and pleaded so much she eventually felt sorry for me and told me to come get my shit.

I called some of my friends and we rode five deep to Ariana's house. I had my friend Tommy drive, because my nerves were a little shaken. Oh, I went in all by myself, but I told my boy to keep the car running. Just in case.

"Hey, Ariana," I said. "I'm sorry if you misunderstood me this morning."

"I don't think I misunderstood you, Johnny."

"I really care about you, Ariana, I really do."

"Whateva!" Ariana responded. "Just get your shit and get the hell out of my house, okay?"

"Okay." I reached for my keys and wallet, which she was holding in her hands.

"Hold on one second, mister!" Ariana said. "You think you can play with women's emotions and get what you want and then drop them like a hot potato, don't you?"

"I don't know what you're talking about," I said, still holding my hand out.

"You are a selfish, mean, rude pig!" Ariana said. "Here!"

Ariana slammed my keys into my hands. I could have just walked off and left things as they were, but I couldn't. I was pissed off and I wanted her to know she was wrong.

"Maybe the next time you should know a man longer than a month before you have sex with him," I said. "Maybe then, you won't be so disappointed when you find out that's all he wanted."

"What?" Ariana asked. "What did you just say to me?"

"Look," I said, sensing homicidal anger. "I think it's best if I leave."

"No!" Ariana said, running to the back. "No, you stay right there, mister!"

"Oh shit!"

I ran out of her house and jumped in the backseat of the truck.

"Go! Go! Go! Go! Go!" I shouted.

"What's up?" Tommy shouted.

"Man, just go!" I yelled. "She's getting a gun!"

Tommy sped off as Ariana was running to my truck with a gun in her hands, screaming at the top of her lungs.

"Man, what you do to that chick?" Tommy shouted.

"Nothing man, just go!" I shouted, ducking as much as I could beneath the dashboard.

We sped away and I considered it to be another unfortunate incident with a woman. I never gave it a second thought.

CHAPTER TWO

Monogamy and I didn't mesh, so I wanted to explore my wild side. I wanted to try an alternative lifestyle. The pleasure of having sex with women just for the sake of having sex was no longer a challenge for me. I knew what to say to the groupies for a one-night stand if I was in the mood. I knew what to say to women in relationships who had to make it seem as if they were having problems with their husbands or boyfriends. And I knew what to say to single women looking for a relationship. I told them all the same thing, or made them think the same thing: I loved them.

I had mastered the art of communication with women. Once I realized what type of man the object of my affection fantasized about having, I listened, studied, and became that man. I knew eventually I would disappoint them but my objective was to make love, not friends.

I felt no guilt! No sympathy! Nothing! It was not my fault that women could not accept men for being men. They had to make us into unrealistic fantasies. So, I became that fantasy.

As I said, my next thrill would be an alternative lifestyle. I wanted to explore the world of homosexuality. I know what you're thinking, but hell no! I wasn't referring to me and another man. I wanted to make love to a lesbian. I felt that had to be the ultimate challenge.

Playing in the National Football League had its advantages. My fame attracted those who may not normally be attracted to me. For example, Trinity. I met her at a sports bar, a gay and lesbian sports bar called The Ass Bar and Grille. I went with a bisexual friend of mine, Greta, who had told me it might be a great place to pick up a male-curious lesbian.

We sat at the bar for a long time just chatting with each other. Trinity and her girlfriend walked in and sat beside us. My lesbian friend, Greta, who was actually bisexual, pointed them out. Greta was a six-foot, blonde bombshell from Sweden. She had endless long legs, huge firm breasts and deep blue eyes. She was an international model introduced to me at a celebrity party in New York.

She and I met and had sex during my one-night-stand phase. She was one of the few who actually understood the terminology of a one-night stand. Because she was bisexual, and not totally homosexual, she didn't count. She did teach me how to properly perform oral relations on a woman. It was like a class. Lights on, visual presentation, and then the oral test for my final grade. It was given on her, so she was happy with her teaching and my learning skills. Greta taught me to be passionate, patient, and unselfish.

Although Greta was a wonderful experience, I needed a bona fide, woman-only lesbian to satisfy my desire. The way Trinity was swinging on her girlfriend's arm, she had to be a straight lesbian, so to speak. And boy, was she gorgeous!

Greta got their attention and invited them to come over and drink on our tab. Who turns down free booze? They joined us and we hit it off. They were familiar with who I was and knew plenty about football.

"I can't believe I'm talking to Johnny Forrester!" Trinity said.

Trinity was white, with brunette hair and a tight, fit body. She had to be a former athlete. That body couldn't have been natural. Her girlfriend, June, wasn't bad looking, either. The more we talked as a group, the more our conversations became one on one. June and Greta had their own conversation and Trinity and I had ours.

Trinity was a financial advisor and that was our excuse to swap telephone numbers. I asked her a lot of personal questions. She made it perfectly clear that she was happy with June and our relationship would be strictly business. She also told me she had never been with a man and had no interest in being with another one.

She kept her word until I told her I was falling in love with her. I used her logic against her. She told me on one occasion that love shouldn't be restricted to men and women. Love should be shared between two people who love each other, regardless of the gender. I told her that she was being hypocritical because she would not allow herself to love me because I was a man. I finally got through to her and she started to have feelings for me.

I asked Trinity why she loved June so much. She told me June was very attentive, very passionate and understanding. This was the same information other women had told me. After receiving that information, I became much more attentive and passionate. I made everything about *her*. I sent flowers for no reason. I planned spontaneous romantic getaways. I did everything June did and more. Eventually, Trinity was telling me she loved me and she had to figure a way to get out of her relationship with June.

She broke it off and invited me over for a romantic evening to consummate our relationship. We had a nice romantic dinner and then headed for the bedroom.

"Oh, Johnny," Trinity said as I placed myself between her thighs.

"You ready, baby?" I asked.

"Oh, God, yes!" Trinity said, opening her thighs. "I want it all, Johnny! I want to feel every inch inside of me!"

"Put it in."

Trinity took the head of my manhood and guided it into her wet vagina.

"Wait!" Trinity said, squirming around. "Wait a minute, it hurts!"

"Okay!" I stopped and then entered slowly. "Is that better?"

"Aw, yeah," Trinity said. "Go slow, like that."

Trinity and I moved slowly until she became used to having a man inside of her instead of a strap-on.

"Give it to me, baby!" Trinity shouted. "I want it deeper! I want all of that black stick inside of me!"

She asked for it, so I gave it to her, hard and deep. She screamed, shouted, yelled, bit me, scratched me and then cried.

"I love you!" I shouted as my orgasm hit.

"I love you, too!" Trinity screamed. "I love you, too, Johnny!"

After we had our orgasms we continued to hug and kiss. I wanted to watch television but Trinity wanted to ask questions, questions I really didn't feel like answering.

"So, this is what it's like to be with a man, huh?" Trinity asked, rubbing on my chest.

"Yes."

"This feels good. I feel like I want to be around you twenty-four hours a day. I want to spend every minute with you."

"Uh, okay."

"What's the matter?" Trinity asked.

"Nothing," I lied.

"Something's the matter, you're acting strangely."

"I think we need to slow down."

"Excuse me?" Trinity said. "What do you mean exactly by 'slow down'?"

"I just think we're moving a little too fast here, that's all."

"Johnny, I broke up with my girlfriend because you said you loved me. I made love to you because you said you loved me. And now you say we're moving too fast."

"I never asked you to do any of those things."

"You're right, sweetheart," Trinity said. "I overreacted." Trinity kissed me on my neck and then rubbed my chest. "I love your manly chest."

"Thank you, baby."

"You ready for round two?" Trinity asked.

"Yup!" I said. "You?"

"Oh, yeah, baby. I'll be right back."

Trinity went into the bathroom and then came out and straddled me. She started to grind on me and my manhood began to rise. Trinity lowered herself on top of me and leaned forward and kissed my neck.

"Aw, you feel so good inside of me," Trinity said.

"Ride it, baby."

Trinity lifted my arms above my head and placed my hands together. The next sound I heard was not that of seduction, but entrapment.

CLICK!

"Hey, what's that?" I could feel tight handcuffs around my wrists.

"Do you think you're going to ruin my life and just walk out on me?"

"Trinity?" I said. "What are you doing? Take these things off!"

"You're the master of deception, Johnny. Manipulate your way out of those handcuffs!"

"This is not funny, Trinity!"

"You're damn right it's not funny!" Trinity started to put on her clothes.

"Where are you going?" I asked.

"I'm going to find my woman!" Trinity replied.

It was almost five o'clock in the morning and this woman was going to find her ex-lover. Leaving me handcuffed to her bed. I was afraid and uncertain of what was going to happen. Night turned to morning, and then morning turned to afternoon. All the while, I was lying naked in Trinity's bed, exposed and waiting for her to return.

I heard the door open downstairs and then I heard her walk upstairs. She passed the bedroom I was in, but did not enter. I heard her scrambling around in the bedroom next door. Next, I heard her walk downstairs and then out of the door.

I tried to use brute force to break the handcuffs but I couldn't. My legs were free but they couldn't do me any good. Because of the way I was handcuffed, with my arms above my head, I couldn't get any leverage to use them to my advantage. I twisted and turned, jerked and pulled, but no matter what I did, those handcuffs wouldn't budge.

I realized I wasn't gaining anything. I was only losing energy. I was hungry, tired, and exhausted. I decided to reserve my energy just in case Trinity returned with some hired hands to finish me off.

I couldn't believe what was happening to me. I tried to be optimistic about getting out of Trinity's house without incident. But how could I? Surely she knew I was going to be pissed off and she was going to protect herself.

Saturday afternoon became Saturday night and then Saturday night became Sunday morning. I hadn't eaten in almost two days but as much as I resisted, Mother Nature consumed me and I relieved myself. It was an incredibly uncomfortable situation but I had no alternative.

Around ten o'clock Sunday morning, Trinity walked in and unlocked the handcuffs as if nothing had happened. She walked downstairs and out of the door. I wiped myself and quickly put on my pants. I was weak from the lack of nutrition over the last couple of days, but I had enough strength to put my clothes on and get the hell out.

On my way to my car, I kept looking around waiting for someone to come out of the shadows. I couldn't believe she just unlocked me and wasn't afraid that I would retaliate or at least call the police. I got in my car and drove off, looking in my rearview mirror waiting for someone to appear.

After that humiliating experience, I left women alone for a while and tried to focus on my football career. I was introduced to my first wife, Deirdra, at church, and we started to date. I fell in love, at least, I thought I fell in love, and we were married.

One year after our marriage, my daughter, Brittany, was born. She was the joy of my life. I slowed down slightly with my obsession for women, but I didn't stop. I had a wife and child at home and a woman in every city.

Deirdra began to find out about my affairs and threatened to leave if I didn't stop. I was so arrogant I believed that in spite of my many affairs, she was not going anywhere. She tried to be a good wife and stay by my side, but the women became too much a part of our private lives. One day when I arrived back in town from an away game, she had packed her bags and left.

She asked for a divorce and I didn't fight her on it. Not having Deirdra and Brittany at home, my sexual appetite was at an all-time high. I started to miss practice because I was having orgies in my home in the afternoon. My coach called me into the office and told me I was suspended from the team for an indefinite amount of time. That indefinite time became the rest of the season. Right before mini-camp of the next season, I was released.

My sexual addiction had caused me to lose my family and my job. I was a professional football player with multiple pro-bowl honors. But I was also a multimillionaire, single and out of control. My preoccupation with sex dominated my mind making everything else secondary.

Although I was still in my prime as far as football was concerned, no other team wanted to gamble on me because of my problems off the field. I was considered a character risk and I never played another down in the NFL.

The reality of being out of football was an eye-opening experience for me. I decided to seek counseling to try to regain control of my life. Fortunately for me, the result of that counseling transitioned my obsession for women to atonement for my past.

I sincerely wanted to make amends for the female victims I had emotionally destroyed as objects of my affection. I needed to understand what made me behave the way I did; contrarily, what made those women allow me to behave the way I did. I thought that by understanding my own psychological inadequacies I could somehow constructively redeem my past. That motivated me to go back to school and further my education, where I attained my master's and doctorate degrees.

But as much as I would love to say that I was completely cured of my addiction, I'd be lying to you and myself. It will always be a daily battle, a battle that takes tremendous strength and resistance; a battle that I have won on some days and have lost on many others.

One may ask: why would a sex addict place himself in such a vulnerable position in terms of temptation? Some say that if women are your addiction, why do you opt to counsel *"only"* women? The answer is both simple and complex. Simply put, my sexual addiction was caused by my obsession to gain the attention of women. Women had always been the validation of my manhood, beginning from my very first experience.

Consequently, women served as the source of my self-esteem. Not my family! Not my friends! Not my coaches! Women! As a matter of fact, my lack of self-esteem stemmed from my parents' emotional neglect and inability to show real affection.

I was born the younger of two boys in Buena Vista, Michigan. It's a small automotive town located near the city of Saginaw. My parents were religious fanatics. They believed in two things, heaven and hell. If I followed their beliefs, I was bound for heaven, but if I did not, I was on a fast track to hell. As far as I was concerned, hell couldn't have been much worse than growing up in my parents' house. Even though I screamed for their love, I received no positive affirmation from them.

Well, my mother wasn't the problem. Ma was an angel. My problem with her was that she allowed my father to chastise and bully me. In my mind a mother should protect her child and Ma should have prevented Pop from terrorizing me.

In Ma's defense, she showered me with love when Pop wasn't around to antagonize us. Pop, on the other hand, was brutally critical of me. Nothing I did was ever good enough for him. He never expressed any sense of pride for me or in me. Pop and I never really got along, but for my mother's sake, we got by.

Although I pretended not to want his approval outwardly, I needed his approval and also his love. He was emotionally unwilling to give me either one of them. So, out of spite, if I couldn't get his loving approval, I would rebel and make his life a living hell, just like mine. I tried everything under the sun to upset our perfect little household. Lying, stealing, robbing; anything I could do, I did it. In my constant battles with Pop, Ma usually ended up being the casualty.

Thank God my counseling allowed me to find peace within myself. That inner peace inevitably gave me the understanding to find peace with my father.

As rebellious and defiant as I was, my brother, Michael, on the other hand, was academically inclined, obedient, and couldn't find trouble if it was in his front pocket. He was a good kid but he didn't take shit off anybody. He didn't allow anyone to push him around. Not even Pop! He stood up to the man and Pop never as much as raised his voice to him. Don't get me wrong; my father didn't fear Mike in any way, but he respected him.

It was pretty apparent at an early age that I was going to have Ma's sensitivity, and Mike was going to have Pop's toughness. Although I excelled in sports, always dated women, you know, all the things considered to be masculine, my father never acknowledged my masculinity. He constantly emasculated me because of my sensitive nature.

The fact that I was the largest person in the house by the age of fifteen didn't make it any easier. In retrospect, I think Pop viewed my gigantic size as a threat and he reacted accordingly. He was small in stature but he was ferocious and very confrontational. He was well respected in our neighborhood, or maybe just well feared. I don't know if he was overcompensating for his lack of size but he challenged everyone who said a cross word to him, especially those who were larger than him. And the larger I grew, the more he resented me. I was soft to him. Big and soft! He was determined to toughen me up. Even if it meant tearing me down.

If it wasn't for Mike, there's no telling where I would have ended up. He believed in me, and stayed on my back until I finally decided to straighten up and get my life together. As some siblings do, we grew up and apart, losing that close brotherly connection. But life brought us back together.

That brings me to my point. Mike, who is a novelist, recently wrote a best-selling book titled *The Office Girls*. In his book, Mike secretly documented the lives and issues of his female co-workers at a company called Upskon.

He wrote intimate confidential information about these women that he would later regret. When the book was about to be released, Mike had a choice to make. He could reveal his name as the author and receive worldwide acclaim, but by doing this he would be revealing the identities and private lives of the office girls. His other option was to conceal his name as author, remain anonymous, and protect his relationship with the office girls. He chose the latter, and things worked out for the better.

I didn't realize the enormity of my brother's celebrity until I accompanied him on a West Coast tour of his next book. I was used to getting attention by playing professional football but watching the attention he received seemed much more personal and intimate. For example, one of his book signings was hosted by a club in Los Angeles. The name of the book club was the Reading Divas. They treated him as if they really knew him and the characters in his book. I was marveled by his charismatic way of charming his audience.

Over time, I built a relationship with the office girls as well. As a matter of fact, my brother and I married two of the women from that office. He married Cynthia and I married Alicia.

I met my second wife at a New Year's Eve party my brother was hosting. I was an uninvited guest. As soon as I saw Alicia, I knew I had to have her. She was gorgeous. She had naturally golden hair and an hourglass figure. She had a beautiful delicate face and a heart of gold.

Alicia and I fell in love instantly. We were married less than a year after our introduction. My daughter came to live with us after Deirdra lost her lengthy battle with cancer. Brittany and Alicia connected as well. Alicia adopted her and we became the family I always wanted.

As I became closer to the office girls and studied the history of my new patients, I found their behavioral patterns intriguing. The actions and reactions of both groups, surprisingly, were concurrent with the other. By medical definition, there was no exception between the two groups. Romantic relationships, family issues, financial burdens or financial prosperity, the reactions and resolutions to these issues were eerily similar among those women who claimed to need therapy and from those who claimed not to need it.

The more I examined the similarities of these two different

groups, the more captivated I became with the natural behavior of women, not just the psychological, but also the physiological. My personal life as well as my professional life became consumed with the female species.

I had counseled hundreds of patients, but my demographic was predominantly male. Fortunately, I had my administrative assistant, Rosemary Dewitt, to rely upon. Rosemary was very sharp and kept my office running smoothly. Remarkably, she had never worked a day in her life before I hired her.

From my understanding, as a child, Rosemary was tested and her intelligence quotient was rated as one of the highest in the world. She was revered as a genius by other so-called geniuses. Her academic resume was impeccable. She had degrees from Princeton, Oxford, and Cambridge, one of which was a doctorate in psychology.

I couldn't understand for the life of me why a woman of her academic background would want to work in a small mental health office. Judging by the Mercedes-Benz she drove to work every day, she wasn't hurting for money. As a matter of fact, it looked like she could afford to loan me a couple of dollars.

She wandered into my office one day while I was painting the walls and asked me if I was hiring. I wasn't at the time, but she seemed to be qualified to help so I offered her a job and she accepted.

Rosemary was a very light-skinned black woman, early forties and very thin. Her hair was jet-black and straight, with a part down the center of her head. She wore conservative long skirts and sweaters practically every day, even on those days when the weather was hot. But to her credit, she also wore a big warm smile. She spoke softly, with a delightful Southern drawl.

Rosemary and I worked diligently to have the office ready for our first day of operation. We wanted the office to appear as if we had been up and running for a while. The first patient had arrived and was sitting in my office. I was nervous as hell but Rosemary was as cool as a cucumber.

I smiled at her as she handed me the file. I quickly scanned the information, took a deep breath and prepared for my entrance.

CHAPTER THREE

My first patient would be Ms. Anise Lawrence. Anise had been diagnosed with a mild case of OCD or Obsessive-Compulsive Disorder. OCD can range from mild to severe. When OCD affects a person mildly, it can be treated and controlled. But if it goes untreated, it can destroy a person's ability to function at work, school and even in the home.

OCD is an anxiety disorder where an individual becomes trapped in a pattern of repetitive thoughts and behaviors that are senseless and distressing but extremely difficult to overcome.

In Anise's case, she has a particularly hard time letting go of intimate relationships. She manipulates the men in her life into staying with her until she decides to move on to the next man. During her transition, she prefers to leave the former lover in a fit of rage. She somehow misconstrues this rage as love.

Generally, I listen to my patients and let them dictate the flow of the conversation. But I felt that if I followed that procedure with Ms. Lawrence, it would not serve her well. I thought that she needed to be encouraged to speak openly without the threat of judgment before she would be able to address her controlling issues.

As I walked into my office, I could see the back of Ms.

Lawrence's head. She had light-brown hair and every strand seemed to be in place. As I walked closer, I paused to get a better view of her before she could get an eyeful of me. She was wearing a black business suit with a white butterfly collar. Her figure was noticeably shapely, even sitting in the chair. When she finally appeared within my peripheral view, I noticed her skin tone matched the color of her hair, perfectly. She had golden hair and beautiful golden skin to match.

Her hands were folded neatly on her lap and her legs were crossed comfortably right over left. Despite the position of Ms. Lawrence's body, she still maintained an upright posture.

"How are you today, Ms. Lawrence? I'm Doctor Johnson Forrester." I shook her hand.

"How are you, Dr. Forrester? Don't be so formal, please call me Anise."

"Good morning, Anise." I took Anise's file out of the folder. "Well, for starters, I want you to know that we can discuss whatever you want. On the other hand, we don't have to discuss anything you feel uncomfortable discussing. I also want to assure you that everything spoken in this office is completely confidential. Sounds good?"

"So far, so good."

"Tell me a little about yourself, Anise."

"Well, I'm not here because I'm crazy," Anise said, laughing lightly. "I'm not crazy and I don't need any medication. I just need to talk to someone who won't judge me."

"Crazy is a term that I'd rather not use, Anise, and it's not for me to judge anyone."

"Thank you, that makes me feel a lot more comfortable."

"Good. I feel comfortable knowing you feel comfortable."

"Well, seems like we're both comfortable!" Anise joked.

"Are you ready to begin?"

"Sure," Anise said.

"Ending a relationship can be difficult to overcome. Do you have a hard time ending relationships?"

"Who me?" Anise laughed. "No, not at all."

"Have you ever had your heart broken before?"

Anise paused momentarily, as if she was thinking of the correct thing to say, "Well, of course I've had my heart broken. It wasn't anything traumatic. I was young and he was my first love. The man I was in love with just happened to be married. His wife kind of took offense to our dating and he broke it off. I was interested in other guys as well, so although it hurt, I managed to deal with it."

"Okay, was your reaction rage, pain, or denial?"

"Definitely pain. I respected him for telling me, so I didn't feel rage. And there was no way for me to deny it, because it was right in my face," Anise said with a half-smile.

"Are you skeptical of romance now?"

"I would have to say yes."

"Do you become anxious and excited at the beginning of a relationship?"

"Um, excited and anxious? I would say no. I'm too cautious and too careful. I just try to enjoy the moment. I don't ask for promises, nor do I give them. I want what I want when I want it. And I always get what I want when I want it."

"Okay," I said, surprised by her bluntness. "Do you look for romance with men who may fit the bill that you have ordered in your mind? Or do you look for compatibility in friendship first?"

"I don't look for anybody or anything! I try not to place expectations too high in the romance department—it avoids major disappointment. I date, and right now, it's only in the name of friendship. So I guess the answers to your questions are, no, I don't have a bill to fit, and yes, friendship is a prerequisite for romance."

"Do you measure your friends on the amount of time, money, and interest spent on you?"

"Oh no, of course not. And I'm sure all of my friends would agree with me on that. It's me who gives most of the time and the money."

"Okay, is it possible for you to be physically attracted to a man and maintain a platonic relationship?"

"Platonic? Well," Anise shifted her body for the first time, "I guess that would depend on how attracted I was to him."

"Does the attraction level dictate your actions?"

"That goes without saying."

"I see. Do you confide in your male friends as deeply as your female friends?"

"Probably. I don't have a lot of female friends. Most of my friends are males, so I probably confide more in my male friends than my female friends. Does that make sense?"

"Sure it does," I said and then moved to the next question. "Who's your closest friend?"

"My closest friend," Anise said, pondering the question, "does it have to be male or female?"

"Whichever," I said. "It doesn't matter."

"She's nice," Anise said, "just a nice, beautiful human being. She has a problem with how the world sees her though, and it affects her self-esteem! But she's a wonderful human being."

"If you could change anything about your friend, what would it be?"

"I would change the way she views herself. She is very beautiful inside, but she is so concerned with how she looks on the outside that it really affects her self-esteem. I am a person who truly believes that beauty is only skin deep. I just wish she would believe that."

"Why don't you think she believes that?"

"I don't know, maybe she needs to be sitting in this chair instead of me." Anise chuckled.

"Maybe she does?" I repeated, pretending to laugh, knowing that most of the time when those types of questions are asked, those answering are indirectly referring to themselves. Not in the, *"let me tell you about my friend"* way, but most people select their friends because they are similar to themselves.

I thought Anise and her friend were opposites in this case. My analysis was that Anise's friend had low self-esteem because she didn't believe she was physically attractive. However, I believe Anise had low self-esteem because she believed that she was attractive, and the thought of being a beautiful woman with no substance was more painful than being an unattractive woman with substance.

"Are you close to both of your parents? Or are you closer to one more so than the other?"

Throughout the interview, Anise had flashed her alluring smile, but as soon as I mentioned her family, the smile faded. Her posture, which had been so erect and confident, became slouched and she seemed uncomfortable.

"I don't have a close relationship with either one of my parents," Anise said, while squirming uncomfortably. "I haven't seen either one of them since I left St. Louis."

"Do you find that your family is reliable and trustworthy?"

"No!" Anise answered quickly.

"When you think of your family as a whole, do you think of a haven or hellhole?"

"Hellhole!" Anise responded as soon as the question was out of my mouth.

"You seem uncomfortable when we discuss your family. Is there anything you would like to say?"

"Uncomfortable?" Anise asked. "I don't know what you mean."

She stood up and walked toward the window. She stared outside and didn't respond to my question.

"Is everything okay, Anise?" I asked.

"If you don't mind, can we end the session?"

"Oh sure," I said. "It's up to you."

"I'm sorry, Dr. Forrester," Anise said. "I guess questions about my family are a little overwhelming."

"Sometimes that happens," I said, trying to console her, "it even happens to me."

"Okay," Anise sighed heavily. "I don't want you to think I'm a basket case."

Seeing Anise as she stood by the window allowed me to get a full glimpse of her beauty, and I felt sensations I had not felt for a woman since I met my wife. As a matter of fact, she was the spitting image of my wife. Their likeness was uncanny. Their face, their hair, their shape, their complexion, everything was so alike.

I walked over and stood behind Anise to get her attention. Her body's scent smelled so fresh to my nose. It wasn't the fragrance of perfume, but a subtle touch of aroma from her flesh. I couldn't help but absorb as much of her aroma as I could before I spoke again.

"Should I be sitting down?" Anise looked over her shoulder at me.

"You're fine," I said, walking away purposely to rid myself of her feminine scent, "we'll pick up next week where we left off."

"Okay." Anise walked over to the chair to pick up her purse. "So, is that it? Can I go?"

"Oh yes." I quickly walked her to the door and opened it for her. "Rosemary will set up your next appointment."

"Thank you," Anise said.

❈❈❈

Their voices even had a similar ring. I watched as Anise gracefully walked to Rosemary's desk to make her next appointment. On her way out of my door, she looked back at me and waved. I waved back and then followed her into the waiting room with Rosemary. Anise scheduled her next appointment and left.

"Do I have time to get breakfast before the next appointment?" I asked Rosemary.

"You have thirty minutes," Rosemary responded while looking in the appointment book. "So hurry!"

"Would you like anything?"

"No, I'm fine, but you should hurry."

"I'll be back in a minute," I said while grabbing my car keys and coat simultaneously.

There was a small café located on the first floor of our building that Rosemary and had I frequented while we were preparing to open the office. It served great food and delivered when we were too busy to go downstairs.

As I walked in, I saw Anise already standing in line. There was a huge man standing directly behind her obstructing my view. I walked around him and tried to engage her in conversation, but the rather large gentleman thought I was cutting in front of him and objected to me standing there. Anise told him I was with her and he withdrew his aggression. Obviously, he was with her. Why? I didn't know.

"Hey you," I said.

"Hi, Dr. Forrester," Anise said very warmly.

"I'm used to being the biggest guy in the room, but this guy is ridiculous!" I whispered to Anise.

"He's my protector!" Anise said.

"Protecting you from whom?"

"It's no big deal," Anise said. "So your secretary makes you do your own shopping, huh?"

"Yeah, and it's even worse at home with my wife."

"Oh," Anise said, sounding surprised, "you're married?"

"Uh…" I paused with my mouth wide open. "Uh yes, I am married."

"You sure?" Anise chuckled as she reached the counter. "You seem a little indecisive."

"Oh no," I replied. "I'm certain."

I waited for her to make her order, and thought to myself, *What the hell am I thinking? I'm a happily married man, standing in front of one of my patients and acting like a high school boy with a crush.*

After Anise made her order, she stood to the side and waited. I ordered and silently stood next to her. It was a little awkward, but I found silence to be a better alternative to talking. Apparently, Anise did not.

"So, are you a newlywed?" Anise asked.

"I'm not sure if we should be discussing my personal life, young lady," I replied sarcastically.

"Come on, Dr. Forrester, you know personal information about me; tell me a little about you."

"Ah, but you're forgetting one small element. It is my job to know personal information about you."

"I see," Anise reached for her order and gave me a seductive smile, "then perhaps I need to make it my job to know personal information about you, Dr. Forrester."

Anise continued to look at me as she tucked her food in one hand, and her purse in the other, and walked out of the café. I stared sinfully as she walked out of sight.

This ain't good! I said to myself.

❂❂❂

Over the next week, Anise called the office to speak with me about personal issues she was facing. The office calls turned into cell phone calls because even though I only had five patients—well, six after I offered Wanda a few free sessions for helping around the office—my schedule could not accommodate the amount of time it took to discuss Anise's concerns.

I will admit that our conversations drifted beyond doctor-patient content, so much so that we began to discuss my sexual relationship with my wife. Although I knew this was both unethical and unprofessional, I succumbed to the temptation.

When Anise arrived for her next appointment, I was anxious and eager to see her. Knowing I had violated my professional code of ethics, I tried to rebound by making sure our next session would be strictly medical.

"Good afternoon, Anise," I said, and shook her hand, keeping our introduction professional. "How are you today?"

"I'm fine, how are you, Dr. Forrester?" Anise sat down and crossed her legs, right over left.

She was not wearing a pantsuit this session. She wore a tight miniskirt and a fitted shirt. A shirt that revealed two protruding nipples and a skirt that, when she uncrossed her legs, revealed a nicely shaven vagina. Despite the bulge in my pants, I pretended not to notice the strip show Anise was providing. I won't deny that I peeked momentarily. What man wouldn't? And then I quickly turned my attention back to the session.

"Let's pick up where we left off last week," I said while opening her file. "We were discussing your family, but..."

"I'm still not ready to discuss my family at this point," Anise interrupted. "I want to discuss romantic relationships."

"Romantic relationships?" I asked. "Is there any reason in particular you would like to discuss romance?"

"Love. I want to know how love feels."

Smiling, I asked, "What do you mean, you want to know how love feels?"

"I have never been loved," Anise said. "I've been raped. I've been molested. I've been used by men in every physical way imaginable, but I have never been loved. And I want to know how that feels."

"I thought you said you were in love with a married man before?"

"I did. But that doesn't mean that he was in love with me."

"I understand, uh, you mentioned being raped and molested. How old were you when that happened?"

"I was molested when I was twelve and then I was raped at the age of fourteen. Both were by the same man."

"Would you like to discuss it?"

"I'd rather not."

"Does it still hurt?"

"Yes."

"Was it someone you trusted?"

"Yes."

"A relative?"

"No. A friend of the family."

"Who did this to you?" I said, becoming too emotionally inquisitive.

"You told me that I could discuss what I felt comfortable discussing. I do not feel comfortable discussing this," Anise said, turning away.

"That's fine," I said. "Relax."

"Tell me, Dr. Forrester, you're married," Anise began, "what does it feel like to love someone and to have that love reciprocated?"

"We're not here to discuss me, Anise, we're here to discuss you."

"But if you tell me about you, it may tell me things about myself."

"Why do you think that?"

"Why? I think that you are an amazing man, a man who listens. A man of desire, a man filled with love."

"I am truly appreciative of your compliment, Anise, but that is a conversation we should not have as doctor and patient. This is neither the time nor the place. We should get back to our session."

"Let's not bother, the session is over. Here," Anise handed me a card, "meet me at this hotel at noon. I will be sitting in the lobby waiting for you. Perhaps that's a better place to discuss it."

Anise stood up and walked out of my office, leaving me sitting there with the card in my hand. I threw the card in my top drawer and slammed it shut, frustrated with myself for not ending our flirtatious dialogue right then and there. I felt myself reverting back to a time when my flesh controlled my life and I wasn't going to allow it to happen again. I reached in my drawer and ripped up the card.

Moments later, my seventh patient, Stacey Hemphill, knocked on my door. Stacey was one of my few female patients when I was working at the clinic, shortly before I started to work for the prison system.

Stacey was white, forty-one years old, and still had an amazing figure for her age. She stood about five feet, ten inches tall, thin but with curvy hips, especially for a Caucasian woman. She had short, straight, sandy-brown hair that was cut right below her ears. Her earrings were barely noticeable, and had it not been for the occasional sparkles shining from her diamonds, I would not have noticed them. She was very low maintenance, but beautiful in her own way. She had a masculine look. She always wore business suits—suits that men wore, not women. Her shoes even looked like men's shoes.

We first met at the MARTA Lindbergh Station while we were commuting and she started a conversation. We were both new to the Atlanta area. Our offices were in the same building so we became friends, nothing romantic, just friends. One afternoon we ran into each other at a restaurant and shared a table for lunch. The rest is patient confidentiality history.

I never diagnosed her with any medical disease. Basically, she was as normal and competent as anyone I've ever met, present company included. I did, however, diagnose her with "girlfriend syndrome." Translated: she lacked people skills and didn't have a girlfriend to gossip with or confide intimate details. She paid me to play that role, and I was more than happy to sit and listen.

In her professional life, Stacey was well on her way to becoming one of the most respected criminal attorneys in the city of Atlanta. Her ambition as an attorney greatly contributed to her inability to excel in other areas of her life.

Her current dilemma was that she was torn between her husband and her career. He was an attorney as well, but had not come close to achieving her success.

Stacey was an aggressive overachiever who pushed her husband as much as she pushed herself. Her husband, although accomplished in his own right, did not share Stacey's aggressive ambition. The difference in their professional philosophies was causing a strain on their marriage.

"Dr. Forrester?" Stacey peeked around the door.

"Good afternoon, Stacey," I said. "Please, come in."

"Thank you," Stacey said before walking over to the patient's chair and sitting down. "How are you, Dr. Forrester?"

"I'm fine, and you?"

"I'm fine, too," Stacey said with a huge grin.

"Hey, somebody's having a good day."

"Well, I am. I finally got my husband to open up and talk to me a little bit."

"Good for you. Did you discuss your careers?"

"He wasn't ready to discuss the issues. He was only willing to admit that we had issues. I'll take it one step at a time."

"Is he willing to discuss your starting your own firm?"

"No, not yet."

Smiling, I asked sarcastically, "And why not?"

"I don't know," Stacey smiled back, "I don't want to damage his ego any further; he was just promoted to junior partner and then I start my own firm. I don't want to seem like I'm grandstanding him!"

"Grandstanding?" I almost shouted. "Shouldn't he celebrate your accomplishments just as you celebrate his?"

"Sure, but mine have come more often than his, so I don't mind if he gets the attention all to himself sometimes. There's nothing wrong with that."

"I understand. But how does it make you feel when you replace your jubilation with his?"

"I feel perfectly fine," Stacey said. "And as I said, we celebrate mine all the time. It's a small price to pay to restore my husband's confidence."

"And by doing this, how is your confidence affected?"

"It has absolutely no effect on my confidence."

"So when do you plan on discussing your excitement for your firm with him?"

"Soon," Stacey said, "very soon."

"How do you think he'll react?"

"Hopefully, he'll be accepting of it and excited for me."

"And if he's not?"

"I suppose there'll be more visits to your office." Stacey chuckled.

"That's fine with me."

"Dr. Forrester," Stacey said, "may I ask a question?"

"Sure, go right ahead."

"Why do you think I'm so successful in my career, but I'm such a failure in my social life?"

"A failure? Why do you say that?"

STACEY'S STORY:

"*My father was a career military serviceman and I was an army brat. I was born an only child on a military base in Germany. My mother died during childbirth, turning my dad into a single father—one with no maternal instincts. But desperate times call for desperate measures. My father did all he could to make my life as normal as possible. We traveled the world over until he retired and permanently moved back to his home state of Texas.*

"*He met my stepmother, Charlene, and they married when I was fourteen. I immediately felt her impact on our lives with a woman in the house. My dad became softer and he slacked up a little on pushing me to excel. Please note that I said he 'slacked up', not backed up. He was still a hard-ass.*

"*Charlene was a huge factor in my father becoming a United States senator. She did a lot of hands-on work to make sure he won that seat in Congress. She made sure he walked right, talked right, and behaved right. He owed everything to her.*

"*But as far as I was concerned, being the daughter of a senator was extremely difficult. I was expected to achieve academically, socially, and professionally as well or better than the best of my peers. And I was not allowed to use gender as an excuse to fail.*

"*My father raised me to be the best at everything I attempted, from high school ROTC, to college ROTC, to being tops in my class at Harvard University's law school. That inherited competitive nature did not appeal to men. I was unsuccessful at maintaining relationships because I was always perceived as being too masculine. I had many sexual encounters but that's not what I wanted. I wanted the house on the hill with the picket fence. I wanted two-point-five kids, a boy and a girl, and a whatever. But I couldn't change who I was, even though I tried.*

"*As a little girl, I wasn't raised with Barbie dolls. I was raised with G.I. Joes. I didn't wear pretty dresses. I wore durable jeans. I didn't wear play make-up on my face. I wore war paint. My father was a* very masculine, disciplined man who didn't have an ounce of sensitivity in his body. Unfortunately for me, I was my father's daughter. I was a determined, independent woman.

"Where we differed was that I was also a sensitive, caring woman who wanted to be loved, and who wanted to give love. I wanted to have female friends that I could talk with about men, share intimate details, but that never happened.

"In romance and in law, men always thought of me as an adversary and never an ally. That was, until I met my husband. We had just passed the bar and were working for a small law firm in Austin, Texas. We were friends at first, and then our friendship blossomed into romance.

"I felt completely successful in every aspect of my life but romance. Finally, I had found love! I was ecstatic! We dated for almost a year before we eventually had sex. I was twenty-seven and experienced. He was twenty-five and not so experienced. The sex wasn't all that fantastic, but it seemed to make him happy. And making him happy made me happy.

"We were married three years later with great expectations of starting a family, but our careers got in the way. Year after year, we postponed our pregnancy until it wasn't even a part of our conversations. As of right now, not only am I not sure that we're going to have a baby, I'm not even sure we're going to maintain our marriage."

"I remain optimistic, but I am very concerned about saving my marriage."

"I would like to hear more about that in our next session."

"I look forward to it," Stacey said.

"Let me walk you to the door," I said after shaking her hand.

I escorted Stacey through the waiting room. On my way back, I stopped at Rosemary's desk to confirm my next appointment.

"Who's next?"

"Your next appointment is Wanda Briggs. Sorry, Dr. Forrester, I tried to get her to keep her original appointment but she insisted on moving it up."

"That's okay, Rosemary."

"Almost forgot, you also have a message," Rosemary added while passing me a memo. "Ms. Lawrence called."

"Oh, okay," I said, looking at the note and then quickly folding it in my hand. "Well, I have to step out for a second, Rosemary. I'll be back shortly."

I grabbed my coat and quickly headed toward the door.

"Where are you going?"

"Uh, I have to meet someone. It's very important!"

"Don't forget Mrs. Briggs' appointment!"

"I won't!" I said while hurrying out of the door.

❂❂❂

As I pulled into the parking lot of the hotel, I considered turning around, but only for a moment. I realized what I was about to do was a serious setback in the stability of my recovery, but my mind was made up and I was going to go through with it. I stepped out of my car and walked into the lobby. I wasn't totally sure of what was about to happen, but whatever it was, it was going to have to happen quickly. My next appointment was within two hours and I had to be back in my office.

There she was, sitting in a short dress that showed off her legs. Her open-toed shoes exposed her perfectly manicured toenails. I walked slowly to her, admiring her beauty until I stood directly in front of her face.

"Hi," Anise said with that seductive smile.

"Hi." I stood there amazed by the sensuality of Anise's presence.

It was apparent that Anise and I shared an uncontrollable sexual attraction, which bordered on being animalistic wild, but there also existed a powerful enigmatic romance that had linked us together in such a short period of time. We did not ask for it, it was forced upon us through the interaction of the other's company. What began as a doctor-patient relationship had unpredictably blossomed into an indomitable relationship of spontaneous passion and lust.

I picked up Anise's little duffel bag that was sitting beside her feet and then clasped her hand in mine. We walked silently through the lobby of the hotel and onto the elevator. Once the door was closed, she leaned toward me and rested her head on my shoulder. We stood in that position until the elevator door opened and we walked out.

Once we arrived at her room, she scanned the key and we walked in. I dropped her bag on the floor and we sat side by side at the foot of the bed. I reached for her hand and we sat in silence intertwining our fingers. We leaned backward together on the bed and faced each other. I caressed her face and stared beyond her eyes. We wrapped our bodies together and became one. Without even realizing it, we unclothed ourselves and moved to the center of the bed.

We lay totally unclothed and unconcerned about anything other than the moment we were sharing. Her eyes were looking directly into mine. Her lips and her tongue were passionately and slowly kissing my lips and sucking my tongue. Her breasts clung to my chest. Her navel pressed against my stomach. Her thighs rubbed against mine as they intertwined. Her toes gently slid up and down the top of my feet, but with everything that we were sharing in that moment, we did not share a single word.

I could feel my hands caress the spine of Anise's back. The indention in the rear of her body felt so feminine, so naturally created for my hands to fit. I pulled her closer to me and all that stood between our bodies was my firm manhood.

I turned Anise on her back and she slowly opened her thighs. I placed my manhood at the entrance of her vagina as she moved her hips and raised them slightly to meet me. I lowered my face and began to kiss her on the neck. She turned her head to the side to give me full access. As I kissed and sucked on her succulent neck, Anise moved her hips more rapidly. I could feel the juices from her vagina seep onto the head of my manhood.

She began to moan loudly and then grabbed me by my hips. She tried to adjust our bodies so that my manhood could slide into her soaking wet hole. I pulled away, teasing her, making her legs shiver from anticipation. My kisses moved further south as I sucked gently on her left nipple. Then I moved over to the right breast and engulfed as much as I could into my mouth. Back and forth I went until she was moaning uncontrollably.

I continued to kiss her, moving down to her stomach and licking her navel with long, wet licks. Up and down her stomach. I turned my head to the side and began to lick up her right leg, and then all the way down to the toes on her right foot, sucking them, one by one. I clutched her big toe in my mouth with the suction of my tongue.

Next, I licked her left leg, from her inner thigh down to her toes. On my way up, I stopped at her womanhood and licked the outer region of her vaginal lips. She arched her back and raised her hips. I continued to lick up and down, and then side to side, brushing my tongue against her erect clitoris. She spread her legs far apart and placed her hands at the back of my head.

She pushed my face into her womanhood and began to grind rhythmically against it. I buried my face so deep into her thighs I could barely breathe. Her lustful reaction made me so willing to please her that I continued to lick and suck her relentlessly, not caring if it rendered me unconscious.

From the wild bucking of her hips and the loud moaning of her voice I knew her orgasm was approaching. This made me all the more eager to make sure her orgasm was strong and powerful. I licked even faster and harder, and then side to side with the tip of my tongue. Finally, Anise pushed my face into her again and raised her ass completely off of the bed. She screamed and kept my head in one position until she dropped back down on the bed, gasping for air.

I quickly slid up to her and held her in my arms as her body jerked and moved uncontrollably beneath me. Once her orgasm subsided we looked each other in the eyes, but still, no words were spoken.

After a few moments of recuperation, Anise turned me on my back and straddled me. She lowered herself on top of me and, inch by inch, slid down my manhood. Once I was inside of her, she placed her hands on my massive chest and began to grind back and forth. Her eyes were closed and her mouth was wide open. Her knees were on the bed beside my hips, and her feet were behind her. She continued to rock back and forth on my manhood, faster and faster. The faster she moved, the louder she moaned. Her hips began to move so fast that I had to grab them and guide her to prevent her from causing me permanent injury.

Her breathing became so heavy she had to pause to catch

her breath. I turned Anise on her back so that I could take over the reins. I grabbed her by the ankles and spread her legs as far apart as possible. I grabbed the head of my manhood and slid it inside of her. She gasped as I went as deep as I could possibly go.

Once I was inside of her, I began to slide in and out, feeling Anise's moist wetness. She reached behind me and grabbed me by my ass, pushing me deeper inside. We continued to make love as I slammed between her thighs. Our bodies clung together from the stickiness of our perspiration.

After a while, I raised Anise to her knees and positioned her on all fours and then I stood behind her. She grabbed her ass cheeks and separated them to allow me access to her pulsating womanhood.

I slid my manhood inside and pulled her back into me by her waist. I watched, again, as she rocked back and forth, crashing backward into me harder and harder. I began to smack her ass every time she slammed backward. Every time my hand hit her ass, her legs would quiver and she would scream loudly.

She lowered her head and arched her back. She pulled the sheets from the corners of the bed and bit the pillow. I continued to slap her ass and ram her until I felt a huge orgasm approaching.

I pushed her onto the bed and closed her legs tightly. As my orgasm erupted, I rammed my manhood inside of her over and over and over. My muscular body completely covered hers as she lay on her stomach. She wrapped her feet around my ankles and lifted herself as much as she could against my weight and matched me stroke for stroke, slamming backward into me. I turned her head to the side and kissed her wildly.

I poured so much juice into her it started to overflow. After my orgasm, we lay together in the same position. She lay on her stomach, with me on her back, and my manhood still inside of her. We eventually fell asleep in that same position.

When we woke, I hurriedly got up, grabbed my clothes and ran into the bathroom. I took a quick shower and then she followed. Once we were dressed, we stood face to face in the middle of the room. I took her face in my hands and slowly kissed her forehead. *My God*, I thought, staring into Anise's eyes, *she looked just like Alicia.* Then I put my hand in hers and led her out of the room.

We walked back to the elevator, still not uttering a word. Once the elevator door opened, we stepped inside patiently and watched it close. Anise leaned toward me and rested her head on my shoulder. We stood in that position until the elevator door opened and we walked out. We walked silently through the lobby and back to her car.

"Bye," Anise said with that seductive smile.

"Bye." I was still amazed by the sensuality of Anise's presence.

CHAPTER FOUR

When I arrived back at the office, both Rosemary and Wanda, my next appointment, were sitting and waiting. I tried to ignore their stares of disapproval over my tardiness, but Wanda wouldn't allow it.

"Hey," Wanda said, throwing her purse over her shoulders and following me into my office, "my time is very valuable, don't be keeping me waiting!"

"I sincerely apologize for my tardiness, Wanda," I said while holding my office door open for Wanda to walk past.

Wanda walked into my office and then sat on the couch. Wanda was a character. She was the sarcastic one of the office girls. She approached me with an idea to help build my clientele. Her plan was to receive five free therapy sessions in exchange for helping me renovate the office. When I asked her how that would help build my clientele, she told me she was crazy as hell, and if I could cure her, I could cure anybody!

Wanda looked very rugged. She had a deep voice and big bold eyes. I'd say she was about five feet, six inches tall. She was top-heavy with slender legs.

"Uh, that won't be necessary, Wanda, you can sit on the chair," I said, pointing to the patient's chair opposite my desk. "We won't need that right now."

"Why not? I been waiting all my life to lay on somebody's couch and have some psychologist tell me about me! So come on, man, let me lay my fat ass down!"

"Okay, Wanda. I'll come to you." I moved my chair to the side of the couch.

"Hey, Johnny," Wanda said, turning her head around to look me in my face, "just because you got all this fineness in front of you, it don't mean you have to act on it. Try to control yourself, if not for you, then for Alicia! 'Cause once I whip this whip appeal on you, you gon' wanna leave everything you have and camp right outside my front do'!"

"Wanda!" I shouted and tried to keep from laughing. "Can we please proceed with the session?"

"Sorry about that, you know how I am once I get going!"

"No problem, are you ready?"

"Yup!" Wanda said. "But please, please be gentle."

"Okay, Wanda, I want you to relax and get comfortable."

"I can't get no more comfortable than this! This couch is about to put my ass to sleep. What is this? A Posturepedic?"

"We want comfort, not sleep."

"I ain't going to sleep, just ask me some questions!" Wanda said with enthusiasm.

"Where do you want to begin, Wanda?"

"I want to begin with my husband."

"What about your husband?"

"Not my husband now," Wanda said, "my first husband. My husband now is the bomb!"

"So tell me, Wanda, why do you think your second marriage is successful, but your first marriage wasn't?"

"I like my husband this time!" Wanda laughed.

"And is the intimacy greater or lesser?"

"Damn! You just get straight to the personal, don't you?" Wanda asked.

"Wanda," I said, "are you going to take this session seriously or not?"

"Okay, I'm sorry! I promise I'm going to be serious! Ask me whatever you want."

"Okay, let's start over. How does your second marriage differ from your first marriage?"

"Well, my second husband talk to me more than my first husband. And he don't run around in the streets, he's a family man. He love staying home with me and the kids."

"What do you think the difference is in making this marriage work, and the failure of the first marriage?"

"I don't think my first husband ever wanted to really be married. I don't think he understood how much work it was going to take to make a marriage work. The day he left was the worst and best day of my life."

"Why do you say it was the worst and the best?"

"'Cause even though it hurt me, I mean really hurt me," Wanda said in a melancholy way, "I guess it forced me to let him go."

"Did you have any children while you were married?"

"No, I didn't, but he did. He had a couple of children out of wedlock, but I stayed with him anyway. I know it sound crazy, but I was trying to keep my family together. And if he hadn't left when he did, there's no telling how long I would have let that fool get away with making a fool out of me."

"So did your relationship with your first husband leave a lingering effect on your perception of future relationships?"

"I guess so," Wanda said while lying with the full length of her body relaxed and her hands behind her head. "But it didn't only affect my relationship with men, but women, too. I don't trust nobody! And I mean nobody! I always felt like people was trying to make fun of me, or talk about me. And before my husband left, I always thought of myself as weak for taking it. But when I was forced to deal with the fact that he was gone, I saw myself in a different light. I felt like, if I can deal with that niggah leavin', I can deal with anything! And now, I don't take no shit off nobody! Now I attack people before they attack me."

"Why would anyone want to attack you, Wanda?"

"I don't know why, they just do."

"Have you felt this way your entire life?"

"Yeah," Wanda said reluctantly. "Kinda."

"Then there has to be a reason."

"I don't know, I guess it's because since I don't have a model-type body, people think they can say whatever they want to me."

"What does your body have to do with how you're treated?"

"Don't act like you don't know how people with my type of body gets treated. I used to get all upset about what people thought when I wore certain clothes, or stood beside a smaller woman. So now, even if I think somebody is looking at me funny, I tear into their ass!"

"Do you think that's fair?"

"Fair to who?"

"To those you attack based on an assumption, when their intention may be purely nonjudgmental."

"I'm sorry, but that's a chance I gotta take. Better them than me!"

"So would you say that you have a naturally aggressive personality, or do you think it was acquired?"

"I guess it was acquired. I used to take shit, now I give shit!"

"Okay, one last question before we finish this session. Do you love yourself more today, with your aggressive personality, than you did with your passive personality?"

"I won't say I love myself, it's more like I respect myself."

"Understood," I said. "Very good, Wanda. Good session!"

"Uh-huh," Wanda said while sitting up. "You got me on this couch pouring out my inner-most secrets. I need a drink! What you got up in here?"

"Sprite, Pepsi, tea, what do you want?"

"I don't want no dam' soft drink! I want somethin' that's gon' burn my chest. I need some liquor! Hard liquor!"

"Wanda, it's three o' clock in the afternoon; you don't need to be drinking that stuff."

"Man, if you only knew." Wanda stood up to leave. "I need a drink twenty-four hours a day dealing with that shit in my house!"

"Let's go, Wanda," I said, taking her arm in mine and leading her to the waiting room. "Rosemary, can you make an appointment for Wanda's next visit?"

"Sure, no problem," Rosemary said. "Is next Friday at noon okay, Mrs. Briggs?"

"That's good," Wanda said. "Johnny, you might wanna hit the liquor store before I come up in here the next time."

"Okay," I replied, now embarrassed that Rosemary was listening.

As Wanda closed the door behind her, Rosemary looked at me and I smiled and shrugged my shoulders. I walked back into my office and waited for my next appointment.

It wasn't fifteen minutes later before Rosemary was knocking on the door.

"Your next appointment is here, Dr. Forrester, are you ready for her?" Rosemary asked.

"Sure, send her in."

"Okay," Rosemary said, then looked back over shoulder into the lobby. "He's ready for you, Ma'am, come right on in."

Rosemary stepped to the side to let Ms. Kimberly Mathis pass. Kimberly was a tall woman, well over six feet, and walked with a slight limp. She was dark-skinned with dark bushy eyebrows. Her posture was poor and that made her seem slightly hunchbacked. Her face was round and puffy, but she was not obese at all. Her hair was uncombed and sticking from beneath the hat she was wearing to keep it in place. Her clothing was tattered and not very well kept. Her shoes did not match, but Kimberly did not seem to be concerned with any of her inadequacies. She was much too preoccupied with other distractions.

Kimberly walked past, nodding her head in courtesy to Rosemary. She stood by the door clutching her bag as Rosemary stepped out of my office and closed the door behind her.

"You may have a seat, Kimberly." I pointed to a chair.

"Thank you, doctor." Kimberly walked nervously to the chair and sat down. "You can call me Kimberly, that's what everybody call me."

Still clutching her purse, Kimberly smiled very faintly, an obvious sign that she was trying to forcibly put herself at ease.

Kimberly had originally been diagnosed with schizophrenia. But before I began therapy, I needed to be certain that she had been diagnosed correctly. Schizophrenia is a chronic, severe and disabling brain disease. Approximately one percent of the population develops schizophrenia during their lifetime. Although the disease affects men and women with an almost fifty-fifty rate, it appears in men earlier, generally, in their late teens to early twenties. Women, however, are affected in their late twenties to early thirties.

Schizophrenia's most common symptoms are emotional expressions, normal versus abnormal behavior, hallucinations, illusions, delusions and disordered thinking. In some cases, schizophrenia and substance abuse are confused as one and the same because the symptoms of both are quite similar.

The first signs of schizophrenia may be confusingly shocking to friends and family members. These psychotic symptoms are referred to as an acute phase. They are dramatic in the behavioral differences and personality changes. Despite popular belief, schizophrenia is not the same as *"split personality."* A split personality disorder is when an individual exhibits the characteristics of two or more independent personalities.

Psychosis is also a common psychiatric condition that affects people with schizophrenia. It causes a person to lose their sense of reality and cling to fantasy.

Unfortunately, Kimberly was one of the most severe cases I had ever seen. Before diagnosing her with schizophrenia, I had her take a series of mental and physical tests. They included urine and blood tests to eliminate the probability of substance abuse. I also eliminated the possibilities of depression or bipolar disorders through psychological analysis. After the final tests, the original diagnosis was confirmed that Ms. Kimberly Mathis suffered, scientifically and undeniably, from chronic schizophrenia.

"Good afternoon, Dr. Forrester," Kimberly said.

"Good afternoon, Kimberly."

"Well, here I am." Kimberly was almost embarrassed to open her mouth completely and reveal her not-so-glamorous smile.

"Has the new medicine Dr. Glover prescribed for you been working?" I asked.

"Well, I guess so. I've been behaving more like my old self, so I guess it is." Kimberly chuckled.

"Are you ready to begin?"

"Okay."

"Where would you like to begin?"

"Can we begin with my boyfriend?"

"Sure," I said. "Let's begin with your boyfriend."

"I am very excited about my new man." Kimberly adjusted her hat to fit her head appropriately. "His name is William."

"I would like to know a little about William, if you don't mind."

"What do you want to know about him?" Kimberly asked.

"I don't know," I said, twirling a pencil in my hand, "what would you like for me to know?"

"Um, well he's nice, very sweet. Everything I always wanted in a man. He's handsome. He's distinguished."

"He seems like a good guy, so do you think you two have a future?"

"Well, I think so, but there is an issue of our interracial relationship. And also, there's the issue of, um, his wife."

"So, William is married?"

"I know I'm wrong, but he loves me, and I love him."

"Does his wife know about the affair?"

"Oh no, Dr. Forrester! No! Nobody knows but the two of us."

I was amazed at the progression of Kimberly's reaction to the medication. Her sense of awareness, and thought processes were keen and more normal than in the initial telephone interview. In that interview, she spoke with an obvious speech impediment that seemed to have totally disappeared.

"Do you think William will ever leave his wife?" I asked.

"I don't know, but if we're meant to be together, we'll be together."

"Well said."

"Would you like to see a picture of him?" Kimberly dug into her purse.

"A picture of who?" I asked.

"William."

"Well, sure," I said, feeling slightly uncomfortable, "if you have one."

"Well, of course." Kimberly pulled out a photo. "Here he is."

My mouth dropped and I couldn't believe the man I saw in the picture.

"Excuse me, is this William?" I asked, while taking the picture out of her hand.

"Yes, that's William."

"You mean, your William? The man you've been talking to me about?"

"Yes, this is my Bill." Kimberly took the picture out of my hand and stared at it proudly, holding it away from her body. "He likes for me to call him Bill."

"You're serious, aren't you, Kimberly?"

"Yes, of course!"

"Did you ever tell Dr. Glover about William, I mean, Bill?"

"Yes, he thinks the world of him." Kimberly smiled broadly and put the photograph back in her purse.

"Interesting," I said, "when was the last time you saw Bill?"

"I saw him a couple of days ago."

"Where?"

"At the shelter."

"I see," I said, "Bill came to the shelter?"

"Yes."

"The man in the picture that you just put back in your purse, came to the shelter?"

"Uh, yeah," Kimberly said, seeming to lose the articulation skills she had moments earlier.

"Did he come in a car? In a taxi? How did he arrive at the shelter?"

Kimberly looked away and started to shake her legs rapidly.

The right side of her face twitched slightly from nervousness.

"In a box that sit on the table in the break room at the shelter," Kimberly said, looking as sincere as anyone I've ever seen in my life.

"That box on the table in the break room, is it called a television?"

"Yeah!" Kimberly said, "I believe some people call it a television. Yes they do!"

"Do you know who the man in that picture is, Kimberly?"

"Yes," Kimberly said, clutching her purse and straightening her hat, "he's William Jefferson Clinton. Bill for short!"

"Do you know that he was once the president of the United States?"

"I don't care, even if he was, I still love him." Kimberly was looking very sincere. "It doesn't matter who he is, he loves me for me, and I love him for him."

"I understand, Kimberly," I said while looking at the clock, "I can't wait to hear more next week. Let's get Rosemary to make you another appointment."

I walked her to the lobby and had Rosemary schedule the next appointment. I also had her double Kimberly's dosage of medication. She was improving, but she still had a long way to go before she could function in society.

CHAPTER FIVE

L ater that day, I was on my way from a friend's house when I received a telephone call. Once I saw that the call was coming from a restricted identification number, I should have hung up, but I didn't.

"Hey!" Anise said.

"Oh, hi, Anise," I said reluctantly.

"Where are you?"

"I'm on I-85, going south," I said. "Where are you?"

"Stuck on I-20 going east near downtown," Anise replied. "Dr. Forrester, I can't stop thinking about this afternoon."

"I'm sorry, Anise," I said. "That should have never happened."

"I wanna see you."

"I'm sorry, I can't."

"May I tell you why I got that hotel room today, Dr. Forrester?"

"Okay. Why?"

"To take my life."

"Why would you want to do something like that, Anise?"

"Why do you think? I'm tired of living this pitiful life!"

"Stop talking like that! You hear me?"

"That's easy for you to say. You're going home to your family. But I'm going home to a lonely hotel room. Every night, the same old thing! I can't take it anymore!"

"Anise! Listen to me!" I said, raising my voice. "Stop talking like that!"

"When you touched me today it was the first time in my life I felt that a man was touching me because he cared about me. It made me feel alive. But once you left, I felt that same emptiness. If I go back to that empty hotel room, I don't know what I'll do."

I am a well-trained mental therapist who knew the mental history of a patient exhibiting all the symptoms of OCD. I was well aware of her manipulative ploy, but instead of ignoring her for the sake of her mental health, I pretended to be gullible because I needed a reason to see her one more time.

"Where are you, Anise?"

"I'm almost downtown."

"Okay, meet me in Gwinnett County so that we can talk."

"I'll meet you anywhere!" Anise said.

"Keep on I-20 east to I-85 north, and just drive until we reach the same exit and get off," I said while passing my designated exit and continuing south near Suwanee.

"Will you make love to me?" Anise asked very softly.

"No!" I said. "I can't! That can never happen again!"

"Please, Dr. Forrester, I know it's not right, but I cannot go to that empty hotel knowing what we shared earlier!"

"I'm sorry, Anise."

"Did you not enjoy this afternoon?"

"This afternoon was amazing, but I have a wife."

"Didn't you have a wife this afternoon?"

"Yes, but," I said while thinking of a rational response. "We can't keep doing this. It's not right! I don't want to go back to that life!"

"It's too late! You already have."

We held the phones in silence, waiting for the other to give in.

"Didn't I feel good to you, Dr. Forrester? Didn't you like the way I felt wrapped around you?"

"Of course, but I have a wife!" I said. "Please, let's stop this."

"Are you aroused thinking about being inside of me?" Anise ignored my request to stop talking about sex. "Do you want me?"

"Of course, but please, we can't do this!" I was practically begging her to stop because I knew I couldn't at that point. My addiction had defeated my love for my wife.

"Oh God, Dr. Forrester, I'm lifting my skirt," Anise said. "It's almost to my panties."

"Anise!" I panted, growing more aroused by the minute. "Stop this!"

"I'm touching myself, Dr. Forrester!"

"Please," I said, rubbing my hand across my bulging manhood.

"I'm touching it, Dr. Forrester." Anise sighed. "It's soaking wet."

"Oh God," I said, conceding to my lust.

"I can feel you inside of me, Dr. Forrester." Anise sighed heavily in my ear. "Oh, you feel so good."

The more Anise talked, the hornier we became. My manhood was so hard I had to adjust its position. Anise told me several times along the way that she was going to touch her soaking wet vagina until I could fill it all the way up.

When we realized we were approaching the same exit, we decided to meet beside a QuikTrip gas station on Beaver Ruin Road. Coming from the north, I passed the Highway 316 exit, then the Pleasant Hill Road exit, then got over to my right and exited onto Beaver Ruin Road.

Anise, coming from the south, passed the Jimmy Carter exit,

then the Indian Trail exit, and got over to the right and exited onto Beaver Ruin Road. She had to wait on traffic to make a left turn and then go back over I-85.

I arrived first and pulled into an isolated area on the side of the store where the cars were scarce. It was dark by then and, fortunately for us, I had borrowed a friend's van to move some small furniture.

"Where are you?" Anise asked.

"I'm on the side of the store in a dark-blue van."

"I think I see you, flash your lights." Anise waited for me to flash the lights.

"Can you see me?"

"Yeah, I see you, I'm going to park next to you," Anise said, and then pulled beside me.

"No," I said, "park a few spaces down and walk over here."

"Okay."

Anise parked a few spaces down and quickly walked back to the van. I opened the door to the passenger seat and she climbed in.

"I had to see you," Anise said.

She wasted no time sticking her tongue in my mouth. We began to fondle each other immediately. She reached right for my manhood, pulling it out of my loose-fitting sweat pants, and I slid my hand beneath her pantyless skirt. She was so moist my fingers were drenched. I continued to finger her as she squirmed and moaned.

She leaned over to my side of the van and lowered her mouth onto my manhood. I watched as her head went up and down and then side-to-side. I thought I was going to explode right there.

"Oh, that feels good," I said with my head leaned back and my hands guiding her head. She was making nasty slurping noises that reverberated off the inside walls of the van.

After a while, I grabbed her hand and we went to the back of the van where a pullout seat more than accommodated our mission. I snatched her clothes off, and she pulled down my pants and I lay on my back. She straddled me and put her legs on either side of my waist, then lowered herself.

"Oh shit," Anise said, "I'm so freakin' wet!!"

"Oh yeah, that feels so good!" I said while grabbing her ass.

"You like it, baby? You like it when I do it like that?" Anise was slowly grinding on me.

"Oh yeah!" I said, not really sure if I was answering her questions properly. I was saying the first thing that came to my mind.

"Oh shit!" Anise started, moving her hips faster. "Give it to me!"

"Yeah, ride it like that!" I watched Anise's small waist and her big round ass move faster and faster.

I quickly flipped Anise over and put her on all fours, lifting her ass in the air. I opened her ass cheeks and slid my manhood into her wet womanhood. We didn't waste any time trying to get a rhythm. We were both so horny she started to slam her ass backward into me. I rammed her as fast and hard as I could. I could feel the van bounce so vigorously that I thought it was going to tip over.

"Give it to me! Give it to me, baby, please!" Anise shouted, turning her head sideways and looking over her shoulders to watch me ram her from behind.

"What you looking at?" I shouted and smacked her right ass-cheek.

"OH SHIT!" Anise yelled, shaking momentarily, then pushing backward into me harder. "Oh shit, that feels good! Smack that ass, baby!"

I continued to ram Anise deep and hard, smacking her ass until I could see my hand print.

"Ugh!" Anise groaned, ramming backward as hard as she could.

The harder I pounded, the lower her body moved on the seat. Eventually, she was flat on her stomach and I reached around and put my arm beneath her neck like in a wrestling move.

"You ready to come? Huh?" I shouted.

"Yeah, baby! Give it to me! I'm almost there! Faster! Faster, baby!" Anise shouted. Her body jerked beneath me as if she was having a severe epileptic attack. "I'm coming! OH SHIT! OH SHIT! OH SHIT!"

Her orgasm triggered mine and I exploded. I pushed my manhood in deep, pressing her face against the inside of the van's wall. She placed her hand on the wall and pushed backward. I kept slamming her head against the wall with the impact of my deep strokes. Thank goodness it was carpeted. We continued to grind until I was completely spent. Once I was finished, we lay there and caressed each other's bodies until our tremors subsided.

"Oh shit, Anise," I said, "that was good. That was real good."

"It was good to me too, baby," Anise said, breathing heavily. "But I want more."

She turned on her back and opened her thighs and, like magic, I instantly became hard again. She took the head and slid it to her entrance. I guided it in, and we lay in the missionary position and looked in each other's eyes. We moved slowly and gently until we shared another long, powerful orgasm.

Afterward, I did not say a word. I was consumed with shame and guilt as a husband and as a psychologist. I slowly put on my clothes and waited for her to leave. Anise kissed me on the cheek and stepped out of the van. I watched her until she got in her car and drove away.

❁❁❁

I made a couple of stops on the way to my house to explain why I was arriving home late. I walked in and my beautiful wife was sitting in the den watching television with my sister-in-law. She greeted me with a hug and a big, warm loving smile.

"Hey Johnny," Cynthia said. "Well, I better be getting home to my ol' baldhead husband."

"Don't leave on my account, Cynt." I kissed her on the cheek.

My sister-in-law was a little cutie! She was about five feet, three inches tall, long straight hair with a gorgeous little shape and an absolute sunshine personality. She was always smiling or making someone else smile. Just a wonderful person; my brother was a lucky man.

"I was supposed to be home a long time ago. Mike is at home taking care of the baby. I know he's about to lose his mind."

"Tell Mike I said what's up, Cynt," I said.

"Okay," Cynthia said, "I'll see y'all later."

Alicia walked Cynthia to the door and, as soon as she closed the door behind her, she came back into the den and gave me another long hug.

"Hey, baby! How was your day?" Alicia kissed me on the cheek.

"Wonderful! Just wonderful!" I sat down in my chair.

"Are you hungry?" Alicia asked.

"I'm not hungry. I picked up something on the way."

"You're coming home later and later, Johnny."

"Well, people need me, baby, what can I say?"

"Very funny, Dr. Phil!" Alicia said sarcastically. "Wanna watch *American Idol* with me?"

"I have two words for you," I said, taking off my shoes, "*hell* and *no*."

"That's okay," Alicia said. "I have something a little better in mind anyway."

Alicia walked over to me and sat on my lap. I didn't know if she could smell the stench of sex on me, so I gingerly pushed her away.

"Baby, I'm tired, can I have a rain check?" I asked.

"You're always tired, baby," Alicia said before hitting me on the chest.

"No, I'm not, I'm just tired tonight."

"I guess I better go take a cold shower then, huh?"

"I'm sorry, Alicia, I'm just too tired."

"Well, I work every day just like you, but it doesn't stop me from wanting to make love."

"Alicia, we make love all the time," I said. "Opening up that office has zapped a lot of my energy."

"I started my own business, too, Johnny. But it hasn't affected my libido."

"There are three of you and only one of me," I said. "Even the good Lord took one day off to rest! Why can't I?"

"Okay, Johnny," Alicia stood and walked upstairs, "I know when I'm not wanted."

"Alicia! Alicia!" I shouted as she stomped up the stairs one by one. I took the remote and began to change the channels rapidly. "Damn!"

❁❁❁

The next morning, I got up and went jogging. I ran a little farther than usual because I couldn't get the thought of Anise out of my mind. Throughout my professional career, I had been successful at burying my addiction, but my lust for this patient had me regressing back to my days of nymphomania. I loved my wife and I loved my practice, but this developing uncontrollable desire for this woman was placing both of them in jeopardy.

The drive to the office was long and aggravating, however, I still thought I would arrive shortly before my first appointment. Rosemary, as usual, had everything prepared for me. My file was sitting on my desk. My coffee was sitting on the warmer. And my patient was sitting on the waiting room's couch.

"Good morning," I said as I rushed into the office. I extended my hand to shake the patient's hand. "Sorry I'm late, ran into a little traffic on the way in."

I was taken aback by her unusual size. She was about five feet eight inches tall, but weighed one hundred pounds soaking wet.

Veronica was a thirty-two-year-old white woman whose hair was long, stringy, and blonde. She had blue eyes, a pointed nose and thin lips. Her strong cheekbones kind of reminded me of Sarah Jessica Parker's.

"That's okay, I'm Veronica Taylor."

"Hi, Veronica, can you please come with me into my office?"

"Sure," Veronica said, following me.

I placed my items on a chair and sat down at my desk. Mrs. Veronica Taylor, former state beauty queen, now suffered from an eating disorder known as anorexia nervosa. Anorexia is an obsessive psychological condition that begins with the notion of dieting to lose weight. The objective of becoming thinner becomes secondary to the obsession of controlling and the fears relating to one's own body. The dieter continues the destructive cycle to the point of starvation and in some cases, death.

Approximately ninety-five percent of those affected by anorexia are female, and though the numbers are small, men as well, are affected by the disorder. Caucasians, particularly those in the middle and upper socioeconomic groups, are more affected than other racial groups. The most at-risk groups are athletes, dancers, actors, and models. As a former beauty queen, Veronica was a prime candidate. In her initial session, I was determined to get her to admit the source of her eating disorder.

"How are you?"

"I'm fine, how are you, Dr. Forrester?"

"Great," I said. "Today, I want you to tell me a little more about your past. I want you to relax and tell me whatever you feel comfortable telling me, okay?"

"Okay, I'll try," Veronica said.

VERONICA'S STORY:

"I was born in Albany, Georgia. My parents were socialites in the Albany area, if that's what you want to call them. I was the youngest of three girls. My oldest sister, Eve, who was six years older than me, and Reese, who was two years older, were beauty pageant winners, so there was tremendous pressure for me to follow in their footsteps.

"Being thin was easy for them; they appeared to be naturally slender people. I had to work a lot harder at it. Even though I dieted, worked out, the whole ball of wax, I just couldn't stop gaining weight. I became depressed because I knew I was disappointing my family. I didn't want to be an embarrassment. The ugly child! The loser! So I started to look to alternative ways to keep the weight off.

"My first experience with vomiting after eating was on Thanksgiving Day, my junior year of high school. I accidentally walked in on my sister, Reese, bent over the toilet. She was on her knees, with her ponytail clutched tightly in her hand to prevent the splatter from getting in her hair. I will never forget the way her eyes were bulging and her face was sunken in. I ran to her thinking she was sick. She pushed me away and I watched in horror as she coughed up the meal she had just eaten.

"Reese was tall, about five feet eleven inches. She had naturally blonde hair and the deepest blue eyes. She had broad shoulders and slender hips. Her lips were also naturally full which gave her an exotic look. She was a joy to look at, up close or afar. But seeing her on that bathroom floor was an image I never wanted to see again.

"Get away from me," Reese said before sticking her face further in the bowl.

"What's the matter with you?" I said in disbelief.

"Get out of here, Ronnie!" Reese shouted. "Get out!"

"No! What are you doing?" I shouted back.

"Ugh!" Reese groaned, spilling her meal into the toilet again and then rolling over and sitting up. "Why didn't you knock?"

"Why didn't you lock the door?" I shouted back.

"Are you happy now?" Reese screamed, wiping her mouth.

"No! I'm not happy! What are you doing?"

"Welcome to the real world, little sister," Reese said. "This is how you win beauty pageants, Ronnie!"

"What?" I said before turning to walk out of the bathroom, "I'm telling Mom and Dad!"

"Get back in here!" Reese shouted, jumping up and pulling me back into the bathroom. "You think Mom and Dad don't know I do this? Don't be naïve, Ronnie! They know! They just don't care! As long as I'm their little debutante and win their little pageants, they couldn't care less how I do it."

"Please, this isn't healthy, Reese. You're small enough! Look at you, you're beautiful!"

"That's just it, Ronnie," Reese said sadly. "You're never really small enough. Instead of killing myself with working out and dieting, this is easy, and it's effective."

"In a matter of minutes, Reese was back in the kitchen eating more food, laughing and talking as if nothing had happened. It wasn't long after that when I began to vomit after eating. I wasn't doing it regularly, but I was doing it enough to get results. The weight came off quickly and stayed off. My popularity skyrocketed and I started to place in the top three in local pageants. Shortly thereafter, I started to win, and then winning became expected of me. The more I won, the more I vomited.

"I don't know if it was the success of winning or the convenience of knowing I could eat without fear of putting on weight. But for whichever reason, my obsession spiraled out of control and I never recovered.

"Throughout all of the madness, I met my husband in college and we married and had children. Just as I thought of my sisters, he thought I was naturally thin. It took him a while, but he finally realized my thinness was not normal. His curiosity made him peek into my personal life and he found out some of my dark secrets. And that's why I am here..."

"I weighed one hundred twenty pounds the first time I vomited. That is the most I've weighed since. Even after watching Reese starve herself to death, I continued to force myself to lose weight. I loved my sister! I love my family! Please help me, Dr. Forrester."

✪✪✪

Later that afternoon, I had an appointment with Mrs. Betty Amos. Betty was African-American, with about a five-foot-five or six, slender frame. She was what we would call voluptuous. Big Ass! Big Boobs! Big everything! She wore a neat, short, round natural 'do speckled with gray. She was very dark-skinned. She reminded me of the actress Esther Rolle, who played Florida Evans on the sitcom *Good Times*. I can't help it if my patients resembled celebrities.

Betty was previously diagnosed with a disorder known as Münchausen's. Münchausen Syndrome is a factitious disorder in which a person pretends that she or he has a physical or mental illness. Actually, the symptoms or results of the symptoms are self-inflicted. Münchausen's, named for Baron von Münchausen, an eighteenth-century German officer who was known for embellishing stories of his life and experiences, is the most severe type of factitious disorder.

In most cases, people with this disorder pretend to have these symptoms to gain the sympathy or attention of physicians, friends or family members. Many people go as far as to cause bodily harm to themselves. There are those willing to undergo painful and risky operations. Some of the most common physical symptoms are chest pains, stomach problems and fever.

People with this syndrome deliberately produce or embellish symptoms in a variety of ways. They lie or fake being ill, hurt themselves, or alter their diagnosis. The possible warning signs are dramatic but inconsistent medical history; drastic change once treatment has begun; predictable relapses following improvement in the condition; extensive knowledge of hospitals and/or medical terminology, as well as the textbook descriptions of illnesses; presence of multiple surgical scars; appearance of new or additional symptoms following negative test results; presence of symptoms only when the patient is alone or not being observed; willingness or eagerness to have medical tests, operations, or other procedures; history of seeking treatment at numerous hospitals, clinics, and doctor's offices, possibly even in different cities; reluctance to allow health care professionals to meet with or talk to family, friends, or prior health care providers; problems with identity and self-esteem.

Betty was a prime example of Münchausen's. She was forty-five years old and just had her first child. During her pregnancy, Betty received the traditional attention given to a pregnant mother. In addition, she received attention for being a middle-aged mother. Also, she was heralded by doctors for the miracle of her child's birth. That came after having been diagnosed as barren. The attention was overwhelming and subsequently difficult to surrender.

After the healthy delivery of a baby girl whom she named Audrey, Betty continuously took the child into the emergency room for mysterious illnesses. However, doctor after doctor found that these illnesses had ephemeral symptoms that were not prevalent when the child arrived at the hospital.

Suspicion arose when Betty's husband, David, walked into a hospital emergency room with Audrey unresponsive to cardio-pulmonary resuscitation. It took several attempts to revive the child, and only by the grace of God were they finally able to get the baby to breathe on her own. As heroic as the doctors and nurses were, much to their chagrin, Audrey was left with mild brain damage.

The incident was investigated as possible child abuse. Upon the investigation results, enough evidence was presented that the police thought it was in Audrey's best interest to be taken away from David and Betty.

Fortunately, David was cleared of any involvement in Audrey's previous visits to the hospital and she was returned to him after he and Betty filed for a divorce.

In order for Betty to have regular visitations, she would have to undergo a psychological examination. She flat out refused and was denied further contact with Audrey. David convinced her to seek counseling for post-partum depression. Although she was reluctant to receive psychological treatment because she felt she was innocent of the allegations against her, for the sake of spending time with Audrey, she agreed.

In my professional analysis of Mrs. Betty Amos, I was convinced that she did not suffer from post-partum psychosis, but was a classic case of Münchausen's. Understanding the circumstances, I was expecting Betty to be a hostile patient, and she certainly did not disappoint me.

"Good afternoon, Mrs. Amos," I said. "May I call you Betty?"

"Call me whatever you want," Betty said.

"How are Audrey and David?"

"They're fine, why do you ask?" Betty answered defensively.

"No reason, just being courteous."

"I know why I'm here, so don't try to pick my mind!" Betty snapped.

"I'm not here to pick your mind, Betty, I'm here to listen, and listen only," I said, trying to make her feel comfortable. "You seem to be reluctant to engage in your therapy. May I ask why?"

"Because I don't want to be here!" Betty said. "I'm only here because I want to see my child! And prove once and for all that there's nothing wrong with me."

"I understand."

"Do you?" Betty asked. "Do you really understand what it's like to have your friends, the police and your entire community believe that you would harm your child?"

"I can't say that I do, Betty. But I can try understanding how you feel."

"Listen to me! I don't have time for your psychological bullshit, so say whatever it is you have to say so I can get the hell out of here!" Betty lit a cigarette.

"I'm sorry, Betty, but this is a smoke-free facility."

"What?" Betty snapped, appearing to be very annoyed.

"You're not allowed to smoke inside of this building."

"Well, I'll be back."

Betty stood up and stormed through the waiting room and out of the office. I followed her until she slammed the door behind her.

"What was that all about?" Rosemary asked.

"Believe me, I have no idea," I said with my hands in the air.

"Has she completed her session?"

"I don't know," I said while walking back to the office, "I really don't know."

A few minutes later, Betty returned smelling like a smokestack, still just as defensive as she was when she left.

"Okay, how much more time do we have?" Betty asked.

"That's up to you."

"Do you realize I'm a registered nurse?"

"Yes, I am aware of that. May I ask why you asked that question?"

"Because I have been a nurse for over twenty years and I know when a child is sick. Especially mine!"

Betty stared at me intensely, to the point that the silence became uncomfortable. I took advantage of the moment and asked the difficult question.

"Can you tell me what happened the day Audrey was rushed to the emergency ward?"

"Yes, she stopped breathing."

"Why? What happened?"

"I'll tell you the same thing I told everybody else; it was an allergic reaction!"

"An allergic reaction to what?"

"I don't know!"

"By your own admission, you're a seasoned registered nurse who recognized an allergic reaction in your own child. Shouldn't you then be able to determine what caused it?"

"It's not that simple!"

"Okay," I said, pausing momentarily, "but I'm curious to know why, after all the trips to the emergency ward with Audrey being turned away untreated, why after all of those times, did you decide to let David take her, and not you?"

"Are you a therapist, or a detective?"

"I apologize if I sound accusatory, Betty. I'm simply trying to understand the core of the problem so that we can discuss it."

"The core of the problem is that I'm frustrated! Frustrated that everybody believes that I tried to kill my daughter!"

"Do you think the accusations are unwarranted?"

"Unwarranted?" Betty shouted. "You bet they're unwarranted!"

"And how does that make you feel?"

"How do you think it makes me feel? I'm pissed off! Angry! As a nurse and loving mother, when I see any symptoms harmful to my child, I'm not going to wait until she's fatally sick. I'm going to take precautionary measures to ensure her health and I don't give a damn what anyone else thinks!" Betty was so frustrated her lips were shivering. "Do you have any children?"

"Yes, I have a daughter."

"How would you feel if you were being accused of hurting your most prized possession?"

"I don't know, Betty, I never considered my child as being one of my possessions."

CHAPTER SIX

The next afternoon, Kimberly's and Wanda's appointments were back to back. I didn't like for my appointments to run so closely together because I didn't want my patients to interact at such an early stage in their therapy. I thought it was safe for Wanda because she didn't suffer from any mental disorders. In fact, I was curious to see how Kimberly would interact with a supposedly normal person.

After Kimberly's session, I walked her into the waiting room. I asked her to wait as I pretended to be taking care of business with Rosemary. She walked around nervously and then sat in a chair.

Wanda was sitting on the waiting couch with two more of the office girls. I presumed Valerie and Darsha had come for entertainment purposes.

Valerie was tall with long legs, nice shape. Her hair was cut short. She had a dark complexion. She wore a man's business suit, but it was very appealing on her.

Darsha was light-skinned, with stylish shiny hair and young! Her eyes were shaped similar to an Asian's. She also wore youthful stylish clothes.

At first, Kimberly was timid and nonsocial. But it didn't take her long to start interacting with the office girls. I was pleased with the activity until Kimberly began to suffer from delusions.

She began talking out of her head about William, or Bill, as she referred to him, and the office girls could not make sense of her. I tried to alleviate the confusion by stepping in, but by that time it was too late. The office girls got up and quickly walked outside.

"Oh shit," I mumbled to myself, following them out of the office.

"Johnny, what the hell is wrong with that crazy-ass woman in there?" Wanda said, screaming at the top of her lungs.

"Wanda, she's not crazy, and please lower your voice," I said.

"Lower my voice? You got us up in there with that fruitcake!"

"Stop calling her names!" I said.

"Johnny, I ain't gon' lie, she had me scared as hell!" Valerie said.

"Me too, that woman is in there talking about Bill Clinton is her boyfriend! And you don't think that's crazy?" Darsha asked.

I lowered my head figuring it would be easier to just let them rant themselves out than to try to get them to be quiet.

"What the hell is that?" Wanda said. "A freakin' giant?"

"Ain't that bitch big?" Valerie asked.

"That bitch bigger than you, Johnny!" Wanda said.

"Stop it!" I shouted. "Stop calling her names!"

"Okay, man!" Wanda said, laughing along with Darsha and Valerie. "We gon' leave you and your *one flew over the cuckoo's nest* alone."

"Thank you!" I said sarcastically.

"But you better call security before that big heffa get loose up in there," Darsha said.

"I'm telling you, because if she get pissed off and snap up in there, even yo' big ass ain't gon' be able to stop that *National Geographic*!" Valerie said.

"If that giant run up on me, she gon' get her ass maced!" Darsha said before reaching into her purse and pulling out a can of mace.

"Mace ain't gon' stop that woman! Not even an elephant gun gon' stop that big bohemian." Wanda laughed.

As they were laughing, Kimberly wandered into the hall, mumbling to herself.

"Johnny, get her," Wanda said and moved behind me.

"I'm getting the hell outta here!" Valerie said and went scampering onto the elevator. "Wanda, I'll wait for you downstairs!"

"Girl, wait for me!" Darsha caught up with Valerie and jumped on the elevator before the doors closed.

As Wanda was trying to escape, Kimberly stood between her and the elevator. Wanda stood in her tracks, closed her eyes and screamed loudly.

"JOHNNY! HELP ME!"

"What's wrong?" Kimberly asked very softly.

"Get away from me!" Wanda shouted.

I started to walk toward Wanda slowly, because I did not want to startle Kimberly. Kimberly looked at me, and then at Wanda.

"Is she hurt?" Kimberly asked.

"No, Kimberly," I said, "she's fine."

"Then why is she yelling like she hurt?"

"Don't worry about her, she's fine. We were only playing a game."

"Can I play?"

"No!" Wanda said quickly.

Kimberly stared back and forth at Wanda and me.

"Are you mad at me?" Kimberly asked Wanda.

"No," Wanda said apologetically, "no, I'm not mad at you."

"Then why can't I play with you?"

"Well, the game is over. Maybe you can play with Dr. Forrester later."

"I can?" Kimberly asked excitedly.

"Sure you can," I said.

"Thank you, Ma'am!" Kimberly said to Wanda, before turning to me. "Thank you, Dr. Forrester."

"My pleasure, Kimberly."

"Are you my friend?" Kimberly asked Wanda.

"Uh, yeah," Wanda said. "Yeah, I'm your friend."

"Here," Kimberly said, pulling a flower from out of her huge hat and handing it to Wanda.

"Thank you," Wanda said, taking the flower.

"Are you my friend?" Kimberly asked again.

"Yes, I'm your friend," Wanda answered, finally relaxing.

"You're my friend, too!" Kimberly said, grinning from ear to ear.

"Shouldn't you hurry to catch your bus, Kimberly?" I asked.

Kimberly ignored me and continued to talk to Wanda.

"Before I got like this, I used to be pretty. Real, real pretty, just like you," Kimberly said. "And, and, and, I may not be as pretty as I used to be on the outside, but my friend says I am still pretty on the inside."

I couldn't have written a better ending. Wanda didn't have a response to Kimberly's remark, nor did I. Her behavior, though strange, was more dignified than that of any of the rest of us.

She proved that the line between sanity and insanity is as thin as the words that we speak.

"Okay, well," I said, "I guess I'll be seeing you next week."

"Bye-bye!" Kimberly said, waving at Wanda and me as she stepped onto the elevator.

Wanda and I waved back and Kimberly continued to wave until the elevator doors closed.

"Next time, come alone, Wanda," I said while leading Wanda back into my office.

"Okay," Wanda said, "but let's hurry up and get in your office before them elevator doors open and the '*Green Mile*' get back off that elevator."

"Get in there!" I opened the door and watched Wanda walk past.

❁❁❁

Later that day, we met at Mike's house for dinner. Alicia and Cynthia and another one of the office girls, Pam, were in business together. They had become quite successful in the short time since launching their marketing firm. CAP Public Relations and Marketing, an acronym for Cynthia, Alicia, and Pam, targeted mostly female clientele with a "woman-power" campaign.

Pam was distinctively attractive to me. She had a very sculptured body and a sculptured face with an elegant haircut. And an ass that could be defined only as phenomenal! Her negative attribute, without question, was her horrible disposition.

Atlanta was a hip-hop city with a hip-hop culture, and CAP wanted to take full advantage of the potential budding stars.

They had recently been negotiating a contract with a young superstar in the entertainment business. The young woman's stage name was Gizelle. I had never heard of her, but apparently she was a hot commodity and they really wanted to sign her. She was going to be the guest of honor for the dinner and they were expecting to sign her to a contract at that time.

Cynthia had gone all out to make their house look like an executive mansion. The dining room had elegant candles, tablecloths, and servers. Do you hear me? Servers! I had been to Mike's house a million times and was quite familiar with the decor. That night there was plenty of furniture, decorations, and people I had never seen before.

Mike and I were in the basement watching television and waiting for the arrival of their big superstar. We had kindly been moved from ground zero, and removed to below ground, period. But you didn't get a complaint out of us, we were happy with the arrangement. We wanted to stay as far away as possible from the rat race pressure of their dinner party.

As usual, Cynthia and Alicia did most of the legwork; Pam normally came in at the end and made sure everything was intact. Don't get me wrong; this was a practice that served their business quite well. When Pam swooped through, it was with diligence and authority. Her no-nonsense attitude was the glue that kept the firm together.

Mike and I were stretched out on separate couches with our legs kicked up, relaxing. There was no conversation, just the ever-melodic sound of the television. Brothers don't need dialogue to enjoy each other's company. Most times, a mutual television show will suffice.

Somehow, and neither Mike nor I would ever admit to being the culprit, the station was stuck on the Lifetime channel and not on ESPN where it began. Our silence was a code of acceptance and denial. If neither of us spoke of our effeminate attraction to the chick flick that had us so enthralled, neither one of us had to admit it. Not until we heard the sound of Cynthia's feet rushing down the stairs.

"Hey, man!" Mike said. "Turn the station!"

"Huh?" I said, not reacting fast enough.

"Man, turn the station, Cynthia's coming!" Mike jumped up quickly, looking for the remote.

"Where's the remote?" I said, jumping up, too.

"It's over there!" Mike shouted. "It's over there by you!"

"I don't see it!" I said, tossing pillows around.

"Uh, fellas," Cynthia said while walking over to the television and changing the station manually, "the next time, all you have to do is walk over to the television and just change the station with your hand."

"Boy, you and your jokes, Cynt," Mike said.

"Oh, is that what you call them?" I said sarcastically.

"Anyway," Cynthia said, "we need you two to get dressed."

"Get dressed?" Mike asked. "We still have two hours left."

"Yeah, but you two need to shower and get freshened up."

"SHOWER?" Mike and I shouted simultaneously.

"I've already showered once today," I said.

"Me, too!" Mike added.

"That was today, now you need to take one tonight," Cynthia said.

"I'm sorry, baby, but hell no!" Mike said. "I told you when we were married that I was committed to one ass-wash a day. I have fulfilled my commitment, now please allow me to live in peace as a man."

"You better quit trying to show out in front of your brother and get your butt in that shower, Mike," Cynthia said, looking at him seriously.

"Don't be a hero, man," I said sarcastically, "live to fight another day."

"I'm only doing this for my little brother, Cynt; don't think you're running anything up in here! This is my house!" Mike said jokingly.

"Whatever you have to tell yourself is okay by me; just get your butt in that shower. You too, Johnny," Cynthia said, snapping her fingers, "get to cleaning!"

"Hold it! Hold it! Hold it now!" I stood up. "I'm not your husband. Your two showers a day rule does not apply to me."

"Boy, if you don't get your butt up there in that shower!" Cynthia said, putting her hands on her hips.

"Don't be a hero," Mike said sarcastically, "live to fight another day. She's small, but she's wiry!"

"Man, whatever," I said, before stomping up the stairs behind Mike with Cynthia closely on my heels.

"Hup, two, three, four! Hup, two, three, four!" Cynthia marched toward us.

"Cynt," I said jokingly, "I can have Rosemary make an appointment for you next week. I can fix this for you!"

"You better be worried about your appointment for dinner tonight!" Cynthia said, still marching and swinging her arms back and forth. "Hup, two, three, four! Hup, two, three, four!"

Mike and I showered, dressed and prepared for the CAP dinner. We went back to the basement to watch more television until we were summoned. This time we made sure the station stayed on ESPN.

It wasn't long before Cynthia was calling us upstairs to help with some of the final accessories. As we were winding down, the doorbell rang. Pam had arrived. Mike and I walked to the door to greet her. Mike's mouth dropped to the floor when he opened the door and saw Pam standing there with her date. Guess who's coming to dinner?

"Hey, Mike," Pam said, hugging him.

"Hey, what's up, Pam?" Mike stared at Pam's date.

"This is my friend, Christopher," Pam said, pointing to her date. "Christopher, this is my friend, Mike, who I was telling you about."

"Good to meet you, Christopher," Mike said, shaking Christopher's hand.

"Hi, nice to meet you, Mike," Christopher said. "You can call me Chris."

"Okay, Chris it is," Mike said, stepping to the side. "You guys come in."

Pam and Chris walked into the dining room. I watched Mike's reaction as well as Cynthia's and Alicia's to Pam's date. It was as if everyone was ignoring the pink elephant in the center of the room. Pro-black, Afrocentric, non-European Pam was on a very important dinner date with a Caucasian man, and no one thought to ask a question. Well, I took it upon myself to get to the core of her racial metamorphosis from black to white.

"So, where did you two meet?" I asked.

"I met Christopher at a conference for young entrepreneurs," Pam answered.

"Okay, interesting," I said. "So, where are you from, Chris?"

"I'm originally from Toronto, Canada," Christopher said. "But I was raised in Texas."

"Oh, Canada!" Mike said sarcastically, singing the opening bars of Canada's national anthem.

"Good rendition," Christopher said back.

"How did you guys meet at the conference?" I asked, switching back to my inquisition.

"I, uh, I sat next to Pam at the conference. We began a conversation and decided to stay in contact."

"Interesting," I said, folding my arms and tapping my lips with my fingers.

"Okay, that's enough of that, Johnny," Pam said. "Don't pay any attention to him, Chris. He's a psychologist; it's just his nature."

"I understand." Christopher laughed.

"I talked to Gizelle on my way over and told her the limo was on the way to pick her up."

"Limousine?" I asked. "You ladies are going all out, aren't you?"

"Yes, baby, we got a limousine! Gizelle is big! Really big! She's going to be our biggest client! I'm so excited!" Alicia said.

"I can see!" I said. "Hope everything goes well tonight."

"Oh, this is a done deal!" Pam said. "By the end of the night, Gizelle will be the next client of CAP!"

"Toast!" Mike said, lifting his glass.

The doorbell rang at the same time as we were lifting our glasses and we were forced to delay our premature celebration.

"I'll get it!" Cynthia said, lowering her glass and running to the door.

"Ooh, it's her!" Alicia said anxiously.

"Baby, calm down before you blow a gasket," I said.

"I can't help it!" Alicia said, jumping up and down.

"Alicia! Would you stop it?" Pam said. "We want her to think we are just as important to her as she is to us. We can't be jumping around like we're her fans!"

We could hear the voices coming around the corner and nearing the dining room. Everyone stared at the dining room door awaiting the first sight of Gizelle. But to our disappointment and elation, it was Tina and Curtis. Tina was a former office girl as well.

Tina was dark-skinned, slightly overweight, with long black hair. Although she thought people couldn't notice, she never wore her natural hair. It was either an extension or a wig. She had a cute face, but no particular feature jumped out at you. Her personality was unmatched though. She was the happiest person I've ever met. Never in a bad mood, and never allowed anyone around her to be in a bad mood.

Curtis was about five feet ten inches tall, close neat haircut, but he was balding at the top. He had a close-shaven moustache and beard. He was dark-skinned, with thin lips and a broad flat nose. He wasn't a favorite of the office girls at first, but after they saw how he was treating Tina they couldn't maintain their hostility.

Tina and Curtis had had problems in the past, but despite all of their issues, their marriage managed to survive. Curtis had abused Tina throughout their marriage, but had made a three hundred-and-sixty degree turn and now worshiped the ground she walked on. He had become a minister and a devout Christian, a triumphant story of redemption.

"Hey, y'all!" Tina said, waving her hands in the air. "I'm sorry I'm late! Is Gizelle here yet?"

"No, but she's on her way," Alicia said.

"Good, we ain't too late!" Tina said.

"How's everybody doing this evening?" Curtis asked.

"We're fine, how are you, Curtis?" Alicia said.

"I'm feeling fine."

"Hey, Curtis, I forgot to drop off those clothes at the shelter, but I'll get to them this weekend, I promise," Mike said.

"That's okay," Curtis said, "we'll take 'em when we can get 'em."

"Curtis received approval for his loan to build for the church today!" Tina shouted. "God is blessing us, ain't He?"

"Curtis, you got the loan, man?" Mike shouted.

I was surprised to see Mike's enthusiasm for Curtis. He rarely expressed emotions, even when he was excited. For some reason, he had an unexplained affection for Curtis. In my opinion, I think Curtis was his last connection to Ms. Virginia.

Ms. Virginia was the darling of the office where they worked. She was tragically murdered on the job by her ex-husband. I really didn't get the chance to know her, but by the way they talked about her, she was truly a saint. Anyway, she was responsible for introducing Curtis to Christ and getting him cleaned up and back on his feet.

"Yes! Praise the Lord!" Curtis said, balling his fists.

Pam, Cynthia and Alicia shared hugs with Curtis and Tina in a congratulatory celebration.

"Oh my God, I'm so happy for you, Curtis!" Cynthia said, hugging him again.

"Thank you, Cynthia!" Curtis said, slightly embarrassed. "May the glory be to God."

"Toast!" Mike shouted again.

"Oh no, this is y'all night, not mine!" Curtis said, pointing to the girls.

"I don't care who we're toasting, I just need a glass!" Tina said.

"Tina," Curtis said, "Don't give in to temptation."

"Come on, baby, can I have just one drink?" Tina asked. "Come on, it's a celebration. Pleeeeeease?"

"Okay, sweetheart," Curtis said, kissing her on the cheek. "One drink!"

"Pass the sauce!" Tina shouted, lifting her glass.

"Curtis, what would you like to drink?" Cynthia said.

"I'll take a soda," Curtis said. "But in a wine glass."

Cynthia filled Curtis' glass; once again as we lifted our glasses, the doorbell rang.

"Damn!" Pam said. "We're never going to finish this toast."

"Hold on, I'll be right back!" Cynthia went running to the door again.

Again, we could hear the voices approaching as they neared the dining room. This time when Cynthia stepped around the corner, she was accompanied by the beautiful Gizelle. Behind Gizelle stood a jolly black giant. I am considered to be large by most, but this guy dwarfed me in comparison. He looked familiar, as if I knew him from somewhere. As I took my attention off the Sasquatch, I looked closer at the superstar. My eyes popped, my heart stopped, and my mouth dropped. My wife's first star! My wife's bread and butter! My wife's big catch! Just happened to be my mistress, Anise Lawrence.

"Hi, everybody!" Anise said, smiling at everyone.

"Hi, Gizelle!" Alicia said, hugging her.

"Hey, Alicia," Anise said, hugging her back.

"Okay, how was the ride over?" Pam asked.

"Nice, very nice," Anise replied. "I'm going to get one of them."

Cynthia led Anise around the room, introducing her to those of us who had not made her acquaintance. Well, at least to those of us she thought had not yet made Anise's acquaintance.

"This is my brother-in-law, Johnson Forrester," Cynthia said. "We call him Johnny."

"Good evening, Dr. Forrester," Anise said.

"How did you know I was a doctor?" I said, quickly recognizing that Cynthia did not introduce me as a doctor. Not sure whether someone else may have picked up on Anise's blunder, I tried to cover her tracks by pointing to the monogram on my sports coat. "Did the monogram on my jacket give me away?"

"Absolutely," Anise said, smiling wickedly.

"Everybody sit down so we can eat," Cynthia said.

We took our seats and sat down for dinner. I didn't say a word during the meal. I kept my head down and my eyes up. The conversation flowed throughout—I was not a part of that flow, but it flowed just the same. Eventually, the saga was over and the ladies moved the party to the patio for Anise to sign the contract. Candles were lit, wine was drunk, and I was sweating like a fevered pig! Tina took a group photo of Alicia, Pam, and Cynthia as they surrounded Anise.

"Say cheese, y'all!" Tina shouted.

"CHEEEEEESE!" the ladies said in unison.

There was another round of congratulatory drinks and then the ladies took a ride in the limousine with Anise, dragging Tina along with them. Curtis and Chris left in their separate cars as Mike and I waited for our wives to return.

My head was still spinning from the would-be catastrophe and I was developing a serious headache. My wife and my mistress were in the same vehicle saying God-knows-what to each other.

I sat down at the dining room table and put my head in my hands, thinking to myself that once again, I had let my addiction ruin my life. Mike walked in with the caterers as they were beginning to clean up and noticed me sitting in pitiful despair.

"Damn, Johnny, what the hell is wrong with you?" Mike asked. "You're sweating profusely! Are you okay, man?"

"I don't think so," I said, keeping my head down.

"What's up?" Mike pulled out a chair and sat next to me.

"Man, I got myself into some serious shit," I said.

"Okay, what's up?"

"I don't even know where to begin."

"Like you always tell me," Mike said, "begin from the beginning."

"Well, you know that nice young lady that just left out of here with our wives?"

"Yeah, Gizelle," Mike said. "What's up with her?"

"I know her as Anise Lawrence; she's a patient of mine."

"For real?" Mike said excitedly.

"Yeah," I said. "But that's not all."

"What?" Mike looked at me curiously.

"Well, Anise and I have been having an affair."

Mike sat back, took a deep breath, and then stared at me.

"Man, damn, Johnny!" Mike said.

"I know," I said. "It's bad."

"Johnny, are you telling me you're cheating on Alicia with a patient?" Mike asked in disbelief.

"Yes." I rubbed my temples. "Oh, I have a headache!"

"You're going to have more than a headache if Alicia finds out!"

"She probably knows by now."

"If Alicia knew, believe me, my front door would be kicked in."

"Aw boy," I said, sitting back, "damn!"

"So what are you going to do, Johnny?"

"I keep trying to break it off with her, man, but it's like she reminds me so much of Alicia. The only difference is that Anise is freaky as hell. She'll do anything sexually, man! Anything!"

"If you have the real thing in Alicia, why do you need someone who reminds you of Alicia?"

"I don't know. I can't explain it, Mike!"

"You better get out of this shit, man, before you lose your family!"

"I want to!" I said. "But Mike, it's so good. It's so, so good!"

"Get a-hold of yourself, man!" Mike shouted.

"You're right! You're right! You're right!" I said.

"Johnny, how did you cross the line from doctor of psychology to doctor of love?" Mike asked. "What happened?"

"I don't know!" I said. "Nothing happened! It just happened!"

"No," Mike said. "Sex doesn't *just happen*. Something started this!"

"I don't know, I guess we flirted, one thing led to another, and here we are. I can't explain it any better than that."

"You can and you will," Mike said. "You're bullshitting! You're the most logical man I know, Johnny. You know what you're doing. You've thought about it. Analyzed it! Rationalized it! And now you're trying to bullshit me into thinking this was some random act of emotion. That's not you and we both know it. So what the hell is up?"

"Okay, man," I said. I knew it was time to confess my addiction to Mike because if I didn't, he was going to drive me batty with all of his questions. "I've been suffering from a sexual addiction called erotomania since I was in high school. This shit has been haunting me my whole life, man. After I was kicked out of the league, I got help and, up until now, I've been successful with battling it.

"Kicked out of the league?" Mike asked. "I thought you had a career-ending injury."

"I did," I replied. "It was sex!"

"How bad is it, Johnny?" Mike asked. "Are you some kind of freak?"

"No, man," I said. "I just love having sex with women. Normal sex! But a lot of sex! From a lot of different women."

"Is Alicia a freak like you, too?" Mike whispered.

"I'm not a freak!" I snapped and then lowered my voice. "Neither of us are freaks. I just had a minor setback, that's all."

"That's all?" Mike asked. "You're having an affair with a superstar and you think it's a minor setback?"

"It's a major setback, huh?" I said, lightly biting my lip.

"Yeah, my brother," Mike said.

"I have to call Alicia!" I said, standing up nervously. "I need to know what they're talking about in that limousine."

"Look, I told you, if Gizelle had told Alicia about you and her, this house would be raided by those office girls. Relax! You're a psychologist, get a grip!"

"You're right! You're right! I need to get a handle on things."

"Okay, we have to figure out what we need to do to get you out of this."

"Damn, man, I don't believe I got myself into this position!"

"Well, I saw Gizelle's body, and being a man myself, I have to say that I'm not saying that you're right," Mike said, "but I understand!"

"Mike, she's so beautiful, so intelligent, and so mature. Looking at her is like looking at Alicia," I added, still very confused. "This is going to be hard, man!"

"I know, man!" Mike said. "But you have to do it."

"You're right. I have to break it off!"

"You damn right you have to break it off!" Mike snapped. "If Cynthia finds out about your infidelity, it's going to ruin my household, too."

"I, uh, I'll talk to her on Monday and get to the bottom of

this, if Alicia hasn't killed me by then," I said. "Hey man, I'm sorry to disappoint you like this."

"Don't worry about what I think, man, my life ain't been no crystal stair, either."

"Life ain't been no crystal stair? What the hell does that mean? Have you been watching BET or UPN?"

"That's a line from a classic poem, fool," Mike said. "I can't condemn you; I'm just getting myself together. But anyway, go home and get some sleep. You can't do anything tonight."

"Some things change, some things stay the same, huh? I'm still the little brother running to big brother to help solve my problems."

"You listen to people's problems every day, Johnny, but who listens to yours? We all need to share our burdens sometime, even a psychologist like you. Everyone needs somebody, sometimes."

"I appreciate that man."

"Okay, now get out so I can go enjoy some porno before my wife gets back home."

"Okay," I said, managing a smile and standing to leave, "I'll see myself out."

CHAPTER SEVEN

It was a long, agonizing drive home. I went straight to bed but I kept thinking about Anise and Alicia talking and swapping stories about me. I tossed and turned until I finally fell asleep. I woke up to Alicia turning on the bedroom lights and standing over me with a pair of scissors.

"OH SHIT! Wait a minute!" I screamed, throwing my hands in the air to protect myself from any immediate slashes.

"What's wrong with you, boy?" Alicia asked.

"What are you doing standing over me like that with those scissors?" I sat up and reached for a pillow to cover my family jewels. Just in case she was still planning a sneak attack.

"Here, can you cut the price tag off of this nightie for me?" Alicia said, handing me the scissors.

"Oh, sure, no problem," I said, removing the pillow and taking the scissors out of her hands.

"Were you having a bad dream?"

"Yeah, something like that."

"Tonight was one of the best nights of my life!"

"I'm happy for you, sweetheart!"

"I'm sorry for bailing out on you at the dinner party, but I thought this would make up for it," Alicia said while pulling the nightie completely over her body. "Come here."

She stared at me as she lifted her nightie above her head, revealing her sexy, perky breasts. She seemed to have glided out of the negligee with the simplest of ease, dropping it to her toes, and then kicking it to the side.

She took me by my hand and led me to my comfy chair, a huge winged-back chair where I sat when Alicia wanted to give me special attention. She turned down the lights and began to dance seductively, rubbing her ass up and down on my manhood. It sprang up instantaneously, almost bursting through my boxers. She turned around and faced me, taking her breasts in her hands and putting them in my face. As I puckered up to taste her nipples, she moved them away. The way she teased me drove me wild and she knew it.

She reached inside of my underwear and fondled me, stroking up and down. When I started to moan and move my hips to her rhythm, she moved away again and danced over to what we call the entertainment center. It is most commonly known in some bedrooms as the "stripper pole." It was her idea to install the pole to spice up our relationship. I must say that pole has brought more peace of mind in this bedroom than I could ever hope to accomplish in my office.

Alicia began to dance around the pole, grabbing it with one hand and letting her body fall backward. Her head dropped toward the floor as she leaped in the air and wrapped her legs around the top of the pole. She was suspended momentarily in an upside-down position, head to the floor and feet to the sky. My manhood jerked as Alicia's body slowly slid down the pole.

As her knees hit the floor, she leaned completely backward with the pole between her legs and started to grind. She had her legs beneath her, as she lay on her back, rising up to the pole, grinding, and then falling back down. She held the pole with both hands and continued to grind on it, up and down, up and down. It must have started to arouse her as well because her moans were becoming increasingly louder. At one point, I think she was totally oblivious to my presence. I know my wife, and I know how she reacts to an orgasm.

She bit her bottom lip and stuck her hands in her panties. She sat upright and opened her legs and placed them on either side of the pole. Her fingers were moving quickly inside of her panties, as her other hand cupped one of her breasts.

"Ah," Alicia said, very softly, "Ah! Ah! Ah! Ah! Ah!"

It was about all I could stand watching her beautiful body spread out as she pleasured herself. Her body started to tremor and she turned on her side in the fetal position and shook convulsively. Her fingers were still moving rapidly inside of her panties.

I dropped my shorts around my ankles and lay beside her on the floor. While she was still having her orgasm, I slid my manhood inside of her from behind. I lifted her leg in the air, holding her by the ankles, carefully targeting every stroke. Going in as deep as I could go, and then bringing it out as far as I could go, slowly and deeply, over and over.

She turned her face toward me and licked me wherever she could. Her kisses felt so moist, so wet, so damn comforting. Being inside of her let me know the difference between love and lust. I loved this woman very much. I would give my life in an instant to save hers, but for some sick reason, I couldn't be faithful to her to save my life.

As I released myself inside of her, she continued to say how much she loved me. The more she talked, the guiltier I felt.

"Oh baby," Alicia moaned, "I love you so much."

"I love you, too, baby."

"Don't move," Alicia said, "I want to just lay here with you inside of me."

"Alicia," I said, "you know there's not even an adjective to describe how much I love you, right?"

"Do you really love me that much, Johnny?" Alicia turned on her back and looked into my eyes.

"Until my daughter was born, I never knew I could love anyone as much as I loved her. But then, that was my child, my baby, so that explained that special love between us. I never thought for a moment that I could fall in love with a woman and feel that special kind of love. I never felt that way until I met you, and I've been head over heels ever since."

"Oh, that's so sweet."

"Get some sleep; you have a busy day tomorrow."

"Okay," Alicia said, snuggling in my arms and closing her eyes. "Good night."

"Good night," I said before covering Alicia's body with the comforter from our bed.

After Alicia fell asleep, I couldn't help but rub her beautiful face as I lay peacefully on the floor. I held her close to me and caressed her body for the remainder of the night.

❊❊❊

The next morning, Alicia awoke early from excitement. They were scheduled to have lunch with Anise for a photo shoot. By the time I got up, breakfast was cooked, Alicia was dressed, and Pam and Cynthia were already sitting in my kitchen when I walked into it.

"Good morning, ladies." I yawned and opened the refriger-ator.

"Good morning, Mr. Forrester," Cynthia said.

"Good morning, Mrs. Forrester," I said back.

"What's up, Johnny B. Goode?" Pam said sarcastically.

"Nothing much," I looked at Alicia, "just trying to get a meal." I poured a glass of milk and leaned against the counter.

"Oh, Mike told me to tell you that he would be over here in a little while to pick you up to go golfing," Cynthia said.

"Golfing?" I said, pausing in the middle of a drink. "Mike?"

"He's been watching the Golf Channel lately and he said he feels he can be as good as Tiger Woods."

"What time did he say he was coming?"

Ding-dong!

"Um, about now," Cynthia said.

I went to the door and couldn't help but laugh when I saw Mike standing there in plaid and checkers.

"Mike, you're breaking every fashion law known to man." I chuckled.

"What? You don't like this?" Mike showed off his clothes. "This is what golf is all about."

"You look like a clown, Mike."

"Let's go shoot eighteen, or thirty-six, or however many it is! I'm ready to do this!"

"Not with me! I'm not going anywhere with you looking like that, and it's not shoot, it's play. Let's go play eighteen holes."

"You play, I shoot!" Mike walked through the house. "Where's my wife?"

"In the kitchen," I said, following him.

"Good morning, Charlie's Angels," Mike said, walking into the kitchen.

"Oh, my eyes!" Pam covered her eyes.

"Cynthia, how could you let Michael come outside like that?" Alicia said.

"Michael Forrester, what are you wearing?" Cynthia asked, turning around and looking at Mike from head to toe.

"This is my Tiger Woods gear, baby!"

"You're not going out in public looking like that."

"This is classic wear, Cynt," Mike said. "I'm talkin' Ben Hogan!"

"Ben Hogan?" Pam said. "He's a wrestler, right?"

"No, Pam," I said. "That would be Hulk Hogan."

"I don't know who Ben Hogan is, but if he dresses like that," Cynthia pointed to Mike, "he needs to be ashamed of himself, too."

"Come on, big boy, let's go," Mike said, patting me on the back.

"I don't feel like going anywhere, man." I sat next to Alicia at the table.

"Man, you bug me to death about playing golf with you and when I go out and buy all this gear, you don't wanna play?"

"I want to play," I said. "Just not today."

"Mike, you look like a Harvard white boy!" Pam said.

"Look who's talking about a Harvard white boy. You didn't have a problem with bringing that Harvard white boy in my house last night."

"Yeah, what was that all about, Pam?" Alicia asked.

"It was something different. He was nice, and I'm just so tired of black men it's pitiful."

"So, is Christopher your flavor now?" Cynthia joked.

"Yup!" Pam said. "He respects me as a woman! I don't have to worry about him not having a job! Cheating! Lying! None of that baby-mama-drama shit. We're just kicking it. I never thought I could ever have something serious with a white guy, but I don't know, girl."

"Before you become consumed with jungle fever, I told you I have a friend I want you to meet, Pam," Mike said.

"Is he black?" Pam asked.

"Of course."

"Then naw, I'm cool," Pam said. "Black men need to get themselves together before I date another one."

"Huh?" Mike said. "Get themselves together? What do you mean by that?"

"Don't trip. You know what that means." Pam took a sip of orange juice.

"Here we go," Mike said, rolling his eyes. "No, I don't know what you mean. How about you tell me, Pam?"

"Well, black men are bossy, lazy, deceitful, and I'm tired of dealing with that bullshit."

"So, Your Majesty, you haven't found one black man that you feel is deserving of your love?" Mike asked.

"Nope! Every black man I get involved with is sorry! And I'm tired of dealing with that."

"I don't know, I'm not a psychologist or anything, but Johnny," Mike said, turning to me, "if a person develops a socially destructive pattern, does that come from without or within?"

"Don't drag me into your argument; I'm an innocent bystander."

"Man up!" Mike said. "Defend yourself!"

"She's not talking about me," I said.

"The hell she's not," Mike said. "You're just as black as any other black man; don't let your degrees fool ya!"

"I'm not getting in it!" I said.

"Pam, what the hell is wrong with you?" Mike asked.

"Why do you and Johnny always use that term, Mike?" Alicia asked.

"What term?" I asked.

"'What the hell'?" Alicia said. "You two use that term for everything!"

"I know, right?" Cynthia agreed.

"I get it from my daddy!" Mike said. "Now Pam, what the hell is wrong with you?"

"There's nothing wrong with me," Pam said before crossing her legs.

"Let's analyze this for a minute," Mike said. "If you continue to attract lazy, bossy, and deceitful black men, perhaps it's not so much them as it is you."

"I don't think so! It ain't me! It's their lazy asses! I don't even know why you're even arguing with me. You know it's true!"

"I can't speak about all black men, but as for me, I'm not lazy! I'm not bossy! And I'm not deceitful! So that bullshit you're talking is not true with me and I am definitely a black man."

"Well, I just see you as a man."

"What do you mean you just see me as a man? I'm a black man. So see me as a black man!"

"Well, if you want me to see you negatively, then I will," Pam said.

"Wait a minute, so you're saying that if I'm seen as a black man, it has to be negatively, and in order for me to be seen positively, I have to be seen as just a man? That's bullshit, Pam!"

"That ain't bullshit, it's the truth!" Pam shouted.

"It's that type of ignorant-ass talk from our women that hurts us more than anything!"

"That's how I see it, Mike, you can't tell me how to think!" Pam yelled.

"I'm not telling you how to think! I'm saying what you're saying is bullshit!!" Mike shouted back. "What you're saying doesn't make sense, Pam!"

"How come it doesn't? Because you don't agree?" Pam yelled, standing up.

"Pam, calm down," Alicia said and patted her hand.

"I am calm!" Pam shouted.

"Well, it's like this, Pam. I'd appreciate it if you keep your opinions about black men to yourself when you talk to me. It's disrespectful and I don't want to hear it."

"Mike, this is my mouth and I can say whatever I want to say!"

"I know whose mouth it is, but I'm asking you to respect me as a black man, and as a friend, and keep your negative opinions to yourself!"

"You can't tell me what I can say!"

"Pam!" Mike screamed, and then he spoke softly. "Pam, listen to me, please. I am a black man, and when you say such negative things about black men, you are talking about me, Johnny, and every other decent black man in this country. Johnny can sit over there and act like he's not black, but if he does, he's settling for that stereotypical rhetoric himself."

"Why are you dragging me into it, man?" I asked.

"You're the weak link, man!" Mike said. "Back to you, Pam. I have a wife that I love and respect. I have children that I love and adore. I am not a criminal! I am not lazy! I am not bossy! I am a proud *'black'* man who wants to be respected for being a *'black'* man. Shit, I'm black! I'm not invisible! Respect me for being black!"

"I can respect you as a man, but not as a black man," Pam said. "So I guess we can agree to disagree."

"No, no, we can't. Not on this. There is no agreeing to disagree. You either respect me as a black man and this I ask as a friend, or we can't be friends."

"Mike, you can't tell me what I can or cannot say, man! And you can't change how women think!"

"Who are you supposed to be, Pam?" Mike asked. "The queen of women? Your bitter, mean ass don't represent every woman in America! It's only the bad-ass-attitude broads who can't find a man to put up with that bullshit!"

"Mike!" Cynthia said. "Don't talk to her like that!"

"Oh, that's okay," Pam said. "He's showing his true color right now. He's just a niggah like any other black man!"

"I got your niggah." Mike kissed Cynthia on the cheek. "I'll see you later, sweetheart. Johnny! Alicia! I'll see you two later."

"So I guess I'm off the hook for golf then, right?" I asked.

"I guess so," Mike replied.

After Mike walked out, we sat in silence momentarily and then Pam spoke.

"What's wrong with Mike?" Pam asked.

"What's wrong with Mike?" Cynthia snapped.

"What's wrong with you?"

"What do you mean what's wrong with me?" Pam snapped back.

"Mike's right! You don't represent all women! Just because your bad-attitude ass can't keep a man, don't run around here acting like you're a spokesperson for all women!"

"Would you two stop?" Alicia said.

"Why are y'all trippin'?" Pam said. "All I did was bring a

white dude to our dinner party and y'all acting like I bleached my skin like Michael Jackson or something!"

"Lay off Mike!" I shouted.

"We're tripping because it's insulting to Mike, or any other black man for that matter, to hear someone say to their face that they're lazy and deceitful."

"Cynthia, Mike knows I wasn't talking about him," Pam said. "He just wanted to talk shit."

"To him, you were talking about him! His skin ain't clear, Pam, he's black! He's a black man! And he wants to be viewed and respected as a black man!"

"That's too bad, I can't help what I've been through, and my opinion is based on my experience. That's how I see black men."

"If that's how you see them, then that's how you see them! But Mike doesn't want to hear your constant complaining and bashing of black men because you can't get along with them. And to tell you the truth, I'm tired of hearing it myself."

"I'm sorry but I'm going to say what I want to say."

"Are you really that bitter? Huh, Pam? You're so mad that you're willing to lose your friends because you're too damn stubborn to stop insulting them?"

"Again," Pam said, "what is the big deal? Johnny is not upset!"

"That's Johnny!" Cynthia said. "If he doesn't mind listening to you insult black men, that's something he has to deal with. Any man with a spine should speak up when being insulted."

"Hey!" I said. "I can hear you, Cynt."

"I'm sorry, Johnny. Don't take that personally, baby," Cynthia said.

"I don't see any other way to take it," I joked.

"Anyway," Pam said. "Mike will get over it, Cynthia."

"Naw, I don't think so, and I don't think he should. And I'm going to tell you right now, if you don't apologize to him, I won't get over it either."

"And what is that supposed to mean?" Pam said. "Is that supposed to be a threat?"

"If you can't respect my husband, then I can't respect you. It's as simple as that," Cynthia said. "Look, I better go!"

Alicia probably wanted to step in and stop the argument like I did, but we were both so flabbergasted by the intensity of the conversation we could only look on in amazement. That changed when Cynthia stood up to leave.

Pam and Alicia realized how important Cynthia was to their relationship with Gizelle and how important Gizelle was to the success of CAP's PR and marketing firm. It was Cynthia who had convinced her to sign with their firm.

Alicia, Pam, and Cynthia brought different skills to their company. Cynthia was the recruiter; she had a wholesome, trusting personality that made their potential clients feel comfortable. Alicia was the seller; she was glamorous and charismatic and reflected the image of their marketing firm. Pam was the closer, she was aggressive and savvy and made the clients feel as if they were always getting the better of the deal, even when they weren't. They needed all three of those aspects to keep their newly found goldmine on board. Alicia and Pam knew it, and unfortunately for them, so did Cynthia.

"Where are you going, Cynt?" Alicia asked.

"Home!" Cynthia said.

"No you're not; we have a photo shoot today!" Pam said.

"Pam, I don't give a damn about a photo shoot when it comes to my family!"

"See, that's what I'm talking about right there!" Pam said. "You're willing to ruin your own happiness to please your husband."

"I'm not ruining anything, you are!" Cynthia said. "My family comes before anything, Pam. Business! Friends! Anything!"

"I bet your husband won't put his career before you!" Pam snapped.

"Hold on, let me tell you something!" Cynthia said, putting her hands on her hips and pointing her finger in Pam's face. "As far as my husband is concerned, not only would he put me before his career, he would put your mean, black ass before his career, too!"

Alicia stood between Cynthia and Pam to try to get the situation under control. I sat quietly and enjoyed the entertainment.

"What is wrong with you two?" Alicia said. "We have never argued like this, and we're not going to start now! Cut it out!"

"Excuse me, ladies," I said, "but if I may interject?"

Pam and Cynthia ignored me and continued to fuss.

"Please help me out over here, baby!" Alicia said.

"Hey! Hey! Hey!" I shouted, getting their attention. "Cynthia, I know you made a vow to Mike to never tell the office girls about what happened with his book. But perhaps you should explain why Mike feels the way he does, and why you feel the way you do."

"I don't know if I should, Johnny. Mike would probably get upset."

"Cynthia, tell them!" I said.

"Okay," Cynthia said, sitting down. "Do y'all remember when Mike's book, *The Office Girls* came out and we were talking about how much it reminded us of us?"

"Uh-huh," Pam said, waiting for more information. "And?"

"Well, it reminded us of us," Cynthia said, "because it *was* us."

"What you talkin' 'bout, Willis?" Pam said jokingly.

"Mike wrote that book under the name of Cora. Cora was Ms. Virginia's real name. He uh, he started off writing the book because Janine had gotten him fired at this other job, and he was pissed off about it. She had written a negative article about black men and Mike didn't care too much for it, so he asked her to revise or retract it. She didn't want to do it, so he wrote an article in response to hers. A lot of women must have found his article offensive and protested to have him fired and he lost his job. I don't know how he found Janine, but he ended up working in our office. He knew who she was, but she didn't know who he was.

"Anyway, long story short, Mike wrote the book to get even with certain women. He got information from us to write his book. But when the time came for him to release the book, he couldn't do it. He loved us too much to do it! He was willing to sacrifice his career for our sake! So forgive me if I want to stand up for him."

"But Cynthia, he shouldn't have been using us in the first place," Pam said.

"Maybe he shouldn't have, but that's beside the point. When he was faced with his career and the people he loved, he chose the people he loved."

"I know he had to make some money off of this book," Alicia asked.

"Yes, he did," Cynthia said. "That book was an international bestseller, and no one but a small group of us knew Mike wrote it. That book would have made him famous. Fame is just as important as sales in the entertainment business, Alicia, you know that. Mike sacrificed his fame for our anonymity."

"I know I better not be in that damn book!" Pam said, laughing and rolling her eyes.

"Sorry, babe, you're chapters three and four," Cynthia said, "and Alicia..."

"I don't even wanna know!" Alicia interrupted Cynthia.

"And neither do I," I said. "Keep that shit to yourself."

My brother Mike had been lucky enough to have partaken of sexual activities with all three of the women present in my kitchen. Of course, that would include my wife. Their affair happened before we met, I had accepted it, and it didn't have any effect on our marriage, but I was not interested in knowing the details.

"Okay, it's been a very entertaining morning, and you ladies have a very important shoot to get to," I said, "so as my mama used to tell my friends, you don't have to go home, but you got to get the hell out of here!"

"Whatever!" Pam said.

"So, is everything okay with us?" Alicia asked.

"Pam, is everything okay with us?" Cynthia asked as well.

"Yeah, I'll call the bald eagle and apologize to him! But that Negro has some explaining to do," Pam said as she reached into her purse for her cell phone.

"Oh, no!" Cynthia said, grabbing Pam's cell phone. "Don't be going off, Pam! As a matter of fact, don't say anything about it at all! Just say I'm sorry and that's it!"

"All right, girl!" Pam said. "But you know I must really love you and your husband to bite my tongue like this."

Pam dialed Mike's number and walked out of the kitchen for

privacy to apologize. Alicia looked back and forth at Cynthia and me and then smacked her head with her hands.

"Duh!" Alicia said. "Mike was our first client! If he wrote that *Office Girls* book, why haven't we marketed it? Do you know how popular that book was?"

"Yes, of course I know." Cynthia laughed. "I see the evidence every time he gets a royalty check."

"I think we need to discuss this later, sister girl," Alicia said. "But right now we need to be getting ready for that shoot."

"All right," Pam said while closing her flip-up cell phone on her way back into the kitchen. "I apologized, I didn't mention the book, and Mike and I are cool again. So can we get to our photo shoot now?"

"Let's go, heffa!" Cynthia walked over to Pam and hugged her tightly.

"Hey, what did you ladies talk about when you were out on the town last night?" I said, trying to get information. "How was that Gizelle girl?"

"She's sweet," Alicia said.

"So everything went well, huh?"

"Yeah," Alicia said. "She really enjoyed being one of the office girls. She was happy to be part of a regular crowd."

"Oh, okay," I said, feeling a little better. "I think I may just call Mike back and see if he's still up for a round of golf."

"Okay, do that, we're about to get out of your way," Alicia said.

"See you later, Johnny," Pam said, waving as she walked out.

"All right, brother-in-law," Cynthia said as she hugged me, "I'll see you later, take care."

CHAPTER EIGHT

The women left, leaving me all alone to mull over my inexplicable behavior. I lowered my head on the kitchen table and closed my eyes. The sun was shining through the window directly on the back of my neck, leaving a burning sensation. It felt unusually hot that morning, as if hell was introducing me to my future.

I was startled when my cell phone rang. The number came up as restricted and, again, I went against my better judgment and answered.

"Dr. Johnson Forrester speaking," I said with authority.

There was a long pause, and then I heard a soft voice on the other end. "Hi. How are you?"

"Anise?" I asked.

"Yes, this is Anise. Last night was bizarre, huh?"

"Bizarre? What type of game are you trying to play? My wife is on her way to meet you!"

"I know."

"What is the matter with you?" I said. "Get off the damn phone!"

"What's the matter?" Anise chuckled. "Don't you wanna talk to me?"

"Look, I'm getting ready to hang up." I said. "Good-bye!"

"Don't you dare hang up this phone on me!" Anise snapped. "Nobody hangs up on me! Nobody! And if you do, you're going to wish you hadn't!"

"Is that a threat?" I asked. "Huh? Are you threatening me, Anise?"

"Don't make this difficult, Dr. Forrester," Anise said. "I told you, I want what I want when I want it. And I get what I want when I want it. Do you understand me?"

"I'm sorry, Anise. But you can't get everything you want! Especially not me! So stop acting like a child!"

"Acting like a child?" Anise screamed through her cell phone. "Who the hell are you talking to? I'm a grown-ass woman and I do whatever the hell I want to do."

"Are you insane?" I shouted.

"Come on, Dr. Forrester, you are just as addicted to me as I am addicted to you and you know it!"

"Stop talking like that! As a matter of fact, first thing Monday, I'm going to give your case to another doctor."

"Another doctor can't help me," Anise said. "Only you can help me."

"There are plenty of well-qualified doctors to handle your session."

"No, I don't think there are," Anise said. "Not until I say so."

"I'm not going to argue with you on this, Anise," I said. "I have to go. My wife is on her way to meet you for a photo shoot, so perhaps that's where your attention should be."

"Yeah, I'm on my way, but I have to make a stop first."

"Okay, good-bye."

"Good-bye, Dr. Forrester."

✪✪✪

Minutes later, Anise was knocking on my front door. Reluctantly, I opened it. She walked in and smiled. I don't know if it was her actual beauty or the taboo of the situation, but Anise looked absolutely gorgeous.

"How do you know where I live?"

"Take your clothes off!" Anise snatched my head down and kissed me.

Every thought of fidelity, morality and integrity left me once she hugged me tightly and stuck her tongue in my mouth. Our bodies pressed against one another and we both knew that this session would be filled with lust and passion.

I immediately grabbed her around the waist with both hands. We started kissing very slowly and passionately. We moved our hands up and down each other's bodies. We walked backward and fell against the wall. Our tongues never stopped wrestling as our heads turned from side to side.

We immediately stripped ourselves of our clothes right there in my foyer and fell to the floor. We were totally naked with Anise straddling me. I grabbed her by the ass, making sure her womanhood was planted directly on top of my manhood. She leaned forward on top of me and continued to grind.

She began to moan loudly as my manhood and her woman-hood met in the middle of our hard grinds. I lifted myself and started to suck her breasts, one by one.

I rolled her over on her back, and continued to suck her breasts, taking my hand and slipping it between her legs. I maneuvered my fingers inside of her and I could feel the wetness of her vagina. She opened her legs wider to allow my finger access to go in and out. I started to kiss her again very passionately as I fingered her faster and faster. My fingers became drenched with her juices.

She reached for my manhood and slid it inside of her. She groaned and wrapped her legs around my ankles. I gave her a few long, deep strokes but I wanted to move from the foyer and into one of my bedrooms.

"Come on, let's go upstairs," I said, pulling my soaked manhood out of Anise.

"Oh baby, I don't want to wait, I want it now!" Anise rubbed between her legs. "Put it back in! Please!"

I didn't have to respond verbally. I positioned myself between her legs and shoved my manhood back inside of her.

"Oh yeah, baby!" Anise moaned and raised her shoulders off of the floor. Her head dangled in the air as I plunged into her. "Oh my, God!"

"You want it now?" I said, ramming Anise hard, and covering her mouth to keep her screams within the walls of the front door.

"Yeah, give it to me!" Anise replied with my hands still covering her mouth.

I reached my hand beneath Anise's ass and lifted her in the air. That seemed to turn her on even more as she started to buck her hips uncontrollably.

"Oh shit, I'm almost there, Dr. Forrester!" Anise shouted, grabbing my face and kissing me wildly. "OH GOD! OH GOD! OH GOD!"

I slammed so deep and so hard into Anise I thought I was going to knock a hole through her back.

"Oh God, I'm coming! Don't stop! Don't stop!" Anise wrapped her ankles around my legs and pumped up and down.

"Open your eyes, Anise! I want to see your orgasm through your eyes!"

"Oh damn, Dr. Forrester!" Anise said, wiggling her body beneath me as her juices leaked from inside of her.

I kept pumping until Anise stopped wiggling and squirming. I looked at our bodies, still intertwined, and the sexy image of her legs still wrapped around the base of my back.

"Oh my God! Oh my God, that felt so good," Anise said.

I slowly stood up and grabbed my pants. "Do you need a towel, Anise?"

"Uh, no, I don't have time. I'll take a shower at the photo shoot location."

As Anise was sliding her underwear up her curvaceous hips, her phone rang.

"Hey, girl," Anise said, "I'm sorry, I'm running a little late. I'll be there in a few minutes, okay?"

I stood silently and listened as Anise discussed her meeting with my wife.

"Okay, see you in a few, Alicia, bye-bye!"

"That was my wife?" I asked nervously.

"No, that was my PR firm," Anise said. "When she's with you, she's your wife, but when she's with me, she's my PR agent."

"Wait a minute, no matter where she is, she's always my wife," I said, a little pissed off.

"Then what was she five minutes ago when you were between my legs?" Anise kept putting on her clothes.

"Get out of my house!"

"Okay, Dr. Forrester," Anise said before opening the door and trying to kiss me on the cheek. "See you on Monday."

I moved my face away when Anise tried to kiss me. She smiled and patted me on my chest. I walked back into my kitchen and sat down at the table. I lowered my head and closed my eyes as I had before my phone rang.

The sun is known to rise in the east and set in the west. The sun above my house was in the same position as it was before Anise arrived. And the heat burning down on my neck had increased in temperature and intensity. Instead of moving away, I sat there and allowed the sun to blister my skin, a small return for my huge guilt.

❂❂❂

On Monday, my first appointment was with Veronica. I had kept a close eye on her to make sure she was not relapsing with her recovery.

"So how are you this morning, Veronica?" I asked.

"I'm fine." Veronica crossed her frail legs.

"And how is it going with the diet?"

"I've had a couple of setbacks, but my husband keeps at me."

"What did you have for breakfast?"

"I, uh, well, I haven't had breakfast yet."

"Are you hungry?" I asked.

"No, no, I had a heavy dinner last night so I'm still stuffed."

"What time was dinner?"

"Uh, I don't know, maybe eight, or eight-thirty last night," Veronica said nervously.

"And it's now," I said, looking at the clock, "eight forty-five in the morning. It's been twelve hours since you've eaten. Is your nutritionist aware of this?"

"No." Veronica slumped into her chair.

"Are you going to tell her?" I asked.

"It's no big deal, Dr. Forrester. I shouldn't force myself to eat, that's as bad as forcing myself not to eat."

"Don't you think someone with your condition should eat as often as possible?"

"Of course! I agree with you one hundred percent. But my condition is not that grave."

"But haven't you been placed on a diet to assist in weight gain?"

"Yes I have, but it's not like I'm sick or anything. I'm like anyone else who's skinny. I just need to lose weight! No big deal!"

"Did you just say that you needed to lose weight?"

"No. I said that I needed to gain weight."

"Okay, well, that's neither here nor there," I said. "Does your husband think your weight is no big deal?"

"We discuss it often and he never complains. He loves my body."

"May I ask your current weight?"

"Why?" Veronica asked nervously.

"Because I'm concerned."

I waited patiently as Veronica fidgeted with her bony hands. She stared down at them as she rubbed them over and over. She finally lifted her head and with tears welling in her eyes spoke very softly, "I weigh, uh, I weigh eighty-eight pounds."

"Eighty-eight pounds?" I asked, obviously disturbed.

Although I could see that Veronica was very thin, it was still upsetting to hear her say that she was only eighty-eight pounds. She had lost ten pounds since our first conversation. This woman was wasting away to nothing, and nobody seemed to be able to stop her.

She lowered her head and began to cry. I walked around my desk and wrapped my arms around her. She turned her head into my chest and cried even more. I stood, bent toward her, and let her cry until she ran out of tears. Once she pulled away and started to wipe her eyes, I felt it was safe for me to return to my desk.

"I'm sorry," Veronica said. "I'm sorry for crying like this."

"There's no need to apologize, Veronica."

"I just don't know what to do. The guiltier I feel about losing weight, the more I try to eat. And the more I try to eat, the guiltier I feel about gaining weight. It seems to be a never-ending cycle of guilt. I'm consumed with guilt for losing weight and I'm consumed with guilt for gaining weight."

"I understand," I said while tapping the point of my pencil on my desk.

"Dr. Forrester, I don't want to die!" Veronica said, starting to cry again. "Please, can you help me?"

Knowing that I should never make a medical promise to a patient, I acted on my sympathetic emotion and said, "Yes, yes, I will."

❦❦❦

My next appointment was with Betty. I had to get a strong cup of coffee to prepare myself for that one. When she walked into my office, I was taken by surprise by her pleasant demeanor. She wasn't defensive. She wasn't aggressive either and by the time she left, I thought we had had a breakthrough.

"Good morning, Betty," I said.

"Good morning, Dr. Forrester."

"How are you feeling this morning?"

"I'm feeling pretty good and you?'

"Very well."

"Good," Betty said, with a quick flash of a smile.

"So, how's your family?"

"They're fine."

Previously when I asked that question, Betty snapped at me in defense. This time she was calm and courteous.

"Audrey is responding well to her developmental tests. But they keep trying to say there's something wrong with her! I don't think for a second my daughter has brain damage, Dr. Forrester!" Betty said. "She's one year old, for Christ's sake! Children develop differently and my child is no exception. Her development is slow, but progressive."

"I understand. Is she crawling or walking?"

"She is just now learning to crawl. I'll admit, most children are walking at her age, but it's not uncommon for babies to take their time crawling and walking."

"I was a late bloomer myself. I think I may have been almost two years old before I started to crawl. But look at me now," I said jokingly. "So I understand firsthand what you mean."

"And you turned out pretty good!" Betty laughed. "And you're not bad to look at, either."

"Thank you."

"And like you, I was a late baby bloomer myself, if I can borrow your terminology."

"You were?"

"Oh yes," Betty said. "And it seems like I've been trying to catch up my entire life."

"Interesting," I said. "What does that mean exactly?"

"This is not going to be easy, but here I go."

BETTY'S STORY:

"I was born in rural Kentucky in a small town named Middlesboro. I was the oldest of seven girls. My parents were very conservative. Living in the mountains was restrictive enough, but when your parents think rock and roll is the devil's music, or wearing jeans is dressing like a hooker, life can be downright miserable.

"There was a ten-year difference between me and the next youngest sibling. Because of the big gap, I became an instant babysitter. I was never given an opportunity to enjoy my teenage years. I was the surrogate mother to six children. When they were sick, I nurtured them back to health. When they were hungry, I fed them. I got them dressed in the morning! Made sure their homework was completed! At the end of the day, they grew up and were married and had children before I left my parents' house. My youth was stolen!

"I suppose something wonderful came out of it though, my desire to nurture and care for others. Becoming a nurse was fulfilling and made me feel as if I had a purpose in life.

"Searching for my own identity, I sought the attention of others to find out where I fit in. During my search, I dated a lot when I was young. I wouldn't say I was a whore, but I sure as hell wasn't a virgin either. One thing for sure, I never really had a serious relationship until I moved to Atlanta. I was engaged to a man that I later found out was still married. Obviously that didn't work out. I continued to date but, as I said, nothing serious.

"But then I met my husband when he was a patient of mine at Grady Hospital. As his nurse, I spent a lot of time with him and we just developed a bond. We just seemed to have a lot in common. I was new to Atlanta and he was new to Atlanta. He was single and I was single. Well, one thing led to another and we just hit it off.

"We got married and we tried for years for me to get pregnant, *but the doctors said I could never have children. But we kept pray-ing to the good Lord that he would bless us with a child and one day I woke up sick. I knew immediately what was wrong with me, but it took David some time to be convinced.*

"Well, you should have seen his face when that doctor finally showed us the sonogram. He was jumping up and down in that office. The whole world seemed to share our excitement. People were always telling me how beautiful I looked. They said I had that motherly glow. Beautiful? Can you imagine that? It was a wonderful experience. An experience I wasn't used to having.

"Getting rid of my pregnancy weight was an entirely different story. There was nothing wonderful about that. Instead of losing weight, I kept gaining. But I still had my precious little girl. And people always talked about how pretty she was. She was a little angel.

"But for some odd reason, she kept getting sick. I couldn't figure out for the life of me why she kept getting sick! And every time I took her to the doctor, they couldn't figure out what was wrong with her, either.

"Being a nurse, it was hard to watch all those doctors and nurses see after my little girl, but I knew it had to be done. Even though those quacks couldn't find anything, they had to admit that Audrey was an angel! And guess what? I was the angel's mother..."

"You know, Dr. Forrester," Betty said. "When you've been stepped over and stepped on as much I have, you really appre-ciate it when the world starts to show you attention for the first time."

"I understand."

"Sometimes, it may even get to the point where a person enjoys the attention so much as when the attention starts to fade, they may continue to do things to maintain that attention. Things they know they shouldn't be doing."

"Can you explain what you mean?"

"You know what I mean don't you, Dr. Forrester?" Betty asked, wanting me to confess her sins for her rather than force her to confess them herself.

"I don't want to assume," I said. "Please, explain."

"I guess," Betty said, then repeating herself, "I guess what I'm trying to say is that I may appear to be crazy to you, but I'm not! I love my child and I would never intentionally harm her."

"Have there been any more instances where Audrey has been ill?"

"No, Dr. Forrester! And there's not going to be."

"And you?" I said. "How are you feeling?"

"I feel better than before." Betty smiled again. "But there are still some things I need to deal with and, uh, get them out in the open."

"Absolutely. Would you like to discuss these things?"

"Well," Betty said, "I have this guilt, this unbearable guilt, that I may be responsible for the lack of development of Audrey's motor skills in some way."

"In what way?" I asked.

"Okay, I'll tell you, but I want to make something perfectly clear. I have never harmed my child. I have never given her any medicine, any drugs, nothing to harm her! I have never abused her! Hit her! I've never done anything to put her life in danger! She is a beautiful child and I don't want her to grow up feeling unloved and unattractive as I did! That's a horrible, lonely place. But maybe I enjoyed getting attention for being her mother so much that I wanted her to remain a newborn longer than I should. But I would never hurt my baby!"

I took Betty's statement as a confession of guilt for Munchausen's, but nothing more. I don't think she was admitting in any way that she was guilty of harming her child.

"What happened the day David rushed Audrey to the hospital?"

"Okay," Betty sighed, "I had just worked twelve hours at the hospital and I was home with Audrey. I was unbelievably exhausted. David helped me out by cleaning and feeding Audrey before he went to work. After he left, Audrey and I fell asleep.

"I checked on her periodically when she slept, even if I wasn't awake. So while we were napping, I still awoke from my sleep to check on her as well. I noticed Audrey's chest was not moving up and down. I checked her pulse and it was barely even faint. I tried waking her, but she didn't respond. Then I applied CPR and she was still unresponsive."

Betty lowered her head and started to cry. I was careful not to get emotionally involved with this patient. I wanted to show that I was concerned, but not to the point where it appeared that I condoned her behavior. She was still part of a criminal investigation for the abuse of her child.

"Please, take your time," I said.

"I, uh," Betty continued, "I called David and asked him to meet me at the hospital. He was totally panicked! He felt that it would be better if he took her into the emergency room because I had brought her so many other times with no documented illnesses. He felt they would take him more seriously. I got there a minute or two before David and waited for him to arrive. I don't know, maybe waiting that extra time caused Audrey more harm than good."

"You said that you believe Audrey suffered from an allergic reaction. Was that a professional or personal opinion?"

"Professional," Betty said with total confidence. "Her eyes were swollen! Her throat was swollen! Her lungs were clear! Her chest was clear! There was nothing physically present to explain her difficulty with breathing. I don't know what triggered it, but it was an allergic reaction, Dr. Forrester! I did not do anything to harm my child!"

"When was the last time you saw Audrey?" I asked.

"This past Saturday," Betty said. "I get weekly visits, my last visit was on Saturday."

"How does being divorced affect your relationship with David and Audrey?"

"We still love each other and we express our love whenever we can. But in order for us to get our family together again, we have to be apart for now."

"So does he keep you informed about Audrey as much as you would like?"

"Well, not as much as I would like, but as much as he can without putting himself at risk of losing custody."

"Is this very difficult for you?"

"This is the most difficult situation I've ever experienced in my life," Betty confirmed. "At first I was angry. Very angry! But I suppose, for Audrey's sake, the authorities are doing what's best for her."

"Are you still angry?" I asked.

"No, I don't think I'm angry anymore," Betty said. "I'm lonely. I miss Audrey. I miss Audrey and David."

I was astonished by the contrast in Betty's demeanor from her last visit to her current visit. I wasn't certain if her sense of loneliness had overtaken her defensiveness, but either way she appeared to be on her way back to some form of normalcy.

CHAPTER NINE

My next appointment was with Anise. She had called while I was in my meeting with Betty and cancelled. Not long afterward, she called me on my cell phone and asked if she could have her session in her hotel room.

She told me that she was busy preparing for an interview with a major magazine. The interview was arranged by Alicia, and if she missed it, it could bring negative press to herself and CAP's marketing firm.

I suggested we cancel the session and all future sessions. I offered another therapist. But she became irate and told me she would expose our relationship if I discontinued our therapy.

I tried to reason with her, but she was unreasonable. She screamed, she threatened me physically, and with all of the red flags being waved directly in front of my face, I still went to her hotel room.

I told Rosemary to reschedule my afternoon appointments for an hour later. I met Anise at an upscale hotel in Buckhead. When I entered the restaurant, I noticed Anise's very large bodyguard sitting nearby. I didn't say much, I sat at the bar and pretty much listened to her. She was very excited and kept the conversation going. We made small talk for a while, and then Anise made her move.

"I love when you make love to me, Dr. Forrester, but right now I want you to take me upstairs and sex the shit out of me!" Anise said. "I am so hot right now! I'm soaking wet!"

"Anise," I said, "we have never made love, and we will never make love! We had sex, and it's going to stop! Right here! Right now!"

"I don't think so, Dr. Forrester."

"What do you mean, you don't think so?"

"Like I said," Anise said, rubbing her hands between my thighs and then grabbing my crotch, "I like the way this makes me feel, and I'm going to have it whenever I want until I get tired of it."

"Are you crazy?" I snatched her hands from my crotch and tossed them to the side. "What the hell is wrong with you?"

"You tell me. You're my therapist!"

"I'm sorry," I stood up to leave. "This is over!"

"You sit your ass down right now before I call your precious wife and describe every single inch of your body!" Anise looked as if she were possessed by a demon.

"What is wrong with you?" I said in a much calmer tone. I sat back down and tried to appeal to her sensibility. "You're a beautiful young lady with your whole life ahead of you. You can have any young man on this planet. Why do you desire a man you can't have?"

"A man I can't have?" Anise repeated sarcastically. "I have you in every way that I need. I don't need a husband. I don't need a boyfriend. I need a lover! And you're my lover! And you're going to be my lover until I say I don't want you anymore."

"Anise, stop this! Please!"

"Look, don't act like you're not getting anything out of this," Anise said.

"What am I getting out of this?" I asked. "Sex?"

"Not just sex! Great sex!" Anise said. "But there are fringe benefits as well."

"There are no benefits in this at all for me."

"Do you think I would actually sign with a looney-tune marketing firm like CAP if I didn't have my own interest at stake? They can do nothing for me, but I can do everything for them. And they owe it all to this." Anise grabbed my crotch again.

"Stop it!" I moved her hand away.

"I don't have much time, I have to meet your wife in a few minutes, so let's hurry up and get upstairs before she gets here."

"No. I'm not going anywhere with you!"

"Stop whining like a little bitch and get your ass upstairs!"

"Look, you do what you have to do, but I'm not going anywhere with you."

"Oh, okay," Anise started to dig into her purse, "Excuse me for a second, Dr. Forrester."

Anise pushed a button and then placed the phone to her ear and waited for the person on the other end to answer. Of course I knew she was trying to bluff me into thinking she was calling Alicia, but I wasn't buying it. I wasn't buying it until I heard my wife's voice echoing through that teeny, tiny phone.

"Hi, Alicia, this is Gizelle, how are you?"

Hearing Alicia's voice brought the situation to a frightening reality.

"I'm great, how are you?" Alicia said.

"I'm wonderful! Guess who I'm sitting here with?" Anise looked right at me.

"Who?" Alicia asked, very excitedly.

"NO!" I whispered nervously. I reached for Anise's phone, trying to take it out of her hand. But she turned her back and moved away. "Anise! No! Don't do this!"

"He's a cutie!" Anise said.

"Well, who is it?"

"Uh," Anise said, waiting for my reaction. "Who is it?"

"Okay," I surrendered, sat back in my chair, and pounded the counter. "I'll go upstairs."

"Uh," Anise said, "the guy from the magazine. He's a cutie, girl."

"Well, if he's as cute as you sound, you should really enjoy this interview."

"How long is it going to take you to get here?" Anise asked.

"Shouldn't take more than thirty minutes. I have to pick my daughter up from school and drop her off at daycare, but I'm on my way."

"Okay," Anise said, "take your time."

Anise hung up the phone and then looked at me.

"I'm glad we got that taken care of," Anise said. "Let's go upstairs and, uh, talk."

We got up from the bar and went to her hotel suite. As we stood up, so did her bodyguard. He didn't say a word; he just quietly followed us to her room. Her bodyguard stopped at the door and we went inside. Once we were inside, Anise stripped completely naked and stood in front of me. Her body was so mature, so well formed.

I was sitting on the edge of the bed and she stepped closer, teasing me with her beauty. Without warning, she started to pull at my tie. She took both of her hands and ripped the buttons from my shirt.

I pulled Anise to me and she grabbed a handful of my manhood. I lay her on the bed and wasted no time kicking out of my clothes and sliding deep inside her.

"I want you to kill it! Like an animal! Wild and nasty!" Anise shouted, grabbed her ankles, and spread her legs apart. "You better get it! And you better get it right!"

"Oh!" I moaned, getting more and more excited with every word that came out of her mouth.

I slammed into Anise's wet vagina and she started to dig her fingernails into my back, which made me slam even harder. She started to slide her fingernails up and down my spine, deeper and deeper into my skin.

After continuous hard, deep strokes, Anise turned me over and straddled me. "Watch me slide up and down on you!"

"Oh God!" I watched her tight body slide slowly up and down.

"Grab my ass, Dr. Forrester!" Anise moaned. I grabbed her ass and moved in time with her grinding.

I sat up and started to suck her breasts, first one, and then the other. She started to hump on me like an animal. Breathing hard and pushing me back down on the bed. She placed her hands on my chest and, again, dug her nails into my skin.

"Oh shit! Right there, baby! Right there!" Anise shouted. "Give it to me! Give it to me!"

I grabbed Anise, turned her around and threw her on her back again. I lowered my face down to hers and we started to kiss. She opened up her legs and I lay between her tight muscular thighs. We kissed slowly and passionately as my manhood came closer to exploding.

"Oh shit!" I shouted, pushing deep inside and pressing against the inner walls of her vagina, filling her with my juice.

"Oh God!" Anise said. "Oh my God!"

Her legs slid up and down the back of mine as she wrapped them around me.

"I can't take it!" Anise said, "Oh God, I'm coming!"

I stuck my finger and my tongue in her mouth simultaneously. She sucked them both wildly until her orgasm subsided. Anise kept on moving, and my manhood kept on rising.

"Damn, baby!" Anise said. "You still want more, huh?"

"I got to go!" I tried to pull out of her.

"Don't move! Don't move!" Anise squeezed my manhood with her vagina muscles. "Oh shit, you feel that?"

"Oh," I moaned, not wanting to answer.

"You know you like that, don't you?" Anise stared me in the face and continued to squeeze my manhood. "Feels good, huh?"

"Oh my God!" I said, conceding to Anise's sensuality and stroking her harder.

I kissed Anise up and down her neck. The more I kissed, the louder she moaned. She closed her eyes and bit her lip. We found the same rhythm once she placed her hands on my hips and guided me in and out. I would go in as far as I could, and then pull it out until only the tip remained. Then I'd push it back in again.

I gave one slow deep thrust, and then pulled it out again. Anise reached behind me and smacked my ass. That motivated me to move in at a downward and then upward motion. I could feel her juices rolling down her thighs and sticking to mine. The lubrication allowed me to go deeper. Anise opened her thighs wider and wrapped her feet around my lower back, planting her heels on me for leverage. She let out an ear-splitting squeal and her body shook as if she was having an epileptic fit.

"OH SHIT!" Anise shouted. "OH GOD, I'm coming again!"

"Ah!" I said, not wanting to let Anise know how good it actually felt. In my mind, no words meant no passion.

"Oh shit, it feels so…" Anise said, not completing her sentence.

"Shit!" I shouted.

"Get it, baby!" Anise yelled. "Get it!"

All I can say is, I've seen sunlight and I've seen rain, and that day I saw both at the same time. I can't explain why, but that was one of the most powerful orgasms I had ever experienced. I couldn't breathe. I couldn't speak. All I could do was shake, and I mean shake convulsively.

"Damn! What are you doing to me?" I screamed as I grabbed the headboard and shoved my manhood so deep inside of Anise it started to bend.

"OH SHIT! YOU IN THERE, BABY!" Anise screamed and dug her nails deep into my arms.

"OH GOD!" I moaned, as I felt my manhood explode inside of her again.

"Damn, baby!" Anise kissed me all over my face.

"SHIT!" I pulled out of Anise, and let my juice squirt uncontrollably all over her body. "Damn!"

KNOCK! KNOCK! KNOCK!

Anise covered herself with a towel and ran to the door. She looked through the peephole and then looked back at me. "Guess who?"

"Shit! Where the hell is your bodyguard?" I said, jumping to my feet and quickly putting my pants on. "Is there another way out of here?"

"We're on the seventh floor. The only other way out of here is out of the window."

"What am I going to do?" I asked, grabbing my clothes.

"Go in the bathroom!" Anise said.

❀❀❀

I ran into the bathroom and climbed in the shower, quickly sliding the shower curtain behind me. I looked around my environment and wondered how a happily married, established doctor could put himself in such a stupid position.

Meanwhile, I heard Anise open the door and let Alicia inside. I could feel my heart beating through my chest as I listened to Anise explain to Alicia that she will be doing the interview in a conference room where the magazine team is waiting. The thought of my wife on the other side of that bathroom wall almost made me hyperventilate.

My composure worsened when I heard Alicia ask Anise if she could use the bathroom. Under the circumstances, Anise could easily have suggested using the bathroom in their interview room, but then that would have been too safe and too easy.

The next sound I heard was Alicia entering the bathroom. I strained my left eye, focusing through the crack between the curtain and the shower wall. I could see Alicia, but she could not see me. There she was, checking her makeup in the mirror. She washed her hands thoroughly and walked out. I think I held my breath the entire time.

I remained perfectly still until I heard their voices fade out. I slowly walked out of the bathroom, tiptoeing to the door. I peeked out of the peephole and saw no one. I very cautiously opened the door, and stuck my head out. I looked left, and then right.

I tried to button my shirt as I quickly tiptoed to the elevator.

I put my suit coat on and continued to button my shirt. I didn't have time to knot my tie so I shoved it into my pocket. I pushed the down button and continued to button my shirt.

As the door opened, I tried to walk into the crowded elevator. But I had to stand to the side and wait for two women to pass. I had my head down and wasn't paying attention to the women as they exited.

I took a deep breath thankful the nightmare was over. As long as my wife was not on that elevator and I could see that she wasn't, I was fine. At least, I thought I was fine until I heard a familiar voice ringing through my ear.

"Johnny, what are you doing here?" The voice was right beside me.

I was so surprised, I couldn't think of a word to say. Finally, without even turning around, I said, "Lord, have mercy."

I wanted to jump on the elevator but I couldn't. I had to address why I was in a hotel without my wife. Watching the elevator door close in front of me like prison bars, my last escape was gone. And then the voice repeated, "Did you hear me? What are you doing here?"

"I can explain,"" I said while turning around and looking like I just got caught with my hands in the cookie jar. "Where's my wife?"

"I don't know," Pam said. "We're looking for her, too."

"Aw, that's so sweet," Cynthia said. "Are you here to support your wife, boo-boo?"

"Yes." I nervously walked back toward Anise's room. "I played hooky from my afternoon appointments to surprise her."

"We might as well get back on the elevator if they're not up here." Cynthia stopped in her tracks.

"Come on, let's go back downstairs." Pam turned around

and headed back to the elevator. "And what's wrong with your clothes?"

"Oh, I just loosened my clothes to get more comfortable."

"That's more comfortable?" Cynthia asked.

"It is for me," I said.

"Hmm." Pam looked at me suspiciously.

We walked back to the elevator and waited for it to open. By the time we found the conference room where the interview was being held, it was time for me to return to my office. I kissed my wife good luck and rushed back to my office.

When I arrived, Rosemary couldn't wait to tell me the news about my next patient. It was a patient simply referred to as Patient Number Five. Patient Number Five would be one of my most interesting subjects.

Patient Number Five was an eighty-something Pulitzer- and Nobel Prize-winning author of psychological studies. I was reluctant to accept her as a patient because I was not privy to her personal background. Her name, city of birth, and background for the first forty-odd years of her life were omitted from her file. The only information listed pertained to her Nobel and Pulitzer awards. However, the case was so bizarre that my curiosity convinced my skepticism to give way and I agreed to give her therapy.

She was diagnosed as suffering from agoraphobia. Agoraphobia is the fear of being in a situation where one might experience anxiety or panic and where escape from the situation might be difficult or embarrassing.

People with agoraphobia might feel anxious about being home alone, leaving home, crowded places, public transportation and in an enclosed elevator, anywhere that it might be difficult or embarrassing to find a way out. To avoid the anxiety associated with these places, they refrain from putting themselves into such situations.

The severity of agoraphobia is quite variable. Some people with agoraphobia live essentially normal lives as they avoid potentially anxiety-provoking situations. However, in severe cases of agoraphobia, people are homebound. These people work very hard to avoid any and all situations that might cause them to become anxious.

About twice as many women than men report that they experience agoraphobia. Frequently, people report that the onset of their agoraphobia followed a stressful or traumatic event in their lives. The most common age for agoraphobia to begin is when a person is in his or her mid-twenties. Less than one percent of the population suffers from agoraphobia. There are no laboratory tests required to confirm a diagnosis of agoraphobia nor are there any physical conditions to make that determination.

Severe cases of agoraphobia can be very difficult to treat and can last many years. There are four common ways of treating this disorder: therapy, medication, a combination of therapy and medication, or behavior and cognitive therapy.

I was at a distinct disadvantage because I didn't have the benefit of the patient's medical background. The only information I had was that she was a recluse, and no photos had been taken of her in over forty years. She refused to come into the office and told Rosemary that if we were to have our sessions, they would have to be in her home. I was anxious to start the sessions with Patient Number Five, so I jotted down her address and took off without as much as saying good-bye to Rosemary.

Patient Number Five lived in a huge mansion in an exclusive

exurban neighborhood. I wasn't familiar with the area at all. Actually, I didn't even know the area existed. But I did know that whoever lived in that neighborhood was loaded, not doctor loaded, but old money loaded.

As I pulled up to the entry gate I was met by a young man sitting in a booth. He gestured for me to pull forward and I followed his command.

"May I have your name?" he asked.

"My name is Dr. Johnson Forrester and I am here to see, uh," I said, pausing as it suddenly occurred to me I didn't know my patient's name by anything other than Patient Number Five. "I'm, uh, here to see the lady of the house. I am her therapist."

"Uh, what is that name again?" the man said, picking up his clipboard.

"Dr. Johnson Forrester," I said, becoming impatient. "Is everything okay?"

The man didn't respond to my question. He pushed a button and the gate started to open. I stared at him as he walked back to his chair in the booth and sat down.

I drove through the gate cautiously and then drove through the narrow path that led to the front of the main house. I was amazed at the statues and artifacts that lined her perfectly manicured yard. I was also amazed at the many security guards stationed around the property.

When I got to the house, I didn't see a place to park so I parked alongside the curb and cut my car off. I peeked up at the gigantic mansion from the inside of my car, and I couldn't see the top. I picked up my recorder and a notepad and stepped out of my car.

I walked up what seemed like as many stairs as at the Capitol building and pounded on the door. The lion-framed latch was enormous, even for a man with huge hands like me.

I knocked a couple of more times and then I walked off of the porch and looked upstairs. I saw a curtain close in one of the windows and I knew that somebody in that house knew I was outside. I went back to the door and pounded again, this time harder.

Finally, a man opened the door and spoke, "May I help you?"

"Yes, I'm here to see, uh, to see the lady of the house."

"And what is your name, sir?" the man asked.

"I am Dr. Johnson Forrester. I have an appointment with the lady of the house."

"Please come in."

The man stepped to the side and allowed me to enter. "I will inform the madam that she has a visitor."

The man smiled and disappeared into one of the rooms. I stood silently and took in the scenery. There were several old paintings of the same black man hanging on the walls. Other than that, the decor was solely Colonial furniture and decorations. I thought I had been transported back two hundred years or more. The only sign of contemporary life was the electricity burning throughout the chandelier.

The man returned after a short while. "The madam is ready to see you, sir. Please come with me."

I couldn't believe how the man was talking, *"the madam is ready to see you, sir,"* and if I didn't know any better, I would have sworn I was in Great Britain!

Anyway, I followed him up three flights of spiraled stairs until we came to a pair of doors. Along the way, I got a glimpse of the decor of each floor, which did not waver from that of the first floor. I marveled at what I saw. But little did I know, the best was yet to come.

The man took a key from his jacket and reached to open the door, but just before he stuck the key in the lock he looked at my hands. He turned to me and said, "I'm sorry, but you are not allowed to bring that recorder into this room. You cannot bring any technological instruments that will record visual images or sounds. However, you are allowed to bring a pencil and a notepad."

I was slightly uneasy about the interview from the moment I pulled into the gate, but now I was really becoming concerned.

"I don't have a pencil, all that I have is a pen and a pad," I said, holding up both items.

"If you would be so kind as to wait here until I return." The man walked over to a small cabinet and returned with a pencil and a notepad. "This should suffice."

He handed me the items and unlocked the door. Before I could enter the room he said, "There is a chair in the north end of the room. Please sit there, but say nothing until the madam has addressed you. When the madam is ready, she will speak. Is this understood?"

"Uh, yes."

"On the right side of the chair, there is a flashing button. Please summon me when you are prepared to leave."

"Okay," I said while walking into the room.

"Good day, sir."

"Uh, good day," I said back, thinking to myself, *who says, "good day"?*

I walked into the pitch-black room. All light disappeared as the man closed the door behind me. It took my eyes a moment to adjust, and even when they did, I still couldn't pick out objects in the dark. I could see the red flashing light and found my way to the chair the man had mentioned. I sat for nearly thirty minutes before a scraggly, old voice penetrated the darkness.

"It is said the admission of ignorance is the beginning of wisdom."

I was slightly startled and did not respond when she initially spoke. I turned my head in several directions, trying to find the location of the source of the voice.

"Are you going to just sit there, or are you going to speak?" Patient Number Five asked.

"Good afternoon," I said, while staring in the dark, trying to focus my eyes in the direction of the voice.

"Do you know who I am?"

"Not by name," I said. "Who are you?"

"Who I am is not as important as who you are!" Patient Number Five said.

"Do you know who I am?"

"You are Dr. Johnson Forrester."

"You have a beautiful house, Ma'am."

Patient Number Five did not respond. I thought quickly to ask another question before the silence became uncomfortable.

"Were you born in Georgia?" I asked.

Patient Number Five still didn't respond. Sitting there in the darkness, I realized this was not just about therapy. I didn't know exactly what it was about, but I knew therapy was not the sole purpose for my visit.

"Do I make you uncomfortable?" I asked.

"Do you make me uncomfortable?" Patient Number Five

asked, barely enunciating her words. "You sit in the darkness and hear the voice of an old woman you can't even see. You don't know what is to your left or what is to your right. I am familiar with every single inch of this room. So dear sir, I have no reason to be uncomfortable. You do."

It was a good thing the room was completely dark because Patient Number Five could not see my mouth moving and no words coming out.

"I assure you, I am not uncomfortable," I said.

"What is it that makes you most uncomfortable? My voice?" Patient Number Five mumbled, "Or the darkness?"

"Neither," I said, trying to sound confident.

"How long have you been a mental clinician, sir?"

"Long enough to know that I should be asking the questions."

"Ask," Patient Number Five said.

"Have you been in this house for the past forty years?"

"I have been in my mind for the past forty years!"

"What does that mean?" I asked, thinking to myself that I was talking to someone completely out of her mind.

"It means whatever you want it to mean," Patient Number Five responded.

There was a long pause and then I heard her voice speaking directly into my ear, "What do you think it means, sir?"

Her voice being so close to my ear startled me.

"Oh shit!" I said and moved away from the voice.

I started to push the button over and over until the door began to open very slowly. When there was enough light for me to see where I was going, I made my way out to the hall.

"Are you all right, sir?" the man asked.

"No, I'm not all right!" I shouted, walking past the man.

"I'll see you out, sir."

"Don't bother, I'll see myself out!" I practically ran down the three flights of stairs.

I jumped in my car and zoomed through the gate. Fortunately, the gate started to open before I sped through. On my way out, I took a good look at the house because I knew I would never enter it again.

CHAPTER TEN

O n my way home, I stopped by the office to go over upcoming appointments with Rosemary, but she had gone for the day. I stayed for a while trying to figure out why I'd become a psychologist in the first place.

The events of the afternoon had me not only questioning my profession, but my sanity. I sat in the darkness until late in the evening. When I couldn't find any answers, I woefully went home to my wife and child.

When I got home, I looked in on Brittany, who was asleep in her bed, and kissed her good night. I quietly took off my clothes and slipped under the covers with Alicia. I snuggled behind her and pulled her close to me.

I began to caress her body, her shoulder, her waist, her hips and legs, everything. Up and down, and up and down. She pushed her ass against my manhood to let me know that she was awake. I responded by letting her feel the fullness of my rock-hard stick. She turned around to face me and I lowered my mouth to her mouth and began to kiss her. We kissed very slowly, not wanting to miss one drop of pleasurable saliva.

We lay on our sides and continued to caress each other as we kissed. Although I was having an affair, I loved my wife deeply. Making love to her was so gratifying. I felt like our souls were connected. It felt so wonderful that touching just didn't seem like it was going to satisfy us. I started to kiss her on her neck, biting softly, and then sucking it more aggressively. Touching her felt so comfortable, so familiar.

She started to squirm from the pleasure, squeezing my body tighter. I kissed her shoulders, then moved over to her breasts, sucking her nipples thoroughly in my mouth, back and forth, then round and round.

I continued downward to her stomach, curling my tongue, and licking her navel. She arched her back slightly as I continued downward to her inner thighs, licking back and forth from one to the other.

I teased her as I brushed over her womanhood, letting only the moisture from my lips touch the edge of her vaginal lips. She started to grind slightly as I licked and kissed down her legs to her ankles, then up again.

"Oh baby, that feels good," Alicia moaned, moving her hips up and down on my face. "Oh, that feels so good!"

I continued to lick and kiss Alicia's thighs, teasing her with my lips until she grabbed my head with both of her hands and pushed my face into her. I pushed her legs backward to have a clear path to her soaking-wet womanhood and then I curled my tongue and licked upward in one long, wet motion.

"Oh shit!" Alicia moaned, jerking her legs.

I gave her another long, wet stroke of my tongue, and she began to grind wildly on my face. I softly bit her vaginal lips, making her tighten her thighs around my head and squeeze excruciatingly hard.

"Give me your tongue, baby!" Alicia said while grinding on my face.

The way her body twisted and turned made my manhood even harder. The more I licked, the more animated she became, moving around trying to escape my tongue.

When I felt her orgasm approaching, I licked her relentlessly, not even raising my head for air. She grabbed my head, and raised her hips from the bed. I could feel her toes stretching far apart from the powerful magnitude of her orgasm.

"OH SHIT, BABY!" Alicia shouted. "Damn, that feels good! SHIT!"

Alicia rolled from side to side, trying to feel every vibration of her orgasm. Not wanting to miss the moment, I turned her on her stomach while she was still shaking, and slid my manhood in from behind. I slammed her legs together, and quickly rammed her as she bit the pillow, trying to prevent her own screams.

Although she lay exhausted, I lifted her to her knees and continued to ram her from behind. Not wasting any time I continued to ram her, grabbing her by the waist and slamming her backward into me. She turned her head to the side and opened her mouth. There were no sounds coming out, just an opened mouth. Eventually, she broke her silence and screamed out loud.

"Oh, baby! Oh baby! Oh baby!" Alicia moaned incoherently, "That feels so good!"

"Oh God, I love you so much, baby!" I shouted back.

I turned Alicia's face to mine and rubbed my cheeks against hers as I poured all of my juices inside of her. We fell asleep with my manhood still inside of her and my cheek pressed against hers.

We woke up the next morning as excited as we were the night

before. We fondled each other until I was fully erect and she was fully flooded. I turned Alicia on her back and opened her legs. I put the head at the entrance of her womanhood and tried to enter her.

"Go slow, baby." Alicia separated us with her hands. "It's still sore from last night."

"I will, baby," I assured her, "I'll go real slow."

"Take it easy, baby!" Alicia grimaced, tightening even more. "Go slow."

"Relax, baby," I said, "relax, and I promise it won't hurt a bit."

"You promise?"

"I promise," I said while placing Alicia's feet on my shoulders. I pushed the head in slightly, and stopped.

"Oh Johnny, it hurts," Alicia said. "It's sore."

"Relax, baby." I stopped all movement. "I love you, baby. This is love. I want to make love to you like I have never made love to you before."

"Oh, I love you, too, baby." Alicia raised her head so that I could see her face.

"See there, it doesn't hurt anymore does it, baby?" I cautiously slid my manhood in and out.

"No Johnny," Alicia moaned, "it feels good. Make love to me like that, baby, slow and easy."

I slowly slid my manhood into Alicia, inch by inch. Finally, it became comfortable, and we slowly made love, eye to eye, mouth to mouth, chest to breast, manhood to womanhood, leg to leg, and feet to feet. Our bodies totally became one.

"I love you, baby," I said.

"Are you okay?" Alicia asked.

"Yeah, I'm okay," I said, still stroking her in rhythm.

"Oh, Johnny," Alicia moaned, sucking my manhood inside of her, "you've never told me you loved me this much."

"I know, and I'm sorry." I lowered my head beside hers, and gave her long, deep strokes.

"Oh my God, make love to me like this all the time, baby," Alicia said.

"I love you, Alicia," I whispered.

"Oh baby, I'm coming!" Alicia tightened her body.

When I felt my orgasm approaching the tip of my manhood, I pulled out, leaving Alicia's body convulsing in the air. I was trying to delay my explosion but I was too far gone. I hurriedly shoved it back inside of her and pumped rigorously. We hugged, shook and squeezed each other until our orgasms subsided.

That morning, Alicia and I did something we had not done since the very first night we spent together: we showered and cleaned each other's body. Nothing sexual, just pure appreciation of each other's love.

❊❊❊

My first appointment of the day would be Kimberly. She was wearing one of her unusual hats, but I had become accustomed to her style so they weren't as peculiar as they were originally.

Kimberly was very nice and cooperative as usual. She was courteous and answered every question I asked. She even volunteered answers to questions I didn't ask.

"How are you today, Kimberly?"

"I am doing good! I can't complain at all." Kimberly smiled from ear to ear. "The Lord woke me up this morning clothed in my right mind."

"Thank God," I said, not knowing what else to say.

When Kimberly took her medicine on schedule, she was bright and articulate. When she did not, she was delusional and almost incomprehensible.

"Dr. Forrester," Kimberly said, "may I ask you a question?"

"Sure."

"Do you believe in God?"

"Do I believe in God?" I asked. "Why do you ask?"

"Because sometime I wonder why I'm like this."

"Why you're like what?"

"Why I can't think right. I want to say certain things some-time, and even though I have the words in my head, I can't make them come out of my mouth. Why does God make some people smart, and some people dumb?"

"You're not dumb, Kimberly."

"I sure feel dumb sometime."

"Let me tell you something, Kimberly. You are not dumb! You are a very kind and warm person."

"But that doesn't mean I'm not dumb, Dr. Forrester."

"'Dumb' is a relative word, Kimberly. Some people know some things that other people don't know, but you can be sure that the people who know some things don't know everything. They probably don't know things that you know."

"Huh? See, I don't know what you mean."

"Don't worry about it." I chuckled. "I don't either, but there was a point in there somewhere."

"Can I tell you something else?" Kimberly asked.

"Absolutely."

"I wasn't always like this. I was smart, real smart, until that accident happened."

"What accident?" I was now very confused. There had been no mentioning of an accident in her file. I didn't know if she was telling the truth or if she was being delusional.

"The car that ran into my mama's car and made my head bleed real bad. And I couldn't walk and couldn't talk for a long time."

"Please, Kimberly," I said, "tell me how you were before the accident."

KIMBERLY'S STORY:

"I was born in East St. Louis, Illinois. It was just me, my mama and my little brother. I didn't know my first daddy. My mama said he lived far away. My second daddy died when I was a little kid. I can't remember a lot about him, but he was a nice man. He used to kiss me, and pick me up and play with me. He was a very nice man. He used to say I was pretty. He said I was his pretty little girl.

"Everybody used to say I was pretty. I was tall, and I had pretty hair that my mama used to comb all the time. I was skinny, too. People used to say I was skinny. All the boys used to say I was pretty. They would always ask me for my telephone number, but we didn't have a telephone so they couldn't call. The boys treated me nice, real nice.

"I used to have lots of friends. Olivia, Jackie, Janet, and Christy. We went to Emerson Elementary School from the first grade to the sixth. And then we went to Central Junior High School together. We were best friends! They were nice to me! Very, very nice!

"My brother was nice and my mama was nice, too. We used to have fun together all the time when I was little. But when I got big, my mama and my brother died. They died together when that car ran into my mama's car.

"My mama was driving with me and my brother in the car. I think

about that night all the time. It was nighttime and me and my brother were asleep in the backseat. I was sixteen years old and my brother was twelve.

"When I woke up, I looked out the window and I could see that car was coming fast. Real, real fast. I tried to call Mama to tell her to go faster, but before I could yell, the car ran into us. I remember rolling over and over and over. The sky kept flipping up and down, and up and down.

"I was knocked out for a while, and when I woke up there were police lights all over the place. I was in the ambulance and we went flying down the street. Zoom! Zoom! Zoom!

"I stayed in the hospital for a long, long time. When I got out of the hospital I had to move to Atlanta, Georgia with my grandma because I could not walk and could not talk. And I did not look pretty anymore.

"I used to ask my grandma what happened to my mama and my brother. She told me they died when that car ran into us. She said they went to Heaven to be with my daddy. My whole family went to Heaven and left me all alone, but not my grandma.

"I was so, so sad. I missed them very, very much. But I loved Grandma, because she loved me and was nice to me. She was a very nice woman. She used to take care of me and feed me, and let me sleep in her big ol' house with her. But she got sick and then she died, too. Even Grandma went to Heaven and left me alone. I was very, very sad.

"One morning when I was asleep, that man came to my grandma's house and told me I had to leave. I was sad and I started to cry, but he said if I did not leave he would call the police on me. I ran out of that house real, real fast. I was scared of the police.

"I did not have a place to sleep for a long, long time. It used to be *real, real cold so I started to sleep under a bridge to get warm. Three bad men came to me and hurt me.*

"One man grabbed my arms. One man grabbed my legs, and one man lay on top of me. And then that one man let my legs go and lay on top of me while his friend grabbed my legs. It hurt me real, real bad. I did not sleep under that bridge never ever again.

"Those three bad men said they hurt me because I was not pretty. People don't say I'm pretty anymore. Nobody ever tells me I'm pretty anymore.

"But I met my friend at the bus station and she is very nice to me. She takes care of me and she doesn't let anybody hurt me. She is a movie star and she is on the television all the time.

"She is my only friend and when I can't see her I get very, very sad. She is my only friend in the whole wide world…"

"Why people scared of me?" Kimberly mumbled under her breath.

"Why do you think people are afraid of you, Kimberly?"

"Because of how I look and how I act."

"Who acts afraid of you?"

"Everybody," Kimberly said. "I try to be nice to people but people treat me very, very mean."

"Sometimes Kimberly," I said, "people are mean to me, too. But it doesn't mean that there's something wrong with me. Just like when people are mean to you. It doesn't mean that there's something wrong with you. And it surely doesn't mean that you're not a pretty girl."

"I want to be pretty, Dr. Forrester. I want to have friends. I want somebody to love me." We stared at each other momentarily, and then Kimberly continued to speak, "If somebody keep living without a friend, or without somebody to love them, what's the use in living?"

"You," I said, sitting upright in my chair, "you're the use in living."

"Sometime I don't think I love me, either."

"Didn't you say that you had a friend who takes care of you?" I asked, convinced that this friendship was a figment of her imagination just like her relationship with Bill Clinton.

It was time for our session to end, so I walked Kimberly to the lobby and said good-bye. When I returned to my office, I sat in my chair as I came to the conclusion that Kimberly had not developed mentally since the day of her accident, and maybe, just maybe, her condition was more physical than mental. Her condition could be more treatable through operations and medication than therapy.

After waiting over an hour for my next patient to enter my office, I stopped by Rosemary's desk to find out the delay. "Who's next?"

"Oh, I rescheduled today's appointments until tomorrow because Patient Number Five called and she wants you to stop by this afternoon," Rosemary said.

"I'm not going back to that house!"

"She made it perfectly clear that she wanted to see you today, Dr. Forrester."

"I'm sorry, but that is a situation I do not want to find myself in again."

"What happened over there?" Rosemary asked.

"First of all, getting through her security was like going through customs at the airport. And then I had to drive a mile to get to the front door of her Addams Family-looking house!"

"You don't say," Rosemary said, giving me her complete and undivided attention.

"That's the sane part of the story," I said. "When I finally get inside of the house, Mr. Belvedere takes me up a hundred flights of stairs to the attic or wherever we were and unlocks the door of a pitch-black room."

"You're exaggerating, Dr. Forrester." Rosemary chuckled.

"No I'm not," I said, sitting on her desk. "Mr. Belvedere instructs me to go to a certain chair and be seated until Her Majesty summons me to speak. I sat there for maybe a half an hour and then she starts to speak out of nowhere. Scared the living shit out of me! And then from out of nowhere I hear this maniac speaking directly into my ear."

"What did you do then?" Rosemary asked, laughing more openly.

"I got the hell out of there!"

"Well, you must have made a good impression on her somehow because her staff has called several times today requesting your return."

"Nope!" I said, standing up from Rosemary's desk. "That woman and her whole staff are nuts! They don't need therapy; they need straitjackets."

"Come on now, she can't be that bad," Rosemary said.

"Rosemary, that house and those people are not even in the twenty-first century, they're not even in the twentieth century! The house still has pictures of some slave on the walls. There's nothing that even resembles modern times. The butler, or whatever he is, is not even American!"

"That's a prejudicial comment, Dr. Forrester."

"No, that's a realistic comment, Rosemary!"

"I don't mean to push, but this lady could be very important to your career."

"I don't understand," I said, confused and bewildered. "How could this old woman be important to my career?"

"She hasn't been interviewed or photographed for over forty years, and she's granting you that opportunity."

"I'm not a member of the paparazzi, I'm a psychologist!"

"Either way, this woman is too important for you to refuse therapy," Rosemary said. "Do you hear me?"

"Rosemary, this woman is nuts!" I said, trying to plead my case.

"Perhaps she is a bit eccentric, but once the world finds out you've had access to her, you're going to be as big as Dr. Phil."

"Big as Dr. Phil, huh?" I started revisiting the possibility of returning to the house on Haunted Hill.

"Bigger!"

"Okay, I'll go back out there, but if I'm not back by six, call the cops!"

"You'll be fine."

"What time is the queen expecting me?" I asked.

"Whenever you get there!"

"Well, I guess there's no time like the present." I snatched my blazer off of the coat rack.

Rosemary started to prepare to leave as I was leaving.

"Where are you going, ma'am?" I asked sarcastically.

"There's no need for my sitting here if there are no more patients scheduled."

"So, are you taking a sick day or a vacation day?" I asked sarcastically.

"I'll let you know after I do payroll."

"Lock up," I said, laughing at Rosemary's payroll joke, "I'm off to see the wizard!"

"Good-bye." Rosemary chuckled. "Get out of here."

I arrived at Patient Number Five's house determined not to be startled by any of the peculiarities inside. My mentality was to expect the unexpected, but everything was pretty much the exact same routine as the day before.

As I sat in the darkened room awaiting the sound of Patient Number Five's scraggly voice, with pencil and pad in hand I felt more like a reporter than a psychologist.

The pencil and pad made no sense to me. The room was too dark to write anything legibly. But I knew I was not going to be able to remember every account, so I had to attempt to write as much as I could as legibly as I could.

Expecting to hear Patient Number Five's voice reverberate from afar, I sat erect, waiting and listening. I turned my ear in the direction I thought the voice would come, and tilted my head to the side.

From out of nowhere, I could feel someone's breath upon my skin and, without time to react, I heard the ghastly sound of Patient Number Five whispering directly into my ear again. "It is said the admission of ignorance is the beginning of wisdom."

I jumped out of the chair, turned in the direction of the voice and yelled, "What are you doing?"

There was no response. Moments later, the voice came from what appeared to be from the other side of the room.

"Are you alarmed?" Patient Number Five asked.

"Of course not."

"You seem to be very timid for such a large man."

"I'm not timid!" I said, trying to justify my reaction. "Anybody would have been startled by someone approaching them in the darkness."

"So tell me, sir, are you always this timid?"

"I'm not here to discuss me, ma'am. I'm here to discuss you."

"Is that so?"

"Yes."

"What is it that you would like to discuss?" Patient Number Five asked.

"Why don't you tell me what you would like to discuss?" I said, taking control of the session.

"Before we go any further, could I ask a question?"

"In regards to what, ma'am?"

"Psychology."

Not knowing where she was going, I figured it would be best to just let her ask the question so we could continue the session.

"Okay, one question," I said. "Ask."

"Do you think the brain controls the mind or the mind controls the brain?"

"What kind of question is that?"

"It's a very elementary question in the field of psychology, sir," Patient Number Five answered. "Now what is your answer?"

"I'm not going to answer that ridiculous question!"

"Is it because you do not know the answer to the question, sir?"

"There is no logical answer to that question and you know it."

"There is always a logical answer to any question," Patient Number Five replied. "Your professional objective should be to rationalize the irrational."

"Please don't tell me what my professional objective should be."

"Then you tell me, sir. Do you think the brain controls the mind or the mind controls the brain?"

"They are one and the same."

"So, are you saying that the brain and the mind exist as one entity?"

"Yes, I am."

"Is it possible to touch the human brain?" Patient Number Five asked.

"Of course."

"So," Patient Number Five said, "by your theory, it is also possible to touch the mind."

"Of course not! I never said that."

"If they are one and the same, how is it possible to touch one, but not the other?"

"Because one is physical, and one is mental."

"Which, is which?"

"I am not going to continue this conversation!" I said, becoming more and more frustrated.

"Are you frustrated, sir?"

"Absolutely not," I said, composing myself. "It's just that I'm curious to know if you invited me to your home for therapy or to challenge my psychological acumen?"

"I must tell you, sir," Patient Number Five said. "Your psychological acumen has not been much of a challenge."

"Okay," I said, scribbling down as much as I could in the dark. "I think that maybe we need to discontinue your session because it's become very apparent that we're not going to make any progress here."

I pushed the flashing button for the butler to come get me. But as the door opened and I began to walk out, it suddenly closed. As the darkness quickly consumed the room again, I stood unsure of what was going on and where I was in the room. The flashing light near the chair had been extinguished.

"Do you make it a habit to walk out on all of your sessions, sir?"

"This is not a session!" I said, feeling my way through the darkness. "Now please, open this door!"

"I will open the door when you answer my question," Patient Number Five said. "Now, do you think the brain controls the mind or the mind controls the brain?"

"The brain," I said, reluctantly answering the question, "the brain controls the mind!"

"Why is that your answer?"

"Because the brain is the living organism that harbors our consciousness, and our intelligence. Without it, we have no soul, no spirit and, subsequently, no mind. Now please," I said, very frustrated, "open this door!"

There was complete silence in the room. I saw the red flashing light over by the chair begin to blink again, and then the double doors to the bedroom slowly began to open.

I walked out of the house, this time pissed off! I knew I would have to return again, if for no other reason than to show this woman that I was a qualified doctor, qualified enough for her, and anyone else.

CHAPTER ELEVEN

Throughout the week, Anise continued to threaten me if I did not meet her for a private getaway. She had made the arrangements and told me that all I needed to do was convince Alicia to let me have one night away from her.

Alicia had no problem letting me out of the house, especially after Anise had conned her into thinking they would have a nice all-girl weekend at the location that she had reserved for her and me. Once Alicia gave me the okay to go, Anise called her back and cancelled their getaway.

I drove my car to the airport and parked in the overnight parking area. I stood on the curb until Anise's stretch limousine pulled in front of me.

"Waiting for me?" Anise slid over to give me room.

I'd made a decision to end this relationship on the drive down from Atlanta to the coast, even if it meant exposing my infidelity to Alicia.

Anise and I had plenty of erotic conversation, and with each word I knew that I wanted to have wild and nasty sex one final time. And then I'd go home and make love to my wife for the rest of our lives.

We arrived at our bed and breakfast inn, located within walking distance of the shore, and quickly made ourselves comfortable. We freshened up and headed for the beach. We stopped at several pubs and restaurants along the way just to see what was inside.

Before we knew it, it was late evening, the sun was going down and the shore was quite cool from the breeze blowing off of the ocean. It was quite romantic, but we were not looking for romance. We were two people looking to enjoy the moment.

Later that evening, we went to a popular jazz club in nearby Savannah. Savannah is about twenty miles inland of Tybee Island, where we were staying. We really enjoyed ourselves. The music was vibing, we talked, we laughed, and the next thing we knew they were shutting the place down.

When we got back to Tybee Island we weren't ready for bed so we went to the beach instead. Anise grabbed a bottle of wine, I grabbed a blanket along with some candles and away we were. It didn't take long for us to find a remote location isolated from the other beach denizens.

We spread the blanket, lit the candles and lay side by side. The cool breeze made us cuddle closely. I looked at her and I thought to myself, this woman is beautiful, but that's not why I'm attracted to her. God knows I've had more than my share of women, even to the point of embarrassment, but there was something about her that struck me differently. Watching her long hair blowing in the wind, her big, beautiful soft eyes, and her small traceable lips, I realized exactly what it was. She was accessible and susceptible to my addiction. Taboo, yet tantalizingly tempting. The contradiction was fascinatingly stimulating.

"Is this supposed to be our last rendezvous?" Anise asked sarcastically.

"It has to be."

I laid Anise on her back and began to kiss her gently on the neck.

"Umm," Anise moaned, smiling, probably grateful we didn't waste our time on a discussion that would mean absolutely nothing to either one of us. "What was that for?"

"That was for me," I said, and then started to kiss her on both sides of her neck, "but this is for you."

I slid my legs between hers and split them apart so that I lay directly in the middle of her thighs.

"Oh, Dr. Forrester," Anise moaned, "oh, shit."

Anise's hands reached under my shirt and she squeezed my chest muscles. Her thighs began to undulate, grinding up and down and pressing into me. I pulled her shirt above her head and tossed it to the side. I started to kiss her shoulders and then moved down to her breasts, kissing and sucking her hard, pointed nipples one at a time.

Her breathing became harder and her moans became louder. I held both of her breasts in my hands and ravaged them, lightly biting them with my teeth.

As I squeezed her breasts in my hands, I curled the tip of my tongue and licked downward to her navel, and then further down to her thighs. I removed the remainder of her clothing, and then removed all of mine. And there we were, totally unclothed.

I opened her thighs wide and began to lick up and down her legs, and then between her inner thighs. I inched closer and closer until my soft, thick lips touched her soft, wet vaginal lips. Her legs stiffened at the point of impact. I slid my tongue along the outer edges of her vaginal lips, up and down, stopping now and then to suck them into my mouth.

She began to toss her head from side to side and move her hips wildly.

"Oh, don't tease me, baby," Anise moaned. "Lick it, baby, lick it, lick it!"

"Shh!" I said, trying to get her to lower her voice.

"Oh yeah, baby!" Anise said, grabbing my head and pushing it into her thighs. "I can't take it anymore, lick it, baby!"

I took my time licking and sucking between her thighs, and then jabbing her vagina with my tongue and licking vigorously inside. Every time I felt her on the verge of her orgasm, I would stop and let her hips convulse.

"I can't take it, baby!" Anise moaned loudly. She grabbed my head, then elevated her hips off of the blanket and wrapped her legs around my neck. She held me there until her orgasm hit. And boy did it hit!

"OH MY GOD! OH MY GOD! OH SHIT!" Anise shouted while falling back to the ground but still holding my face in one place. "DAMN BABY!"

As her orgasm began to subside, I broke her powerful thigh-grip. I quickly raised myself, folded her legs backward, and rammed my manhood deep inside of her. She was certainly moist enough.

"Oh, God, you feel good, Dr. Forrester!" Anise sighed, spreading her legs as far apart as they could go.

"Feels good, Anise? Huh? Feels good?" I shouted as I pulled out almost all the way, and then I rammed her like a pallet jack. "Huh? You like it when I ram you?"

"Oh, slow down, baby, it hurts!" Anise said. "Slow down!"

The passion and the pace were both intense. I had Anise in a position where I could hurt her and I tried my best. Despite the pain, she matched me stroke for stroke. As her feet dangled beside my head, I could see her toes spread further and further apart. I slowed down and pushed my manhood deep inside, and then I pulled it almost completely out, and then back in again. This drove Anise insane. She grabbed my ass and begged me to give it to her hard.

"Oh, it hurts! Oh, it hurts so bad!"

I sped up the pace again and began to drill her even harder. I was no longer striving for pleasure. I wanted to hurt her. I mean, physically hurt her!

"Oh, slow down, baby! It hurts too bad."

"Shut up!" I yelled, still ramming her.

Anise tried to slow me down by placing her hands between us. I slapped her hands away and continued to pound as hard as I could.

"You want it, right? Well, take it!" I said while pushing Anise's body off of the blanket with my thrusts and pushing her onto the sand.

During our wild session, I could hear the sound of people approaching. I could also feel my orgasm approaching, faster and faster, deeper and deeper, and harder and harder. And then it hit me like a force of nature. BAM!

At the same time, I could hear the voices much clearer and much closer, but it was too late for me to stop. I began to ooze what seemed like cups of man-juice all over the place.

"OOOOOOOOOOOOOOOOH, shit! Damn, baby!" I yelled so loudly that Anise pushed my head into her breasts to muffle my screams. My last time having sex with Anise was the first time I ever referred to her by an affectionate name.

Once my orgasm was finally finished, and my toes were

realigned with the rest of my feet, Anise and I scrambled to cover as much of our bodies as possible. We pretended to be asleep as the couple passed.

"Aw," the woman said, "isn't that romantic?"

"Romantic?" The man said, "That's exhaustion from sex."

"Shh! Be quiet before you wake them up," the woman said before covering the man's mouth.

After the couple was out of sight, or at least out of hearing range, Anise and I wrapped ourselves in the blanket.

"I thought you were Mr. Conservative, Dr. Forrester," Anise said sarcastically. "You got pretty wild that time."

"I am a lot of different things to a lot of different people, Anise."

"So what are you to me?"

"Tonight, I'm your lover and friend."

"And what will you be tomorrow?"

"I'll be a memory," I said while lying back, but not taking my eyes off of her. "You know why I'm attracted to you, Anise?"

"My ass?" Anise asked sarcastically.

"No!" I said. "You're like me. You are looking for everything and nothing."

"Meaning?"

"Let me try to explain this." I paused to find my words. "I am a happily married man with a wonderful wife but, for some reason, it's not enough. I am not satisfied with being satisfied. I need more. So, I allow a woman half my age to seduce me into having an affair. It makes me feel young, attractive, and desirable."

"How does that make us alike?" Anise said, flashing that mischievous smile.

"You're famous, beautiful and rich but, for some reason, that's not enough for you. You can have any single young man you want, but you choose to seduce an older married man. Because it makes you feel mature, secure, and validated."

"Validated?" Anise asked. "Who am I trying to validate myself to?"

"Yourself."

We looked at each other and then cuddled together under the blanket. As we lay under the light of the moon, we agreed to end the relationship. She told me she had had her fun with me, but now she had her eye on another prize. She told me he would be a challenge, but she would definitely get him, just as she had gotten me. *Poor sap*, I thought to myself, *better him than me*. We laughed, snuggled together and fell asleep.

The next morning, we made the long ride back to Atlanta. I suppose the finality of the relationship put her at ease, and she began to open up and tell me what I believed to be the truth about her past.

ANISE'S STORY:

"I was born in St. Louis, Missouri, the gateway to the West. I had no siblings, well, none in my immediate family anyway. I was told my father had illegitimate children, but I never ran into them.

"My family had problems before I was even born. My mother was white and my father was black. That alone made it difficult for me. I'm sure you had multiracial friends and, if you did, you know we were easy targets for blacks and whites.

"It didn't help that my father was an alcoholic and my mother was a workaholic, meaning, she wasn't around enough to stop him from smacking me around when he got drunk. He didn't hit her though. She wasn't going to tolerate that shit from him or any man. He hit

her one time, and she nearly killed him. If she had known he was beating me, she would have caught a case, quick! But she couldn't stop
what she didn't know.

"My father's friends used to come over when my mother was gone
and play cards with him. When my father wasn't drunk, he was as
nice and gentle a man as you could find. But when he and his friends
were drinking, they would get totally out of control and my father
would be oblivious to anything other than the next swallow from his
liquor bottle.

"For years, his friends would fondle me in front of his drunken face
as if they were my loving uncles, and that idiot didn't even notice. I
kept all of that to myself until I was fourteen and my so-called Uncle
Frank took me in the bathroom, covered my mouth with a towel and
viciously stole my virginity.

"He left me feeling ugly and disgusted. I felt cheap and dirty,
thinking my body had been damaged forever. It wasn't the physical
violation that did the most damage, it was the emotional violation.
I thought no other man would ever want me.

"I was afraid to tell my parents because I didn't have any proof and
I thought they wouldn't believe me. I couldn't tell them, but I couldn't
live there anymore, either.

"Early the next morning, I stole enough money from my mother
to catch the Greyhound bus to Atlanta and have a little for my pocket.
When that bus pulled off from the station, I promised God and myself
that I would never let another man take advantage of me again.

"I was on the bus for over three days. The longer I sat, the angrier
I became. I created a self-destructive monster that was on a collision
course with death. I didn't give a damn about me, and I sure as hell
didn't give a damn about anyone else. In my mind, it was me against
the world.

"The first couple of weeks were rough. I didn't have a place to live, or food to eat, so I hung around the bus station. I met a couple more runaway girls on the streets and they showed me the ropes, which was how to live in unlivable conditions.

"I didn't have much pride or dignity. How could I, begging for money? But I had enough to make a promise to God and myself that no matter how hungry or desperate I got, I would never sacrifice my body for a handout. Never!

"After being on the street for about a year, I started to develop beyond my age. When I was younger, my features were more Caucasian dominant, but as I got older, the niggah came out! My hips! My butt! My shape all over was straight-up sister! I could sing, dance, everything! My rhythm is what got me off the streets and into the strip clubs of Atlanta.

"I had to grow up, and I had to grow up in a hurry! I lied about my age, faked my identification, and became Gizelle, the most popular figure in Atlanta's adult-entertainment industry. I received many high-priced proposals for sex, and I won't lie, some were very tempting, but when I make a promise, I keep it!

"When I was sixteen, this guy came in and told me he wanted to go to the VIP room for a private show. He was doing all of this talk about being some big-time music producer, but I wasn't buying it. He tried to convince me to go back to his hotel room, but I told him he didn't have enough money in the bank to pay for me to do a private show like that.

"I think my resistance made him even more determined to get me. He started coming in more and more, and we became close friends. I still didn't believe he was a producer until he asked me to be in one of his videos. When I saw how important he was in the industry, I was like, DAMN! I've literally been sitting on the lap of a goldmine!

"After the first video, he asked me to do more, and shit, the money was good, so I did. He stopped trying to get in my panties and acted as if he was genuinely concerned with my welfare. And of course, once he backed away, it turned me on. I eventually fell in love with him. We did everything together. At one point, we even discussed marriage. There was one problem with that though, his wife.

"I felt guilty about our affair at first. But then, after I met her a couple of times and found out she was a pompous bitch, them being married really didn't matter to me.

"The first time we had sex was amazing! He took his time and made me feel like a woman. We started to do it so much that we became careless and his wife caught us in the bed together. That chick went ballistic! She tried to attack me, but he wouldn't let her. I just laughed in her face.

"And guess what? I still didn't care! The thought of her catching us only turned me on more. I liked being free to do whatever I wanted with any man that I wanted, but at the same time, have control over another woman's man. That's why I selected married men, or men who were in serious relationships, because they can only do and say so much. And the taboo of the sex was always great!

"After his wife busted us, he wanted to end it, but I wasn't having it. We weren't going to stop until I said we were going to stop. Luckily for me, that fool really loved his wife. I gave him an ultimatum: he could either use his influence to get me a contract with a music label, or I would show his wife the photos of us having sex in their house.

"He pulled some strings and got me a contract. All I needed was a foot in the door, and once I got that foot in the door, I knocked the damn door down!

"Now I'm bigger than he is. He was a fool, anyway! His wife left him and took half of his shit. He tried to call me but I didn't even return his calls. Do I feel sorry for him? Hell no! Nobody felt sorry for me when I struggled!

"The only thing good about my first couple of years was that I met *my only real friend. She was from the streets, too. We were like night and day, but she had a heart of gold. When I needed a friend, she was always there for me. So when I made it, I went back and found her. I tried to get her off of the streets but she was too far-gone. She is a part of the streets and she's scared to leave. But I love her just the same."*

"Anyway," Anise said, "you're free now so what are you going to do? Go to Disneyland?"

"Ha! Ha!" I laughed. "I'm going to try to warn your next victim."

"Ah, that's none of your business, Dr. Forrester," Anise said. "You better be glad I'm turning your ass loose."

"Okay! You're right," I said, "but we're going to be friends, right?"

"Yeah, you've been a good sport. Don't worry, I have no problems with you."

"What about my wife's PR firm?" I asked. "Is everything intact there?"

"Turns out, I may have to go in another direction," Anise informed. "I'm sorry, it's just business."

"That's not fair!" I said. "You can't do that to her!"

"Nothing's fair in this business!"

"But you signed a contract, Anise."

As Anise was about to speak, the limousine pulled up to the curb of the airport.

"My attorney will make that contract null and void by Monday morning. It's been fun, and uh, I don't think I need any more therapy."

The driver got out, came around and opened my door.

"This is not right!" I said while standing on the curb.

Anise waved good-bye and the driver closed the door. I stood and watched as they drove out of sight. After an extensive search, I found my car and headed home to my wife.

When I arrived home, Alicia and Brittany were sitting in the kitchen eating lunch. I walked in and dropped my bag on the floor.

"Hi, Daddy!" Brittany shouted and then came running to me.

"Hey, baby!" I picked her up in full stride. "How's my angel?"

"I love you, Daddy!"

"I love you, too, baby," I held Brittany in my arms and walked over to Alicia. "How are you doing, sweetheart?"

"Oh, I could be better," Alicia said. "Gizelle just called and said there's a problem with the contract."

"A problem with the contract?" I pretended I didn't know what she was talking about.

"Yeah, Gizelle asked if she could meet with us on Monday. She said her attorney needs to discuss the contract with us."

"Is everything okay?" I sat down with Brittany in my lap.

"I don't know," Alicia said, "she was kind of rushing me off the phone."

"Seriously?"

"Yeah, I hope everything is all right. I'm going to see her at her hotel and get this straightened out."

"I'm sure everything is okay." I sat Brittany in the chair beside me.

"We've invested a lot of money in luring Gizelle to our company. I hope she's not trying to renege on our deal," Alicia said. "That would destroy us financially."

"It'll be okay, sweetheart," I said. "Don't stress yourself out."

I kissed Alicia on the cheek, and then turned her face to me and kissed her on the lips.

"It's going to be okay," I said. "Okay?"

"Okay," Alicia replied and stirred her tea.

"Guess what, Daddy?" Brittany jumped up and down in her seat.

"What?"

"Brimone and Alexiah are coming over!"

"Oh, they are?" I jumped up and down with her.

"Yes! Yes! Yes!" Brittany shouted.

"Pam, Cynthia and Tina are bringing the kids over tonight," Alicia said.

"So, is this going to be a girls' night in?" I asked.

"Yeah, but we're going to be discussing business, too, not just having fun. After I come from Gizelle's, the girls are going to meet me here."

"Are you taking Brittany with you?" I asked.

"I'm dropping her off at Cynthia's. She's going to bring her back when they come over tonight."

"I'll see what Mike is doing, maybe we can catch a game together."

My pager went off and it was Rosemary calling. She never called on the weekends, so I knew it had to be of major importance. Before I could respond to her page, she was calling on my cell.

"Good afternoon, Dr. Forrester. I just received a call from Veronica Taylor's husband," Rosemary paused momentarily before saying, "Veronica's at Emory University!"

"Oh, my God!" I responded. "What happened?"

"She was found passed out in her car in front of the Hotel Grand. Someone saw her and called the police."

"Did she have an accident?"

"I'm not sure," Rosemary said. "She has bruises, but there was no damage done to her car."

"Did he give her condition?"

"Yes," Rosemary said, "she's in critical condition."

"Okay! I'm on my way!"

When I arrived, Veronica's husband was leaning against the wall outside of her room. Judging by his demeanor, I prepared myself to receive the worst news.

"Good afternoon, Mr. Taylor," I said, "I'm Dr. Johnson Forrester."

"Oh, thank God you're here! I'm Veronica's husband, Tim."

"Sorry to hear about this, Tim. Veronica is such a lovely person," I said. "How's she doing?"

"They were able to bring her back around and she can speak now. I was out here thanking my lucky stars when you walked up. She's a fighter!"

"What happened?"

"I'm not sure. She was coming from the Hotel Grand and I guess she passed out."

"The Hotel Grand?" I asked, remembering that it was the hotel where Anise was staying. "What was she doing there?"

"I have no idea," Tim said. "She was supposed to be bedridden."

"Wow. That's strange. Can she have visitors?"

"Only family," Tim said. "And her therapist! Go on in, she'll be happy to see you."

"Okay, good."

I slowly pushed the door open and saw Veronica lying there with cords running in and out of her body. I felt somehow responsible for her being in this condition. If I hadn't been so involved with Anise and our affair, perhaps I could have been more attentive to Veronica's needs. The woman was crying for me to help her and I was basically telling her to help herself. And now she lay before me barely clinging to life.

"Hey, how are you doing there?" I said, taking her hand.

"Better," Veronica said faintly.

I looked at her feeble, young body and knew there was something I had to do, something more than wait for her to visit my office and discuss her problems.

"Hey kiddo," I said, "we're going to get you well. You hear me?"

"Yes."

"Okay," I said, rubbing her hand, "you get some rest. I'll be back to visit you tomorrow and I better see a smile on your face."

"Help me," Veronica said, "please."

"I will," I answered, patting her on the hand. "Good-bye."

I walked out of the hospital room fighting back tears. I put my hand on Tim's shoulder and, with all the sincerity I possessed, I promised to help in every way possible to get Veronica healthy. "I don't know exactly what I can do, but I am going to do something! I'm not God, but I do know God! And He will help Veronica get through this."

"You don't know how much that means to us." Tim shook my hand.

"I, uh, I'll stop by tomorrow and check on Veronica to see how she's doing."

"Thank you," Tim said, "this situation can be so emotionally and physically exhausting. I don't know how much I have left in the tank. But I'm not giving up until I have nothing left."

"Don't worry," I said, "everything will be okay."

I walked away believing in my own words. As a psychologist, I'm used to saying those words out of habit, but this time I meant it. I had to; a woman's life depended upon them. And I'd be damned if I was going to let her die.

Before I could get in my car to leave, I received another phone call from Rosemary. I didn't hesitate to answer this time.

"Yes, Rosemary, please tell me you're a bearer of good news this time."

"It depends on how you look at it."

"How may I help you?"

"Patient Number Five would like to meet with you."

"When?"

"Now."

"That's impossible! I have too much on my plate right now."

"I think you may want to go, she's not taking no for an answer."

"Dammit!" I said. "I can't drop everything and run to this patient every time she calls for me, Rosemary!"

"Don't shoot the messenger!"

"I'm sorry."

"You okay?"

"Yes, I'm fine," I said. "I guess I gotta do what I gotta do."

"Keep me informed."

"I will."

CHAPTER TWELVE

After I pulled into Patient Number Five's gate, I had become so familiar with the routine that it took only moments before the butler was unlocking her door and letting me in. My usual extensive wait for her to begin speaking did not take as long this time. It was only a matter of minutes before I heard that unique voice force its way into my ears.

"It is said the admission of ignorance is the beginning of wisdom."

"To what do I owe this honor?" I asked.

"Honor is earned, not owed."

"Okay, in layman's terms," I spoke very calmly, "why am I here?"

"You have had quite an interesting day," Patient Number Five said.

"How do you know what type of day I've had?"

"Because, even in darkness, I can still see."

"Okay," I said, very frustrated, "You win! You are much more philosophical than me. Now please tell me, why am I here?"

"You are a doctor of psychiatry, are you not?"

"No. I'm a doctor of psychology."

"Is there a difference, sir?"

"You're a Pulitzer- and Nobel Prize-winning author in the field of mental disorders," I said. "You know exactly what the difference is."

"And what would that difference be, sir?"

Even though I knew the question was a ploy to play on my ego, I couldn't resist the temptation to boast of my intellectual prowess.

"Psychiatry is the branch of medicine dealing with disorders of the mind, including psychoses and neuroses," I said, convinced that my definition was undeniably accurate. "Psychology, on the other hand, is the science dealing with the mind and with mental and emotional processes. It's the science of human and animal behavior."

"So, do your patients have mental disorders?" Patient Number Five asked. "They include psychoses and neuroses?"

"Sure," I said, knowing the question was a set-up. "But…"

"So, by your own definition, sir," Patient Number Five said, "you are a psychiatrist and not a psychologist?"

"It's not that simple and you know it," I said. "Sometimes the treatment intertwines."

"So what is your indulgent obsession with the tautology of the title of psychologist over psychiatrist?"

"I do not have an indulgent obsession. I'm just stating the facts."

"Until you are defined by your work, and not your title, all that you are is a name on a door with the word 'doctor' as a prefix."

"Who the hell are you to judge me?" I asked. I had become frustrated by Patient Number Five's condescending remarks and I was ready to confront them. "You sit in a room surrounded by darkness, afraid to exist outside of the protective walls of this attic! Yet you give unprovoked, nugatory remarks on something you know absolutely nothing about! Until you leave this room and go out and face my world, don't you dare sit in judgment of me! Do you understand me, madam?"

There was a short silence and then Patient Number Five spoke very softly, "I think it is time for you to leave, sir!"

"Fine!" I pushed the flashing button and, in a matter of seconds, the double doors opened.

I left Patient Number Five's house again, frustrated and angry. I was supposed to be the therapist, and she the patient, but time after time after leaving our session, I felt confused and incompetent. I felt as if I was the patient searching for answers.

I tried to forget my visit with Patient Number Five and place concern where it was needed most, on my family and my true patients. I called my wife to take my mind off some of my stress. Just the sound of her voice made me feel better.

"Hey you!" I said.

"How did it go today, sweetheart?"

"Not good. Not good at all," I said. "Veronica is battling for her life."

"That's a bummer!"

"Yeah, I probably don't need to be discussing this."

"You're not telling me her intimate secrets or anything like that," Alicia said. "What's the big deal?"

"I don't know. I guess I just need to deal with this myself before I discuss it with anyone else."

"You sound really upset, sweetheart," Alicia said, "are you going to be okay?"

"I'll be okay," I said. "Where's my sorry brother? He was supposed to meet me tonight so we can hang out together."

"Oh, good news!" Alicia said. "I saw Gizelle today and she is going to write a book and wants Mike to write it for her."

"Why is she writing a book?"

"Who cares? She said if we can get Mike to help her write her book, she would sign a long-term contract with CAP."

Something didn't sound right about this. Anise had never mentioned writing a book to me. I was curious to know her motivation behind this book. I couldn't believe writing a book was her sole interest.

"Hopefully, they can seal the deal tonight," Alicia said.

"What deal?"

"Mike is on his way to her hotel to negotiate a deal for writing her book," Alicia said. "We're going to have a little celebration when he gets back!"

"Mike is on his way over to Gizelle's hotel room?" I asked.

"Yeah, he just left," Alicia said. "What's up?"

"I'll call you back!"

"What's the matter?"

"Nothing! I'll call you back in a minute!"

I didn't wait for Alicia to say good-bye, nor did I say good-bye to her. It suddenly hit me. Mike was the new object of Anise's affection. I should have known she had a devious plan when she agreed to break it off with me. I was not about to let my brother go through what I had just experienced. I believed it was her way of getting back at me for wanting to end our affair.

I sped through traffic getting to Anise's hotel. I didn't even bother with the elevator and ran up the flights of stairs and swung open the door. My adrenaline was flowing. I was breathing hard, my heart was pounding, but I couldn't stop running.

When I got to Anise's suite, I started to pound on her door.

As I knocked, the door came open on its own. I slowly walked in, leaving the door ajar. I walked through the sitting area of the suite and into the bedroom. Anise was asleep on the bed, still wearing the same clothes she was wearing when they dropped me off at the airport.

Mike had not arrived, so I had a little time to ask Anise to leave him out of our scandalous sex game. I sat on the edge of the bed and tapped her on the feet.

"Anise, wake up. We need to talk."

She didn't budge, so I nudged her again. She still didn't budge, so I stood up and walked to the head of the bed and turned her over.

"Anise, wake up," I said, getting a clear look at her face. I could see blood flowing from her head. "OH SHIT!"

I stepped away, covering my mouth. I accidentally knocked over the lamp making a loud noise. I panicked and started to run out of the room. As I was approaching the door, Mike walked into the suite.

"What the hell are you doing here?" Mike asked. I could tell by his tone that he was disappointed and pissed off.

"Mike! Man, look, I didn't do it! I didn't do anything!" I said nervously.

"What's wrong with you?" Mike said. "Where's Gizelle?"

"She's back there, man! She's dead! She's dead, Mike!"

"What?" Mike said, pushing past me and into the bedroom. I followed Mike into the bedroom, pleading my innocence.

"Oh my God!" Mike ran to Anise and then started shaking her body for any signs of life. "Man, what have you done?"

"I didn't do anything! She was like that when I got here!" I shouted. "I swear to God!"

"Gizelle! Gizelle!" Mike shouted, shaking her body. "Call the police, Johnny!"

I wanted to move but I couldn't. I couldn't move a muscle.

"Johnny!" Mike shouted. "Call the damn police!"

"Okay! Okay!" I shouted. I walked slowly to the phone and picked it up.

"What are you waiting for?" Mike held Anise in his arms. "Dial the number!"

As I started to dial, Mike told me to hang up the phone. I slammed the phone down and paced the floor.

"What happened, Johnny?" Mike asked.

"Mike, no matter what kind of trouble I've gotten into. I have never lied to you, man! I did not do this!" I said. "I swear to God! I did not do this!"

"What were you doing here in the first place?"

"I came to save you from her." I pointed at Anise's body. "She was going to seduce you and blackmail you into having sex with her, just like she did me. I couldn't let that happen!"

"Go!" Mike shouted. "Go! Get out of here, man!"

"I'm not leaving you, man, are you crazy?"

"If they find you here and it comes out you two were having an affair, you're going to jail."

"So!" I said. "I'm not leaving you."

Mike ignored me and dialed the police.

"Atlanta Police Department, how may I assist you?" the dispatcher said.

"My name is Michael Forrester, and I just discovered a body," Mike stated.

"Where are you?" the dispatcher asked.

"I'm in the Hotel Grand on Peachtree Street in Buckhead!"

"You say someone is dead?"

"Yes, Ma'am."

Mike gave them additional information and hung up the phone. He continued to try to convince me to leave. But this was my brother and I loved him. I could not stand the thought of him being in this situation for my sake. His concern for me turned to anger when I refused to leave. Granted, I was much larger than Mike, but he was still the older brother and that psychological factor made up for and exceeded the size difference.

"Johnny," Mike said in a calm, yet serious tone, "I'm not going to tell you again. Get out of here!"

"I'm not leaving, Mike!"

Mike jumped up and physically pushed me out of the door. We could hear the sound of the police sirens nearing and I began to panic again.

"I'll be downstairs," I said.

"Go! Go! Go! Go! Go!" Mike repeated.

I ran down the hall to the exit sign, passing the elevator. I heard the elevator door ring; sounding that it was about to open. I swung open the stairway exit door and looked through the small window after it closed. I could see the police getting off the elevator and going toward Anise's suite.

I wanted to turn back and run to Mike's rescue but he would have kicked my ass. I sped down the stairs and into the lobby. I slowed down when I saw people walking around so as not to seem suspicious. I was still breathing hard, but apparently no one suspected a thing.

I called the girls back at the house to let them know Mike and I would be getting in late. They chastised me at first, but we were able to get clearance from our wives. I sat in the lobby with my heart about to leap out of my chest, waiting for my brother to walk out the elevator and tell me everything would be okay.

I wasn't waiting long when Mike stepped out of the elevator surrounded by police officers who were holding him by both arms. I stood up and started to walk toward him. He looked at me and shook his head no, gesturing for me to back away.

As I watched them put Mike in the back of the patrol car, I came to a disappointing realization. My family, my career, and my reputation were utterly and completely in jeopardy of being destroyed.

❋❋❋

On the drive home, I tried to figure out how I could explain to Cynthia that Mike was at the police station. I needed time to build up my nerves. I went over a variety of scenarios several times in my head. The closer I got to my house, the stronger the pressure felt. Before I knew it, I was out of time. I was pulling into my driveway, out of time and out of ideas.

As luck would have it, or bad luck would have it, the other office girls were still there. Out of all the nights they decide to stay late, it had to be this one. I stood outside of my house for a minute or two before I mustered the courage to enter.

The office girls—Tina, Cynthia, Pam, and Alicia—were huddled in my living room, very much awake. I walked in with my head down and sat between Alicia and Cynthia.

"What's the matter, baby?" Alicia asked.

"Whoo!" I said, taking a deep breath. "We have a problem. We have a serious problem."

"What's wrong?" Alicia asked.

"It's Mike."

"What's wrong with Mike?" Cynthia asked anxiously.

"Mike's in jail."

"Mike's in jail?" Cynthia laughed. "For what?"

"I don't know exactly."

"You're not kidding, are you?" Cynthia removed the smile from her face.

"I wouldn't play about something like this, Cynt!"

"Where is he?" Cynthia said while putting on her shoes.

"The police station."

"What are we waiting for?" Tina screamed. "Let's go!"

"Maybe just Cynthia and I should go."

"Have you lost your damn mind?" Pam said. "You think we're going to sit around while Mike is in jail?"

"I don't care who comes! Let's go!" Cynthia shouted. "I got to get to my husband!"

"Y'all go! I'll call Curtis and let him know I'm staying here with the kids till y'all get back!" Tina said.

"Thanks, Tina," Cynthia said.

"Come on, Cynt, let's go!" Pam said.

We made a few calls and found out where Mike was being held. The office girls and I loaded into my truck and we drove to the police station. A police officer explained to us that Mike was not under arrest but was only being detained for questioning.

Another detective explained the reason for the detainment was for a murder inquiry. He would not give us the name of the victim because the next of kin was being notified to come to the morgue and identify the body. He said there was no identification found at the scene. Mike had informed them of her identity but they still needed formal identification.

As the detective was talking, my cell phone rang. I looked at the number and it was Rosemary calling again. I excused myself from the room and walked to a quiet area.

"Sorry to be calling so late, Dr. Forrester," Rosemary said.

"No problem," I said, "now what's the matter?"

"I just received a phone call from the police."

"Okay," I said curiously. "And?"

"Well," Rosemary said, "they found an unidentified body in the Hotel Grand and your number was given as a point of contact."

"Okay," I said. "What does that have to do with me?"

"The police want you to identify the body."

"Why do the police want me to identify a body?"

"They believe it may be one of your patients."

"What?" I tried to pretend that I was surprised by the news.

"Dr. Forrester!" Rosemary shouted. "Dr. Forrester! You there?"

"Yes, I'm here," I said, "Where, uh, where am I supposed to be going?"

"Do you have a pen? I can give you the number for the detective and you can call him back."

"Sure, hold on," I said, "I have to find something to write with."

I went to an officer's desk and asked for a pen. She gave me a pen and ripped off a corner of a sheet of paper and handed it to me.

"Okay, I'm ready, Rosemary."

Rosemary gave me the information and I hung up. I didn't hear Alicia walking up behind me as I was calling the detective.

"What's that all about, honey?" Alicia asked.

"Oh, nothing!" I slammed my cell phone shut.

"You okay?"

"It's just one of my patients."

"This time of the night?"

"Yeah," I said, "Veronica is not doing very well."

"I'm sorry, honey," Alicia said. "This has not been one of your better days."

"I know, but it'll be all right. "

"Is there anything I can do?" Alicia asked.

"I'm fine," I said. "Cynthia probably needs you more than I do."

"Okay," Alicia said, kissing me on the cheek.

After Alicia was out of clear view, I called the detective to get specific information about why I was making a trip to the morgue. He wouldn't say much over the phone, just that it would be explained to me when I arrived. He told me it would take a while to get dressed but gave me directions where to meet him. I told Alicia I had to run out to pick us up some coffee and that I would be back shortly. She didn't question my leaving because she was too focused on supporting Cynthia.

I was always under the impression that a morgue operated as a nine-to-five business. I guess death happens twenty-four hours a day, so the morgue has to accommodate its schedule.

I had never been in a morgue before it smelled of medicine and was unusually quiet. The detective met me and led me to the room where the body was waiting.

I was nervous, very nervous! We passed several rooms, and with each passing I took a sigh of relief knowing that was not the room. But then my heart would accelerate again in anticipation that the next room could be the room where Anise's dead body waited for me. Finally, the detective stopped in front of a room and then turned to me.

"You ready, Doc?"

"Ready as I'll ever be," I replied.

"Here we go!"

The detective opened the door and I followed him into the room. I stared nervously as I saw a body covered from head to toe beneath a perfectly clean white sheet. The outlined physical features were so apparent. The nose, the mouth, the arms, the toes, everything seemed to be so humanly recognizable beneath the sheet.

The detective grabbed the sheet at the head of the body and paused to give me time to prepare. As he pulled the sheet down and revealed the face of the body, I closed my eyes and prepared again to pretend to be surprised. But when I opened my eyes, my heart stopped and my eyes flooded. There she was, peacefully asleep. The body of the woman I had just had sex with earlier that day was lying before me, dead!

"Is this your patient?"

"Yes," I said, overwhelmed with sadness, "yes, it is."

"Sorry to hear that."

"Do you know what happened to her?" I asked, wanting to get as much information as possible.

"As far as we could tell, this was a homicide. There are signs of a defensive struggle. The victim had a number of external injuries, bruises, marks, to reflect foul play. There was physical evidence that someone else was around the body when she died. In cases like this, we generally request an autopsy to try to determine a definite cause of death. But until we get the results from the autopsy, we won't know for sure."

"I don't know, maybe as her doctor I should have suspected something wasn't right."

"Don't beat yourself up over this," the detective said. "Things like this can't be predicted."

"This didn't have to happen." I shook my head. "It just didn't have to happen."

I stared at Anise lying on the table until the detective covered her face with the sheet.

"Does she have a next of kin for us to contact?" the detective asked.

"No, no, she doesn't. At least none that she mentioned."

"Well, is there anyone we can contact who may want to possess the remains?"

"I will," I said, not certain what that responsibility entailed.

"Are you sure?"

"Yeah. I'm sure."

"Well, let's go upstairs and get everything taken care of," the detective said, patting me on the back, "sorry for your loss."

"Thank you."

CHAPTER THIRTEEN

I was so engulfed by the surreal events of the day that I started to play into the nightmare. I knew I was obstructing justice by not telling the police everything I knew, but I couldn't. I was too afraid.

By the time I got back to the station, Alicia, Cynthia, and Pam were sitting in a room waiting for me to return. I passed them the cups of coffee which I picked up on my way back and sat next to my wife. As the hours passed, we spoke only when necessary. There was no conversation, only stares and tears. Every time a door opened, we looked in its direction, hoping Mike would emerge from beyond it.

Pam held Cynthia's hand while we sat and waited. She only released her hand one time. That was when she stepped away for a moment to make a telephone call.

When she returned, she held Cynthia's hand again without saying a word. Maybe an hour later, Wanda, Lisa, Darsha, and Valerie walked into the station. Wanda was still wearing her nightclothes. I knew Mike was close to the office girls, but even I was surprised to see their loyalty to him.

It's not like they kept in contact with one another on a regular basis. But when one of the so-called office girls was in distress, they came a-running. All of them!

"Somebody better get to explaining why I'm at the police station in the middle of the night!" Wanda said with her hands on her hips.

"Mike is being questioned for a murder," Cynthia said.

"Murder? Mike?" Wanda asked. "Come on now."

"Who was killed?" Lisa asked.

"Gizelle," Pam said. "The singer."

"Gizelle?" Darsha shouted. *"The Gizelle?"*

"Yeah," Alicia said, "she was our new client and wanted Mike to help her write a book. Mike went over to help her and that's all we know."

"Y'all know Gizelle?" Darsha asked.

"We knew Gizelle," Pam said.

"So why are they questioning Mike?" Lisa asked.

"We don't know, they won't tell us anything more than that," Alicia answered.

"You okay, Cynt?" Valerie asked while sitting beside her and rubbing her back.

"No!" Cynthia said, wiping her eyes.

"It's going to be all right, baby," Valerie said. "You know Mike don't have nothing to do with this."

"I'm scared, Val," Cynthia said.

"Hey, look," Wanda squeezed between Cynthia and Valerie, "ain't nothing gon' happen to Mike. You know that straight-ass niggah ain't did nothing wrong."

"I appreciate y'all coming down, but this might take all night," Cynthia said. "I don't expect y'all to stay here all night with me. Go home and get some sleep."

"I ain't goin' nowhere!" Wanda said.

"Me neither!" Valerie said.

"Me neither!" Darsha agreed.

"I'm not going anywhere, either, Cynt," Lisa said.

"And you know you better not even look over here at me," Pam said.

"Now, how do you like your coffee, black or cream?" Darsha asked.

"I've already had coffee," Cynthia said. "But thanks anyway."

"You can get me some," Wanda said.

"Hey, get me some, too," Val said.

"You better bring your ass on, girl," Darsha said.

"You was gon' get Cynthia a cup," Val said.

"You ain't Cynthia!"

"You make me sick, you stankin' heffa!"

"Yo mama!"

"Will y'all go get the coffee and shut the hell up!" Wanda said.

"Okay, girl, shut up," Darsha said. "We'll be right back."

"Hold on, I'll come with you," Valerie said.

For the remainder of the night, the office girls talked, paced and cried, while I sat quietly and didn't say a word. I didn't know how to console them. Or myself.

What I did know, however, was that the past twenty-four hours had created an eye-opening analysis for me. I was forced to see the man I truly was, an emotionally selfish person who had been a self-pitying, self-righteous coward who never had the balls to stand up for himself.

I had bullshitted my way through life and, for the most part, gotten away with it. My facade as a mental clinician was no different. My ostentatious use of my intellect camouflaged my ignorance to my patients. They misconstrued my smile and my sagacious use of big words as clinical therapy. But how can one be a clinician to others when he, himself, is in emotional ruins? It's just not possible.

Sitting there in that police station, I tried to come to terms with the reality of my past and my future. I was at the crossroads of sanity and insanity. If I continued to live my life passively and non-confrontationally, I would inevitably lose my mind. I could no longer accept the collapse of my professional and personal life. But logic told me that I should not expect my environment to change until I first change the conditions within it. Beginning with myself. Logic also told me that it was much easier to contemplate one's ideas than to activate them.

A little after daybreak, I decided to find out what was taking so long with Mike's release, since he wasn't under arrest. I asked around and was passed from officer to officer. I was becoming annoyed with their runaround so I made a call to rectify the situation.

Thirty-minutes later, Stacey walked through the door of the police station. She was suited up and ready for business. She wasn't smiling and she wasn't happy.

"How long have you been down here?" Stacey asked.

"Since about nine last night," I said.

The office girls, all of whom were asleep on top of each other, overheard our conversation and began to wake up.

"Are you telling me your brother has been getting interrogated since last night?"

"Yeah," I said, not fully understanding Stacey's frustration.

"Has he been placed under arrest?"

"No, not to my knowledge. To my understanding, he has only been detained for interrogation."

"This is unacceptable!"

Stacey walked off in a huff. She went to the front desk and then she and another officer disappeared behind a set of double doors. The office girls were confused as to who she was, and why she was there.

"Who was that, Johnny?" Cynthia asked.

"That's a friend of mine."

"Is she here to help Mike?"

"I don't know, Cynt, but we're about to find out."

We sat for almost hour and then Stacey came from beyond the set of double doors. Once she had passed through, she held the doors open and Mike came through next. Ironically, the two had studied law together at Harvard University and were already well acquainted.

The office girls ran to Mike with Cynthia leading the way, asking a barrage of questions.

"Baby, are you all right?" Cynthia asked, kissing Mike over and over.

"Yeah, I'm fine," Mike said. "I just need to get some rest."

"You okay, man?" I asked.

"Not right now," Mike said, staring at me momentarily, "but I will be."

"I was worried about you back there," I said.

"I know you were," Mike replied evenly.

"Boy, you bet' not ever scare us like this no mo'!" Wanda said.

"Oh, I got it now! A brother has to go to prison to get a visit from you chicks, huh?" Mike said sarcastically.

"Shut up, niggah!" Wanda laughed.

"Forget all that small talk," Valerie said. "Why you in jail?"

"It's a long story," Mike said. "I'm about to go home and get some rest. If you want to hear, you better come now. 'Cause like the song says, I'm not one to repeat gossip, so you better be sure and listen close the first time."

"You better tell us now, Mike!" Darsha said. "I can't wait!"

"My house! I got to get some rest," Mike responded.

We piled out of the police station and followed Mike to his house. Stacey told me that if we needed her legal assistance, she would be more than happy to represent Mike. I thanked her and told her I didn't think it would be necessary. I thought our nightmare was over, but it was just beginning.

❂❂❂

The sun had completely come up and we were gathered in Mike's living room. Everybody was clustered head over foot to fit into the tight squeeze. Alicia and I sat against the wall with her between my legs.

Mike explained how he had gone to Anise's room and found her dead body. He told them that was the reason he was detained. The whole story was unbelievable. The office girls thought Mike was embellishing it. And if I hadn't been there in the room, I would have been skeptical myself. But Mike was not embellishing. In fact, he was omitting some of the story. He never once mentioned that I was there, too.

"Mike, how did you feel when you realized she was dead?" Lisa asked.

"I was like," Mike said, "I was like, this can't be happening."

"Were you scared?" Darsha asked.

"I really didn't have time to be scared. Everything happened so fast."

"Well, we know what your next book is going to be about." Lisa smiled.

"And what's that?"

"Murder mystery," Lisa said.

"I wanna be in it!" Valerie said.

"Y'all know I got detective skills," Wanda said. "When Ms. Virginia died, I was the one who figured it out."

"Is that supposed to be a joke?" Pam snapped.

I didn't know exactly what triggered Pam's reaction but it wasn't long before I found out.

"Huh?" Wanda said.

"Why would you try to make a joke over somebody's death?" Pam shouted. "That shit ain't funny!"

"First of all, stop yelling at me! And second of all, we know Ms. Virginia was your mother, but you didn't love her no more than nobody else!" Wanda said.

"So what! She was my mother!" Pam shouted.

"You was the one always trippin' on her, Pam!" Wanda shouted back.

"Kiss my ass, Wanda!"

"Kiss my ass, Pam!" Wanda said. "Who you supposed to be?"

I saw firsthand, the defensiveness of Wanda's personality as discussed in my office. She was becoming the aggressor in this conversation instead of being sympathetic to Pam's sensitivity.

"That's enough, Wanda," Cynthia said. "Pam, you too."

I looked at Wanda and she looked at me. I shook my head in disapproval, letting her know her behavior was excessive. But to my surprise, she had already recognized it herself.

"I'm sorry, Pam," Wanda said. "I should have been more sensitive."

"Is this a joke?" Pam asked.

"No, it's not a damn joke, would you stop saying that? I'm trying to be a kinder, gentler Wanda, so work with me."

"Damn!" Pam said, looking around. "You must really know your job, Johnny, if you can get Wanda to apologize."

"See, if y'all keep talking shit to me, I'm gon' have to set if off up in this piece!" Wanda said.

"Hold up!" Valerie said. "If you can get Wanda to act like that, Johnny, maybe I need to come see the wizard."

"I don't think even the wizard got something in his doctor bag for gayness." Wanda laughed and blew Valerie a kiss.

"Shut the hell up, Wanda!" Valerie said. "Every time you say something to me it's got to be about being gay!"

I had never been considered one of the office girls, understandably so; I didn't share what they experienced in that office. But I was accepted into their group by association with my wife and my brother.

They did not gather together that often. But when they did, and I witnessed it, I saw that they shared an impregnable bond. They argued, they laughed and then they made up. They genuinely enjoyed being together. It was always a sense of family, a family in turmoil sometimes, but a family just the same.

"Back to Mike!" Alicia said. "Is this over with?"

"I certainly hope so," Mike said.

"Well, you know we got your back!" Darsha said.

"Of course!" Mike said.

I couldn't help but envy Mike's relationship with the office girls. These women loved this man. Not for sex! But for love, pure love! Everything I'd been searching for my whole life, this man had it delivered to him on a silver platter without even trying.

The office girls chatted for a little while longer and then they dispersed, saying their emotional good-byes. Alicia and I went home and I passed out before I could take my clothes off.

I slept for a few hours and woke up ready to confront my issues. I had a brother questioned for murder, one patient found dead, one near death, one out of her mind, and one accused of abusing her child.

I took a long shower and contemplated how I would resolve some of the issues. When I was finished with my shower, I felt refreshed. But I still didn't have any resolutions.

I knew for certain that the first thing I would do is visit Veronica at the hospital. I relieved Tim of his duty and he went home to freshen up. I sat beside Veronica's bedside and we talked. Not patient-to-doctor conversation, just conversation.

"So, you ready to get up and run the marathon with me?" I joked.

"Oh, I think I may need a few extra days." Veronica smiled faintly.

"You know you have a lot of people concerned about you."

"Oh yeah," Veronica said, "I guess I'm a lucky person, huh?"

"Luckier than most."

She smiled again, this time broader than before.

"Don't you have something else to do besides spend your Sunday afternoon with an invalid?"

"You're not an invalid," I said. "You're a beautiful young woman."

"Please!" Veronica said. "Stop lying to me! I'm freakin' dying and you're telling me I'm beautiful!"

"You're not dying." I stood up and walked away.

"I want you to tell me the truth! I'm tired of people lying to me. I want somebody to look me in the eye and tell me the truth for once."

"Okay, Veronica," I said, "I say this not as your therapist, but as a friend. You are sick! Extremely sick! You need to put weight on your body or we are going to lose you. And frankly, I can't allow that to happen, sweetheart."

"What can I do?" Veronica started to cry.

"I'll tell you what."

"What?" Veronica replied.

"Do you like spinach?"

"I was raised in the country. I don't like it, I love it!"

"I'll make a deal with you. I hate spinach. Hate it! It makes me want to puke! Here's the deal. I promise to come here every day and I'll eat that nasty, horrible spinach if you promise to eat a smidgen of it with me. Deal or no deal?"

"You got yourself a deal, mister!"

"Okay, so when do we start?"

"I don't think I can start for a few more days. I have to be nourished through these tubes first before I start eating regular food," Veronica said, breathing heavily.

"That's okay. We can start in a few days," I assured her. "You sound a little exhausted so I'll let you get some rest."

"I guess I'll see you in a few days, huh?"

"You wish! I'll be here first thing in the morning to relieve Tim."

"Seriously?"

"Absolutely."

"Why?"

"I don't understand," I said. "What do you mean, why?"

"Why are you coming to see me every day, Dr. Forrester?" Veronica asked.

"Because you're my hero," I replied.

"How can I be anyone's hero?"

"Because you're a fighter, Veronica! You could have left us but you chose to fight. I don't know that if I was in your position I'd have the strength to fight like you're fighting."

"Thank you," Veronica said, "you don't know how much that means to me. You really don't."

"Look, I have to go!" I said. "Everybody can't afford to lay up all day and have people wait on them hand and foot. Some of us have to go out in the workforce."

"Well, I guess I'll be seeing you tomorrow morning."

"I guess you will. Good-bye!"

"Good-bye!"

As I was walking out, the nurse was walking in. She almost dropped her pan when she realized who I was.

"Dr. Forrester, what on God's green earth are you doing here?"

I didn't want to reveal my relationship with Veronica, nor did I want Veronica to know my relationship with Betty.

"I'm here visiting a friend," I said. "Do you work here?"

"Yes, Veronica is my patient."

"I didn't tell him a thing," Veronica said, now barely able to speak.

"You two know each other?" I asked.

"Yes," Betty said, passing by me to fluff Veronica's pillows, "she's my patient."

"Okay," I said. "I guess that cat is out of the bag."

"I guess he thinks we're ashamed to be seeing a psychiatrist," Betty said.

"Psychologist," I said, correcting Betty. And then I remembered Patient Number Five's badgering me about my tautology of the word. "Psychologist? Therapist? It really doesn't matter."

"Are you ashamed, Veronica?" Betty asked boldly.

"No," Veronica whispered.

"Neither am I," Betty said.

"See you tomorrow, Veronica," I said. "Betty, may I speak with you privately, please?"

"Sure." Betty followed me into the hall.

"Are you aware of the severity of Veronica's condition?"

"I'm her nurse." Betty put her hand on her hip.

"I didn't mean to offend you, I was just asking."

"I am going to give you the benefit of the doubt and just come out and ask you," Betty said. "Are you here for Veronica, or are you here to check up on me?"

"What?" I was thrown off by Betty's question. "Check up on you? I didn't even know you worked here. Veronica is my patient and she is very sick!"

"What kind of therapist visits a sick patient in the hospital? That's for a physician."

"I don't know," I said. "I suppose the answer to your question is the same therapist who cares enough to believe a mother who has the look of love for her child in her eyes, and not one of harm."

Betty smiled and hugged me tightly. She covered her mouth and started to cry.

"Oh my God!" Betty said. "You believe me! You really believe me!"

"Now, I want you to believe me," I said, pointing to Veronica's door, "I am here for her, not to check up on you. I am afraid that if I stop coming, she may never eat. Her husband loves her, but he is not helping her. I need your help, Betty."

"Sure, what do you need me to do?"

"I need you to help me save that woman's life."

"Don't worry, I have no plans on losing her." Betty smiled with confidence.

"Thank you."

"She's not going anywhere, Dr. Forrester," Betty said. "At least not on my watch."

"What a relief. I'll be back tomorrow."

❀❀❀

It was almost dark before I got home. When I turned the corner where I lived, I could see my driveway still had cars in it that did not belong to the residence. I was not in the mood for company or socializing so I was going to go straight to bed.

When I stepped into my house, I was greeted by Brittany and my two nieces, Brimone and Alexiah. Their happy faces momentarily took away my disappointment and sadness.

Brimone and I were very close because I was around when she was born. I didn't know Alexiah as well, but I loved her the same. She was absolutely adorable!

"Hey, Daddy!" Brittany ran to me and jumped into my arms.

"Hey, big girl!" I held her high above my head and then put her back on the floor.

"Hi, Uncle Johnny." Brimone grabbed my left arm.

"Who are you?" I said sarcastically.

"Your niece!" Brimone said.

"No, my niece is a teenager! You're a grown woman!"

"Hi, Uncle Johnny!" Alexiah grabbed my right arm.

"Hey, little lady! Look at you! You're as big as your sister!"

"Can you play with us?" Alexiah asked.

"Yeah, Daddy, play with us," Brittany urged.

"I'll play with you on one condition."

"Okay!" Alexiah said.

"We have to eat some," I said, pausing and then tickling Alexiah's and Brittany's stomachs, "ICE CREAM!"

"YEAH!" Brittany and Alexiah shouted in unison.

"I don't want any ice cream," Brimone said, folding her arms.

"Oh, that's right, you're grown now!" I said jokingly.

"No, I'm not." Brimone laughed.

"I know what you want; you want a beer, huh?"

"No, I don't want a beer! That's nasty! Yuck!" Brimone said, making a face.

"It's nasty? Oh, so you know what beer tastes like? I'm going to tell Cynthia!" I said while walking toward the kitchen.

"No! Don't do that, Uncle Johnny! You know I don't drink that nasty stuff!" Brimone was trying to stop me from passing her. "Y'all help me!"

"Okay!" Alexiah shouted. "Come on, Brittany!"

Brittany and Alexiah grabbed both of my legs, and Brimone climbed up my back and I dragged them into the kitchen.

"Get off of me!" I shouted, grunting playfully.

"What are y'all doing on your Uncle Johnny?" Cynthia asked.

"He's trying to get me in trouble, Ms. Cynthia!" Brimone said, hanging from my back.

"Brimone drinks beer!" I said.

"No I don't!" Brimone shouted.

"What are you doing to my babies, Johnny?" Cynthia asked.

"Nothing!" I said, "Whoa! You're about to make Uncle Johnny's back give out!" I slowly lowered Brimone to the floor.

"Tell him to stop lying on me, Aunty Alicia!"

There was no place to sit down so I sat on the kitchen floor and the three girls surrounded me. Pam and Tina were also taking up space.

"Stop lying on her, Johnny," Alicia said.

"And I'm doing fine," Tina said sarcastically.

"Forgive my manners, ladies," I said. "How's everybody doing?"

"You are too little, too late, Mr. Pied Piper!" Tina said. "How you gon' walk in here and not speak to us?"

"I was preoccupied with my nieces and my child, excuse me," I said sarcastically.

"You're not that preoccupied, you see us," Pam said.

"That's right, speak to your company!" Tina said.

"I will, when I see company."

"Okay then," Pam said.

"Where's Mike?" I said.

"He's in the living room waiting for you," Alicia said.

"Why didn't anybody tell me?" I said.

"You were preoccupied with your nieces and your child, remember?" Tina said.

"Whatever," I said before pulling the girls off of me.

I got up and went into my living room where Mike was waiting. The girls followed me, still holding my arms.

"Hey girls," Mike said, "can Daddy borrow Uncle Johnny for a second? We need to do some grown-up talk."

"Okay, Daddy!" Brimone said. "Come on, y'all."

Brittany and Alexiah followed Brimone into another room. The living room had two entrances, but both were viewable. If Alicia or anyone entered the room we could see them before they could see us so we spoke quietly, but openly.

"Now, do you want to tell me everything that happened between you and Gizelle?" Mike asked.

I placed my hands on my knees and sat back. I took a deep breath and began to talk.

"Well, um, of course you know we had an affair," I said, "and every time I tried to break it off, she came up with something."

"Came up with something like what?"

"She threatened to tell Alicia about us," I said. "Or, she threatened to leave their firm high and dry with a bogus contract. Man, they put everything they had into that company."

"Damn, Johnny!" Mike said, sitting back. "We are in some deep shit, man!"

"I know."

"The police are not going to just let this go away, you can believe that."

"But they've already questioned you, what else can they want from you?"

"They want a suspect! They want a conviction! That wasn't some thug rapper the police could care less about. That was a young bright star the entire community cared about," Mike said. "And she was found by a nationally known author; they're going to come after me. And they're going to come after me hard!"

"I won't let that happen!"

"Let's not go through this again, Johnny."

"You've been protecting me my whole life, Mike. We're not kids anymore. I have to clean up my own shit now, man."

"Don't be stupid, Johnny!" Mike said. "We have witnesses who know why I went to visit Gizelle. We have an alibi for me. A fool-proof alibi! If you try to prove your independence on this one, you're going to jail."

"Wait a minute, Mike." I leaned forward, looking very disappointed. "Do you think I killed Anise?"

"Johnny," Mike said. "It doesn't matter what I think. What matters is what the police will think."

"No, you're wrong. It does matter," I said. "Do you think I'm capable of committing murder?"

"That's not the point."

"Answer my question!"

"I think you need to lower that volume, man!"

"Answer my question," I said, lowering my voice, "big brother."

"If you want the truth, I'll tell you. I think that under certain circumstances anybody is capable of murder."

"Wow!" I shook my head. "My very own brother thinks I'm a murderer."

"This is not the time to try to step up and be a man, Johnny," Mike said. "You have to act like you don't know anything about this whole matter. Because at this point, I can get in trouble for obstructing justice."

"I know," I said. "The police already know that Anise was my patient."

"And?" Mike said, cutting me off before I could get all of the words out of my mouth.

"And they're going to ask questions."

"So what? If they ask questions about your relationship with her, you keep it simple and focused on your therapy. Can you do that?"

"I don't know, Mike."

"Well, Johnny, 'I don't know' won't get it," Mike said. "You have to know!"

"But what if someone has seen me with her?"

"Seen you where? What were you doing with that girl?"

"Nothing," I answered. "But what if they ask me if I ever saw her outside of work?"

"Tell them yes," Mike said. "Is it suspicious for a doctor to see his patient outside of the office? No. I don't think so!"

"What about the bodyguard?"

"What bodyguard?"

"Anise's bodyguard that came to your house."

"Did he see you two behaving in an unprofessional way?"

"I can't say for sure, but he sure saw us a lot."

"Well, there's nothing we can do about that right now. Let's focus on what we can do. Like stick to our story. Is that understood?"

"I guess so."

"Johnny!" Mike said. "Is that understood?"

"Yeah, Mike."

"Okay, let's just get through this and we'll be fine."

"I hope so."

"I love you, man," Mike said. "You're my little brother and I'll do anything for you."

"I know you'll do anything for me," I said. "That's the problem."

CHAPTER FOURTEEN

Later that night, Alicia and I were getting ready for bed. Once she finished her nightly ritual, she slid in the bed behind me. To my surprise, she was unclothed and ready for action.

"Come on, baby," Alicia said. "I want some."

I turned around and faced her and then we started to caress each other's bodies. I kissed her up and down her neck. She started to moan and wrapped her body around mine.

"Oh, keep doing that, Johnny."

I pulled her closer to me, pressing my manhood against her vagina and grinding. Her moans became louder, and she reached behind me and grabbed my ass. Her breasts were squeezed against my chest as we became as close as two bodies can get without my manhood puncturing her kidney.

Alicia lay on her back and opened her legs. She reached between my legs and grabbed my manhood. "What's wrong?" Alicia asked, holding my very flaccid manhood in her hands.

"What do you mean?" I asked, knowing exactly what she meant.

"You're not ready."

"Okay, give me a minute!" I was very embarrassed.

I continued to grind on Alicia's vagina, trying my best to make my manhood rise to the occasion.

"Can I help?" Alicia asked.

"Okay."

Alicia rolled me on my back and slid down my body. She started licking and kissing my chest. Steadily moving downward, she started licking my stomach and then twirling her tongue around my navel area. She kissed my inner thigh, which was my sensitive area, and I stiffened from the pleasure.

"You like that, baby?" Alicia asked.

"Oh God, yeah." I rested my head backward and sighed out loud. I could feel my manhood starting to swell.

Obviously, Alicia could feel my manhood, too, so she slid her mouth closer to it and started to taste. I watched her mouth and my manhood become one entity. Her head looked so sexy, bobbing up and down and then side to side. She paused momentarily to breathe and then went back to work.

I was at full strength by then, if you know what I mean. She took her mouth off of my manhood long enough to speak.

"Seems like you're ready now!" Alicia said.

"Oh yeah," I said. "Lay down, baby."

Alicia turned on her back and opened her legs again. Reaching between my legs she grabbed my manhood and feeling its hardness, she smiled at me and prepared for me to enter her.

As usual, it felt fantastic as I slid it in. She pulled my head down to hers and we began to kiss passionately. I could feel her moisture and the sensation of her vaginal muscles gripping my manhood.

Just then, that warm, moist feeling seemed to diminish more and more. I continued to grind but it just wasn't there.

"What's the matter, Johnny?" Alicia asked. "Are you stressed out or something?"

"No! I'm not stressed out!"

"Then why can't you make love to me?"

"I can! I just need time!" I shouted, rolling over and turning on my back.

"Time for what? I'm here, naked, in all of my glory! What do you need time for?" Alicia shouted.

"I don't know!" I shouted back. "But I know putting pressure on me is not the answer!"

"Well, what's the matter?"

"I don't know, Alicia, I want to do this very much. But something is going on here that I can't explain."

"Johnny, what's going on? I'm horny as hell!"

"I want to make love to you, too, baby," I said. "But there's something going on in my head that I can't explain."

"Can't explain to who? You? Or me?"

"Right now," I said, "both!"

I reached for Alicia and pulled her onto my chest. We stared in the darkness and I wondered what Alicia was thinking. She answered my thoughts with her next question.

"Are you having an affair, Johnny?"

"Are you serious?"

"Well, what am I supposed to think when I don't seem to be able to turn my husband on? There are normally two things that are going on when that happens," Alicia said. "An affair or loss of interest. Which one of those is the case here, Johnny?"

"Neither," I said. "Perhaps it's just stress like you said. I've had a lot of emotional incidents the past couple of days. Maybe I need to just relax and relieve my mind of some of the issues surrounding me."

"Are you sure?"

"Absolutely!"

"Okay, this better not happen again!" Alicia said. "You hear me?"

"Of course it won't."

Of course it won't is what I said to Alicia, *but I hope it won't* is what I said to myself.

I had always been extremely attracted to Alicia and nothing had changed. Internally, I was aroused as usual, but for some unexplained reason, externally, my manhood would not respond to my urges. The next morning we tried again, and it ended with the same results. I could tell Alicia was frustrated but, for my sake, she pretended the situation didn't bother her.

❂❂❂

The next few days went without incident. I visited Veronica every day and once the doctors cleared her to start eating solid foods, we kept to our agreement and ate spinach.

Betty was instrumental in making sure she ate an adequate amount of vitamins and minerals. Remarkably, we could see the difference within a week. Her face was full, her bones were not as revealing, and she was actively stronger both mentally and physically. But to ensure there would be no relapse, I maintained my visits.

Since I assumed legal responsibility of Anise's body, I was placed in the position of finding the executor of her estate. I spoke with her attorney and he told me that Anise had no immediate family contact information, and her Last Will and Testament clearly stated that none of the members of her entertainment entourage should be selected as the executor of her estate.

I told him I would assist in locating her family in Missouri to let them determine the executor. He told me that there was no need to look any further than the man in the mirror because I was the executor. I was floored when those words came out of his mouth.

Anise was becoming more confusing in death than she was in life. I don't know why she would select me as her executor. She was much younger than me. I was puzzled as to why she thought I would live longer than her. She must have suspected that she didn't have much longer to live. I just didn't know why.

As Anise's attorney and I went over her Will, I was stunned even more when we went through the names of her beneficiaries. The very last name stated, and the primary recipient of seventy-five percent of her assets, was her sister. Her mother, and only living relative, had no knowledge of the sister's existence. As I scanned over the Will, the sister's name seemed familiar but I didn't give it a second thought. I was too focused on just how impossible it was going to be to find the mysterious sister.

After I left Anise's attorney's office, I went home and took a nap in my den. It wasn't long before I was awakened by the noise of constant doorbell ringing. Alicia ran to the door as quickly as possible when she heard Cynthia banging loudly. She opened the door and Cynthia walked past her looking for me.

"Where's Johnny?" Cynthia shouted.

Although I could hear every word they were saying, I stayed hidden straightening my clothes to make myself presentable before I stepped around the corner in full view.

"What's the matter, Cynthia?" Alicia was becoming panicked herself. "What's wrong with you?"

"Mike has been arrested for murdering Gizelle!"

"What?" Alicia shouted. "Johnny!!!"

I stepped around the corner tying my housecoat string. "What's going on?"

"They took Mike to jail, Johnny!" Cynthia said, stomping her feet.

"Why? Why would they take Mike to jail now?"

"They said they found evidence against him!" Cynthia said. "Oh my God!"

"Sit down, girl!" Alicia said.

"I can't! I have to get Mike out of jail!"

"Do something, Johnny!" Cynthia shouted at me. "Your brother is in jail!"

"Okay!" I shouted back. "Everybody just calm down so we can think this through!"

"Think what through?" Cynthia yelled. "My husband is in jail and I want him out!"

I can't say that at that moment I experienced the one and only epiphany of my life. But I can say that I did realize I was about to start practicing what I preached. I had to become the master of my domain, so to speak.

At that moment I felt fearless. I felt courageous. Determined. Relentless. Any adjective that could define triumphant applied to me. Never in my life had I felt confidence in facing crucial situations without advice and confirmation from someone else, be it personal or professional. I always needed someone else to save me, or love me, or validate me. But not in that moment!

"Johnny!" Alicia shouted. "What are we going to do?"

"We're not going to do anything," I said. "I'm going to get my brother out of jail."

I walked upstairs and changed my clothes. When I went back

downstairs Cynthia and Alicia were standing by the front door waiting.

"Let's go!" I said.

"Thank you!" Cynthia said.

"It's going to be all right, Cynt," Alicia said.

Once I pulled off, Alicia opened her cell phone to make a call. I could see Wanda's name pop up. As much as I liked the office girls, some things are just family issues, and the family should solve them.

"Please, don't call them this time, sweetheart."

"I'm about to call Wanda and let her know we're about to go to the police station and have the office girls meet us up there," Alicia said.

"Why?" I asked.

"Because they need to know."

"But that's just it. Mike doesn't need them right now."

"How come he doesn't?"

"Look, if we can't help Mike, they surely can't help him," I said. "We don't need an entourage filling up the police station on Mike's behalf; it will hurt more than help."

"So are you saying you don't want me to call them at all?" Alicia asked.

"No, I'm saying let's see what's going on and then tell them."

"If it was me, I would want to know," Alicia said. "Wouldn't you, Cynthia?"

"Huh?" Cynthia asked, not really paying attention to our conversation.

"If something were to happen to one of the office girls, wouldn't you want to know?"

"Yeah."

"See," Alicia said.

"So you think we should tell the office girls to meet us at the police station?" I asked while looking at Cynthia's face in my rearview mirror.

"No," Cynthia said. "This is about my husband right now, not the office girls. I don't want to be comforted; I want my husband out of jail."

"But wouldn't you wanna know, Cynt?" Alicia asked again.

"Yeah, I would wanna know, but I would also want to respect whoever's privacy, too."

"So you don't want me to call them?" Alicia asked.

"For what?"

"Okay," Alicia said, putting her phone back in her purse.

"Johnny," Cynthia said, leaning forward between the two front seats. "Please, bring my husband home."

"I'm not leaving without him."

❂❂❂

I called Stacey on our way to the police station. She told me she would meet us out front. When we got there she was waiting with both barrels ready to fire. However, she wasn't the only one waiting. I think Stacey was just as surprised as we were to see the amount of paparazzi snapping pictures.

"What are they doing?" Cynthia covered her face as we stepped out of the car.

"Just get inside!" I tried to shield Cynthia and Alicia from the photographers.

I was finally able to locate Stacey, who was also trying to make her way inside of the station.

"Is all this fuss over Mike?" I asked her.

"It's more about Gizelle's murder, than Mike's arrest, but let's get inside so that we can talk."

The ladies followed me as I forced my way through the crowd. Once we were inside we were met by police officers that kept the paparazzi outside.

"Is there anywhere we can go?" I asked.

"Yeah, come on," Stacey said. "Follow me."

Stacey whispered into the ear of a police officer and he took us into a small room for privacy. Alicia and Cynthia followed closely behind us.

"Okay, we have a serious situation here, Dr. Forrester," Stacey said. "The state seems to think they have more than enough evidence to bring a case against Michael for murder. I will tell you now, it doesn't look good, but we plan on fighting this tooth and nail."

"What evidence do they have?" I said. "Mike did not do this!"

"It's not that simple," Stacey responded.

"Mike is innocent!" I said.

"Unfortunately, being innocent does not make you not guilty."

"What do I have to do to get my brother out of here tonight?" I asked.

"There's nothing you can do to get him out of here tonight," Stacey said. "He'll be arraigned first thing tomorrow and bail will be set. Hopefully, the judge will allow bail and we can have him out by tomorrow afternoon."

"Tomorrow afternoon? Can't we do something to get him out tonight?"

"I know you're concerned about your brother but you have to let the legal process play itself out. If you push it, it'll push back."

"So my husband has to be in here all night?" Cynthia asked.

"Ma'am, let's just hope and pray your husband has to *only* be in here all night. There are very serious charges against Michael and he's going to need you all to keep level heads and support him no matter how grim the situation may look. If he sees you falling apart, it may destroy his optimism as well."

"How am I supposed to be strong knowing my husband is locked up like a caged animal?"

"I don't know," Stacey said. "But you have to try."

"Can I see him?" Cynthia asked.

"I'll see what I can do," Stacey said.

Stacey left and returned a while later. She had arranged for us to visit Mike. Only Cynthia and I were allowed to visit, and that was one at a time. Cynthia went first, and when she came out her eyes were filled with tears.

"I can't stand seeing him locked up like that, Johnny."

"I know, Cynt, but we're going to have to be strong," I said.

"I tried, but I can't!"

"I understand," I said. "But why don't you and Alicia go home and get some rest."

"Yeah, there's nothing you can do by staying here," Alicia said.

"I'm not going anywhere."

"I know how you feel, Cynt, but somebody needs to go talk to Brimone and Alexiah before they see their father on the television arrested for murder."

"Okay," Cynthia said, "but I'll be back. There's no way I can sleep in that house without Mike."

"You're not going home, Cynt," Alicia said. "After we talk to the kids, we're going to my house."

"Everything is going to be okay, Cynt," I reassured her.

"Let's go, sweetheart." Alicia reached for my hand.

"I'm not going," I replied.

"There's nothing you can do here, either."

"Maybe not, but I said I wasn't going to leave this place without my brother and I meant it."

"So you're going to stay here all night?" Alicia asked.

"Looks that way."

"Baby, what are you trying to prove?"

"Nothing," I said. "If the situation was reversed, he'd do the same thing for me. That's my brother, Alicia! Let me do what I have to do."

"I guess this is what you have to do, huh?" Alicia kissed me on the cheek. "Call me."

"Bring my man home," Cynthia said.

"I promise."

Cynthia and Alicia were escorted home by police officers. I stayed at the station and slept sitting up on a bench. When daylight came, I bought a snack from the vending machine. It actually tasted pretty good. The coffee, on the other hand, was strong and bitter.

At approximately eight in the morning, Stacey walked by reading documents she had in her hands. She was dressed very sharply and ready for business. She saw me in my not-so-ready-for-company attire and laughed.

"Have you been here all night?" Stacey chuckled.

"Yes," I said.

"Why?"

"I couldn't leave him," I said.

"I have good news that should make your morning a tad bit sunnier."

"How long have you been here?" I asked, wondering how she could have good news this early in the morning.

"Long enough to know Michael is on his way to be arraigned

as we speak, and there should be no problem with posting bond."

"Thank God!" I said.

"He was transferred to the courthouse a few minutes ago," Stacey said. "We're on our way now."

"Can I ride over with you?"

"Sure, let's go."

I rode over to the courthouse with Stacey but she refused to discuss any of the details of the case. It was a media circus outside of the courthouse. Stacey seemed to absorb the attention of the press and use it to her advantage. I tried to stay in the background and away from the cameras.

Once we were in the courtroom, I sat in the first row behind the defendant's seat. Mike was already seated along with other inmates, waiting for his name to be called.

The proceeding didn't last nearly as long as I thought. Stacey pretty much did all the talking to the judge. Mike only had to say two words. The judge asked him, "How do you plead?"

Mike answered by saying, "Not guilty."

After Mike's plea, the judge set bond at one hundred thousand dollars. The bail was high, but manageable. Before Mike was taken back to his cell, we shared an eye-to-eye glimpse with one another. He smiled at me, and I smiled back. And then he disappeared behind a small door.

Stacey and I went to work to have Mike bailed out of jail. We wanted Cynthia to get some rest, so we kept Mike's bail status private until we were ready to pick him up. It took until the late afternoon, but finally he was released. When he walked out, we hugged one another as if we had never hugged before, and then Stacey gave Mike and me a ride to my house. Mike quickly established his role as the elder Forrester on the drive there.

"Damn, man," Mike said. "You look worse than me. Did Alicia kick you out of the house?"

"Aha, very funny," I said. "I stayed there to keep those big boys in the big house off of your ass."

"Man, please," Mike said. "I ran that joint!"

"We have a busy day today, fellas," Stacey said. "You guys need to go home and get some rest. Michael, we have a meeting in my office later today."

"Believe me, I don't need any rest," Mike replied.

"Sure you do," Stacey said. "You're running on adrenaline."

"I'm just ready to get this over with."

"It's not going to be that simple, Michael," Stacey said. "You know that. We have a lot of work ahead of us."

"Well, let's get started."

"So, do I get to see you in legal action, Mike?" I asked.

"No, that's for my attorney."

"I can't believe you guys went to law school together."

"Yeah, we were fierce competitors," Stacey said. "We vied for the number one seat in our class until we completed law school."

"Who won?"

"Stacey won hands down. She was tenacious!"

"He's being modest!" Stacey said. "He was just as tenacious as I was. He and our professor used to battle all the time."

"The man couldn't stand me, Johnny."

"That's not true!" Stacey said. "You were his favorite."

"What class were you in?" Mike asked. "The man despised me."

"You have to be kidding me!" Stacey laughed. "He picked you out of the class and made sure you excelled and reached the top."

"No," Mike said, "he didn't pick me out of the class like it was something good. He picked on me in the class because I was the only black student and he didn't want me to look foolish because he was black, too."

"You ingrate!" Stacey said. "That man is the reason why you're a lawyer."

"You couldn't be more wrong," Mike said. "That man is the reason why I'm an author."

I couldn't quite figure it out, but I decided there was much more to their story than I was hearing.

CHAPTER FIFTEEN

Stacey dropped me off first and then took Mike home to Cynthia. Later on, I visited Veronica at the hospital. She was up and taking small steps, thanks mostly to Betty's nurturing. Betty was excited about Veronica's health improvement and so was I. Betty had become a miracle worker. Her natural tendency to nurture had helped save a woman's life. It's too bad she couldn't save herself from the judicial system. Although I was still convinced that Betty suffered from Münchausen syndrome and had sought attention by taking her daughter to the emergency room quite frequently, I was also convinced that there was no way in hell she would harm her child in the process. No way!

"Good morning, Betty," I said.

"Good morning, Dr. Forrester."

"How are things going with your daughter?"

"I have a hearing coming up soon."

"Why didn't you tell me?"

"I was going to."

"Let me know w hen it is, maybe I could come for moral support."

"Actually, you can do more than that."

"Sure, anything."

"Can you be a character witness for me?"

"Are you sure?" I asked.

"One hundred percent sure."

"I guess so."

"I would really appreciate that," Betty said. "Thank you, Dr. Forrester."

"I look forward to being there."

Betty and I talked a little longer as Veronica slept. She asked questions about Mike and his case. My brother was quickly becoming a celebrity albeit for all the wrong reasons.

I stayed until Veronica woke up so I could tell her good-bye. Her recovery was remarkable and I could feel her turning the corner to being in perfect health again. She wasn't totally out of the woods, but she wasn't very far away from the road back home, either.

Around noon, Mike called and asked me to meet him in Stacey's office. He felt that I should be there to listen and make sure our stories would stay consistent. I agreed, but I told him I had appointments toward the latter part of the day.

Stacey's office was huge! I was very impressed. If the size of her office was any indication of her success as an attorney, I had but one word to say, "Wow!"

Mike and I were the first to arrive. Stacey welcomed us and led us to a conference room. Stacey apologized for having to step away and then left us sitting in the room. Her paralegal, Jenny, scampered around taking files out and bringing files in. Jenny was in her early twenties, blonde and thin.

Finally, Stacey rushed in with her zoom, zoom, zoom ready to go mentality. Once Stacey was there Jenny took a seat and got the hell out of the way to let her do her thing. Stacey talked at a very high speed as she set certain files on the table before certain chairs.

"Good morning, guys!" Stacey said. "We're waiting for my partners to arrive. They should be here any minute."

"That's fine," Mike said.

"Jenny, can you get Ms. Hattley and Ms. Carroll and let them know that we're ready, please?"

"It'll be my pleasure!" Jenny said, getting up and leaving.

"We'll be ready to go as soon as they get back, guys!" Stacey smiled. "As a matter of fact, I think I'll go rush them a bit."

Stacey got up and dashed out of the room. I took that time to drop the bomb about our parents to Mike.

"Hey man," I said, "Ma and Dad will be coming down."

"Coming down where?" Mike asked.

"Down here!"

"For what, man?" Mike said while spinning his chair in my direction.

"You."

"I am not in the mood for all of their sermons."

"Man, they're not coming down here to get on your back! They're coming down here to support you. Those people have never been on an airplane before in their lives. They're scared to death. But for you, they'll risk it. And your whining ass is sitting down here complaining."

"I'm not complaining, I'm just saying," Mike said.

"Hey, you guys!" Stacey said, bursting into the room. "I want you to meet my husband, he's just stopping by to say hello."

Stacey's husband, who was following close behind, walked in a few seconds later. He stopped dead in his tracks when he saw Mike and me sitting there. Mike smiled and waved at him.

"Christopher," Mike said sarcastically.

"Do you guys know each other?" Stacey asked.

"Yeah," Christopher said, looking like the cat caught swallowing the canary.

"Where from?" Stacey said, still scampering about.

"Uh," Christopher said, "where did we meet?"

"It was a conference, right?" Mike said.

"Yeah, I think you're right."

Mike couldn't stop smiling. After all the talking Pam had done about her great white hope, he turned out to be a cheating, deceitful liar, just like us black men. I guess men will be men no matter what their race.

"We're here." Jenny opened the door and two black women entered.

"Well, I guess that's my cue to leave," Christopher said.

"See you at the next conference, Chris!" Mike said sarcastically.

"Yeah." Christopher waved good-bye.

"Gentlemen," Stacey said, "I would like for you to meet my esteemed partners."

"Good afternoon, everyone," Ms. Hattley said.

"Hello." Ms. Carroll waved as she sat down.

Mike and I spoke to the ladies. We looked at each other and then looked at them. They were stunning. Ms. Hattley was a light-skinned black woman with sandy-brown hair. She had light-brown eyes and full lips. She was short, maybe not even five feet. Her figure was shaped like an hourglass. She reminded me a lot of Alicia...or Anise.

Ms. Carroll was a tall black woman, five feet ten inches, maybe taller. She, too, was gorgeous. Her hair was naturally curly. She had an Afrocentric build, to say the least. She had an enormously round ass and curvaceous hips. Her breasts were pointed and her flat stomach made them that much more noticeable.

Ms. Hattley sat next to me, and Ms. Carroll sat next to Mike. I could feel Mike looking at me trying to get my attention so that we could ogle the women together, but I refused to look his way.

"How are you holding up, Mr. Forrester?" Ms. Carroll asked.

"I'm doing fine, ma'am."

Ms. Carroll patted Mike on the knee. "Don't worry, we're going to do all that we can to get you out of this mess."

"Thank you," Mike replied.

"So," Ms. Hattley said, "what do they have on us?"

"They don't have much, but what they do have is a whopper!" Stacey said.

"And what is that?" Ms. Carroll asked.

"Michael's DNA matched the semen found in Ms. Lawrence's body," Stacey answered.

"That's impossible!" Mike shouted. "I never touched that woman!"

"Then how do you suppose your semen was found in her body?" Ms. Hattley said.

"I have no explanation for that."

"There has to be some explanation because it's there," Ms. Carroll countered.

"I have never had sex with her," Mike said.

"Somebody did," Stacey said. "And the evidence says it's you, Michael."

"Did you voluntarily give your DNA sample?" Ms. Carroll asked.

"Yes," Mike said. "I know how this may look, but I did not kill that girl."

"Okay," Ms. Hattley said while writing down notes.

"Okay what?" Mike asked.

"I believe you," Ms. Hattley said.

"Are you just saying that or do you truly believe me?" Mike asked.

"If I didn't believe you, I wouldn't have said I did."

"Why?" Mike asked. "Why do you believe me?"

"Because Michael," Ms. Hattley said, "maybe an ignorant man would have voluntarily given his DNA. Maybe even a guilty man who feels he has nothing to lose would have voluntarily given his DNA sample. But a man who knows the law, and pleads not guilty, would never do anything as foolish as voluntarily giving his DNA without legal representation. And from what I hear, you know the law very well."

"Knew the law," Mike said.

"Is that all that they have, Stacey?" Ms. Carroll asked.

"That's all that they need," Stacey joked.

"And who are you?" Ms. Hattley asked me.

"I'm Dr. Johnson Forrester, Michael's brother."

"Are you a part of the team?" Ms. Hattley asked.

"No, I'm just here because..."

"With all due respect, Mr. Forrester, can you please excuse yourself from the room?"

"Well, I'm," I stuttered, "I'm his brother."

"I understand that," Ms. Hattley said, "but the information we are exposing in this room is purely confidential. You could unwittingly divulge information to the prosecution that you have no idea is pertinent."

"Uh," I said, "I, I understand."

"No," Mike said. "Johnny stays."

"I agree with Ms. Hattley. Your brother being here may not be in your best interest, Mr. Forrester," Ms. Carroll said.

I stood up in embarrassment and started to walk out of the room.

"Johnny," Mike said. "Sit down."

I looked at Ms. Hattley and Ms. Carroll and then I looked at Stacey.

"I don't want to jeopardize my brother's case in any way, but if he wants me here, I'm staying."

"I guess that's the client's decision." Ms. Carroll turned toward me. "So you're the brother, huh?"

"Yes."

"And you're a psychologist?"

"Yes."

"Okay, since you're determined to stay, is there any reason why you have not mentioned that Ms. Lawrence was one of your patients?" Ms. Hattley said.

"Uh." I was paralyzed with shock.

"Would you care to explain that, Dr. Forrester?" Stacey said, folding her hands.

"Uh," I repeated, still unable to speak.

I was trying to come up with something quick, but my brain would not cooperate with my mouth. "Look, I think there's something you should know."

"Johnny!" Mike said, trying to cut me off.

"Look Mike," I snapped, "hiding information is not going to help you!"

"What are you hiding, Michael?" Stacey asked.

"Nothing!" Mike shouted.

"Listen! I was in the hotel room with Anise before Mike arrived the night she was murdered!" I shouted before Mike could interrupt.

"Okay," Stacey said before standing up and putting her hand on her forehead as if she had a migraine headache. "Michael, if you want us to represent you, you better tell me the truth and I mean the entire truth, right this minute!"

"Thanks a lot, Johnny!" Mike said. "Johnny was in Ms. Lawrence's hotel room when I got there. I told him not to say anything because I thought the police would question me and then that would be it."

"You thought it was okay to withhold evidence?" Ms. Carroll asked.

"I thought no one would find out," Mike said.

"How could you possibly think that?" Stacey snapped. "If we can find this information as easily as we did, Homicide is surely going to make the connection!"

"Anise," I said, "That is, Ms. Lawrence, and I were having an affair."

"What?" Stacey shouted. "Are you kidding me? She was your patient, for Christ's sake!"

"I know, Stacey."

"Do you know what type of implications that will bring?"

"I know! I know!" I said. "I made a mistake!"

"And how long were you two going to withhold this information from us?"

"Johnny wanted to tell the truth all along, but I wouldn't let him," Mike said.

"Wouldn't let him?" Stacey said. "He's a grown man! A huge, grown man! How can you stop him from telling the truth if that's what he wants to do?"

"Dr. Forrester," Ms. Carroll said to me, "are we defending the wrong man?"

"You sure are, but I promise you, I didn't kill Ms. Lawrence, either!"

"Let me ask both of you a question." Ms. Hattley turned to me. "Do you think your brother is innocent?"

"Yes," I said without blinking an eye.

"And you, Mr. Forrester," Ms. Carroll said to Mike, "do you think your brother is innocent?"

Mike looked at Ms. Carroll and then looked at me. He opened his mouth, but nothing came out.

"Mike?" I was appalled. "Mike!"

"I'm sorry, Johnny," Mike said. "I don't know, man. I really don't know."

"How can you say you don't know?" I shouted. "I'm your brother!"

"This whole thing has to be re-evaluated," Stacey said. "There's a strong possibility that one of you may have killed a beautiful young woman! And right now because of all of your family secrets, I'm not so sure that it wasn't both of you."

"We didn't kill anybody!" I shouted.

"Do you realize how much humiliation you could have caused this firm if this little scandal would have come out, Michael?"

"That was not my intention, Stacey," Mike said.

"So, do you want to go to jail? Are you trying to use this as material for your next book? Huh?" Stacey snapped. "Our careers are at stake here!"

"Do you think I give a damn about your careers?" Mike yelled back. "My life is at stake!"

"Okay, everybody calm down," Ms. Carroll said. "Now that we've gotten to the truth, let's find out what our strategy is going to be."

"We have to start from ground zero now," Stacey said.

"I agree, Stacey," Ms. Hattley said.

"And where is ground zero?" Mike asked.

"Ground zero is your brother submitting his DNA to the police," Ms. Hattley replied.

"No," Mike said. "He can't do that."

"I'll do it as soon as possible," I said.

Mike sighed and shook his head in disagreement.

"Once we get the results back from the lab to determine whose semen it is, then we begin building a defense," Stacey concluded.

"It's my DNA," I admitted. "I had sex with Ms. Lawrence earlier that day."

"How do we know that?" Stacey asked. "For all we know, you could be lying for Michael, just like he lied for you."

"I'm not lying," I said.

"If Dr. Forrester truly had sex with Ms. Lawrence, at least that would explain why they found your DNA, Michael," Stacey said.

"What do you mean?" I asked.

"Well," Mike interrupted, "because we come from the same genetic pattern, my DNA result would resemble yours. And sometimes the lab may not find a perfect match, but if the result resembles the sample enough, a perfect match is superceded by the similarity."

"You knew that all along didn't you, Mike?"

"If Johnny's DNA matches the DNA found on Ms. Lawrence's body, how do we proceed from there?" Mike asked Stacey while ignoring my question.

"We get those charges dropped against you and then the District Attorney would most likely file charges against you for obstruction of justice and against Dr. Forrester for first-degree murder."

"What are the chances of these charges being dismissed against Johnny?" Mike asked.

"It's hard to say," Stacey said. "The likelihood of these charges being dropped is very low. The state had evidence against you but not a direct motive and yet they felt strongly that they could get a conviction. The state would have a motive as well as physical evidence against your brother, so getting the charges dismissed will be very difficult."

"But what if he didn't do it?" Mike asked.

"What if?" I asked incredulously. "*What if*, Mike?"

"I guess my question is, if we're saying neither my brother nor I did it, then how do we prove who did?" Mike said.

"Come on, Michael, has it been that long? You know it's not our job to prove who did it. We're not prosecutors. It's our job to show a reasonable doubt that you or your brother did not do it."

"Anybody have any ideas?" I asked. "My own brother believes I'm guilty."

"I never said that," Mike said.

"Once we have everything laid out in front of us, we'll know exactly how to attack it," Stacey said.

"If I may interject…" Ms. Carroll raised her hand.

"It's your floor, ma'am," Stacey said.

"A woman is unlike a man in so many different ways. Her lovers, her friends, her family, they all take on slightly different meanings than they do with a man," Ms. Carroll began. "Let's assume that one of you is a victim of unfortunate circumstances, Dr. Forrester, and you had nothing to do with the young lady's death. If you didn't do it, someone else did. We have to find out what was going on in that young lady's life at the time of her murder."

"Are you thinking this may be a crime of passion?" Mike asked.

"The crime scene evidence supports that this homicide was indeed an act of passion. But maybe the person who killed her was not trying to hurt her. Maybe it was an accident. There was blunt force trauma causing serious bodily injuries. There were defensive wounds that would indicate she was under attack, but the room did not look as if a fight had gone on there. So maybe she wasn't being attacked, maybe she was the attacker," Ms. Hattley said.

"We need to find some physical evidence to support the presence of someone else in that room other than you two," Ms. Carroll added.

"If we can somehow prove that someone else was in that room, I think we could scientifically counter your DNA," Stacey said.

"How do you counteract DNA evidence?" I asked.

"More DNA," Mike said.

"We keep talking science, but not innocence. Before we go any further with this, I need to know one thing," I said. "Does anyone in this room believe that I did not kill Anise Lawrence?"

Mike and Stacey looked at me but did not answer. Ms. Carroll smiled and told me with complete confidence, "I think it's almost impossible that you killed that young lady, Dr. Forrester. In my opinion, Ms. Lawrence died at the hands of another woman, not a man. I think the key in building a solid defense for you, does not lie in the nature of science...but more so in the nature of a woman."

❂❂❂

Under the advice of my attorneys, I voluntarily submitted my DNA sample to the police. Over the next week I agonized over whether I should tell my wife about my infidelity before it came out publicly. There were several times when I watched her as she slept, thinking that my peaceful little world may be crumbling in a matter of days.

I tried to maintain my focus with my other patients as well. Betty had admitted to wanting attention after she had her child. She was no longer angry and frustrated. She was anxious to go to court to get her child back. Betty's attorney asked me to be a witness on her behalf. It was the first time I had ever been asked to speak as an expert on any case.

The day before I was supposed to appear in court for Betty's hearing, I had a session at Patient Number Five's house. Sitting in my familiar chair, I waited for her to open the dialogue. I had come to the reality that our session would always be a battle of wits. That day was different. Patient Number Five was willing to answer questions.

"The admission of ignorance is the beginning of wisdom," the old, scraggly voice said.

"Good afternoon," I replied.

"Good day, sir."

"May I ask a question?"

"Ask."

"You have many awards. Many achievements. You're a person of esteemed accomplishments. What happened in your life to make you become such a recluse?"

"You sound as if it were a situation of negativity."

"Some people might think that one who hides herself from society might be doing so because she's unhappy with one of two things, society or herself. Wouldn't you say that either one of those scenarios is a negative situation?"

"Quite the contrary," Patient Number Five said. "You forgot one scenario, sir. Perhaps she has unbounded affection for herself."

"Is that your case, ma'am?"

"Perhaps."

"Are you implying that you have achieved such self-love, such self-adoration, that you no longer need or desire the love and attention of other human beings?"

"Perhaps."

"We both know the probability of that being your case is highly unlikely. Don't we?"

"Perhaps."

"When was the last time you were outside of this house?"

"I don't remember exactly," Patient Number Five said, pausing to collect her memory. "I think it was in the 1960s."

"Are you saying no one has publicly seen or spoken to you in over forty years?" I asked.

"Correct. Not anyone outside of this house."

"We've had eight presidents. Three wars. Technological advances that can bring the world into your living room at the touch of a computer keyboard," I said, "and you have no interest in these historical occurrences?"

"Why should I, sir?"

"It's a part of your history."

"No, sir," Patient Number Five countered. "It's not my history."

I paused momentarily and then asked my next question. "Can you recall the morning of the last day you were outside of this house, ma'am?"

"Vividly."

"On that morning when you woke up, did you make a conscious choice that," I paused, "it would be the last day you stepped outside?"

"No."

"Did you make it that afternoon?"

"No."

"Did you make it that evening, or that night?"

"Neither."

"Then when was it?" I asked.

"I have yet to make that decision."

"But you haven't been outside in over forty years. At some point, the decision had to be made."

"I hate to disappoint you, sir. But if I choose to go outside of my home at this very moment, it would be my choice for only that moment," Patient Number Five said, "not for a lifetime, not for forty years, not even for a day. I have lived this long by appreciating every moment of my life. I have absolutely no regrets. Can you say the same?"

"Of course I have some regrets," I said, chuckling in the dark, "who doesn't?"

"I don't."

"You've aged from a young woman to an elderly woman. Haven't you wanted to love or be loved?"

"I am loved."

"By whom?"

"By those who wish to share their love with me."

"What about the affection of a man?"

"I have not had a desire to be desired by a man since the day my husband died."

"And when did your husband die?"

"It was the last day I stepped outside of this house."

I realized the death of Patient Number Five's husband had much to do with her agoraphobia, but I didn't want to push her into discussing it. That approach could backfire and, instead of getting her to open up, I could easily push her into clamming up.

"But you were a young woman, didn't you want to love again?" I asked.

"Some people seek love their entire lives only to find heartbreak and disappointment. But when you find the perfect love, the person who fills your heart with excitement and contentment, it can last a lifetime."

"Has it?" I asked.

"Has what?"

"Has the love between you and your husband lasted? I guess what I'm asking is if you're still in love with him today?"

"Yes," Patient Number Five said very quickly. "I love him as much today as I did the day that he died."

"Fascinating," I said. "Forgive me, but you have to understand that I find it difficult to believe that a woman can still love a man forty years after his death as much as she did the day he died."

"I understand," Patient Number Five said. "But you are a man and, understandably, it would be quite difficult for a man to understand the nature of a woman. It's even difficult for those who specialize in the mental and emotional behavior of women."

"I am not exactly sure what you mean. Can you please elaborate?"

"Your profession is based on the diagnosis of symptomatic behavior of predetermined disorders. Your prognosis is based on the scientific treatment of the aforementioned predetermined disorders. The nature of a woman, in love or out of love, rational or irrational, sane or insane, cannot be predetermined by science.

For it is too unpredictable! How can science predict the unpredictable?" Patient Number Five asked.

"Perhaps science cannot predict the nature of a woman, but it can explain and resolve the aspects of a woman's mental process."

"Sometimes, sir, the logic of a woman's nature may appear to be illogical to a man because he does not understand the reason why she cries, or why she laughs, or why she loves."

"But through communication, consultation and sometimes even medication, scientific treatment resolves most issues."

"I will agree that communication understands the mind. Consultation relieves the mind. Medication controls the mind. So which of those treatments do you prescribe to a woman whose life exists only to love the memory of a dead man?"

I sat in the darkened room unable to speak. Patient Number Five equaled my silence with her silence. On previous visits, she had aggravated me with her condescending remarks about my professional criteria, or lack thereof. She frequently flexed her superior scientific knowledge of the study of psychology. This time she was silencing me with her very practical and logical argument of the validity of psychological research, a complete contradiction of her former arguments. I was prepared for a battle of scientific wits, but instead I received a colloquium on the nature of a woman.

I had the choice to answer the question or continue to sit in the darkness like a bumbling idiot.

"I suppose neither of the three," I said. I changed the subject by asking Patient Number Five a question she had previously asked me. I wanted to hear her answer, but I also wanted to see how challenging the question would be to her. "I would like to ask you another question. It's a little offbeat, though. Is that okay with you?"

"Ask."

"You once asked me if the brain controls the mind, or the mind controls the brain. I gave you my answer, now may I please have yours?"

"Certainly," Patient Number Five said. "The brain is the organism that controls everything that you do and everything that you are. Your soul, your mind, your consciousness and your subconscious are all derived from your brain's functions. So how can a function control its source?"

"I understand," I said. Not getting the puzzling response I expected, I sarcastically asked, "Which came first, the chicken or the egg?"

Without a moment's thought, Patient Number Five went into a full explanation of her theory.

"A chicken is actual, whereas an egg is potential. So it is more logical to suggest that the chicken must have been the original source of existence. Actuality must always take precedence over potentiality."

Trying to be a smart ass, I mumbled, "And if a tree falls in the woods, and there's no one around to hear, does it make a sound?"

Again, without hesitation to ponder the question, Patient Number Five gave her theory with logical cogency.

"No," Patient Number Five said. "A sound must be heard, not assumed as noise."

"Dammit!" I said out loud.

"Are there any more questions you would like to ask, sir?"

"Uh, no, not today."

"Then I would like to retire," Patient Number Five said. "Good day."

"Good day."

CHAPTER SIXTEEN

T he following morning I met with Betty and her attorney at the courthouse. She wore a beautiful dress and she was in the best of moods. The hearing didn't last long. When they called me to the stand I was slightly nervous, but my determination to get Audrey back in Betty's arms was my main concern. I was asked a series of questions about Betty's mental stability. I was anxious to tell my results. I was asked questions by a judge named Neil Caiman. He was a white man and looked to be in his sixties. He had white hair and a thick white moustache with white eyebrows—he was not quite Colonel Sanders, but close.

"Good morning, Dr. Forrester," Judge Caiman said.

"Good morning, sir."

"You can proceed with your medical analysis," Judge Caiman said.

"Well," I said nervously, "I first diagnosed Mrs. Betty Amos as suffering from a mental disorder known as Münchausen's syndrome. Her specific category is known as Münchausen's By Proxy. It is a disease by which the patient manufactures, embellishes, or prevaricates symptoms to appear ill for the attention of others. Mrs. Amos, I found, did suffer from this disorder."

"Thank you, Dr. Forrester," Judge Caiman said. "You may step down."

I looked at Betty and I could see the sense of urgency in her face. That did not go at all as I had planned. I was asked to help her, but instead I may have just added the last nail to her coffin.

"With all due respect, sir," I said, "if I may be allowed to complete my analysis?"

"Go ahead." Judge Caiman gestured for me to continue.

"Although Mrs. Amos did suffer from Münchausen syndrome by proxy, she exhibited no mental indication that she ever intended to cause danger to herself, and definitely not to her child. Her reaction to the attention given to her by others during her pregnancy was brought on by a history of emotional neglect from her family, friends and others close to her."

"But even if it wasn't her intent, couldn't she have caused that child to have real symptoms that would make people think the child was sick?" Judge Caiman asked.

"To my knowledge, none of Mrs. Amos' visits to the hospital resulted in the diagnosis of any physical symptoms for her child," I said. "Not one!"

"How do we know that, if granted joint custody, Mrs. Amos won't repeat her behavior and this time go as far as causing physical harm to her child?"

"I have analyzed Mrs. Amos long enough to comfortably say that she does not reflect any recrudescent signs of this disorder."

"Are you saying you have cured her?" Judge Caiman asked.

"No, sir," I said, looking at Betty. "I'm saying she cured herself."

"Is that all for you, Dr. Forrester?" Judge Caiman asked.

"Yes, sir."

"You may step down."

I stepped down and, as I walked past Betty, she gave me a big smile of approval. I sat in the back waiting for the judge to give his decision. He was laid-back and went about his business in a relaxed but very systematic way.

"Mrs. Amos," Judge Caiman said.

"Yes, sir," Betty said, standing up.

"You can sit down, this is not the Judge Mathis show," Judge Caiman said, laughing and looking around the courtroom.

"Sorry, sir," Betty said, sitting down quickly.

"There has been nothing but circumstantial material presented here today with no grounds of support. I don't see where we need to go any further with preventing you from seeing your child. You have a good day, ya hear?"

Betty jumped for joy. I walked over to congratulate her on her victory. We walked out of the courtroom together and were greeted by a man walking toward us with an adorable little girl in his arms. It was Betty's husband, David. He stopped a few steps away from us before Betty told him that he could come closer.

"It's okay, David!" Betty said. "We won! We won! Bring my baby here!"

"You can come home?" David shouted.

"Yeah baby!" Betty hugged David and Audrey.

I smiled and started to walk away when Betty called me back.

"Dr. Forrester!" Betty yelled. "Dr. Forrester!"

"Yes." I turned around to face her.

"Come here!" Betty waved for me to come back.

"Yes." I stopped in front of her and David.

"This is my husband, David," Betty said. "David, this is Dr. Forrester, my therapist. He is the reason why I'm coming home!"

"God bless your soul!" David said, shaking my hand. "I can't thank you enough! I can never thank you enough!"

"No problem," I said. "Just doing my job."

"Hey, Dr. Forrester," Betty said, holding Audrey so I could say hello. "Look at my baby, Audrey."

"Hey, sweetie," I said, playing with Audrey's cheek. "She's gorgeous!"

"Look at her," Betty said more seriously. "Does it look like there's anything wrong with her?"

"Absolutely nothing." I kissed Audrey and then Betty on their cheeks. "And there's nothing wrong with her mother, either."

"Aw, ain't that sweet?" Betty said.

"I guess I'll be seeing you in Veronica's suite since I won't be seeing you in the office anymore."

"Why not?" Betty asked.

"Why should you come?" I asked. "You have Audrey back."

"If I had been coming to you in the first place, I wouldn't have needed to come to you in the second place." Betty chuckled.

"I couldn't have said it better myself."

"I'll see you around, Dr. Forrester."

"See you around."

That evening when I got home, Alicia was extremely attentive. I guess the incident with Mike made her appreciate our relationship even more. That night, we didn't watch television. We didn't get on our cell phones. We talked. We did nothing but talk to each other.

My parents were going to arrive the next day so we wanted to take advantage of our alone time. After we put Brittany to bed, we hit the sack ourselves. We continued to talk and caress and kiss until we were ready to rip each other apart.

We kicked out of our clothes and I climbed between Alicia's

legs. She took my rock-hard manhood into her hands and guided it into her soaking wet vagina. She was extremely wet. It was probably due to the lack of sexual activity.

"Oh God, I want you so bad," Alicia said, grinding her hips up and down before she could put my manhood inside.

"I want you, too, baby!"

"I want you to give it to me!" Alicia said. "Give it to me, hard!"

I folded her legs backward, placing my hands underneath her kneecaps. Her legs were bent backward so far that her toes were touching the mattress. Her legs began to flail as I drilled her hard and deep.

"What's wrong?" Alicia asked.

"What?" I said. "What's the matter?"

"You're not hard," Alicia said.

I pulled my manhood out and it was flaccid. I held it in my hands and tried to put it back in.

"It's not going to go in like that."

"Give me a minute!" I said, embarrassed and frustrated.

"Just stop!" Alicia was even more frustrated than me.

"Just hold on!" I snapped.

"Something's not right!" Alicia said before rolling over and covering herself with a sheet.

"What do you mean something's not right?"

"I mean what I said! Something is not right and I'm tired of asking what it is! You either tell me what's going on, or I'm going to assume you're having an affair."

"Okay," I said, sighing heavily. "Shit!"

"Is it that bad?"

"Yeah," I said, "it's that bad."

"What?"

"I guess there's no easy way to say it."

"Okay," Alicia said, putting on the lamp, "what is it?"

"First of all, I want you to know that I love you," I said. "I love you more than life itself."

"Look, this is killing me! Would you just come out with it?"

"Okay!"

"Well?" Alicia said, staring at me without blinking. "Go 'head."

"This is so hard for me," I said. "I had an affair, baby, but it meant nothing to me!"

"You had an affair?" Alicia asked in disbelief.

"Yes," I said, hugging her. "I'm so sorry."

"With who?" Alicia asked, removing my arms from around her.

"Does it matter?"

"It does to me."

"Okay," I said, "since you have to know. It was with Anise Lawrence."

"Gizelle?" Alicia said calmly. "That girl? That little girl?"

Alicia jumped out of the bed and started to walk out of the room. I leaped out of the bed and blocked the door.

"Let me explain!"

"Explain what?" Alicia shouted. "That you cheated with a little girl?"

"That's not how it was!"

"Move out of my way!" Alicia screamed.

"Would you please stop yelling before you wake Brittany?"

"I don't even know who you are!" Alicia shouted. "Move! Get out of my way! Get out of my way!"

"Alicia, please! Don't do this," I pleaded. "I need you!"

"You don't need me!" Alicia said, trying to get around me.

"Baby, I'm in trouble! I don't know what I'll do without you! I need you!"

"Get out of my way, Johnny!"

"So you're just going to throw our family away like that?"

"Did you care about our family when you were out whoring around?"

"That's not fair, Alicia!"

"You'll get sleepy before I will!" Alicia grabbed her suitcases and started filling them with clothes.

I sat on the edge of the bed trying to convince her to stay, but she continued to ignore me and pack her clothes. I was desperate and I needed to come up with something quick. I used the only thing I thought would make her stay.

"So what about Brittany?" I asked. "You're just going to walk out on her, too?"

Even though Brittany wasn't Alicia's biological child, you would never have known by the way they loved each other. I kept pressing the Brittany issue and it took her a minute to soften up, but she eventually came around. "You're going to punish Brittany for my mistake?"

"Okay." Alicia threw her suitcase in the closet. "I won't leave tonight for Brittany's sake. But you better not say anything to me! Until I decide to speak to you don't even look my way! You understand me?"

"Yes, ma'am!"

Alicia grabbed her pillow and the comforter and started to walk toward the door again.

"Where are you going?" I asked.

"I'm going to sleep with my baby!" Alicia walked out and slammed the door behind her.

That night, I prayed for the first time in a long time. I mean, I prayed a lot. I don't know if the Lord heard me or not, but I sure had nothing to lose if He didn't.

The next morning I was up and gone before Alicia and Brittany woke up. I headed over to visit Veronica. I guess I was also avoiding Alicia's wrath. Veronica was improving at a much faster rate than we anticipated. She had finally reached a hundred pounds and was moving around with ease.

I stayed for a couple of hours. Betty and I played cards with Veronica. Betty bragged to Veronica that I was her hero for helping her get Audrey back in her life. Veronica bragged that I was her hero for helping to put weight on her body. In reality, the two of them were my heroes for coming to my rescue when I needed comfort and reassurance.

Their words of encouragement prompted me to call Alicia and try to alleviate some of the pain and disappointment she felt. I was surprised when she answered her cell phone, and that she answered it so pleasantly.

"Hi," Alicia said.

"Hi," I said, "I was just calling to check on you to see how you were doing."

"Oh, I'm fine."

"You sure."

"Yeah, I'm sure."

"You don't want to talk about it?"

"I'd rather not discuss it right now."

"Okay," I said. "We'll discuss it when I get home then."

"Okay."

"I love you," I said. "Bye."

"Bye."

❂❂❂

I was so grateful that Alicia had calmed down from the night before. She was her normal mellow self. I was relieved. It seemed like a huge weight had been lifted from my chest.

I went into the office for a few hours and then decided to come home early to try to face my act of infidelity as soon as possible. Unfortunately, she wasn't home when I got there. I walked through the house and started to notice little things were missing.

I ran up to our bedroom and saw that most of Alicia's clothes were gone. I sat on the bed for a minute and then I walked into Brittany's room. I sat on her bed, thinking about how much I would need her.

I looked around her room and noticed items were missing there as well. I snatched open her closet door and all of her clothes were gone. My heart almost dropped to my feet.

I called Alicia but she would not answer her phone. I kept pressing redial but she refused to answer. I ran to my car not knowing where I was going and started driving. Before I knew it, I ended up in Mike's driveway. I ran to his door and started pounding.

"Mike! Cynthia!" I shouted. "Open up!"

"What the hell is wrong with you, man?" Mike said, opening the door.

"Alicia left and she took Brittany!" I said, breathing hard and walking through Mike's house.

"Calm down, man," Mike said. "What happened?"

"I told her about the affair, and when I went to work this morning, she left and she took Brittany with her."

"Why did you tell her, Johnny?"

"Because she needed to know!" I shouted.

"No, she didn't! Not right now!" Mike shouted back.

"Would you prefer if she would have found out on the news, Mike?"

"Of course not!"

"Has she been over here?" I asked.

"No, not today," Mike said.

"Where's Cynthia?"

"I don't know. She left a little while ago and didn't tell me where she was going."

"I bet they're together. Can you call her and see?"

"Yeah, hold on."

Mike called Cynthia on her cell phone but she did not pick up. I watched nervously as he called and called. Instead of calling back she texted him to avoid having to talk.

"They're together," Mike said. "Cynthia thinks she's slick!"

"Where the hell are they?" I asked.

"They can only be in one place."

"Where's that?"

"The batcave!"

"Where's the batcave?" I asked.

"Pam's house."

"Pam's house?"

"Yeah," Mike said. "To the batcave!"

"Let's go!"

Mike and I jumped in my car and we sped over to Pam's house. I let Mike drive because I was too unbalanced. We got there before they could figure out that we were on our way and caught them pulling out of the driveway. The entire office girl posse was there except for Tazzy and Susan.

"Man, you see what you did, Johnny?" Mike asked.

"What did I do?"

"You got my girls blackballing me on our office girls' meetings, man!" Mike said. "I'm guilty by association."

We saw them scrambling around with their cars in confusion.

"What are they doing?" I asked.

"They're trying to run interference for Alicia," Mike said after staring at them a moment.

"Why?" I asked. "I just want to talk to her."

"Johnny," Mike said, "for somebody who's supposed to be an expert on women, you don't know shit, do you?"

"Man, just drive the damn car!" I shouted. "They're getting away!"

There were five cars pulling off at the same time and we didn't know for sure which car Alicia was in.

"Which car?" I asked.

"I don't know!" Mike shouted. "Do you see her?"

"No!" I shouted. "What kind of women do you associate yourself with, Mike?"

"You tell me. We're trying to chase your wife down!"

Finally, Wanda pulled up on our right. Valerie pulled on our left. Darsha pulled in front of us and Lisa pulled in from our rear. They had us completely surrounded. And then, one by one, they started to cut their cars off. We were trapped.

"Hey!" Mike shouted, as he rolled down the window. "Move out the way!"

"We don't listen to cheaters!" Wanda shouted.

"See, this is why I don't fool around with men!" Valerie said.

"Hey, let us out!" I shouted.

"Shut up, cheater!" Wanda yelled.

Mike looked at me. "What kind of Bonnie and Clyde shit is this?"

"I don't know, man, but we're trapped!" I said. "I can't open my door, Wanda's too close!"

I kept pushing against the door, but the weight of Wanda's car would not allow the door to budge.

"Hey! Where's my wife?" I shouted.

"Cheater! Cheater! Pumpkin eater!" Wanda shouted.

"Let me out!" I shouted.

I rolled my window down and tried to climb out. It took me a while to squeeze my large frame through that small hole, but I did. As I crawled out the window I rolled onto the hood of Wanda's car, looking her straight in the eyes. I was looking to kick asses and take names later.

"Whoa, shit!" Wanda said. "Retreat!"

The office girls started their cars and tried to speed away. I walked up to Pam's door and started to bang on it. She didn't answer, so I continued to bang harder. Mike eventually got out of the car and tried to talk some sense into my head.

"Johnny, she's not in there."

"How do you know?"

"Because even if she was in there, she's not in there to you."

"Man, she has my kid!" I started to cry. "That's all I got!"

"I know you're hurting, man, but there's nothing you can do right now."

"But she's got my kid, man!" I said and then sat on Pam's doorstep. I lowered my head and began to cry. There I was, a giant of a man, and I sat there with my head and my tail between my legs and cried.

"Come on, man!" Mike sat down beside me and patting me on my back. "Stop crying, Johnny. Dammit! Some things change, some things stay the same."

After I cried my eyes out, Mike and I headed back to my place. We didn't say much; after my embarrassing Oprah moment, there wasn't much to say.

"I'm sorry for getting soft like that, man," I said.

"Hey," Mike said, "if my wife and child were to leave me, I'd probably break down and cry, too."

"I didn't, like, break down, break down. It was more like a meltdown."

"Breakdown! Meltdown! Whatever!" Mike said, "Don't be embarrassed about it."

"You wouldn't have broken down like that."

"You damn right, I wouldn't have," Mike said. "But you're not me."

"So did I seem a little wimpy to you?"

"No," Mike said. "You seemed a lot wimpy."

"Sorry about that, man."

"What are you apologizing for?"

"You know, I've always been too sensitive, man. I've always been too emotional. That's why I had so many problems with Pop," I said. "This is embarrassing, man."

"What are you embarrassed about?"

"For being so damn sensitive, man!" I said. "It's like I get emotional over everything, but I won't stand up for anything."

"Man, would you stop whining?" Mike shouted. "You're a freakin' psychologist for crying out loud!"

"I know, man, I have to get a grip!"

"Hey, it's all right, man, you're going through a rough time, that's all," Mike said. "It wasn't that long ago when I was going through some serious shit and you talked me through it. So maybe it's my time to return the favor."

"So you're the doctor and I'm the writer, huh?"

"Hell no," Mike said. "It takes skills to be a writer. It only takes money to be a doctor."

"Whatever, man." I chuckled.

"At least I got you laughing," Mike said, pointing to my face. "Seriously though, you'll be okay. If there's anything wrong with you, it's that you care too much. And that's a good thing. You can't help the fact that you care. The world would be a better place if everybody cared too much. That's what makes you who you are, Johnny. Yeah, you're emotional and you're non-confrontational. You're emotional because you care about what happens to people. And you're non-confrontational because you care about hurting people's feelings, not because you're afraid of standing up for yourself. Look at you, man! You're a giant! You can break most people in half if you wanted. But you wouldn't hurt a fly."

"That's interesting." I looked out of the passenger window.

"That was deep, huh?" Mike asked.

"Deep?" I said, still looking out of the window. "I don't know about that. But I find it interesting that you just said I wouldn't hurt a fly, but when asked if I could murder a human being, you're not quite sure."

"That's an entirely different set of circumstances, Johnny."

"How so, Mike?" I stared at him. "When I was asked if I thought you killed Anise, I flat out told them no! But you could not do the same when you were asked that question about me."

"There is a reason for that, Johnny, and you know it."

"What reason?"

"Okay, you were the one who was having the affair with her! You were the one who found her body! You were the one that I found at the hotel with blood on your hands!"

"And I am the one who is innocent!" I shouted. "I did not kill that girl!"

"I want to believe you, Johnny!" Mike said. "I want to believe you so badly! But if you were in my place, what would you think?"

"Mike, I swear to God," I said. "If you were accused of killing someone and you asked me to believe that you did not do it. I don't care what evidence they had against you. I would believe you, stand by you, and fight for you until you were found not guilty! Or until you admitted you were guilty!"

"Okay, Johnny," Mike said. "If you tell me that you had absolutely no involvement in her murder, that's it! No more questions. I'll believe you!"

"Listen, Mike," I said. "I wouldn't ask you to believe me if I was involved in any way, with Anise's death."

"Then no matter what happens from this point forward, we're together!" Mike stuck his fist in the air and asked, "Family?"

"Family!" I said, giving Mike a fisted pound.

CHAPTER SEVENTEEN

Over the next few days my life was pretty routine. But then I received the telephone call from Stacey confirming that my DNA was a perfect match with the DNA found on Anise. She suggested Mike and I come to the police station together to explain the entire, true story.

Mike reluctantly went to the station. Before we went, he contacted his ex-wife's husband, Rob, who was a detective with the Atlanta Police Department. Rob was on his way to the police station anyway, so he agreed to meet with us. He briefed us on what to expect and advised us on what we should say. He was acquainted with Stacey through prior investigations, so he knew that we would be well represented legally. He wanted to prepare us for the interrogation procedure that would take place.

We met in a coffee house a couple of blocks from the police station. Rob sat on one side of the table, and Mike and I sat on the other. I was as nervous as a hog on his way to the slaughterhouse. Mike, on the other hand, was as cool as a cucumber. We explained in absolute detail the events that led up to the moment when Mike walked into Anise's hotel room.

"Damn!" Rob said. "How did y'all get caught up in this?"

"We should have just told the truth from the beginning," I said.

"It's too late for that now." Mike sighed.

"Whose idea was it to fabricate this story?" Rob asked.

"Mike," I said.

"Boy, you're still a rat, huh?" Mike said sarcastically, looking directly at me.

"Why do you have to call me a rat?"

"All right, fellas!" Rob said. "Y'all joking but this is some serious shit!"

"Okay! Okay!" Mike said. "We're serious."

"When you guys get in there, they're going to separate you and look for discrepancies in your stories. Remember, their job is to get to the truth. Not your truth, or your truth," Rob said, pointing at Mike and me. "They want their truth. Their truth has to lead to a conviction. They could give a damn if either one of you spent the rest of your life in prison. They want a suspect. They want a trial. And they want a conviction!"

"But neither one of us killed her," I said. "Will they look for another suspect?"

"I repeat!" Rob said. "They want a suspect, and they have two! They want a trial, and they have circumstantial and physical evidence to move forward with a trial. And then they want a conviction! If they can convince a jury that either one of you is guilty, they will send you to death row and won't think twice about it."

"But we're innocent!" I said.

"Innocent and not guilty are two different things, Johnny," Rob said. "Remember, once you go to trial, it's no longer a matter of you being innocent or not innocent. You're either guilty, or not guilty."

"Well, we're not guilty!" I said.

"Only the court can determine that."

"Mike, why are you just sitting there?" I said. "Say something, man!"

"Let's just get this over with!" Mike said. "Come on, let's go!"

Mike stood up, and then Rob and I followed suit. When we arrived at the police station, Stacey was waiting. As Rob predicted, we were separated and interrogated for hours. Perhaps they were looking for discrepancies in our stories, but I never deviated. I told it as I recalled it.

We stayed all morning and afternoon, and then into the evening. They left me alone for about thirty minutes and then Rob and Stacey walked into the room. *Finally*, I thought, *the cavalry!*

"Thank God!" I said. "Friendly faces."

"I'm sorry, Johnny," Rob said. "You are being placed under arrest for the murder of Ms. Anise Lawrence."

"You don't have to say another word, Johnny," Stacey advised. "You've been a very cooperative witness. Don't say another word!"

"Huh?" I asked, very confused. "What's happening?"

"You have the right to remain silent. If you give up that right, everything you say can, and will be used against you in the court of law…" Rob began.

Although I could hear Rob reading my Miranda rights to me, my mind wandered off and I became incoherently distraught. Stacey had warned me that this would probably happen, but speculation and realization is one hell of a big difference.

I was handcuffed and formally charged with first-degree murder. I was escorted into another room where all of my possessions were confiscated, and then I stood before a camera and had my mugshot taken.

They took me to a large cell which nearly fifteen other inmates occupied. We were huddled so closely together I don't even remember if there were beds. I stood in a corner with my back pressed against the bars, making sure I could see everything that happened. I was not going to stand Jesse James style and have my back to the gang.

Mother Nature started to get the best of me and I had to urinate badly. There was no officer available, so I approached one of my cellmates to inquire as to the procedure of asking permission to use the restroom. He was a young man. Barely looked eighteen. He may have been five feet and a half, maybe not. He was bright skinned. Thin, very thin. His hair was long and braided like a girl's. I wondered if he realized where he was, looking the way he did. He should have at least let his hair down to look as wild and thuggish as he could. But I'll be damned if that boy didn't look like Alicia Keys. Now, I'm not gay or anything like that, but the boy was pretty. He was a pretty man, and that's all that I'm going to say about that. I know he probably had a big-ass boyfriend in there somewhere named Antoine. Anyway, he told me his name was Tayquan and laughed at me when I asked about using the restroom.

"Restroom?" Tayquan said, pointing in the corner. "There you go!"

Peeking around several men, I saw an open toilet.

"What is that, man?" I said, pointing at the toilet.

"That's your restroom."

"But it doesn't have any walls or anything."

"Hey dog," Tayquan said. "This jail, not the Ritz!"

"I understand that, but they expect us to use the lavatory in the open?" I asked. "Right in front of everybody?"

"You either piss in the hole or you piss on yourself." Tayquan laughed.

"Man, I'm not pissing in that thing."

"As big as you are you shouldn't have anything to be ashamed of."

"Ashamed?" I asked. "I'm not ashamed. That's just indecent."

"Look!" Tayquan said, pointing to the toilet. "See?"

I looked in the direction of the toilet and saw a man pissing with no concern for who was watching.

"That ain't shit!" Tayquan said. "You gotta do what you gotta do!"

"Well, I ain't gotta do that," I said, mocking Tayquan. "Not right now, anyway."

"I believe you scared." Tayquan smiled.

"Scared of what?"

"Scared to show what you got," Tayquan said. "I'll show you mine if you show me yours."

Call me slow, but it finally dawned on me that this guy was making a pass at me.

"Excuse me?"

"I ain't stutter!" Tayquan said. "We gon' be in here for a while so we might as well amuse ourselves. Let's go off in one of these corners. Them guards can't see shit if we hide behind one of these big niggahs!"

"Man, what's wrong with you, man?" I said and started walking away.

Tayquan followed me to the other end of the cell and continued to talk.

"Listen, don't be scared. Close your eyes and my mouth will feel just like a woman. They don't call me Jawbone for nothing!"

"Jawbone!" I said, close to losing control. "I am nonviolent, but if you don't back the hell up off of me right now, I'm going to have to knock the shit out of you!"

"You ain't gotta act all like that, Bigman!" Tayquan said, snapping his fingers and waving his hand in the air. "I'm just trying to be friendly."

"I don't want to be your friend, man!"

Tayquan walked away mumbling. Moments later, a big guy approached me. He wasn't tall but he was round, with very long braids, too, although his hair was balding at the top. He introduced himself as Tiny. Tiny, how ironic? A huge man named Tiny.

"Hey, what's up, Bigman?" Tiny said. "The little fella trying to push up on you?"

"Push up on me?" I didn't know what the hell he was talking about.

"Yeah, you know," Tiny said. "Make a move on you."

"To tell you the truth, man, I don't know what he was trying to do."

"Yeah, that's Jawbone. He's like the jailhouse slut," Tiny said. "Don't even waste your time on that."

"Man, I'm just trying to get out of here."

"I feel you on that," Tiny said. "You better watch yo' back though, bro. When these bitches in here get horny, they'll do anything."

"No doubt," I said, suddenly calling upon my limited urban vernacular to make myself fit in with the natives.

"What you in here for?" Tiny asked.

Never in a million years would I have thought that I would be proud to say that I was accused of murder. But if it was going to keep those thugs off of my ass, I would have said I was Charles Manson.

"Murder one," I said, with pride, and then repeated Tiny's question verbatim, "What you in here for?"

"Traffic tickets!"

"Traffic tickets?"

"Yeah, man," Tiny said. "And a suspended license."

This guy is talking like he is John Gotti, king of the jail, but he's in here for traffic tickets?

"Anyway," Tiny said, "who you do?"

"You know the singer Gizelle?" I asked. "They're trying to get me on that."

"Did you do her?"

"Hey, I'll put it like this," I said, still trying to make myself sound tough. "I'm in here for a reason. That's all I have to say on that."

"So you did do it?" Tiny was now very excited.

"Hey, look," I said, "I'm in here for a reason."

"Damn!" Tiny shouted. "What was it like? How did it feel? Did you use your hands? A gun? What?"

"I'd rather not talk about it, Tiny."

"Oh, I feel you! I feel you!" Tiny said. "Hush-hush, huh?"

"Hey, I'm not trying to be rude but I need some time to myself, my man." I felt confident that I would make it until morning.

I stood up the remainder of the night with my eyes wide open, holding my piss and watching everything that moved. I was surprised at the wild activity that was going on. This was supposed to be the county jail, not prison! I had a newfound respect for what convicts have to suffer through.

When morning came, Stacey made sure I was arraigned and released on bond the first thing. Mike and Cynthia were there to greet me upon my release. Of course the other office girls were not there, nor was there a reception at my house like there was for Mike. But I had something much, much better waiting for me, Alicia and Brittany.

I was looking tattered and torn. I hadn't slept in over twenty-four hours, but when I saw my wife and child standing in the doorway when we pulled up, I jumped out of the car and ran to them.

Mike, Cynthia, and Stacey lagged behind to give us time to reunite. I picked them up in my arms and spun them around. Holding them gave me all the security in the world.

"Oh my God, I'm so happy to see you two!" I said, kissing them back and forth on their faces.

"I missed you, Daddy!" Brittany laughed.

"Did you miss me, too?" I asked Alicia.

"Let's not talk about that right now," Alicia said.

"Well, we'll give you two time to relax and I'll check in with you later, Dr. Forrester, okay?"

"Thanks, Stacey," I replied. "Thanks for everything."

"No problem," Stacey said as she got back in her car. "Bye!"

Stacey pulled off and, shortly thereafter, Mike and Cynthia said their good-byes. Alicia and I walked inside the house and met in our meeting room, the kitchen. We didn't want to say too much in front of Brittany, but Alicia made it perfectly clear that she was back to support me as a wife because of my situation, but not to fulfill any other wifely duties, if you know what I mean.

Despite the unexpected sequence of events, I was able to make my daily visit to Veronica. Betty was there and I explained to both of them at the same time the situation with my arrest. They didn't judge me and instead they offered their support and told me they would stand behind me one hundred percent. That was a huge boost of confidence for me.

When I got home, Alicia and Brittany had left. I took advantage of the time alone and went straight to bed. It's funny how being alone can be such a valuable commodity for peace and self-examination. However, after those moments have passed, being alone turns into nothing but loneliness. Loneliness becomes an agonizing nightmare where every thought is magnified one hundred times, especially the painful ones. I know because I had just experienced that nightmare. Just before dark, Brittany jumped on me, waking me from my nap.

"Hey girl," I said. "Can I get a nap?"

"Wake up, Daddy!" Brittany yelled. "Mommy said it's time for dinner."

I looked in the doorway and Alicia was standing there with her hands on her hips.

"Tina and Curtis are on their way over for dinner. So get up and get ready."

Alicia turned around and walked out. No smile. No laugh. Nothing! I felt uncomfortable thinking that I would have to pretend that everything was fine in front of Tina and Curtis when we knew it was not.

"At least my baby still loves me, huh?" I said, kissing Brittany.

"Yes!" Brittany said.

"And I love you, too." I squeezed her as tight as I could without causing physical harm. "Daddy has to get cleaned up, so run downstairs to Mommy until I get ready, okay?"

"Okay, Daddy!" Brittany said before taking off like a jet and running downstairs.

As I showered, I thought about how many dinner parties we were having lately. It used to be special when we didn't see each other that often, but now it seemed like we were seeing each other every week. It's like we had turned into the Huxtables.

When Tina and Curtis arrived, we sat down for dinner and Curtis blessed the food. There was plenty of conversation, but Alicia ignored me throughout. Tina and Curtis pretended along with us that everything was fine.

Brittany went to bed a little while after dinner, leaving the four adults with nothing but time to discuss adult issues. I may not be a genius, but I'm not an idiot, either. I put two and two together and came up with a setup! This dinner was arranged for Alicia and I to discuss my act of infidelity with Reverend Curtis! I didn't like being setup, but what could I say?

"Since we're not doing anything," Curtis said, "why don't we discuss our views on marriage."

"Yeah, why don't we?" Alicia folded her arms.

"What is this?" I asked.

"It's us trying to save your marriage," Tina said.

"Okay," I said, "where do we begin?"

"First of all, we begin with you not acting like a psychologist!" Tina said.

"That's what I am, Tina."

"Not tonight!" Tina said. "You're a husband."

"Brother Johnny," Curtis said, "I can imagine how you may feel. This could be embarrassing. And it should be embarrassing. But we're not here to judge. How can I? I have been the scum of the earth. There is nothing you can do that I haven't probably already done. So, no matter what you tell me, I am in no position to judge you."

"Thanks, Curtis."

"Now, with that being said, do you love your wife?" Curtis asked.

"With every beat of my heart."

"Can you imagine how much you hurt her?" Curtis asked.

"I can, and I am so sorry!" I said. I turned around to Alicia and spoke directly to her, "Baby, I know you probably hate me right now and you have every right, but you have to know that I love you!"

"Why would you do this to us, Johnny?" Alicia pounded her hands on her knees.

"I'm sorry, baby."

"Sorry does not take away the damage you've done," Alicia said. "I want to know what would make you step outside of our marriage!"

"Okay." I lowered my head. "I'll tell you."

"Oh my God, what else?"

"I need to tell you about my past. About me."

"Okay," Alicia said, taking a deep breath, "go ahead."

"Before I met you a long time ago, I was diagnosed as suffering from erotomania."

"Eroto what?" Alicia asked.

"It's a form of nymphomania."

"What are you saying?" Alicia asked. "Are you a sex addict?"

"Yes. No! Not anymore," I stammered. "It's not about the sex, Alicia. It's an emotional inefficiency!"

"Oh my God!" Alicia said, standing up and walking away.

"Alicia," Curtis said, "come back and listen to him, please."

Alicia walked back over and sat down. She shook her legs nervously as Curtis advised me to continue. "Go 'head, Johnny," Curtis said.

"When I was young, I never felt loved," I said while rubbing my hands together unconsciously. "I always felt alone and neglected. I never felt love from my parents. I guess it had a psychological effect on me that made me overcompensate."

"Overcompensate how?" Alicia asked.

"With women," I said. "There were only two things that I was always successful in—sports and women. And I abused them both. Women were always easily accessible, so I tried to make my many meaningless relationships more meaningful by having sex. In some way, that attention made me feel loved and appreciated, even if it was a momentary thrill."

"But why didn't you tell me this before we were married?"

"Because I thought I had conquered my demons and bringing it up would only cause you to worry unnecessarily."

"Obviously, you were wrong on both counts, huh?"

"Okay, Alicia," Curtis said. "Let's remember that we're not here to judge, we're here to confess and forgive."

"Yeah," Tina said, "you haven't given your confession yet."

"What confession?" I asked and looked at the three of them.

"Well," Alicia said, "a month or so after we were married, I had an affair with my ex-boyfriend, Julian."

"You did what?" I rose to my feet.

"I had an affair with Julian." She showed no remorse. Instead, she looked at me with a cold stare of vindictiveness.

I was devastated! I dropped back in my chair and stared back at her. "What?"

Alicia continued to look at me and offered no sign of sympathy. This was her way of hurting me as I had hurt her.

"How could you do this to me?"

"How could you do this to me?" Alicia shouted.

"Alicia, why don't you tell Johnny what happened between you and your ex," Curtis asked.

"Yeah, why don't you do that?" I added.

"Sure," Alicia said, sounding eager to hurt me more, "when we were first married, I felt insecure. I didn't feel that I was good enough for you, Johnny. Julian started to call and I felt comfortable talking to him about our marriage. He was a friend. He told me he would be visiting Atlanta and wanted to meet. We went to lunch and had a few drinks. After that, we went back to his hotel room to look at his portfolio. One thing led to another and we ended up kissing."

"Wow!" I said, shaking my head, "and you never thought to mention this to me?"

"If Gizelle wouldn't have been murdered, would you have mentioned that to me?"

"Alicia, I told you every time we made love. You knew the difference in my touch, my affection. It was only a matter of time before I told you with my lips."

"That's crap, Johnny, and you know it!" Alicia shouted before bending over and putting her head in her hands.

Nobody said a word as we waited for Alicia's response.

"I don't know if we can recover from this," Alicia said.

"We can get through this if we try, Alicia."

"I don't know if I can deal with this."

"Wait a minute," I said, starting to get pissed off, "are you telling me that one month into our marriage you have an affair with your ex-boyfriend and pretend it never happened, but you can't forgive me for doing the same thing?"

"It's not the same thing!" Alicia shouted. "I only kissed him!"

"What difference does it make?" I shouted back. "We both cheated!"

"I kissed a man! And only once! You had a continuous affair, that's different!"

"Both of y'all wrong!" Tina shouted.

"Alicia! Johnny!" Curtis yelled, trying to get us to calm down.

"This is not about who's right or wrong. This is about forgiveness."

"I don't know if I can forgive him, Curtis," Alicia said.

"You can if you want," Curtis said. "If my wife can forgive me for cheating on her and beating on her! Stealing from her! Selling drugs! Using drugs! If my wife can forgive me for that multitude of sins, surely you two can forgive each other for your iniquities."

"I don't know," Alicia said. "I think it's impossible to overcome the lies and deception we've brought into this marriage."

"With man, perhaps it is impossible, but with God, all things are possible," Curtis responded. "I don't want to sound too religious, but a family that prays together, stays together! You have to have more faith in God than you have doubt in man, or us men. I can imagine the pain and disappointment you two feel right now, but time heals all wounds. And time is what you need, not only to heal the wounds but to make a decision on your marriage. You just don't throw it away when things get rough."

"Talk to 'em, baby!" Tina said.

"Unfortunately, our society nowadays makes it so easy to walk away from marriage. It's to the point where, as soon as something happens in your marriages today, big or small, family and friends start to hound you to get out and get a divorce. You're almost ashamed to fight for your marriage because you're afraid of being criticized. But what God has put together, let no man put asunder!"

"But how do we know God put us together?" Alicia asked.

"How do you know that He didn't?" Curtis asked right back.

"I don't."

"Do you love this man?" Curtis asked Alicia, pointing at me.

"Yes."

"And do you love this woman?" Curtis asked me.

"Absolutely."

"Then why would you even question God's gift?" Curtis said. "Instead of questioning it, embrace it. Enjoy it."

"I want to, but I don't know if I can," Alicia said.

"Do you prefer being married over being single?"

"Of course I do," Alicia said. "I love being married."

"Do you prefer love over pain?"

"Who doesn't?"

"A healthy, loving family is difficult to attain and even harder to maintain, Alicia. You have to cultivate it, nourish it and watch it grow. Sure, sometimes it's going to be very difficult. But that's when you have to understand why you're married in the first place. It's not about the individual anymore. It's not about living and loving selfishly anymore. It's about becoming one and forgiving your partner as you would forgive yourself. Do you understand?"

"I understand," Alicia said. "But right now, I'm hurting. Right or wrong, I'm hurting and I can't make myself stop hurting. I want to save my marriage. I just don't think I can."

"Then deal with the pain first," Curtis said. "You have time. Give yourself time to hurt, and then give yourself time to heal. In time, God will make everything all right."

"I don't mean to be selfish, but I'm hurting, too," I joked.

"Don't push it, Johnny!" Curtis said. "Alicia, no one is rushing you, but before you decide to leave your marriage, make sure you've done all that you can to save it."

"Okay," Alicia sighed. "As long as there's no pressure for me to act like everything is fine when my heart knows better. I will stay and try to make this marriage work, but we don't need to sleep in the same room. And I don't want to be touched in any way. Romantically, sexually, I don't want to be touched, period!"

"I don't have a problem with that," I said. "But may I ask one question? That's it! One question."

"So long as it has nothing to do with getting back together."

"It has nothing to do with that. I promise."

"Okay," Alicia said. "What is it?"

"Do you have any romantic feelings for Julian?"

"No," Alicia said. "The last time I saw him I realized two things. One, I have no desire to be with that man, or any other man for that matter. And two, I loved you and I wanted to spend the rest of my life with you."

"And now?"

"And now, I'm hurting."

"Baby look," I said, trying to hug her.

"I can't deal with this right now," Alicia said while pushing me away. "I'm sorry, you guys, but I need to think. Thanks for stopping by."

Alicia left the room and went upstairs.

"Give her time, Johnny," Curtis advised.

"I will, man. At least she's home."

"We better get going, honey," Tina suggested.

"Okay, sweetie!"

"Thank you, guys," I said.

"God bless, man," Curtis said.

I walked Curtis and Tina to the door and they said their good-byes. I sat in my living room and stared at the ceiling. As miserable as I was after being cut off from my wife, I was equally ecstatic to know that we were still under the same roof.

CHAPTER EIGHTEEN

The next morning, I had an appointment with Patient Number Five. I wanted to get back to our last topic. Patient Number Five had opened up and we were discussing our different views on the true nature of a woman. I was a little anxious to begin the session that morning. It became apparent that Patient Number Five was also eager to begin. She wasted no time with her introduction.

"Good morning, sir."

"Good morning, ma'am."

"And what should we discuss today?"

"I'd like to resume our discussion on the nature of a woman."

"Fine."

"From my analysis of our previous conversation, I think the dissimilarity in our perceptions of the nature of a woman stems from your theory based on the unpredictability of a woman's emotions. And by saying that, aren't you implying that women are essentially creatures of emotions and men are rational thinkers?"

"Why, no. I never said the nature of a woman is based on the unpredictability of her emotions," Patient Number Five replied. "Nor did I say men are rational thinkers. Look at your world.

A world of war and death! A world where one nation destroys another merely for the sake of dominance! A world of deceit, destruction and despondency! How rational is that? And that is a world under the influence of man."

"Are you suggesting that men should think more unpredictably, as women do?"

"I am saying that there is a time for rational deductibility and there is a time for emotional accountability. Men sometimes can't distinguish between the two. Sometimes, the power of love should influence the process of logical thinking. But with men, the process of logical thinking tends to influence the power of love and the result is often catastrophic."

"For example?"

"For example?" Patient Number Five said, pausing momentarily, "Are you a married man?"

"Yes."

"Are you a man who is happy to be married to his wife?"

"Yes," I answered, still not certain of where she was leading me.

"Do you think you are capable of betraying your wife?"

"Betraying my wife in what manner?"

"Infidelity."

"Given the right set of circumstances, I think anybody is capable of cheating," I said.

"Not everyone," Patient Number Five said. "People commit acts of infidelity because they succumb to the flesh. Infidelity is not an uncontrollable biological trait infested in the blood of human beings."

"Maybe there is a reason why an individual would commit infidelity."

"If I can borrow from your line of reasoning, what logical explanation can you give to justify infidelity?"

"Abuse, neglect, seduction, vulnerability, there are plenty of reasons why a person would seek the affection of another."

"You are correct, sir," Patient Number Five said. "Those are reasons one may commit infidelity, but they are not justifiable explanations. If one is being abused, if one is being neglected, if one is vulnerable, or if one is being seduced, when they start to feel affection for another, the action of choice should be to leave."

"That looks good on paper, but it's not very logical."

"So tell me, sir, at what point did you make the logical decision to have an affair?"

I was startled by Patient Number Five's question and took my time answering. She sat patiently in the dark and waited for my response.

"I don't understand," I said, understanding fully. "What are you asking me?"

"Your affair, sir," Patient Number Five said, "was your affair a decision based on logic or emotion?"

"What makes you think I had an affair?"

"A man of your knowledge and deductive reasoning would not use such an absurd hypothesis unless he is unable to remove himself from the ideology of the scenario. So at what point did you decide to have an affair?"

"Okay, you got me." I chuckled. "I did not make a conscious decision to have an affair, logically or emotionally. It just happened."

"Nothing just happens, sir. Was your decision one of logic or emotion?"

"I know where you're going with that question, but I can't say for certain if it was either."

"Well, let's analyze your scenario."

"Let's," I said jokingly, now feeling comfortable discussing my marriage with Patient Number Five.

"You are a practitioner of psychological evaluation and treatment, are you not?"

"I am."

"You are an advocate for logic and deductive reasoning, are you not?"

"I am."

"Through your contemplation of having an affair, at what point did you decide that you could deceive your wife and live with the consequences?"

"I don't know," I said.

"Well, I do, sir," Patient Number Five began. "It was at the point when you told yourself the affair was not about love. Your sexual activity with your adulteress was about the need to satisfy a hunger in your soul. You convinced yourself that your affair was nothing you could control. Because it wasn't you, it was the man in you.

"You also convinced yourself that the affair wasn't what you wanted; it was what you had to do. It's the nature of a man. And your nature makes you susceptible to temptation. And once you satisfied your lust, you could go back to your loving wife with a pure heart.

"You convinced yourself that as long as it was your wife that you loved, and not your adulteress, you could privately forgive yourself. But in actuality, you simply prioritized uncontrollable lust over unconditional love. Poor, poor you."

"That's not true," I said while knowing that what she was saying was one hundred percent accurate.

"Oh sir, if you would have allowed the power of love to influence your lust, you would not have rationalized your affair. Love, dear sir, does not need to be rationalized. It only needs to be accepted."

"Like you said, I suppose it's just the nature of a man to sometimes commit acts of infidelity," I said.

"That is preposterous!" Patient Number Five chuckled. "You know that we are not born creatures of uncontrollable habit, unless those habits were inherited from our progenitors. Infidelity is not an inherited trait, it is acquired."

"Oh boy," I sighed heavily. "From your perspective it seems as if all of the issues between men and women fall on the shoulders of men."

"From the beginning of time, women around the world have been oppressed by the decisions of men. So why shouldn't the results of the decisions created by men fall on the shoulders of men? After all, it is a man's world out there!"

"My world is right here and right now! Right here in America, and not around the world!" I said, pointing to the floor, even though I knew she couldn't see me through the thickness of the darkness. "And let me give you a little bit of history, ma'am! I am not one for dredging up the past, but since the existence of this country that we call the United States of America, no other man, or woman for that matter, has been oppressed and suppressed more than the black man! Nobody! So my world as a man is quite different from the world of which you speak!"

"Even in a black man's world, sir, you are still a man!" Patient Number Five retorted. "There is still a responsibility that goes along with being a man no matter what world you live in. Being a man is an inherited trait. One you should not defer or deny."

"I have never deferred or denied my responsibility as a man."

"Are you certain of that?"

"Quite certain."

"Do you think your wife would agree with your assessment?"

"Uh," I said. Wanting to speak with confidence, but not having an intelligent comeback, I added, "You would have to ask my wife that question."

"She is not accessible, so I am reduced to having your opinion," Patient Number Five said. "So, was your act of infidelity one that was responsible or irresponsible?"

"What difference does it make?"

"The admission of ignorance is the beginning of wisdom."

I paused again, seeking an intelligent comeback. But again, I had none. Knowing the battle was lost, I conceded and switched to another subject.

"Okay. I agree. My act of infidelity was irresponsible," I said, conceding all points of my dispute. "Why is it that every time I come here, I am the one under scrutiny? I am the one who is psychoanalyzed?"

"Because I have nothing to prove or disprove, sir!" Patient Number Five snapped.

"And neither do I," I said.

"Oh, it's quite the contrary, sir," Patient Number Five said. "You specialize in the behavior and emotions of women. Your patients' mental stability and recovery depends upon your ability to diagnose and treat their mental disorders. And quite frankly, before you can legitimately psychoanalyze your patients, you must first understand them. You have to understand the nature of a woman."

"You keep stating that I must understand the nature of a woman. That seems to be a contradiction within itself. On one hand you say that the nature of a woman is unpredictable, and on the other you say I have to understand it. To use your own words, how can one predict the unpredictable?"

"Your objective is not to predict. You are a doctor of psychology, not a meteorologist! The way to understanding the nature of a woman is to understand, *not* predict her emotions and behavior. You must listen and react to them. Some psychological and physiological patterns may exist in certain women, but each woman is an entity unto her own self. The risk of behavioral and emotional presumption could be detrimental to your relationship with a woman, be it professional or personal."

"Ma'am," I said, "even without the benefit of my education, I know women well enough to know that they want men to understand how they feel without having to tell us."

"And how has that worked out for you?" Patient Number Five asked sarcastically.

"I get your point." I laughed out loud.

"Do you have your pad and pencil available?"

"Yes."

"Are you writing notes?"

"Yes."

"In the darkness?"

"Yes, in the dark."

"Can you see your notes as you are writing?"

"No, ma'am."

"Then how do you know what you are writing?"

"Because," I said, "once I am in the light I can decipher through my scribbling and understand what was written."

"Finally, we have arrived at the same place at the same time." Patient Number Five chuckled.

"What do you mean?"

"Just as you sit in the darkness of this room scribbling notes, unable to see, unable to predict, unable to determine anything other than the moment itself, this is the same way you should approach the nature of a woman. You listen to what she has to say. You study what she says and how she says it. You decipher her thoughts and her words only after you have heard what she has to say. Do not predict or presume! And this should be practiced on an individual basis, and not as if women were scientific lab rats."

"Wow!" I said, finally understanding Patient Number Five's analysis.

"Wow is correct, sir!" Patient Number Five laughed. "And may I add, your perception of the nature of a woman should hold the same significance in your personal life as it does in your professional life."

"I understand."

"Well done, sir," Patient Number Five congratulated me.

I was about to push the flashing button to request my departure, but I thought that moment was as perfect a time as any to ask a very important question.

"I've listened to you. I've answered your questions, now I have something I would like to ask you."

"Proceed."

"After being underground, so to speak, for so many years, is there anything or anyone that would make you resurface?"

"Um, good question," Patient Number Five paused momentarily and then answered, "I suppose, since it was my love for a man that caused me to hide from the eye of the day, it would have to be the love of a man that would cause me to shine in the eye of the day. But it is more likely that I will meet my wel-comed demise before I meet that un-welcomed man."

I did not respond to her. I merely wrote my notes as legibly as the darkness would allow.

"No more questions, sir?" Patient Number Five asked.

"No," I answered. "None whatsoever."

"Well done."

I could hear Patient Number Five sighing in the darkness; a sound that I interpreted as relief. It was a sound I had so often breathed when I thought I had finally made a breakthrough. For the first time, I felt as if I had her respect as a psychologist and, more importantly, a friend.

❁❁❁

The next morning I was sitting in Stacey's office. My evi-dentiary hearing to determine if my case would go to trial was rapidly approaching. Stacey was upfront and told me that she felt the state had enough evidence to warrant a trial. Stacey also made it a point to say that if I had to go to trial, then more than likely, I would also go to jail. I was disappointed but not disheartened.

Later that day, Rob called to speak to Stacey. He said he wanted to discuss crucial information about another case he was investigating. He told Stacey that my name was also associated with that case and he wanted to question me. Stacey grilled me over and over, thinking I was withholding information, but I was unaware of Rob's allegations.

After Stacey felt comfortable that I wasn't withholding infor-mation, she agreed for Rob to question me, but only in her office. She thought it would be better to talk in a comfortable and not hostile environment. Rob agreed and the meeting was set. However, there was one stipulation. It had to be off the record. By the time Rob arrived, Stacey had left and Ms. Hattley had come in as my representative for the questioning.

"Hey, how y'all doing?" Rob said.

"How's my niece?" I asked, since the meeting was off the record.

"She's fine!" Rob said. "Growing every day. You know how it is…"

"I don't mean to interrupt, gentlemen. I realize this questioning is off the record, but it's still an inquiry. Let's try to keep the family conversation out of it until the meeting is over, okay?"

"Are you married, ma'am?" Rob asked.

"No I am not!"

"Wow! That's a surprise," Rob said sarcastically.

Rob and I laughed, but Ms. Hattley didn't find it humorous at all.

"Okay, Detective," Ms. Hattley said. "You may begin your questions."

"All right," Rob said, still chuckling a little. "Were you two aware that there was another body discovered at the same hotel and on the same day that Gizelle's body was found?"

"Yes," Ms. Hattley replied quickly.

"Okay," Rob said. "The body found behind the hotel was Ms. Lawrence's bodyguard."

"And what does that have to do with my client?"

"I don't know, I was hoping maybe Johnny could tell me."

"I saw the guy a few times with Anise, but I never said a word to him. I know nothing about him, or why anyone would want to kill him. As far as I know, he was just Anise's bodyguard."

"Does that answer your question, Detective?" Ms. Hattley said.

"It answers that question but you know I have more. We can do it now, off of the record, or we can do it later on the record."

"Now seems like as good a time as any," Ms. Hattley said.

"I have nothing to hide," I said.

"What do you think the association between Gizelle's and her bodyguard's deaths could be?" Rob asked.

"How would Dr. Forrester know the answer to that question?"

"I'm just asking," Rob said.

"You're asking as if my client was a suspect in both deaths."

"You have to admit that it's one hell of a coincidence, don't you, Ms. Hattley?"

"Not at all," Ms. Hattley said. "If the man was her bodyguard and she was found dead, obviously the perpetrator had to go through him to get to her."

"I agree, but maybe Johnny can remember something out of the ordinary that could help explain why the bodyguard was not where he was supposed to be that evening."

"My client can assume no more than you and I can assume," Ms. Hattley said. "If the bodyguard would have done his job effectively that day, he and Ms. Lawrence would still be alive today."

I looked at Ms. Hattley and thought to myself that she was one insensitive woman.

"My client does not have to explain why both bodies were found there. That's your job!" Ms. Hattley continued.

"Ma'am," Rob sounded annoyed, "Ms. Hattley, do you know how long I have been doing this?"

"That's irrelevant!"

"No, it's not," Rob said. "Not once have I ever agreed to questioning a suspect off the record, and this is an exception because I happen to believe the man I am gathering evidence on, just happens to be innocent. I am not here to try to manipulate or incriminate Johnny. Two people are dead. I am a police detective and my job is to find out why those people were killed and who killed them. I am not trying to convict an innocent man. I know this man! He is a good man and a good friend! If he wasn't, I wouldn't be here."

"First of all, my client is not a suspect in the death of Ms. Lawrence's bodyguard, so please stop referring to him as such!" Ms. Hattley said. "Now is there anything else, Detective?"

"Yes there is," Rob said. "Let me make something perfectly clear! As his attorney, you see Johnny simply as a client! That's it! But as a detective, I can't just see him as a suspect. As much as you may assume that I am all about my job, it's not easy for me to forget that I have eaten dinner with this man. Or that our children have slept at each other's houses. There is no possible satisfaction in solving a case that would place my daughter's uncle and my friend in prison for the rest of his life! I have a job to do, and if you weren't such a hard ass you would see that I am not only doing my job effectively, I'm doing yours, too!"

"Dr. Forrester, do not answer any questions, I'll be right back!" Ms. Hattley said before standing up and walking out of the room.

"I'm sorry, man," Rob said, "but your lawyer is so busy trying to prove that she is just as competent as the fellas that she is overlooking some pretty obvious variables in your case. I didn't come here to get information from you, man. I came here to inconspicuously give her information. Information that would help you! Information that she should have gotten on her own, and she knows it! That bodyguard is important to your vindication."

"Don't be so hard on them, Rob," I said. "It's not like I can't afford to pay them, but they are taking the case pro bono! That says a lot about them."

"Don't be naïve, man. This is a high-profile case. Your attorney's fee is not comparable to the amount of publicity her firm is receiving," Rob said. "Come on now, Johnny, the publicity or the money? What else would you expect them to do?"

"They could have accepted both the publicity and my money. But they didn't, man."

"So basically what you're saying is, I need to apologize to Ms. Hattley?"

"Basically," I said.

"Dammit!"

Ms. Hattley walked back in, composed and ready for business.

"Okay, gentlemen, where were we?"

"I was apologizing," Rob said. "I was out of line."

"Thanks." Ms. Hattley smiled. "I probably could have been a little friendlier myself."

"You think?" Rob laughed.

CHAPTER NINETEEN

When I got home, I was greeted with Brittany running to my legs and wrapping herself around them. I picked her up and took her into the kitchen. Alicia was cooking, a rare occasion. I initially thought she was coming around and that she was ready to start rebuilding our marriage. But when I saw Mike and Cynthia sitting at the table, it explained the home-cooked meal. Another dinner party! It also explained that she was not ready to spend any alone time with me.

I prepared myself to pretend that I was happy to see them, but before I started my performance, Mike cut me off. "You ready, big fella?"

"Ready for what?" I said while holding Brittany in my arms.

"Didn't you tell me Ma and Pop were coming today?" Mike asked. "What time does their flight get in?"

"Oh man!" I looked at the clock. "Twenty minutes ago. I completely forgot!"

"Man, come on!" Mike snatched my keys out of my hand and rushed past me. "I'm driving!"

We darted through traffic, speeding to the airport. I held on tightly as Mike drove my Escalade like a bat out of hell.

"I'm going to drop you off at the curb and drive around," Mike said.

"Negative!" I said. "Park my truck, man! We're both going in."

"Damn, man!" Mike said. "It doesn't take both of us to pick them up."

"Park my truck, Mike!" I said, pointing toward the parking deck. "Let's pick up our parents together! Like good children are supposed to."

We parked the car and walked to the north terminal of Hartsfield-Jackson Airport. My parents had come in on AirTran Airlines out of Flint, Michigan. We checked the schedule to see if the plane had arrived on time. It had, but not twenty minutes ago as I'd thought; it had landed one hour and twenty minutes ago. I don't know how I'd lost track of my parents' itinerary, but I needed to find them and find them fast.

We looked for them in baggage claim but they were not there. We thought it would be best to split up to cover more territory. We started in the middle of the airport. Mike went left. I went right. Ten minutes later, Mike called my cell.

"I got 'em!" Mike said.

"Where are you?" I asked.

"We're on our way back to the N5 door."

"Do they have their bags already?"

"Yup," Mike said. "We're walking toward the N5. Meet us there."

"All right, I'm on my way."

I arrived at the N5 door before Mike and my parents. When they finally came into view, I was like a child at Christmas. I was overwhelmed with emotion. I hugged my mother, lifting her off of the ground.

"Ma!" I said, kissing and hugging her.

"My baby!" Ma said as she hugged my neck.

"Hey, boy!" Pop said jokingly, "Don't you hurt my wife."

"How you doing, Pop?" I said, extending my hand to shake his.

"Don't put your hand up to me," Pop said, "hug me, boy."

As I hugged my father, I looked over his shoulder at Mike and made a face as if to say, *'What the hell?'*

Mike mouthed back the words, "I know, right?"

I was shocked to say the least. My father had always been unaffectionate and was not a big fan of PDA or public displays of affection. As a matter of fact, he rejected it. He would call us wimps. Well, he called me a wimp and other effeminate names if I displayed any form of sensitivity. But that was the past, and now was now. My father had hugged me for the first time. The first time that I could remember anyway.

"You okay, Pop?" I was still shocked by his hug.

"Yeah," Pop said. "Why?"

"Oh, nothing."

"How my grandbabies?" Pop asked.

"They're fine," Mike said.

"Who is this guy?" I said sarcastically, patting my father on the back.

"What the hell does that mean?" Pop laughed.

"See," Mike said. "Pop's the reason we use that phrase so much, Johnny!"

I would not be exaggerating one iota when I say my family has never laughed together, not that I remembered anyway.

On our way from the airport, I stopped at a gas station. I asked Mike to step out to pump while I went in and paid. He knew there was something going on because we never did that. It was just understood that whoever's car we were riding in paid for and pumped his own gas.

After I paid the attendant, I came back out and stood beside Mike with my back turned to my parents, sitting in the car. I suggested to him, or should I say, demanded, that our parents stay with him during their visit. He fought me tooth and nail but eventually caved in.

I dropped them off and went home to relax. But before I could settle in, Alicia told me we would be hosting a dinner party. She knew I would be irritated, and my irritation meant her jubilation. Anything she could do to aggravate me put a smile on her face. She was only scratching the surface surprising me with the dinner party. I don't know why she thought I would be surprised; I kind of had that one figured out when I walked in and saw her cooking.

I took a shower and got dressed. I took my time coming downstairs trying to avoid contact with Alicia. Eventually, I went downstairs and voluntarily initiated setting the table, something I had never done before. I was doing a lot of things around the house which I didn't normally do.

After the table was set, I had nothing more to do and the silence was awkward so I went back upstairs and waited for our guests to arrive. Once I heard the doorbell ring, I stepped outside of my bedroom and peeked over the balcony. Mike, Cynthia, and my parents had arrived. It was between seven-thirty and eight.

Brittany ran to Ma and Pop and showered them with hugs and kisses. They didn't see each other often, but when they did, it was a sight to see. All of the affection they neglected to give me as a child was being given to my child.

Ma and Pop spoiled Brittany and Mike's kids, too. I don't know where they found the money to buy all of the gifts she received. She enjoyed their attention and they certainly enjoyed hers. I was glad to see them enjoying themselves, but I just wanted the night to be over.

Stacey and her associates, Ms. Hattley and Ms. Carroll, were expected but had not arrived. Mike and I went downstairs to my basement while the rest of my family prepared for dinner.

We briefed Cynthia on Pop's delicate taste for the sauce and made sure he was kept away from all of the alcohol. But unbeknownst to us, Pop had a secret stash in his coat pocket. By the end of the night, we would find truth, anger, fear and alienation in the bottom of Pop's liquor bottle.

My parents and I were already seated at the dinner table when the other guests arrived. Cynthia answered the door and they followed her back to the dining area. They joined us at the table and we said grace. Dinner went smoothly, lots of laughs and talking.

After dinner, we started to discuss the case. It didn't occur to any of us to update Ma and Pop prior to the discussion. As soon as Pop heard Stacey mention that I would have to turn myself in, and place bond if my DNA sample came back positive, he hit the roof.

"If Johnny blood come back positive?!" Pop asked. "What you mean if Johnny blood come back positive?"

"Do you think we should be discussing this in front of your parents?" Stacey asked. "There's going to be very sensitive information involved."

"Hold on, white girl!" Pop shouted. "Don't talk like I ain't in the room! I'm right here! If you got something to say, say it to me!"

"Pop," Mike said. "Stop it!"

"I ain't stoppin' shit!" Pop yelled. "What Johnny blood got to do with anything?"

"Do you really want to know, Pop?" I asked.

"I wouldna asked if I didn't wanna know!"

"Okay," I said. "I was the one who found the girl's body in that hotel, not Mike."

"Aw, hell, Johnny!"

I looked at Mike and he shook his head.

"You?" Ma asked.

"Wait a minute!" Pop said and turned directly to me. "Are you trying to tell me you killed somebody and your brother is taking the rap for you?"

"I didn't kill anyone!" I snapped.

"Somebody did!" Pop yelled. "'Cause somebody's dead!"

Stacey, Ms. Hattley, and Ms. Carroll were looking with embarrassment at our family sideshow. I wanted to stop, but I couldn't. I couldn't as a child and I couldn't as an adult.

"Buddy, please," Ma said while patting his hand.

"Pop! Cut it out, man!" Mike said.

"You still ain't man enough to stand up for yourself, huh?"

"Leave him alone, Buddy!" Ma said.

I lowered my head and stared downward into my plate, reverting back to my youth when I was a timid little boy. This was a familiar place for me, the place where my father drank himself into oblivion and I would suffer the consequences. All at once, the vision of the kind, gentle man at the airport dissipated and the memory of the man my father truly was, became crystal clear.

The man who yelled and screamed at me because he thought I wasn't tough enough. The man who made me wear dresses to school because I didn't want to play football. The man who beat me every time I grew an inch over five feet tall to let me know *he* was still the man of the house! The man I despised!

"Are you gon' have your brother fight your battles for the rest of your life?" Pop stood up and walked toward me. "Huh, Johnny?"

"Buddy!" Ma said. "Leave him alone!"

"This weasel been runnin' with his tail between his legs ever since he been alive! Look at him! He's a goddam' giant and scared of his goddam' shadow!"

"Okay, Pop!" Mike interrupted, "That's enough!"

As usual, Mike stood up to Pop and I backed down. No matter what happened, I always backed down. And there I was, a grown man, in front of my wife, allowing this drunken bastard to take every ounce of manhood I possessed away from me.

My relationship with my father reminded me of a story a psych professor once told my class about the power of psychological influence. It was a story about a trainer and an elephant. As a baby, the elephant was chained to a little spike in the ground to keep him captive. As the elephant grew the trainer continued to use the same spike, even though the elephant was big enough and strong enough to rip the spike and three or four feet of dirt surrounding it completely out of the ground. This was my case with my father. My father had me convinced that I could not and should not ever stand up to him. And he was right.

I kept my head bowed, staring into my plate as if it was a portal that would swallow me up and take me away. Pop increased his antagonizing by bending down and putting his mouth to my ear. He yelled as loud as he could. "You make me sick! You're a yellow-belly, spineless coward whose balls are smaller than the ones you was born with! You ain't no man! You ain't nothin'!"

"Why are you yelling at him like that?" Alicia shouted, jumping up from the table. "Johnny, why are you letting that man talk to you like that?"

I heard Alicia loud and clear and God knows I wanted to speak, but I was too afraid to raise my head. I kept my head down and remained motionless and unresponsive, as if I was in a catatonic state.

"Johnny!" Alicia shouted, "Say something to him!"

"He bet' not say a mumbling word," Pop said. "If he so much as blink a eye, I'll slap the piss out of him!"

I continued to keep my head down. Alicia stood up and ran around the table to where Pop and I were. She pushed Pop out of the way. "Leave him alone!"

"This my son!" Pop said while snatching Alicia by the arm.

Stacey, Ms. Hattley, and Ms. Carroll removed themselves from the table and stood together against the wall. I could hear the sound of people shouting. There was chaos surrounding me, but I couldn't quite understand what was going on. When I saw Pop push my wife, I snapped back, and then I snapped.

"Don't you ever put your hands on her again!" I shouted, grabbing my father by his collar and slamming him against the wall. "Do you understand me?"

"Niggah, I'll kill you!" Pop shouted.

He grabbed my wrists and tried to knock my hands down, but my grip was much too strong. Mike stepped in and pulled me away from my father. Pop reached into his big pants pocket and pulled out his gun. He took a step backward and then aimed the gun at me. "You think you a man, niggah?"

"Oh my God!" Ms. Carroll yelled.

"Somebody do something!" Ms. Hattley screamed.

"Buddy Forrester! You put that gun down now!" Ma shouted. "That's yo' son!"

"He ain't no son of mine!"

"Okay, everybody out!" Mike shouted, directing the women to leave the dining room area. "Ma, you too!"

The women scattered out of the room, leaving Pop, Mike, and me at a standoff.

"Pop," Mike said. "Put that gun down, man."

"You would shoot your own son?" I asked. "What kind of a man are you?"

"Mike," Cynthia said nervously, "do something."

"Give me the gun, Pop!" Mike reached for the gun.

"Move, boy!" Pop said to Mike.

"You think I'm a coward, Pop?" I said. "Huh? Shoot me, then! I'm right here! Shoot me!"

I raised my hands in the air and gave Pop a perfect target. My father cocked the trigger of his gun.

"Put that gun down now!" Ma said while stepping back into the dining area. She stood between Pop and me, shielding me from the line of fire.

"Move!" Pop shouted.

"I ain't moving nowhere!" Ma said.

"Move, Ma!" I said while moving her to the side.

"If you hurt one hair on my baby's head, I swear to God in Heaven the next time you sleep will be the last time you sleep!"

"You stubborn, mean, old, hateful man!" I said. "What kind of a man would shoot his own son?"

While Pop was looking at me, Mike snuck behind him and snatched the gun out of his hand. Pop collapsed to the floor and lay still. My mother ran to him and held his hand. Pop appeared to be unconscious.

"Buddy!" Ma said. "Buddy!"

"Let him sleep it off, Ma," Mike said.

"You all right?" Alicia came running back into the living room and hugging me. "Oh my, God! What is wrong with your father?"

"I don't know," I said, sitting down at the table.

"Is everything okay in here?" Stacey asked.

"Yeah," Mike said. "Pop had a little too much to drink."

"We probably should be going," Ms. Carroll said.

"I'm sorry you had to witness this," I said.

"We understand," Ms. Hattley said. "We'll see you tomorrow in the office. Have a good night."

"Good night," I said with my head in my hands and Alicia rubbing my back. At least one thing good came out of Pop's spectacle. I was receiving affection from my wife again.

After my attorneys were gone, we were left to pull the pieces together of our shattered family. Ma asked for a wet towel to place on Pop's head. He looked so pitiful, drunk and passed out on my dining room floor.

Pitiful or not, this man just pulled a gun on me in my own house. A man who was supposed to love me. I am his son for Christ's sake, and he was going to take my life. I was pissed off and I wanted him out of my house. "I want him up and I want him out!"

"Let him sleep it off, Johnny," Mike said.

"I don't want that man in my house!" I said.

"Johnny," Mike said. "He's drunk. Let him sleep it off."

"He can sleep it off, but not in my house! Get him out of here!"

"If that's what you want, man," Mike said. "Grab his feet."

"I'm not touching him."

"You're tripping!" Mike said. "If you want Pop out of your house, you better grab his feet. Ma and Cynt are not picking him up."

"Who's going to help you take him into your house?" I asked.

"Nobody," Mike replied. "He'll sleep it off in the car. Now grab his feet."

I grabbed his feet and we carried him to Mike's truck. We lay him in the backseat and then I kissed my mother good-bye.

"You gotta stop letting him get away with this, Ma," I said.

"Everybody make mistakes, Johnny," Ma said.

"But does every father want to shoot his son?" I asked.

Ma didn't answer; she just rubbed my face and kissed me on the cheek. "Forgive him, son."

"Not this time, Ma. I can't."

CHAPTER TWENTY

The next morning we had a meeting in Stacey's office. I was embarrassed and wanted to apologize, but my attorneys were very understanding. They refused to discuss the night before and told me that all families had issues. That put me at ease slightly, but the nightmare of my father pulling a gun on me was another issue between the two of us which I would have to resolve within myself.

"We did a background investigation on Kimberly Mathis and Anise Lawrence," Stacey said. "Turns out they did know each other and that they knew each other very well."

"How?" I asked.

"It appears Ms. Mathis showed Ms. Lawrence the ropes on how to survive on the streets. Even though Ms. Lawrence became this big mega-star, she still found a way to stay in contact with Ms. Mathis. I don't know how, but she did."

"If Ms. Mathis lived on the streets then she would not have been hard to find. We may move away, but the streets don't," Ms. Carroll said. "Ms. Lawrence knew where to go. She must have really cared about that girl."

"Once we find Ms. Mathis, we'll find Ms. Lawrence's killer."

"Uh, no," I said. "Kimberly wouldn't have hurt a fly."

"I'm not saying she hurt anyone," Ms. Hattley said. "But if it wasn't her, she knows who it was."

"Whatever she saw that day is keeping her from coming forward," Ms. Carroll said.

"Let's just hope she's alive to speak when we find her," Stacey said.

"Do you think something's happened to her?" I asked.

"I don't know," Stacey said. "We have some of the best private investigators available looking for her and they've come up with nothing."

"I'm optimistic we'll find her, and find her alive," Ms. Hattley said. "And when we do, we'll break this case wide open."

"Yeah, but that's easier said than done," Stacey said.

"We're not going to get anything accomplished just sitting here, so let's get to work," Ms. Carroll said.

"We have two days now!" Stacey said. "Let's find that witness!"

I walked out of that room totally confident their investigators would find Kimberly and I would be exonerated!

❂❂❂

The next couple of days came and went but Kimberly was nowhere to be found. The next thing I knew the state was presenting its case and the judge decided there was enough evidence to move forward with my trial. My family was completely disappointed. My father did not attend the hearing. My bond remained intact and I was allowed to go home until my trial began.

I tried to conceal my anxiety about the trial by laughing and joking more than usual. My family and friends encouraged me to keep my head up saying that because I was innocent, I would be acquitted in the end.

My father went back home to Buena Vista and, against his wishes, my mother moved in with Alicia and me. She refused to leave me in my hour of need. Pop refused to speak to me, even to wish me good luck before he left. My heart was broken, but I had other issues of concern.

My attorneys made sure I was awarded a quick and speedy trial. The jury was selected and a trial date was set. The case received national attention and the media bombarded my house. I rarely went outside and was forced to conduct sessions with my patients over the telephone.

I asked Dr. Glover to temporarily come out of retirement to maintain my practice until my trial was over. He agreed, but told me convincingly that his retirement would be a short-lived one. Once my defense team presented our evidence, I would be found not guilty and free to continue with my life.

The prosecution went first. Their main evidence was the DNA results, as we expected. They also added in their case that I concealed any connection to the murder scene and obstructed justice even after Mike was arrested.

When it was time for my defense to present our case, we countered their DNA evidence with the admission of the affair to explain why my semen was found in Anise.

The prosecution stated that my brother was the witness who placed me at the crime scene. My defense responded that I went to the hotel to prevent my brother from becoming the next victim of Anise's manipulation.

The prosecution stated that I became angry when I found out my brother was going to the hotel to see Anise. They told the jury that I became jealous and, in a fit of rage, attacked Anise and killed her. My defense answered that Anise and I had already broken off the relationship.

The prosecution had their witnesses: the medical examiner; the limousine driver; and the jailhouse snitch. Tiny, my cellmate when I was first held under arrest, testified that I confessed to killing Anise while we were locked up. My attorneys argued that Tiny was an unreliable witness. He was a convicted con man who mysteriously had had his current sentence dismissed. Their last and final witness was their most damaging, Michael Forrester, my brother. He rebuffed their subpoena and vowed that he would be held in contempt of court before he became a witness for the state against me.

He knew that siblings were not protected by the Constitution from testifying against their siblings. Still, he refused to be a witness. He was determined to face jail time instead of betraying me. I convinced him to tell the truth because I was innocent and would be acquitted even with his testimony. Eventually, he realized that he was doing more harm than good by not testifying. His resistance gave the appearance that he had something to hide. He did testify for the state but as a hostile witness.

My defense team said that I arrived only minutes before Mike. Anise had been dead for hours and my whereabouts were accounted for during the afternoon of the murder until Mike and I met in Anise's hotel room. However, the prosecution made it perfectly clear that Anise could have been killed during the time that I was supposed to have been with her.

The most important witness of all was the witness not called to the stand: Kimberly Mathis. She had disappeared from the face of the earth and no one seemed to be able to find her. We didn't know what information she had, but we were certain that it was very important.

After three months, the prosecution and the defense rested their cases. I was happy to have it done and over. The jury deliberated for thirty-six hours. We thought it wouldn't take that long. All of the evidence presented by the state was circumstantial with the exception of my DNA, which was explained.

I had spent the last three months of my life in pure hell, and finally it was coming to a close. I was pissed off and becoming more and more aggravated at the thought of having been dragged through the court system for the benefit of the egos of an over-zealous police department.

Finally, Stacey called and told me the jury was back. Even though I knew the verdict would come back as not guilty, my heart was still beating through my chest.

The judge asked me to stand to hear the verdict. Stacey stood on my left, and Ms. Carroll and Ms. Hattley stood on my right. I looked behind me and I saw Alicia and Ma holding each other by the arms.

"Mr. Foreman," the judge said, "would you please read the verdict?"

"Yes, sir," the juror said. "We, the jury, find the defendant guilty of first-degree murder as charged in the indictment."

I heard the courtroom gasp, and then I heard the loud wail of Ma's cry. I looked over my shoulder and saw her collapse into Alicia's arms. Stacey and Ms. Carroll turned me toward the judge to hear my sentence. I could hear the moans of my mother and my wife echoing through the courtroom. Their pain overcame my fear as I waited to receive my sentence.

"Mr. Johnson Forrester," the judge said, "you have been found guilty by this jury of murder in the first degree. I am allowed by law to sentence you to life with the possibility of parole after a minimum of twenty-five years, or life without parole, or death by lethal injection. Although I would like nothing more than to give you the maximum sentence for this hideous crime, the laws of the state of Georgia prohibit me from administering that sentence if evidence does not support the premeditation of the crime."

I listened without reaction. I was stunned and rapidly approaching the state of being in shock.

"Mr. Forrester," the judge continued, "you will be sentenced to spend the remainder of your life in a state penitentiary without the possibility of parole! You are now turned over to the sheriff's department."

My attorneys hugged me and then the deputies came to lead me out of the courtroom.

"We are going to appeal this right away, Dr. Forrester!" Stacey said.

"This is only the first round," Ms. Hattley added. "We are not giving up!"

"This is not over by a long shot!" Ms. Carroll said.

I looked over my shoulder again and saw Mike fanning my mother. I continued to look at my crying wife and mother until they closed the door behind me.

❊❊❊

On the way to the prison, I sat on the bus in silent disbelief. I observed my fellow inmates and their demeanors. Some acted as if they were going back home, and then some acted as if they were going to hell. I don't know exactly how I looked to them, but inside, I preferred to be going to hell than to prison. Some would say there was no difference.

I had not accepted the fact that I was about to spend the rest of my life in prison. But as the bus pulled through the prison gate, reality started to set in for me. My heart began to beat faster and faster as the bus came to a stop.

Unlike on television, there were no raving maniacs screaming and shouting in anticipation of the new meat. We drove in front of a building and guards waited for us to pile off. One by one, we were escorted from the bus in handcuffs.

The first point of interest for the guards was to inform us that they should never be referred to as guards. They were to be called Correctional Officers, or C.O.s for short. I made sure I took note of that information.

The C.O.s led us to what was called the reception jail for classification. In the reception jail, the first point of action was the property process. This was where we were given our prison uniforms and other materials. Individually, our handcuffs were removed and we were strip-searched. They made us bend over and then did what was called a *"cheek-check."* We had to separate our butt cheeks while the C.O.s inspected our asses. Next, we were told to lift our testicles to have our genitalia inspected. They also checked our mouths for contraband, making us lift our tongues so that they could look around inside. Finally, they checked our feet, looking especially close at the bottom.

Cell Block J was considered the welcome center. All of the new inmates lived there until they were assigned permanent homes. Home is what the C.O.s called our permanent cells. We were assigned homes by the levels of our crimes. I was sent to a level five prison, which was the highest level for criminals in the state of Georgia. But due to the overcrowded inmate population of the state, lower level criminals were also sent there.

The prison levels ranged from one to five. Levels one and two were for crimes such as misdemeanor thefts or habitual minor offenses, although I never met a level one or two inmate while I was there. Level three was for felonious white collar and involuntary manslaughter criminals. Level Four was for violent offenders whose crimes included rape and manslaughter. Level Five was for first-degree murderers and problematic violent offenders inside of the walls. Some inmates entered the prison system at level one. But unavoidable jailhouse circumstances elevated them to level five and an impossible chance of ever seeing the outside again.

Because our bus was late arriving at the prison, it was too late for us to eat dinner. They gave us some old hot dogs and sent us on our way. We were processed, given our prison uniforms and put to bed. My first night was peaceful and no indication of the reality of prison life.

The next morning, I experienced my first encounter with the general prison population. I was a target for several reasons. One, I was a very large man and automatically viewed as a potential threat. Two, I was a former prison psychologist who may have prevented some of these criminals from becoming free men. Three, I was convicted of murdering a major celebrity. Some of the inmates considered a celebrity killer as a trophy for their penitentiary mantles.

As we walked in a double line for our first meal, the whistles and threats began to echo through the chow hall. I tried not to stare back at them, careful not to send any welcoming signals, but it was my nature to observe. I saw blacks sitting with blacks, Hispanics sitting with Hispanics, and whites sitting with whites.

Looking at them surreptitiously, I didn't imagine myself fitting in with any of the groups. I followed the man in front of me in line, step by step. Once our food was on our plates, I followed him to a table. The guy behind me did the same thing, following my lead.

Although I carefully took the time to observe my environment while I was walking through the chow line, I did not use the same inclination when it came to selecting my table. I didn't notice the uniformity of seating arrangements. I did not know that I was supposed to sit next to the man I stood next to in line. And apparently, neither did the guy behind me.

Like idiots, the poor sap behind me and I were just trying to fit in without incident on our first day of prison. Unfortunately, that plan was foiled when we found ourselves sitting at the Aryan Nation's table. The Aryan brothers quickly let us know that we were not wanted.

"What do you think you doing?"

The man was not very tall, but he was wide. His head was bald, and he had tattoos in every exposed part of his body. He had a big, thick moustache and bushy eyebrows. This was the first of many unfriendly confrontations with a man I would come to know as Tank.

"I would like to eat," I said respectfully.

"Not here you not," Tank barked.

Not wanting any trouble, I looked around the chow hall and didn't see an open seat. I did, however, see the black men staring at me, looking to see what my response would be.

It didn't take a genius to know that a man's reputation was a very valuable commodity in prison. But in my position, I knew that if I had tried to stand up to Tank then and there, I would have never made it to see the next morning.

"There's nowhere else to sit," I said pathetically.

"Then stand up!" Tank said. "Both of you! Stand up!"

I stared at Tank and didn't say a word, not because I was attempting some intimidation ploy, I was just so afraid that I couldn't speak. Tank jumped up and turned over my tray. The guy sitting next to him, Twinkle, turned over the tray of the black guy sitting next to me. The black guy next to me stood to his feet. If the C.O.'s saw, they pretended they didn't.

"If you two tryin' to make a name for yourself, you picked the wrong one," Twinkle said in his high-pitched Southern accent.

Twinkle was small, probably half of Tank's size. He was skinny, with a long ponytail. There were several teeth missing in his mouth. His moustache and beard were scraggly. He seemed to be a bit of the opposite of Tank and the other large bald guys sitting at the table. I didn't find him threatening at all; he was more irritating than intimidating.

"Stand up!" Tank said.

I looked at Tank and slowly stood up. I could feel the man standing next to me shake with fear. Neither one of us knew what to do, so we just stood there. Tank and his group went on about their business as if we weren't even there.

A C.O. noticed us standing with our breakfast splattered on the floor and spoke through the public address system. Afraid of being ambushed, the C.O.'s did not come into the general population unless we were on the ground and under control or they had a swat unit available for combat.

"What happened there?" the C.O. said, calling me out.

"It was an accident," I yelled back.

"Well, pick it up," the C.O. yelled back.

"Okay," I said.

I got on my knees and started to put the food back on my tray. I didn't want the C.O. to think that I was going to be a troublesome inmate. While I was picking up the food, I looked over at the groups of black men and all of them seemed to be looking at me. Some were even laughing.

By the time I finished cleaning the mess up it was time for us to leave. We filed out the same way we'd filed in. I kept my eyes straight ahead and didn't mumble a word.

Lunch and dinner were a little better, I suppose, since I wasn't publicly humiliated. I happened to be fortunate enough to sit with the black guys but they weren't very hospitable, either. They practically ignored me. They talked around me, above me, and through me, but not one word was said to me.

I was sleeping well that night until I was awakened by the sounds of C.O.s rummaging through a cell a few bars down from mine. I didn't know at the time what was going on, nor did I care, but I would find out the next morning.

On our way to breakfast, the guy who was behind me the morning before was not in line, the reason being that he'd taken his life in the middle of the night. Suicide happens the most in Cell Block J when inmates first arrive. They try all forms of preventative measures, but somehow, some way, someone always manages to wake up dead.

That particular inmate should have been diagnosed as suicidal before he got off the bus. Stricter measures should have been taken in his case. He showed all of the signs of lethal depression. In my opinion, his death was not suicide but assisted murder by the state.

Within a couple of days, I was given a psychological examination, a job working in the law library and a position as a tutor. I was also given my permanent home address, cell number five twenty-four.

The first time I met my celly, or cellmate, Stone, I tried to make conversation with him. He was not very interested. He had only one thing to say and he meant it.

"Hey, what's going on, brother?" I said, extending my hand to shake his.

"The bottom bunk is mine," Stone said, ignoring my handshake.

"Okay," I said, tossing my stuff on the top bunk, trying not to create another confrontation. "So what is it like in here, man?"

Stone lay on the bottom bunk and said nothing. He was considered to be what was called a shot-caller, or the head of a gang. When something went down between rival gangs, the shot-callers were the ones who got together to work things out or fire things up.

Stone was one of the top weightlifters in the joint, too. That guy's biceps were as big as my thighs. No bullshit! I thought to myself, what kind of criminal machines was our prison system creating? He was a monster!

He stood about six-two or six-three, bright-skinned with a wild Afro. He had a thin moustache with a long pointed beard. He had light-brown eyes and white straight teeth. He was not like most of the hothead shot-callers in prison. He was about business. If you didn't mess with his shit, he didn't mess with you. But if he saw you as a threat, he didn't ask questions, he kicked ass. He eventually took me under his wing, but not at first.

My first night was not my best night with Stone. I jumped on the top bunk and took a deep breath. I stared at the ceiling, still not believing that I was in jail. As evening became night,

I became restless. I tossed and turned all night. Stone became irritated with my constant movement and kicked the shit out of the bottom of my bunk. Needless to say I didn't even open my asshole to fart for the rest of the night.

Later on, I was given what is called *"twenty and four."* That meant that I was locked in my cell twenty hours a day. I was allowed one hour for work, two hours for meals, and one hour for recreation. Every minute and every second of each hour was accounted for.

It would take a week before Stone initiated dialogue between us. Stone and his boys, as he called them, saw Tank and his Aryan brothers confront me again and again. I ignored them as much as I could, but sometimes they made it impossible. As Stone's celly, how I allowed the Aryan brothers to treat me could affect him as well.

"How long you gon' let them white boys make a fool outta you?"

"What do you want me to do?" I said. "Fight 'em all?"

"You gon' have to do something," Stone said. "Tank ain't just picking on you, man. He's going to make a point outta you."

"A point? What kind of point?"

"He's going to kill you," Stone said, "or he's going to kiss you."

"What do you mean, kiss me?"

"You know what I mean," Stone said. "This prison."

"Why would he want to kiss me?" I asked very nervously.

"Because you act like a bitch," Stone said, "so he's going to treat you like a bitch."

"Oh, hell no, man," I said. "Nobody is kissing me."

"You got two choices," Stone said. "You can fight them off of your ass, or you can bend over politely and give it to 'em. Either way, they're going to get it!"

"Why man?" I shouted. "What the hell I ever do to them?"

"You showed fear."

"This is crazy, man!" I said before lying back in my bed.

"You believe in God?"

"Yeah, of course," I answered.

"You better pray that God get you before Tank get you."

I stayed up all night thinking about Tank and his Aryan brothers. I knew I had no protection. When they got ready to get me, they would get me. And there was nothing I could do.

I became so upset that I unknowingly bit a hole through my blanket that night. I was embarrassed to think that I was so afraid of another man that I allowed myself to display such cowardice.

In order for me to deal with my fear of this man, I would have to resign myself to the concept that I would probably die in prison. For death was better than being a coward.

In our cell, Stone and I began to have philosophical conversations. Our perception of one another was that we were polar opposites. I was passive and non-confrontational when threatened. Stone was aggressive and initiated confrontation when he felt threatened, even when we disagreed in conversation. He never displayed any physical aggression, but his words were powerful and definite. He said what he meant, and he meant what he said.

Outside of our cell, Stone would not speak to me publicly because I had not achieved any respect from anybody. I was one of the largest men on our cellblock yet with the least amount of respect. To associate himself with me would be to associate himself with a bitch.

Tank's aggression increased more and more every time he saw me. He began to slap me on my ass when I walked past him.

Since I had not been accepted by any of the groups, I was all alone to defend myself against the Aryan Nation.

One day, I was placing books back on the shelves at the law library. The bathroom was located in the rear of the library. When I pushed my cart toward the back of the library, Tank and five or six of his brothers came out of nowhere and threw a bag over my head.

They took me into the bathroom and slammed me against the wall. I couldn't see any of them. But I knew who it was. I tried to fight back but it was no use; there were too many of them. They pushed me down and pressed my face into the bathroom floor. My arms were held above my head and my legs were stretched apart. I felt my pants being ripped by some sort of sharp object.

I could hear voices but I couldn't make out what they were saying. They started to spank my ass and fondle my manhood through my underwear. Next, I felt my underwear being cut and sliced and snatched off of me. I started to kick and fight, not knowing what to expect next. I refused to accept the reality of being raped. I had prepared myself for death, but not rape!

But then as suddenly as it began, it ended. I could hear the sound of wrestling and they seemed to be arguing amongst themselves. I heard scrambling and the sound of the door opening and closing over and over. After it sounded as if they were gone, and I was alone, I snatched the bag off of my head and pulled up what was left of my pants. I continued to lie on the floor in total embarrassment. Someone knocked on the door and I sat up and leaned against the wall.

"Yeah, give me a minute!" I shouted, trying to make my ripped clothes look halfway presentable.

"Here!" a voice said from outside of the door, throwing a pair of pants inside the bathroom to me.

When I walked out there was no one there. I did not report the incident, which meant I had to stay at the library the remainder of my two hours.

When I got to my cell, I jumped on my bunk and didn't say a word to Stone.

"Everything all right up there, Doc?" Stone asked.

Doc was the name Stone nicknamed me.

"Yeah," I said. "Everything's cool."

"You know you gon' have to kill him, don't you?"

"Kill who?" I asked, knowing exactly who he was talking about.

"Tank," Stone said. "You either gotta kill him or he gon' kill you."

I lay there listening to Stone and asking myself why God would allow this to happen to me. What did I ever do to deserve this? Cheat?

CHAPTER TWENTY-ONE

Like most everyone, I was always cautious of being killed by some nut job. But for the first time in my life, I was more afraid of taking a life than having my life taken. I tried to remain civilized in my mind. I tried to live with the hope that my appeal would be heard and my case would be retried or dismissed before I was killed, or before I was forced to kill. I didn't run out of hope, but unfortunately, I did run out of time.

"I can't believe we're having this discussion," I said.

"Listen, man," Stone said, "they were about to make you into their bitch in that library today. If we hadn't been there today, your asshole woulda been ripped to shreds, babyboy!"

"So that was you?"

"Yeah, man."

"Damn!" I said. "That's embarrassing."

"Until you do something to change it, that's your life."

"Shit," I said, hitting the wall. "Thanks, man."

"Let me tell you how this works," Stone said while getting out of his bunk. "I don't want thanks, Doc."

"Anything I can do for you, Stone, I'll do it. I can't thank you enough, brother."

"I don't want your gratitude, man," Stone said. "Gratitude can't get you shit in here! I want protection money."

"Money?" I asked. "How much money?"

"How much do you think your life is worth?"

"I got money!" I said, trying to assure Stone that I would pay anything he wanted to keep Tank off my back. "How much money will it take?"

"How much? I'll leave that up to you," Stone said. "I guess as long as you alive, you know you payin' the right price. And when you find a knife in your back, or a long, hard prick in your ass, you know you didn't pay enough."

"So will that be check or cash?" I said sarcastically.

"Straight cash!" Stone joked back. "But on the real, man. I can only do what I can do. I can't give you twenty-four hour protection. The Aryan brothers ain't scared of me or no other niggah in here. All I did today was buy you some time. If you want to get them off your back for good, you gon' have to take Tank out, man. That's all it is to it!"

"Man," I said frustrated. "How does a man just take another man's life?"

"If you don't know, ask Tank when he's taking yours," Stone replied.

❁❁❁

A couple of days later, I was visited by Stacey, Ms. Carroll, and Ms. Hattley. They told me the appeal had been filed and we were waiting for the results. Like always, they were honest with me and told me the odds were not in our favor. They also told me they were not going to stop searching for Kimberly.

A couple of weeks later, I received my first visit from Alicia and Brittany. Although seeing them gave me a reason to want to fight for my freedom, it was also very heartbreaking not to be able to kiss and touch them. I was not allowed conjugal visits, so just looking at Alicia made my manhood rise instantly.

I played with Brittany through the glass, placing my hand on the window and pretending to tickle her. She laughed until it was time for them to leave and then she started to cry. I felt so guilty for my baby's tears. I had to get out! I had to live long enough to get out of that prison and hold my family again. No matter what it took!

I waved good-bye to them as they were leaving. As the C.O. escorted me out of the visiting room, I could feel my heart changing inside. The warmth of my family's love had made my heart cold to any son of a bitch that stood between me and getting the hell out of that prison.

When I got back to my cell, Stone wasn't there. I sat on his bunk, which was a definite no-no, and waited for him to come. Frankly, I didn't give a shit anymore. I needed information from him and I didn't want to go through a lot of bullshit to get it. I knew that by sitting on his bed I would capture his attention. If he wanted to fight, we would fight. But one way or the other, he was going to give me the information I needed.

Stone stared at me as he walked into the cell. He put his hands on his hips and then continued to stare at me. He turned his head to the left and looked away from me as if he was trying to control himself. "You know you know better than that, Doc."

"I need some information from you."

"What do that have to do with you sittin' your nasty ass on my bunk?"

"I want you to know I'm serious, man," I said.

"You know there's other ways to get my attention than sittin' your stankin' ass on my bunk, man! Now get yo' ass up!"

"How can I get a shank, Stone?"

"What?" Stone asked, very surprised. "And I ain't gon' tell you again, get the hell out of my bunk! We ain't that damn cool!"

I moved from Tank's bed and sat on the floor.

"Now," Tank said. "How much money you got?"

"However much I need."

"My man." Tank smiled. "We gon' be playing baseball tonight. Sit over by the fence. Have your hands behind your back and don't say a word."

"Oh," I said. "Okay." I didn't exactly know what was going to happen but I was going to follow the instructions to the tee.

Later on at the baseball field, I did as Stone instructed and I felt an object being placed in my hand. I couldn't and didn't want to see who it was. But that was the easiest part. The hard part was getting the object from the field to my cell without being caught.

I was too nervous to try it then so I buried it in a specific spot and would try again when I got up the nerve. Stone explained to me later how to get the shank into the cell without being detected. I thought he was joking at first, but he was very serious. He told me that there were only two ways to get it in undetected, through my stomach or through my ass. I went with my stomach. He then explained that my stomach was more risky because of the vital organs I could damage. Perhaps he was right, but it was a chance I had to take.

I had to disassemble the shank, piece by piece, sitting at the fence with my hands behind my back. That took nearly a week. And then I had to swallow it piece by piece, and shit it out in my cell. During that time, Tank and the Aryan brothers began to apply pressure on me again.

Once I had all of the pieces in my cell, I reassembled it in one night. I was still hoping against hope that there would not be a confrontation between the Aryans and myself, but hope is for fools. They caught me in the library again and beat me senseless.

Stone and his boys were not around to stop them that time. I stayed in the infirmary for almost three weeks. I couldn't write, nor was I able to call Alicia while I was there. I didn't know if Alicia knew what had happened to me and when I asked the C.O.s to contact my attorneys to let them know, they laughed at me. Getting the shit beat out of you in prison didn't get you any sympathy. When I was healthy enough to go back to my cell, I went back mad as hell.

"Why did you go through all that to get that thang if you too scared to use it?" Stone asked.

"Where were you?" I snapped.

"I told you!" Stone said. "I can't watch your back twenty-four hours a day, niggah! You gon' have to protect yourself and stop actin' so damn scary!"

"I'm not scared, man."

"They think you scared," Stone said. "And they gon' keep on whoopin' yo' ass until they take yo' ass!"

"They're not taking anything else from me, man! Not any more!"

"If you ain't scared, act like you ain't scared, niggah! Handle yo' damn business!" Stone replied.

After that night, instead of being stalked by Tank, I started to follow him. I got his routine down to a science. I knew every second he spent alone, even the moment when he slipped off to take a private shit. One day when he was coming back from recreation, I hid in the bathroom and waited for him to come in. The bathrooms were the only areas where cameras were prohibited. I wasn't certain that I had the heart to kill him, but I wanted to hurt him for what he had done to me. Getting my ass kicked was the last straw.

I waited for him and I became nervous when I heard him come in, coughing and hissing from his smoke-filled lungs. He sat down in the stall next to me and started to shit.

My heart started to beat fast. I pulled the shank from inside the toilet where I had hid earlier and clutched it tightly in my hand. I took a few deep breaths and slowly stood on the stool. I looked over the top of the stall's wall and saw Tank sitting there with his pants around his ankles.

I wondered what would happen once the shank pierced his skin. Would he yell? Would he scream? Would he die? Would someone hear him and I'd get caught holding the smoking gun? Through my contemplation, Tank noticed me standing above him and yelled at me.

"What the hell you doing up there?" Tank said.

I stared back at him, but I was too afraid to speak. My adrenaline started to rush and I clutched the shank in my hand.

"I'm gon' kill you, niggah!" Tank shouted, wiping his ass and pulling up his pants.

Without even thinking, I leaped over the stall on top of Tank. I slammed him against the walls of the stalls several times. I covered his mouth and slung him to the floor. I trapped him between the toilet and the wall, slamming his head over and over. I don't recall too much after that. I do remember grunting as I began to plunge the shank into his chest. I continued to stab him repeatedly, becoming angrier at each powerful stroke.

"Die!" I shouted. "Die! Die, niggah, die!"

"Ugh!" Tank said, gasping for breath.

"Hey! Get outta here, man!"

I heard the voice behind me, but I continued to drive the shank deeper into Tank's body.

"You got him, Doc!" Stone shouted. "Come on, let's go!"

Stone grabbed me and snatched the shank out of my hand. He pulled me out of the stall and pushed me toward the exit. On our way out of the bathroom, several C.O.s ran in and threw us to the floor. They cuffed our hands and feet and dragged us away. As they were dragging us side by side, Stone mouthed the words, "Don't say nothing!"

They separated us and grilled us on what had happened in the bathroom. They kept trying to get me to confess. But I wouldn't say a word. I wasn't nervous! I wasn't scared! I didn't give a damn! What did I have to lose?

I knew Stone would be just as stubborn as me or more so. They locked me in solitary confinement. The room was small and dark, but neither the darkness nor the size of the room had any effect on me. Solitary confinement, or The Hole as it was called, was nothing different from being in Patient Number Five's attic.

Each day they asked me to confess and each day I told them to kiss my ass. And then one day the door came open and they asked me to stand to my feet. The light was extremely bright and I had to keep my eyes closed for a while.

I was questioned one more time about Tank's murder and that was it. They asked me to corroborate Stone's story. He had admitted to killing Tank. He told them about the ongoing feud between him and the Aryans. He told them he was blindfolded and attacked in the bathroom of the library, and that Tank was attempting to attack him again and so he defended himself.

When they asked me if I knew anything about his story, even though it sounded as if I was being taken off the hook, I refused to answer. They could have been making it up and trying to get information on him. Eventually, I was released back to cell number five twenty-four and Stone was given an additional five years to his life sentence.

A week later, Stone was released from the hole and returned to our cell. At the first opportunity, I asked him why he'd taken the heat.

"I don't get it, man," I said. "Why did you take the rap for me?"

"Because you have a family out there," Stone said. "Despite what these people might think about us, we're still humans who miss our families. In here, sometimes the thought of having a family is the only thing that separates us from animals. We fight. We kill. It's the survival of the fittest up in here, man. But when I look at that picture you got above your bed and I see that fine-ass wife and that little angel of yours, I can't help but wish I was you. See, in here, I'm the shit! But on the outside, I ain't shit! 'Cause on the outside, I ain't got shit! You do. So what else could I do?"

"Man, I'll never forget what you did for me," I said. "I'm going to repay you."

"If you want to pay me back, get out of here! You don't belong in here, Doc. And when you get out, you gon' have to forget what happened in here. You have to go back to being who you was before you got in here."

"That's just it. I can't go back to being who I was!" I said. "Too much has happened. I'm not the same man. I'm a much different man. I'm a murderer! I'm a cold-blooded killer."

"Don't be so dramatic, Doc," Stone said. "You ain't no killer!

You had to kill, but you ain't no killer! You a man. That's all, a man."

"Yeah, but I'm a different man."

"Okay, you a different man. Prison will change every man in some way," Stone said. "But if you gon' be a different man, be a better man."

As the weeks turned to months, I adjusted more to the day-to-day routine of being in the joint. Stone kept me near and far at the same time. He kept me close enough to watch my back and far enough to keep me out of his jailhouse business. I became one of the boys without having to make their commitments. Once you were in their organization, there was no getting out alive. Stone knew that, so as long as he was the shot-caller I was treated as an honorary soldier. I didn't know what was going on and they didn't tell me. But being Stone's celly made me connected, respected and protected.

❂❂❂

Fighting the urge of depression, the thought of being home with my family went from desperation to motivation. I had to get out for them. I started to use the law library for my own legal office. Stacey and I worked day and night looking for the one clue to set me free.

Stacey came to visit one day and she brought a special surprise, my brother Mike. I talked to him through the glass and the news that he gave me really lifted my spirits. We talked as long as my time allotted. Stacey didn't say much; perhaps she knew my morale was more important than discussing the legalities of the case that day.

"I have a surprise for you, Dr. Forrester," Stacey said. "I have added another attorney to your defense team."

"Okay," I said, waiting for my mysterious guest.

I started to smile when I saw Mike walk around the corner and into my clear view.

"Man, what the hell are you doing here?" I said, giving Mike the fisted pound sign from behind the glass.

"I am here to join your legal team."

"You got to be kidding me."

"No, little brother, I'm not."

"Have you ever worked on a case before?" I asked. "Especially a murder case?"

"Nope!" Mike said emphatically. "But I do have a law degree and I have passed the bar. So I am bona fide."

"Bona fide, maybe," I said, "but what about qualified?"

"Stacey seems to think I'm qualified."

"How?"

"Because you need your family, man. And as your attorney, I could have more private time with you without all of this," Mike said, pointing to the window between us.

"Well, welcome to the team, Mr. Forrester!" I said. "What is your first action as my attorney?"

"My first action is to get you to keep your head up."

"And how do you do that?" I asked, challenging my brother's statement.

"Don't worry about that," Mike said. "Just keep your head up and your ass down."

I realized Mike was joking but he had no idea what I had experienced with the Aryan Nations. I tried to laugh along, but I couldn't. I didn't want him to be concerned, but he picked up my uneasiness.

"Hey, man," Mike said, "everything is okay in here with you, right?"

"Yeah, I'm fine," I said, still trying to manage a smile.

"Nothing has happened to you since you've been in here, right?" Mike seemed very concerned. "You haven't been touched or anything?"

"No man," I said, "I've been tried, but I haven't been touched."

"You sure?"

"Don't worry about me, man. You're going to get tried in a place like this when you first get here. That's just how it is. But you have to man-up and take on whatever comes your way."

"Damn, man, you don't sound like the same Johnny I know."

"I'm not," I said. I was very serious and Mike knew it.

"I don't know if that's good or bad."

"To be honest, Mike," I said. "Neither do I."

❀❀❀

The next week I had another visit from Mike. This time he brought along another special visitor with him. As I sat behind the glass window waiting for Mike to come through the door, my eyes opened wide and the hugest smile a person could have filled my face.

Dressed in her Easter Sunday dress, wig, and hat was Ma. I wanted to burst through that glass and wrap my arms around her. She sat down and picked up the phone. I had to navigate for her because she thought there were buttons she needed to punch.

"Ma, how are you?" I asked, still not believing I was looking at her.

"I'm fine, son. How are you?"

"I'm fine, Ma," I said, "I'm just fine."

"I know you didn't hurt that girl, Johnny! I don't care what anybody say, I know my boys! I know you would never hurt anybody like that!"

My mother was right, the Johnny she knew would never hurt anyone. But the Johnny I had become would kill a man to save his own life. Perhaps, given the circumstances, any man would have done what I did.

"Your father sent his love," Ma said.

"No he didn't, Ma," I said. "You don't have to make up things for him any longer. That man is never going to love me as his son and that's okay. I can't change how he feels so I have to move on."

"Your father is funny acting, but he does love you."

"Ma, that man threatened to kill me! His son! His own flesh and blood! People who love each other don't act like that!"

"You stop talking like that, Johnson Forrester!" Ma snapped. "That man is your father and you better respect him!"

"I'm sorry, Ma," I said. "I don't mean to disrespect Pop, but try to imagine this from my point of view. I have been seeking that man's approval my entire life and he has done nothing but put me down and expressed nothing but disapproval. Never a kind word! Never a pat on the back! Nothing! But all the time he sings Mike's praises."

"There's two sides to every story, Johnny."

"What other side could there be, Ma?" I asked, desperately wanting an explanation. "Huh? Please tell me. Anything!"

"Your father is from another time. Men didn't talk and act the way you do back in his day. He don't know how to take you."

"What do you mean, don't know how to take me?"

"For a long time your father thought you liked boys," Ma said.

"What?" I asked. "Are you kidding me?"

"Your father don't know no better," Ma said. "In his day, men didn't express themselves the way you do."

"Ma, how could Pop think I was gay?"

"Because you was always so sensitive."

"And?" I asked. I was becoming very upset, but where I would normally allow my emotions to take over, I stopped and composed myself. "Ma, I cried and I was afraid because Pop bullied me, not because he thought I liked boys. He was always pushing me around. Challenging me for no reason. And then he would push you around when you tried to get him off of my back."

"Did you ever stop to think that maybe he was hard on you because he loved you?"

"Mama," I said, "I can understand if Pop thought I was a little soft, and he wanted to toughen me up, but he was on my back every day, day and night and he never let up! He never got off of my back!"

"Just like I never got off of Michael's back!" Ma shouted.

Ma looked around and calmed her voice. "Your father was no harder on you than I was on Michael. As soon as you came out of my womb, I felt something special for you. Something I didn't feel for Michael. I'm not saying I loved you more, but I loved you differently."

Although my mother had only a high school education, she was very wise and logical. She had a knack for articulating a point to anybody on any educational level and making that particular person understand.

"Michael used to always say that I favored you. And I gave you all of my attention." Ma chuckled. "And he was right. Your father thought the same thing. He thought I wasn't allowing you to face the world like a man. And he was right, too. I had to learn to let you go."

"But, Ma," I said, "Pop had no right putting his hands on you because he was trying to make me a man."

"What?" Ma asked. "Your father never laid a hand on me."

"Yes he did!" I said. "I remember him pushing you around."

"I don't know where you got that from, but it never happened."

"Ma, are you sure?" I asked. "Maybe you've forgotten, or blocked it out, but I distinctly remember you and Pop fighting."

"Yeah, that's true, we did fight. But he ain't never laid a hand on me. He yelled at me and I yelled at him. Most of the time, I was yelling at him. I'm sure a lot of his frustration with you shoulda been aimed at me. He thought I was not treating you and Michael the same, and Michael thought it, too. And it took me a while to understand how much I was hurting Michael, until I saw how much your father was hurting you."

"So what exactly are you telling me, Ma?"

"I guess I'm saying that if you're going to be mad at your father, you're going to have to be mad at me, too. 'Cause I'm just as responsible for what happened as he is."

"No you're not," I said. "You never yelled and screamed at me. Pop did!"

"And that's the problem. If I woulda been as hard on you as I was on Michael, your father would not have been so hard on you. Do you understand, son?"

"Not really, but I'm trying," I said. "Mike has never said anything to me about the way you treated him. Not one word."

"That's because he's like his father. And you're like me. They handle things a little different from us."

"What's the difference?"

"Well, we laugh when we happy, and we cry when we sad. We express ourselves when we feel emotions," Ma said. "And they try not to express themselves when they feel emotions. Sometimes family members are just that, family. It don't mean that they're the same. We're different, but the same. It's as simple as that."

Again, Ma used the statement of "different but the same". That is where I picked up that line of thinking. By listening to her, I began to understand my relationship with Pop. Not clearly, but I was beginning to see past his rough exterior and understand that our main issue was lack of communication, and not lack of love.

"You know you gave us a lot of trouble growing up, don't you?" Ma said.

"Yeah, I know." I chuckled.

"But there wasn't one time that your father didn't stand by your side, now was it?"

"If by standing by my side you mean, yelling and screaming, then you're right."

"You deserved to be screamed at," Ma said. "You was wrong! But every time you got kicked out of school, he took off work and went up to that school and made sure you got back in. When you got caught stealing at Al's Market, he went up there and paid for whatever it was you stole and they let you back in. When you went to college and you needed money, your father worked extra jobs so that you could have it. He never did that for Michael. But he did it for you."

"He was my father, he was supposed to do that."

"He was Michael's father, too, but he never had to do it for him!" Ma snapped. I could tell that she was becoming angry, so I backed off.

"Ma, I understand what you're saying. But these types of issues need time to heal."

"You can't wait on time, Johnny," Ma said. "Time ain't promised!"

"I understand, Ma. But it took time for this to develop, it will take time for it to be resolved."

"You always thinking like a psychiatrist, Johnny," Ma said. "It's been too long already. While you're sitting in here you need to read your Bible and learn forgiveness."

"Okay, Ma," I said. "I love you, Ma."

"And I love you, too, son. I guess I better go and let your brother come and talk to you a spell."

Ma stood and waved good-bye. As she turned away to leave, I knocked on the window to get her attention. I pointed to the phone and gestured for her to pick up. She sat down and put the phone to her ear.

"Ma?"

"Yeah, baby?"

"Tell Pop I love him," I said softly.

"I'll do that," Ma said with a big grin across her face. "I'll do that!"

"Good-bye, Ma," I said and blew her a kiss.

"Good-bye, baby. I love you and don't you ever forget it."

"I love you, too."

My mother smiled and walked away. I went back to my cell with the hope and excitement of sitting down with my mother and father and resolving all of our family issues. Not as a mental health clinician, but as a son.

CHAPTER TWENTY-TWO

The next week I received another visit from Mike, and this time he brought along Alicia and Brittany. When I saw them walk through the door with Mike, I almost leaped out of my chair from joy.

Brittany ran to me as she always did, putting her hands on the window so that we could play with each other. I noticed Alicia and Mike lagging behind. Neither one of them was smiling. I automatically knew that bad news was going to accompany their sad faces.

I was expecting news about my appeal, but obviously it wasn't going to be the news I was expecting. So I prepared myself for the worst. Brittany picked up the telephone first.

"Hi, Daddy!" Brittany said.

"How's my baby?" I asked.

"I'm fine!" Brittany said, rubbing her hands up and down on the window, trying to catch mine as I moved it around.

We played for a while and then Alicia picked up the telephone. She stared at me and then shook her head, handing the phone to Mike. She blew me a kiss and mouthed the words, '*I love you with all of my heart.*' I mouthed the words back to her and she took Brittany by the hand and walked out in tears. Mike slowly picked up the phone and began to speak.

"What's going on?" I asked, forcing a smile. "It can't be good, Alicia can't even talk to me."

"Johnny," Mike said, "I have some bad news."

I looked in Mike's eyes and saw them filling up with tears. It didn't seem normal.

"Hey, man." I chuckled. "It's all right, just come on out and say it. We can just start over from square one and try again."

"Johnny," Mike said, pausing with his mouth wide open, "Ma died this morning."

Although I heard the words Mike spoke, and I knew he wouldn't lie or joke about our mother, I could not comprehend what he was saying. "What?"

"Ma's dead."

"Don't play with me, Mike!"

"Johnny," Mike said. "She's gone!"

"No, I just saw Ma last week and she was doing fine. You must be mistaken. Go call her!"

"I can't, Johnny."

I stood up and laughed. "Go call her right now, Mike! I'm telling you, she's all right!"

"I'm sorry, Johnny."

"Mike! Please, go call her, man!" I shouted, accepting what Mike was saying and then smashing the telephone against the window. "Just go call her and bring her down here to see me! I just need to see her one more time, man!"

A C.O. walked over to me and tried to get me to quiet down. I snatched away from him and continued to yell at Mike through the window. The C.O. called for backup as I became more unruly. I slammed the phone against the wall, smashing it to bits.

"Okay, that's it!" the C.O. said as he and another C.O. restrained me.

"Johnny! Johnny!" Mike yelled. "Calm down!"

"Let me go!" I shouted, pushing them away. "Mike, go get Ma! Please! Go get Ma!"

Mike could do nothing but watch as the C.O.s dragged me away. I continued to yell and scream until they put me in wrist straps. When I got back to my cell, I told Stone about my mother and I was going to try to get a temporary release to attend her funeral.

Stone warned me that he had no knowledge of a convicted murderer in that prison ever being released to attend the funeral of any relative. That was the warden's rule. The warden was strict, and she showed no favoritism. She implemented rules that were met by every inmate. The rules varied based on the crime and behavior of the inmate.

She rewarded everyone based on anticipated merits. If you achieved those merits then you were granted certain privileges, and being in prison was not as bad as it could have been. But if you didn't abide by her rules, prison could become unbearable. I abided by the rules and stayed out of trouble and received the warden's privileges, but unfortunately, attending funerals was not one of those privileges.

As Stone had warned, my request to attend my mother's funeral was denied and I fell into a state of depression. I stayed in my cell, refusing recreation time and meals. I was content with accepting my years in prison and dealing with the circumstances that came with it. Stone, of all people, became the voice of reason and got on my ass about not fighting for my freedom.

"Hey, Doc, is that it? Is that all you got?"

"Yup," I said. "That's all I got."

"I had you figured to be a man of your word, Doc."

"This is prison. Who gives a damn about a man and his word?"

"So I guess all those speeches you used to give your patients coming out of prison was psychological bullshit, huh?"

"Man, you don't know anything about me!" I said, jumping out of my bunk.

"I know you a self-righteous punk-ass doctor who used to try brainwashing ex-cons into thinking they was somebody when you know they ain't!" Stone said, jumping out of his bunk and yelling in my face.

"Get out of my face!" I said before pushing Stone on top of his bed.

"BITCH!" Stone rushed me and slammed me into the wall.

We tussled for a while, with no one really gaining an advantage to do the other any considerable harm. We kept at it until we were out of breath, sitting against the wall.

"You want some more, niggah?" Stone said with his chest rising up and down from exhaustion.

"You want some more?" I said before barely enunciating my sentence and hoping to God he didn't.

"Hell, nawl." Stone chuckled.

"Me neither," I said, standing up and then reaching a hand down to Stone.

"So, you ready to stop whining like a little bitch and get yo' ass outta here?" Stone said.

"We've done all we could," I said. "I don't see a way out of here, Stone."

"I know you hurting because of your mama, Doc, but you can't let that shit get to your head. You gotta get out of here!"

"Don't let that shit go to my head?" I asked. "That's easy for you to say, your mother didn't just die."

"No, she didn't *just* die," Stone said, "But since I've been locked up my mother *and* my father have died! I have two small children that I can't even talk to because their grandparents won't let me. I got a sixteen-year-old daughter out there and I don't even know where she is! So don't tell me what's easy for me!"

"Damn, man," I said, "I didn't know."

"That's right! You don't know! Yo' situation ain't no worse than nobody else in here! We all in prison! And we all want to get out! So stop feeling sorry for yourself and do something about it!"

"What can I do in here?" I shouted.

"What if I told you that I can find that witness y'all looking for?"

"Kimberly?" I asked. "How can you find her in here?"

"Don't worry about that, Doc. The streets ain't never far from the joint, man. I can find her."

"How? Where is she?"

"It's like this, Doc," Stone said. "I think you a good man and I respect you for it, but to be honest, I don't care no more about a good man than I do about a bad man. I can't afford to."

"Okay," I said, trying to understand where Stone was going with his conversation. "What's your point?"

"I ain't just been looking out for you 'cause I like you. That ain't how it work."

"Yeah, I know, I've been paying you to watch my back!"

"That ain't why I did what I did either."

"So what are you saying, Stone?"

"I told you I got a little girl out there, Doc," Stone said. "I haven't seen her since her mother died. They put her in a foster home and I lost contact with her. That little girl is what keeps me sane within this insanity."

"What do you want from me?" I asked.

"I need you to get out of here and find my child. Right here! Right now! If you promise to find my daughter and bring her to me, I'll have that witness in your lawyer's office first thing tomorrow morning."

"I need to know how you plan on finding her when no one else can?" I asked, starting to believe him.

"Trust me on this, Doc," Stone said, extending his hand for me to shake. "The less you know, the better it is. Now, do we have a deal?"

"Deal," I said, shaking Stone's hand.

"Pack your bags!" Stone said after lying down on his bunk.

❈❈❈

The next day, the day before my mother's funeral, I was told that my lawyers were waiting for me in the warden's office. Two C.O.s escorted me with wrist and ankle cuffs.

My legal team was sitting with smiles on their faces as I walked through the door. My cuffs were taken off and the warden explained that I needed to sign the documents for me to be processed and released immediately.

I didn't know what to say. It seemed too unreal. Stacey directed me to sign where I needed to sign. After signing the forms, the two C.O.s escorted me back to my cell where I gathered my personal possessions. Stone was nowhere around. I was then taken to the exiting unit where I was to be processed and released into the custody of my legal team. Just like that!

I don't know what had happened within the previous twenty-four hours leading up to the moment that I was released, but whatever happened, I was grateful. In twenty-four hours I went from a man destined to die in prison to a free man not knowing where his next step would lead him.

As I walked out of the prison gates, I looked back and thought about the life I was leaving behind. I was a different man with a different outlook on life. I didn't know what to expect, but I was ready for it.

When we got in the car, my attorneys explained to me that my release could possibly be temporary. My case still had to be heard before a state judge to see if the district attorneys had enough evidence to prosecute me again. They were confident the charges would be dropped and I would be a free man forever.

I tried to share in their enthusiasm but they were just as confident of my acquittal in my first trial. I didn't want to get caught up in false hope because I didn't want to deal with the disappointment of having to go back to prison.

"How does it feel to be a free man?" Ms. Hattley asked as we drove away from the prison.

"Unbelievable!" I said, taking a deep breath. "How did you manage this miracle?"

"Your witness came forth a few days ago and gave a statement," Ms. Carroll said.

"Kimberly?" I asked. "You found Kimberly?"

"No, she found us!" Stacey said. "She just walked into a police station and said she knew something about a murder."

"Wow!" I said. "What did she say?"

"She said she was in the hotel room when Ms. Lawrence was killed. She said that she knows for sure it was not you because the suspect was too short for one, and for two, it was a woman," Ms. Carroll said.

"A woman?" I asked. "I guess you were right."

"Yes, Ms. Mathis said she saw a woman."

"How was she talking?" I asked. "Was she coherent? Was she talking sensibly?"

"Of course," Ms. Hattley said, "why shouldn't she?"

"Oh, no reason," I said, knowing that Kimberly was schizo-phrenic.

"Hold it, where's my wife?" I asked.

"She's going to meet you at our office and take you home," Stacey said.

"Where's Mike?" I asked.

"He'll meet us there, too," Stacey said. "He told us about your mother. We would like to offer our condolences for your loss. I didn't know her that well, but she made quite an impression on me."

"Thank you," I said, realizing I had to deal with the death of my mother.

"I'm sorry to hear about your mother, too, Dr. Forrester," Ms. Hattley said.

"We wanted to make sure you made it home to say good-bye," Ms. Carroll said.

"Thank you, thank you, both."

❁❁❁

When we got to Stacey's office, Alicia and Brittany were sit-ting in a room waiting for us to arrive. I grabbed them in my arms and we hugged until Stacey reminded us that we had a little work to do before I left town to attend my mother's funeral.

"I hate to interrupt, Dr. Forrester," Stacey said, "but we need to go over a few things before you go to Michigan."

"Okay," I said, releasing Alicia and Brittany, "I'm sorry."

"I understand."

"So what are our chances of having the case dismissed?" I asked.

As Stacey was about to answer, her cell phone rang.

"Excuse me," Stacey said anxiously. "I really have to take this call!"

Stacey stepped out of the room, leaving the rest of us bewildered and confused.

"What's going on?" Alicia asked.

"I don't know," Ms. Hattley said.

"Stacey is always on the move." Ms. Carroll smiled.

Stacey stepped back into the room looking enthusiastic and optimistic as Ms. Hattley was responding.

"Anyway," Ms. Hattley said, "I think our chances are pretty good."

"Dr. Forrester!" Stacey said. "I think your chances just improved dramatically!"

"Why? What happened?" I asked.

"Well, let's just say if you've been praying for a miracle, now you got two!"

"What do you mean?" I asked.

"It just so happens that my mentor is in town for a conference. I asked him to advise on this case and not only did he say yes, he's on his way up to my office! He's in my office!"

"Who is it?" Alicia said.

"He's the best attorney in the United States of America!" Stacey said. "And you have him on your team!"

"Who?" I asked. "Who do I have?"

"Yeah, who?" Ms. Carroll said with an attitude.

Before Stacey could answer, the door opened and Mike walked

in. Behind him walked a tall, distinguished black man. As he stepped into the office and we could see him in full view, we looked in amazement.

"Good evening, Stacey."

"Thank you for coming, sir," Stacey said, pointing to my family. "These are the Forresters."

"Good evening."

"Um," Ms. Carroll said, still stunned.

"Good evening, young lady. My name is Solomon Chambers."

"Yes!" Ms. Carroll said very excitedly. "I know who you are."

"Yes, but I still don't know who you are," Mr. Chambers said.

Solomon Chambers was one of the most recognized attorneys in the history of the United States. He had led a team of young attorneys in the most significant civil rights decision of the twenty-first century.

"I'm sorry. I'm Tori Carroll, Stacey's partner."

"And you are?" Mr. Chambers said, extending his hand to Ms. Hattley.

"I'm Wendy Hattley. I'm Stacey's partner as well."

"Pleasure to meet you." Mr. Chambers playfully shook Brittany's hand. "And you must be Daddy's little girl?"

"Yes sir!" Brittany said.

I couldn't believe I was in the same room with Solomon Chambers. Mike had mentioned being mentored by Solomon Chambers but I have to tell you, I thought it was all made up. But here he was, live and in color.

"You look like you can use a bite to eat, young lady," Mr. Chambers said. "Are you hungry?"

"Yes," Brittany replied.

"Why don't you take this pretty little girl out and put some food in her belly?" Mr. Chambers said to Alicia.

"I can't eat," Alicia said. She looked at Mr. Chambers and realized he didn't want Brittany to hear their discussion. "On second thought, a little snack might be what we need."

❂❂❂

As they discussed my case, I was impressed with the savvy of my legal team. Mr. Chambers went without saying. But Mike was nothing short of amazing to me. Although he was my attorney in name only, he was meticulous in making sure my attorneys crossed their t's and dotted their i's.

Ms. Hattley and Ms. Carroll eventually left the room to monitor other important cases. My case was simply strategic from that point anyway. Stacey followed them to another room and Mike went to go check on Alicia and Brittany, leaving Mr. Chambers and me in the room alone.

"Wow!" I said. "They have my head spinning!"

"They're the best!" Mr. Chambers said. "My two favorite students. My two best students!"

"I have never seen Mike like this before," I said. "Maybe he should have been an attorney."

"Your brother could have been anything he wanted. And believe me, he is what he wanted to be."

"May I ask a question, sir?"

"Sure."

"What happened between you and my brother?"

"What do you mean?" Mr. Chambers asked.

"He seemed to think that you didn't care too much for him."

"I don't know," Mr. Chambers said. "Looking back, I guess I was too hard on him. I suppose I was a little envious of him because everything came easy to him. In my day, a black man had to work twice as hard to get half as much as a white man. And it seemed your brother didn't have to work hard for anything. When I looked at him, I saw myself. And I wanted him to achieve the same success that I achieved, but I couldn't imagine achieving that success with such a lucky nature. But the fact was, Michael was looking for a different type of success, a different type of achievement. And where I had to work hard and struggle, he didn't. Of course, by the time I realized I was being a stubborn mule, our time had passed at Harvard as mentor and protégé."

"Now I think I understand," I said.

"He told me he would never practice law. And he didn't. I think it was mostly to spite me. That boy probably could have been more than I ever imagined. But he turned out to be a pretty good writer. And I'm extremely proud of him."

"Can you do me one small favor, Mr. Chambers?"

"If I can."

"Do you mind telling my brother what you just told me? I think he'll appreciate it."

"Not at all, son. I can relate to how he feels. I had a mentor who was hard on me just like I was hard on him!" Mr. Chambers chuckled. "Boy, that woman used to make me so mad! But I respected her for what she was trying to do for me. She was an extraordinary woman. She won the Pulitzer and Nobel prizes at a very young age."

As soon as Mr. Chambers mentioned the Pulitzer and Nobel prizes my interest in his mentor increased.

"One day, she mysteriously disappeared and no one has heard from her since."

"What happened?"

"No one knows. She simply vanished after that," Mr. Chambers said with a wistful look on his face. "She used to pick me out of the class and ask me questions she knew I couldn't answer."

"Questions like what?"

"Well, one was, if I thought the brain controlled the mind or the mind controlled the brain?" Mr. Chambers laughed.

"And your answer was?"

"I never came up with the right answer," Mr. Chambers said. "Whatever answer I gave, she disputed the logic behind it."

"If you don't mind me asking," I said, "what was your mentor's name?"

My heart was pounding as if I were waiting to hear the last correct number for my winning lottery ticket.

"Her name was Sofia Dewitt."

The name sounded so familiar. I could not immediately recollect how or why I recognized it, but I did. Perhaps I was so intoxicated with the idea of knowing Patient Number Five's identity that, no matter what name Mr. Chambers spoke, I would have felt I'd heard it.

"Mr. Chambers?"

"Yes, son."

"Do you have time to take a ride with me?" I asked. "There's someone I'd like you to meet. I promise it won't take long."

"Since we're just sitting here waiting for the dream team to return, why not?" Mr. Chambers said.

I wanted to tell him where we were going, but I was afraid that he wouldn't believe me. When we pulled into Patient Number Five's gate, the security guard refused to let us enter. He didn't know Mr. Chambers and would not permit us to pass through the gate. I asked him to inform Patient Number

Five of our arrival and gave him the name of my unexpected visitor. We sat for only a few minutes and then, slowly, the gate opened.

We drove up the long driveway and stopped in front of the huge porch. Mr. Chambers waited for me to get out first and then he stepped out. We walked up the stairs and knocked on the door.

The butler came as usual and opened the door. He addressed me and acted as if Mr. Chambers wasn't even there. When we were about to walk up the three flights of stairs, I asked the butler if there was an elevator or some other means to get to the upper level. I didn't want to burden Mr. Chambers with walking up all of those stairs.

He took us through the kitchen and pulled back a gated door, which revealed an elevator. We stepped onto the elevator without so much as uttering a word and lifted to the upper level.

We stepped off the elevator into an area I had never seen before. We walked down a long hallway that brought us to the front of Patient Number Five's double doors.

We stood in front of the doors until they slowly started to open. I looked at Mr. Chambers' face as we entered the room of darkness. He allowed me to go first. I was familiar with my route to the chair with the flashing light. As the doors closed, Mr. Chambers whispered to me, "Remind me to kill you if we make it out of here alive, son."

"I will, sir."

I led Mr. Chambers to the flashing light and gave him my usual seat. Surprisingly, this time there were two chairs. We sat side-by-side and waited for our cue.

"Good day, Solomon Chambers," Patient Number Five said.

"Good day," Mr. Chambers said. "Do I know you, ma'am?"

"May I ask you a question, Solomon Chambers?"

"I guess I don't have much of a choice."

"Do you think that the brain controls the mind or the mind controls the brain?"

"Oh my God!" Mr. Chambers said. "Mrs. Dewitt, is that you?"

"It's been a long time, Solomon Chambers!" Patient Number Five laughed.

"Ma'am," I said, "may I be allowed to address you by your name?"

"I think that would be appropriate, sir."

From that point forward, Patient Number Five was formally known as Mrs. Sofia Dewitt.

"For what do I owe this visit, Solomon Chambers?" Mrs. Dewitt asked.

"This is just as much a surprise to me as it is to you," Mr. Chambers said. "I guess we can thank this young man sitting to my right, or my left, I can't tell."

"This is a pleasant surprise," Mrs. Dewitt said. "How did you two make your acquaintances?"

"Through legal matters," Mr. Chambers said.

"Oh, what a day." Mrs. Dewitt laughed.

"Can we put on the lights? I would like to see you," Mr. Chambers asked.

Suddenly the room went from dark to dim. It was the first time I had a glimpse of its interior. It was enormous! I realized that the room where I had been sitting all of that time was not a bedroom at all. It was actually outside.

The lighting revealed the screened-in porch and the beautiful decorations of flowers and trees. I was trying to understand how they were able to keep the sunlight out and the darkness in, but I couldn't.

Mrs. Dewitt was sitting on a couch, covered by a sheer net coming from the ceiling to the floor, making it impossible to see what she looked like.

"Mrs. Dewitt," I said.

"Yes, sir."

"Why now, after all of the time that we were sitting in darkness, did you allow the sun to enter? Why didn't you allow the light to enter for me? Is there anything I could have said or done?"

"Yes, sir." Mrs. Dewitt said, "Ask!"

CHAPTER TWENTY-THREE

Mr. Chambers and I kept company with Mrs. Dewitt for only a matter of minutes because we had to get back to Stacey's office. Later that night, Mike and my family flew to Michigan to bury my mother.

Alicia, Brittany, and I stayed in a hotel, while Mike stayed with Pop. My father and I didn't speak while I was there and it bothered me. Usually, I would have badgered Pop to talk to me. But since being released from prison, I wasn't the same man. If Pop wanted to talk, fine. And if he didn't, fine!

After the funeral, we left and headed back to Atlanta. Over the next couple of days, Stacey and Mike were running around like chickens with their heads cut off, preparing for my hearing. Since Mr. Chambers arrived, Mike had taken his advisory role much more seriously.

They were trying to get the district attorneys to drop the charges prior to the hearing, but despite the new evidence in my defense they refused to drop the charges and decided to move forward with the evidentiary hearing. Why? Because they said that although there was a possibility that someone else could have been there around the time Kimberly was there, it didn't mean that I did not kill her earlier in the day.

I wasn't sure if I would be heading back to prison or not, so while I was out I had to make sure I fulfilled my promise to Stone. With help from Stacey's firm, we were able to locate Stone's daughter, Shante. She was still in foster care. We managed to get the Georgia Department of Human Resources to ask the child if she wanted to see her father. She was more excited than we anticipated. She couldn't wait to visit him.

We arranged for me to take her to the prison the Sunday before my hearing. It took a lot of work, but we got it done. I had to go in with Shante because she was underage.

At my first glance, I didn't even recognize Stone. He had cut his hair and shaved his beard, all for his little girl. It's amazing how children can tame the savagery in adults. This man, this killer who could take a life without batting an eye, had washed, cleaned and shaved for a date with his daughter.

"Hey, Doc," Stone said. "How's the outside?"

"Not much different from in here," I joked. Handing the telephone to Shante I said, "I brought somebody to see you, man."

"Hi," Shante said.

"Oh my, God," Stone said. "Look at you."

"I miss you."

"You remember me?" Stone asked.

"Yeah."

"You don't remember me!" Stone chuckled. "What do you remember about me?"

"I remember one time when I was little. I had a dance recital and you were out of town. I asked you if you could watch me. Mommy said you were too far away to come. It was raining and thundering and I just knew you weren't going to make it.

And then after the recital, I saw you standing there with my flowers in your hands. I was so happy I didn't know what to do! Do you remember?"

"Yeah."

"And I remember that time when I was sick, I think I had the measles or something like that. You remember that?"

"Yeah," Stone replied. "I remember that, too."

Shante turned to me so that I could hear what she was saying.

"My daddy had to wear sweaters, and tee shirts, and long pants, because he didn't want to catch the measles. I was sleeping on my daddy's lap for like five days." Shante laughed. "My mommy kept telling him to put me down, but he wouldn't. He spoiled me!"

"How do you remember all that?" Stone said. "You were a baby!"

"'Cause you my daddy!" Shante said, looking at Stone as if he was out of his mind.

"I'm sorry, Shante," Stone said, not even trying to wipe the tears flowing from his eyes. "I should be out there protecting you, but instead I'm in here locked up."

"Why you talking like that?" Shante asked.

"Because I'm letting you down."

"You're not letting me down," Shante said. "You can't change what you did; all you can do is pay for what you did."

"I can't believe you even want to see me."

"Why wouldn't I want to see you?"

"Are you going to come back and see me?" Stone asked.

"Yeah, why wouldn't I?" Shante asked. "You're my daddy."

"You promise?"

"I promise on one condition," Shante replied. "You behave

yourself while you're in here and get paroled so you can be my daddy like you're supposed to."

"Oh, so you're giving orders now?" Stone asked sarcastically, and then saying to me. "She's trying to blackmail me."

"Right!" Shante said.

"In that case, I guess we got a deal."

"You better keep your promise, too!"

"Well, we better be going, Shante," I said.

"Okay." Shante stood up and waved to Stone. "Bye! Oh, I love you, Daddy."

I think she caught Stone off guard. He didn't know what to say. Shante didn't let it stop her. She just repeated her statement.

"I said, I love you, Daddy."

"Oh," Stone said, "I love you, too. I love you so much."

"All right, Stone," I said, "keep your head up."

"Doc," Stone said, "can I talk to you privately?"

"What y'all talking about?" Shante said jokingly.

"You," Stone answered.

"It better be good," Shante said. "I'll wait for you over there, Dr. Forrester."

"Okay."

Shante walked out of hearing range while I stayed to talk to Stone. I sat down and folded my hands on the table, waiting for Stone to speak.

"Hey, Doc," Stone said. "You remember before you left, you told me you owed me. That you would repay me for what went down in here."

"And I meant every word. How much do you need?"

"I don't want yo' money, Doc," Stone said. "I got every dime that you gave me in here, man. That's not my money, it's yours."

"How is it mine?" I said. "You saved my life in here, Stone."

"Now I want to give you that money back to save my daughter's life. She needs to be around good people who are going to do good by her."

"What are you saying?"

"I know I have no right to ask for this, but," Stone said, "I need you to watch out for my daughter, man."

"Is that it?"

"Yeah. That's it. You do that and we're square."

"On one condition."

"What's up?"

"You keep your promise to Shante," I said. "You have a parole board meeting coming up. When you go in there, go in there like you're going for Shante, not to tell them to kiss your ass."

"I'll do my best,"

"That's not good enough, Stone. You have to keep that promise to her."

"Done."

"And by the way," I said, standing up, "you think you're clever. I know your deal with me was bogus."

"What deal?" Stone asked.

"The night before I left we made a deal, Shante in exchange for Kimberly," I said. "From what my attorneys are telling me, Kimberly had turned herself in days before. So that means one of three things. One, you had nothing to do with Kimberly turning herself in. Two, you're one hell of a psychic. Or three, you had already worked out your end of the bargain before the deal was ever made."

"I don't know what you talkin' 'bout, Doc." Stone chuckled.

"Yes you do. What was up with all that, 'I wasn't protecting you because I like you' jazz?"

"I told you. I don't know what you talkin' 'bout, Doc."

"All right, man. But I know better."

"You don't know shit." Stone laughed.

"Keep your head up and your ass down, man."

"You know it," Stone said. "Take care of my baby, man."

"Like she was my own."

❃❃❃

In order for me to keep my promise to Stone, I had to get Alicia to buy into the idea of being Shante's foster parents. Later that evening, I invited Shante out for dinner with us so that Alicia could get an opportunity to meet her. She was an extraordinary young lady who appeared to be unharmed by her past. She was very bright and knowledgeable for her age. She impressed Alicia with her manners and vibrant personality. By the end of the night, Alicia was asking me if we could step in as foster parents. Neither one of the ladies realized they were interviewing and being interviewed by the other.

Before we committed to the responsibility of adding a teen-ager to our family, we discussed all of the possibilities we were facing in our future. Would this be a long-, or short-term decision? What happened if Stone did not make parole? What happened if I went to jail? We discussed all of those issues and decided that we would bring Shante into our home, but not until after my hearing. We agreed she didn't need any further inconsis-tent parenting.

❃❃❃

On the day of my hearing, all of my legal team was present,

including Mr. Chambers, who had used his influence to turn my hearing into a character inquisition. Stacey and I sat together waiting for my name to be called. Alicia sat directly behind me, holding Pam's hand.

Everyone was aware that if the judge decided to move forward, I could be placed under arrest and held for the duration of my trial.

I looked behind me and every last one of the office girls, including Tazzy and Susan, were present. My patients, Betty and Veronica, were sitting next to my secretary, Rosemary. Curtis, Rob, and my ex-sister-in-law, Tonita, were sitting on another bench. I was so overwhelmed by their support I didn't notice that Mike wasn't there. And then in walked Mike along with my father.

I thought Ma probably forced him to come show his support. That couldn't have been it, because Ma was gone. It really didn't matter to me why he came, so long as he was there. I looked at him, and he looked at me, and then he smiled. Pop's presence seemed to give me confidence.

He stood and bent down in front of me. Fearing embarrassment, Stacey opened her mouth to speak to my father, but I tapped her leg letting her know that everything would be fine. I wasn't exactly sure what my father was going to say, but whatever it was, I wasn't going to lower my head. I was going to look him dead in the eyes, like a man.

"I don't know what to say, except I love you, son," Pop said. "And no matter what was done between us, I always loved you. And I always will love you. I pray to God that He get you out of this mess so we can start over."

"Pop," I said, "you just don't know how that makes me feel!"

"You a good boy! No matter what happens in here today, I'm proud of you. You hear me?"

"Yes, sir."

My father stood over me as I was sitting and kissed me on the top of my head. He took a rag out of his back pocket and wiped his nose and his eyes. As my father was sitting down, the doors to the courtroom were opened and we watched as Rosemary wheeled an old woman into the courtroom.

I was shocked, to say the least. I'm not sure that my attorneys even knew why she was there, or what she was going to say. Rosemary rolled her in as far as she could go and the old woman began to speak.

"Good afternoon, sir."

I immediately recognized the voice. It was Patient Number Five, or Mrs. Dewitt, as I had recently started to call her. And then I realized why her last name was so familiar to me. It was the same as Rosemary's. They were somehow related.

"Good afternoon, ma'am," Judge Robinson said.

"My name is Doctor Sofia Dewitt."

"*The* Sofia Dewitt?" Judge Robinson asked.

"I suppose I am."

"Well, I'll be! I have the great Solomon Chambers and the esteemed Sofia Dewitt in my courtroom on the same day! And they say Christmas only comes once a year," Judge Robinson joked. "I'm sorry, ma'am. Please continue."

"It is of grave importance that you know that I have not left my house for over forty years, sir. I have chosen to leave the confines of my house today to come here on behalf of this young man, Doctor Johnson Forrester. The man that you are accusing of the ghastly crime of murder! He could not have been at the hotel to harm that poor young lady because he was at my residence counseling me. Given the short amount of time he had at his disposal to leave my house, arrive at that hotel, murder that young woman and escape, it would be an achievement that defied the laws of physics!"

"I understand, ma'am," Judge Robinson said. "But…"

"Let him go!" Mrs. Dewitt shouted. "Let him go, now!"

"He's not under arrest, ma'am." Judge Robinson laughed.

"You see that he's not!" Mrs. Dewitt shouted. "Rosemary!"

"Yes, mother!" Rosemary said, walking toward Mrs. Dewitt. "I am ready to go home!"

I looked back and forth at Rosemary and Mrs. Dewitt, wanting to scream out loud *What the hell is going on?* But I had to restrain myself until I was out of that court room.

Rosemary looked at the judge, waiting for his approval for them to be dismissed. The judge nodded his head and Rosemary wheeled Mrs. Dewitt away. I tried to make eye contact with Mrs. Dewitt as Rosemary wheeled her out, but I realized she was blind. That explained why she preferred the darkness; it wasn't because she was some nut job. She simply had no need for light.

My defense team brought character witness after witness testifying on my behalf. My family, my friends and my patients, one by one, pleaded to the judge to set me free. Both sides presented their reasons why the case should or should not be brought to trial. And then the judge gave his decision.

"Is there any further evidence on either side?" Judge Robinson asked.

"Well, we feel that Mr. Forrester's DNA found on the victim's body is sufficient evidence to proceed with a trial, sir," the district attorney said.

"I'm sorry, but I don't see it," Judge Robinson said. "All that you have with that DNA is evidence that there was sexual intercourse between the accused and the deceased. And the accused has already admitted that there was an affair between him and the deceased. Now as far as I know, you can't try a man for having an affair. This just sounds too much like a witch-hunt and I want no part of it! At this point, you do not have sufficient evidence to proceed with trying this man for murder. If you can present additional evidence that will hold in a court of law, you are certainly welcome to do so at that time. But for now, this case is dismissed!"

At the sound of the judge's gavel, I felt as if the weight of the world had been lifted from my shoulders. I was a free man! My family and friends rushed to me, fighting to give me their love. Throughout the hearing, the dismissal and the celebration, Alicia never once let go of my hand. I already knew I had a special woman but her unselfish love for me in my most difficult time of trouble only confirmed it. Now it was my turn to prove to her just how good of a man I could be.

Plans were made for us to have a celebration dinner at my house later, but our family and friends agreed to give Alicia and me some alone time before the festivities began.

When Alicia and I stepped inside of our house, we stood in the corridor and hugged. We chuckled like teenagers, and then we hugged again. We put our heads together and sighed. We knew it would be a long way back to where we were in our marriage, but we also knew we were both ready to begin the journey. Alicia took my hand and led me upstairs.

She pulled my suit coat over my shoulders and loosened my tie. She pulled my tie around my neck and tossed it to the side. She unbuttoned my shirt from top to bottom. Then she pulled my shirt off and rubbed my chest. She pushed me on my back and pulled my shoes off.

Next, she pulled off my socks, my pants and then my underwear. I lay on the bed unclothed and unsure of my ability to make love to my wife. We had not made love in almost a year.

I stood up and kissed my Alicia very passionately. My manhood reacted and began to swell, but it had done that before and failed me miserably once our lovemaking session commenced.

I raised Alicia's arms in the air and pulled her tightly fitted dress above her head. I reached behind her and unsnapped her bra, taking it in my hand and throwing it in the air where it landed on top of the chandelier. I turned her around and sat her on the bed. I took her left foot in my hand and unbuckled her leather-strapped, open-toed shoe. Then I grabbed her right foot and unbuckled the strap on that foot. I kissed her perfectly shaped toes and gently nudged her on her back. I stuck my fingers on either side of her panties and slowly pulled them over her hips, down her thighs and over her feet. I threw them in the air where they, too, landed on top of the chandelier.

I held my wife's hand and led her to our bathroom. I put on the Jacuzzi and adjusted the temperature to warm, very warm. I stepped in the tub first, and then guided my wife as she slowly took one step at a time entering the steaming bath.

I grabbed her gently and pulled her to me. I pushed her against the edge of the tub and pressed my body against hers. I opened her legs with my legs, and slid my manhood between her thighs. She closed her legs and I could feel the pressure of her thighs squeezing the middle portion of my manhood as if it was her hand. The head had slipped past the grip of her thighs and slid through. The vibration of the water and the exposure of the head of my penis between Alicia's thighs intensified the sensation.

Alicia took her hand and reached behind her. She slid her hand between her thighs from the rear and massaged the head of my manhood, taking a finger and caressing the split where I piss.

It was such an amazing feeling. I closed my eyes and leaned my head backward and just enjoyed the moment. The soft moisture of her vagina on top of my rock-hard penis could still be felt in the midst of the jet-streaming flow.

Alicia pulled my head down and pushed my face on top of her breasts. I started off sucking her breasts softly. Playing with her nipples, licking them, and tenderly biting them.

"Oh my God," Alicia said, moving my head from breast to breast in the motion she desired. "Suck 'em, baby."

She pulled my head from her breasts and we started to kiss long and passionately. Alicia pulled my manhood from between her legs and aimed it at her vagina. She raised her legs in the water and wrapped them around my waist. I could feel the difference in the moisture of the water and the moisture of her vagina as my manhood slid deeper and deeper inside of her.

"Oh God," Alicia said, gasping in pleasure from the stroke of penetration, "do you love me?"

"Oh, Alicia," I said, "I love you so much."

"You do?" Alicia moved her hips rhythmically, sliding up and down on my manhood. "You love me?"

"Baby, I love you so much!" I said. "Look at me! Open your eyes, Alicia! Look at me!"

Alicia opened her eyes slightly and stared at me.

"Okay, baby!" Alicia sighed, enjoying every single stroke.

I could tell that our involuntary sexual sabbatical had made Alicia incredibly aroused. She was very aggressive with her body movement. It was like she couldn't get enough of my manhood. The more I stroked, the more she wanted.

I stuck my fingers in her hair and pulled her head backward. She groaned and opened her mouth wide. "Oh God," Alicia said, "pull my hair!"

Her golden legs wrapped tighter around my waist and she clamped her feet together. She locked her hands together around the back of my neck and began to ride up and down, making the already vibrating water splash all over the floor. The harder I pulled on her hair, the faster she bucked her hips.

Her feet were kicking so wildly, they were no longer in the water. She was sliding up and down so smoothly it looked as if she was on a see-saw all by herself.

"Shit!" Alicia screamed. "I don't wanna come, baby, but I can't help it!"

"Come for me, baby!" I shouted.

I could feel Alicia's orgasm approaching so I started to stroke her with everything that I had. Normally, she would have asked me to slow down. But she was so excited from pent-up sexual frustration that she encouraged me to go harder.

"Oh shit!" Alicia shouted. "Give it to me! Give to me!"

"You love me?" I yelled, frowning and making the meanest face I could muster. "Huh? You love me?"

"Oh shit! I love you, baby!" Alicia screamed.

Alicia let go of my neck and put her arms behind her to brace herself as she slid over the edge of the tub. I lifted her legs, pushing her all the way on her back. I climbed out of the tub, splashing water everywhere, and plunged deeper inside of her.

I pushed her legs back so far that her body seemed to be folded in half. Her feet were flapping beside my head as I drilled deeper and deeper.

"I'm almost there, baby!" Alicia moaned. "Right there! Right there! Right there! Don't stop!"

I couldn't have stopped if I wanted to because my orgasm was approaching, and approaching quickly.

"Oh God, I'm coming, baby!" I shouted, exploding hot liquid inside of my wife. I was pounding so hard that her body started to slide along the wet floor.

Alicia's legs were twisting and turning, sliding up and down mine as her orgasm took control of her body.

"Oh! Oh! Oh!" Alicia squeaked, digging her nails deep into my back. Her eyes rolled backward into her head, and saliva slid from the side of her mouth. Her words became a series of moans and groans. Her toes were stretched as far apart as the limitation would allow without their falling off. Her juices flowed down her buttocks and mixed with the water on the floor.

When our orgasms subsided, Alicia continued to shake and shiver from the aftereffects. They were involuntary and very powerful. When they struck, she would pull me closely and grind her body against mine until they were alleviated. Her body would still jerk even after the tremors. Between the tremors, she still couldn't speak, she could only moan.

"Oh my goodness!" Alicia said once she was in her coherent state of mind. "My God! That was fantastic!"

"You like?" I joked.

"Oh my God!" Alicia said. "That was awesome!"

"Listen, I love you, Alicia, and if you give me a chance, I promise to be the husband you want me to be."

"You know this is not going to be easy for me."

"It's not going to be easy for me, either," I said. "I am truly sorry for the pain I caused you, but I have to tell you, baby. I'm crushed, absolutely crushed by your affair."

"I know you are and that's what I'm afraid of," Alicia said. "I think that you're so focused on what you did to me right now that you haven't taken the time to deal with my affair with Julian. Maybe one day you'll wake up and realize what I've done to you and you won't be able to handle it."

"That's not going to happen!" I said.

"How do you know?"

"Because what I feel for you is nothing temporary or momentary. It's real and it's strong. I'm never going to leave you, Alicia. Never."

"How do I know that?"

"How do I know that you won't leave me? It's one of the chances of love. We can't spend our lives worried about things like that. That's why we are where we are right now."

"How do I know that you won't cheat on me again?"

"How do I know you won't cheat on me? I don't! We have to believe that our power of love for one another will influence our rationalization of lust for others."

"And what about your sexual addiction problem? How do we fix that?"

"By loving and making love with each other," I said. "You satisfy me in every way. Whatever it was I've been looking for in life, I found it today. In my wife, my family, and my friends. I feel loved. I feel wanted. The only thing that could possibly make me happier would be for you to say you're going to be my wife for the remainder of my life. Do you hear me?"

"Yes," Alicia said, "but I need you to promise you will never ever hurt me like this again."

"You don't have to worry about me. But I need to know that if Julian tries to contact you again, you'll end whatever it is you had for him."

"He has, and I have," Alicia said. "My affair wasn't about my love for Julian. It was my fear of being married. I know you love me but I don't know if you will love me forever. And that scares the hell out of me, Johnny."

"Listen to me, Alicia," I said. "I want this to be the last time we have this conversation. You're my wife and I love you and I'm not going anywhere. You hear me?"

"Yes," Alicia said softly. "I love you, Johnny."

"I love you, too."

CHAPTER TWENTY-FOUR

Alicia and I showered and prepared for our guests. I was hoping this would be the last time we were at a dinner party for a long, long time. As the guests started to arrive, Alicia and I realized we had to move some of them to the back-yard. There was plenty of room.

We had an extended covered patio with decorative tables and chairs already assembled. Alicia had this area built in anticipation of her dinner parties for her firm. It was convenient for that night, but I was not convinced at all that we would get our money's worth from that construction. But for that night, my wife was nothing short of a genius!

"Can we talk?"

I turned around and my father was standing behind me.

"Sure," I said. "Sure, Pop! Let's go upstairs."

My father followed me upstairs and away from the guests. We took refuge in my bedroom. I closed the door behind me. My father and I stood in the middle of the room, man-to-man, face-to-face and eye-to-eye.

"You wanted to talk?" I asked, using my toughest voice.

"Yeah, son."

"Okay," I said, "let's talk."

"You know," Pop said, "you know this is hard for me, don't you, son?"

"I can imagine. But like you always told me, Pop, sometimes life is hard, but then again it's fair, because it doesn't discriminate."

"Yeah, that's what I always said."

"So what is it you want to talk about, Pop?"

I walked in that room ready for battle. Whatever my father had to dish out, I was ready to take it. I had years of frustration I was about to unload on him, and it was between him and his God to make him strong enough to take it.

"I have been a horrible father to you, son," Pop said. "In my mind, I thought I was doing right by you. I thought I was making you a man. But I wasn't. I was making you less than a man. And I'm sorry. I am really sorry, son. I wish I could take back all of them years I wasted riding your back, but I can't! All I can do is say that I love you, and I'm sorry, and I hope you can forgive me."

With those words, all of the pain my father had caused me throughout the years ceased. All of the anger and frustration I had harbored since I was a child evaporated. You have to know my father to know how difficult that was for him. And for him to do something that difficult, to show that much emotion and concern, had to mean that he loved me. For him to stand before me and admit that he was wrong, it meant that he loved me. And then, to ask for my forgiveness, that meant he respected me! Finally, I was a man.

"Pop," I said, "I forgive you, but you have to understand something, man."

"Yeah, son."

"It doesn't make me less of a man if I shed a tear. It doesn't make me less of a man if I don't yell and scream and act a fool to get my point across," I said, practically begging my father to understand. "I am a man! I'm just not like you. Can't you understand that?"

"I understand, son," Pop said. "I understand."

I wrapped my arms around my father and hugged him. He hugged me back, and then he pulled my head down and kissed me on the forehead as he had kissed me earlier in the courtroom.

"I don't know what I'm going to do now that your mother's gone, son."

"Pop, you don't have to live up there in that big old house all by yourself. You can move down here with Mike or me."

"Naw," Pop said, "I'd be better off up there."

"How am I gonna get to know you up there?"

"I don't know," Pop said. "We'll figure it out. Let's get back to the party. I need something to drink."

"Pop!" I said, stopping in my tracks.

"Not that kind of drink," Pop said. "I'll never put alcohol to my lips again."

"Never?"

"Never!"

"Okay, Pop."

We walked downstairs together and then went our separate ways. I walked around my house going from room to room, thanking everyone for their support. I noticed Rosemary sitting alone, isolated from the rest of the party. I sat beside her and thanked her for everything she had done.

"Hi, Rosemary."

"Good evening, Doctor."

"I am so glad you were able to make it."

"I'm glad I could come."

"You know, I have to ask why you kept your mother's identity a secret from me, Rosemary?"

"I understand."

"Why didn't you tell me that Patient Number Five was actually Sofia Dewitt? And more importantly, why didn't you tell me Mrs. Dewitt was your mother?"

"I think that some things are best left unsaid in order for all things to be realized."

"You are your mother's child." I chuckled. "But even if it was your mother, I would have still treated her."

"Treated her?" Rosemary laughed. "She was not your patient, Dr. Forrester, you were hers."

"I was hers?"

"Yes," Rosemary said. "You had disorders that needed to be resolved before you could fulfill your potential as a mental health clinician."

"My infidelity?"

"And there were other reasons."

"And those other reasons were?"

"One reason, I needed you to help my mother get over her final obstacle of remaining in that house until she died," Rosemary said.

"So did your maniacal plan work?" I joked.

"Yes," Rosemary said, "yes, it did. Better than I expected."

We paused our conversation and I stared at all of the people in my house.

"As I look around this house, Rosemary, all of the women here, in some way, made up my journey to myself."

"How is that?" Rosemary asked, looking at the people in her vicinity.

"All of the women in this house are here on my behalf. Some have never laid eyes on each other before. But if I were to be removed from this house, in memory and in body, they would never ever be connected."

"You think not?"

"I'm certain," I said. "One person, one human being can unite the whole world through a mere six degrees."

"Interesting."

"But you know what else is interesting, Rosemary?"

"What?"

"You would think that my discovery of myself would have been determined through the natural order of a man. But it is quite the contrary, I discovered the nature of a man through the nature of a woman."

"In what way?" Rosemary asked.

"I was shown how to love, through the pain of my wife. I was shown how to be courageous, through the fear of my mother. I was shown how to see a woman's soul through the darkness of a woman's eyes."

"Remarkable," Rosemary said.

"But I do have one big question mark about my journey."

"And what is that?"

"You."

"Me?" Rosemary asked. "Why me?"

"Because you are still a question that needs to be answered."

"What would you like to know about me, Dr. Forrester?" Rosemary asked.

"Everything."

"Okay," Rosemary said, "where do I begin?"

"From the beginning."

ROSEMARY'S STORY:

"I was born in an enormous house in the exurban area of Atlanta, Georgia. I was an only child. I had no siblings. I never knew my father; he died eight months to the day before my birth.

"My mother loved him. She constantly told me stories about my father's life and his death. My father was a black man and my mother was white. Although my parents were very educated and wealthy people who contributed academically and financially to all classes, they were not accepted in the upscale community where they lived.

"My mother received international notoriety for her contribution to the study of psychological medicine. She was a Southern socialite from old money and old beliefs. But she had contemporary views and believed in social and political equality.

"My father was one of the rare African-American cardiologists in the United States at that time. When my parents traveled abroad, it was my father who received more acclaim for his brilliant work as a surgeon. But here in America, he was an activist for civil rights and despised by most of his medical counterparts.

"One evening, he was coming home from an operation where one of his patients died on the operating table. His patient was a white man and his family was very distraught. They were so distraught that they followed him to our home and they shot him down. In cold blood!

"Mother heard the gunshots from the house. Having no sight, she had to feel her way from the house to the driveway. When she got to my father's body, he was lying motionless on the ground. She held my father's bloody body in her arms until the ambulance arrived. By the time they arrived, my father was already dead. After they took my father's body away, my mother found her way back to the house. Drenched in her bloody dress. She locked herself in the attic.

"Mother was traumatized. She slipped into a catatonic state and *was mentally unable to arrange or attend his funeral. When she regained consciousness, she had to deal with the reality of my father's death all over again.*

"My father's murder had such an awful effect on my mother's ability to reason that she started to believe that none of mankind could be trusted. She convinced herself that there were people in the outside world trying to kill her. She started to suffer from delusional paranoia and refused to step one foot outside of the house.

"In addition, she had to deal with being with child. After my birth, she began to build a hidden fortress protected by guards and fences. As I grew older, Mother painstakingly sheltered me from any outside contact. She refused to let me outside of the house even to play, thinking that someone was lurking in the shadows.

"She created a playland for me inside of our home. I was also educated in my home by Mother. I became so accustomed to our reclusive lifestyle as being normal, her paranoia transitioned onto me and I, too, started to believe that we were being hunted. I began to see and hear people and voices that weren't really there.

"It wasn't until Mother released me from that house and allowed me to further my education that I truly started to see a different world. One thing about Mother, she was much more afraid of having an ignorant child than a dead child. She knew that even with the most advanced technology, there was only so much she could teach me inside of that house and so I was freed.

"Adapting to learning from someone other than Mother was quite natural. I discovered a slight sense of independence. I excelled to the top of my class from my freshman year of academia until I received my final doctorate. My accomplishments were never fully acknowledged by Mother because she never once attended any of my ceremonies.

"Although my transition to academics in the outside world went

very well, my social skills were at best, inept. My voice sounded strange when I spoke in front of others. It was as if I wasn't myself. My clothes were outdated. I couldn't relate to current issues unless they involved science or literature.

"Mother forbade me from publicly using my true identity. I couldn't discuss our family, where I was born, or where I was raised. Nothing! To the people I met along my journey, I simply appeared and then disappeared. I had one known recognizable characteristic, and that was intelligence.

"The fact that I was known as the smart one, and the smart one only, did nothing to improve my social status. Boys paid me no attention unless they needed to be tutored. Looking back, I guess I really didn't mind. Any attention was better than no attention.

"I spent every vacation and school closing back at that house. Once I came through those gates, I became Mother's captive again. And the rules of my childhood would always be reinforced.

"Over the years, Mother's delusions started to dwindle and she seemed to drift back into the world of reality. Our separation forced us to analyze our own selves. We no longer had or needed the dependency of the other to exist. But as her mind healed, her body deteriorated. And I became a captive of another kind.

"I would spend the next thirteen years caring for Mother's health, and protecting her from the outside world. Her fear was no longer of being harmed. It was of being ignorant. She was afraid that modern science had surpassed her intelligence. Mother would rather die in anonymity and be forgotten as a Nobel and Pulitzer winner than emerge from the darkness and be challenged intellectually by the memory of those awards.

"But I came to the conclusion that if I did allow Mother to have her druthers, it would inevitably lead to my untimely demise. I could *no longer breathe in that house. It had, along with Mother, possessed my soul. To remain trapped in that house one day longer than I did would have meant suicide. It was either death or freedom. If escaping that house meant taking my life I was prepared to do just that…"*

"Eventually, I gathered my nerve and I walked down the driveway, through the gates and down the road."

"How did you end up as my secretary?"

"I kept walking for the rest of that night and into the early part of the morning. When I became tired of walking, I stopped. It just happened to be in front of the building where you were opening your new office."

"Where were you walking from?"

"My mother's house."

"Rosemary," I said, "that had to be a six- or seven-hour walk."

"Dr. Forrester, when you've been locked up basically your whole life, a six- or seven-hour walk seems like six or seven minutes."

"If anyone can relate to you on being locked up, I can."

"Does that answer your question about me?" Rosemary said.

"One more," I said. "I never quite understood why someone with your credentials would want to work as my secretary."

"Well, I didn't need the money, I just needed to escape. I had to get out of that house and start my own life."

"Well, you've certainly done that."

"You may have a hard time getting Dr. Glover to go back into retirement, though." Rosemary chuckled.

"Rosemary," I said. "I've been thinking."

"About what?"

"I have a proposal for you."

"I'm listening."

"Dr. Glover has been a tremendous help with the practice but he really misses his wife and is ready to go back home," I said. "How would you like to take over the practice for a while?"

"Me?" Rosemary said. "I'm flattered, Dr. Forrester, but I don't know if I'm ready to treat patients."

"You've been treating me ever since you came to work for me in the office," I said. "I put my life in your hands."

"I would hardly consider maintaining your schedule as having your life in my hands. That's nothing like those patients putting their minds in my hands."

"You've talked about your mother holding you captive all of your life. I'm beginning to think that maybe it's not so much that your mother needs you, perhaps it's that you need your mother."

"I know what you're trying to do, Dr. Forrester," Rosemary laughed, "but it's not going to work. I just don't think I'm qualified."

"You're more qualified than I am," I replied. "You have the academic background. You have the credentials. What's stopping you?"

"I don't have the experience."

"Experienced is earned. You have to begin somewhere. Why not in a place where you're familiar with the patients?"

"Can I think about it?" Rosemary asked.

"No," I said sarcastically. "If you think about it, you'll only talk yourself out of it. And I really need you to run the office until I am reinstated."

"Do you have any idea when that will be?"

"No, I'm not in any rush. There are a few things I need to

do before I am ready to come back to the practice. So what do you say, ma'am?"

"I guess I have no choice."

"All right, I'm glad we got that settled."

"Thank you, Dr. Forrester."

"Thank you, too," I said, patting Rosemary on the knee.

CHAPTER TWENTY-FIVE

Alicia and the office girls had separated themselves from the rest of the guests, and I knew exactly where they were in my private haven: the basement! On my way down, Mike stepped behind me.

"You sure you want to go down there all by yourself?" Mike joked.

"Not really," I replied, "I'm just going down there to get my wife."

"All of the office girls haven't totally forgiven you, you know?"

"That's their problem, not mine," I said. "But come with me just in case I need some back-up."

"Ten-Four!" Mike said following behind me.

As we walked downstairs I could hear their individual distinctive voices.

"Girl, I'm so glad you got your husband back," Tina said.

"Yeah, we have things we need to work out, but I really love that man," Alicia said.

"Just keep the faith, Alicia, you'll be all right," Tina said.

"I don't know him as well as the rest of the girls, but he seems like a really nice guy," Tazzy said.

"Thank you! I'm so glad you could make it!" Alicia said, hugging Tazzy.

"No problem," Tazzy said, "No problem whatsoever."

"And I thank you, too," Alicia said as she hugged Susan.

"I'm just sorry I can't be here more for you, Alicia!" Susan said.

Mike and I stood at the bottom of the stairs waiting for a pause in the conversation to let the office girls know we were there.

"The good thing is that you have your husband home with you again," Susan said. "And that's all that matters."

"Susan's right, just be happy you got a man!" Lisa said.

"What?" Pam said. "Why should she just be happy to have a man?"

"I'm not even going there with you, Pam," Lisa responded.

"I'm just asking," Pam said, "why should Alicia *just* be happy to have a man?"

"That's not what I'm saying, Pam, and you know it."

"I'm just saying, Johnny cheated on Alicia, went to prison for killing the woman he cheated with, and you're saying she should just be happy to have a man like that. He should be thanking God every minute of the day that Alicia is even talking to him!" Pam snapped.

No longer able to wait for a cue, I stepped off of the last stair and looked at Pam in disbelief. She was embarrassed, but right or wrong, Pam never backed down. Never.

"Not that it's any of your business, but I do thank God every minute of the day, Pam," I said. "I know what I've done. I know how much I shamed and hurt my wife. I know I was wrong. But I still love her and she still loves me. I've apologized for my stupid, selfish act, but what about you?"

"What about me?" Pam asked.

"What is your reason for trying to make her feel stupid for forgiving me? Does it make you feel good about yourself to make Alicia feel bad about herself? Huh? Is that what this is?"

"Don't even come at me like that!"

"No," I said, "answer my question. You are a classic example of the old adage that misery loves company. Since you can't find a man to make you happy, you don't want any other woman to have a man that makes them happy."

"If being cheated on means being happy, then I don't want to be happy," Pam said.

"All right you two, this is supposed to be a happy occasion," Valerie interjected.

"We all family, let them say what they have to say," Wanda said.

"I don't feel like hearing it," Alicia said, shaking her head.

"Yeah, stop starting a fight, Pam," Darsha added.

"I didn't start nothing. I was talking to y'all, and Johnny butted in. If he say something to me, I'm going to say something back."

"Do you have to do this right now, Pam?" Tazzy said.

"Why are all of y'all talking to me?" Pam shouted. "Say something to him, too. I'm just saying what every last one of y'all are thinking!"

"You have no right to speak for me, Pam," Tazzy said, "that's not what I'm thinking."

"You don't represent me neither!" Wanda said. "I got a couple of more free sessions left; I'm staying on Johnny's good side!"

"All I'm saying is this," Pam said. "You got to be your own woman, Alicia. Don't let nobody make a fool out of you!"

"Make a fool out of her?" I asked. "Are you serious?"

Normally on those occasions when people attacked me aggressively, I would try to rationalize or reason with their hostile approach. The last year of my life had taught me that acting rationally has its place, but so does acting emotionally. The trick is to maintain control of both.

"Pam," I said, "you wanna talk foolish? Do you realize the

gentleman you've been parading around as your white knight in shining armor has a wife?"

"Oh snap!" Wanda said, covering her mouth.

"Day-um!" Darsha said.

"Please," Pam said.

"Your Christopher is my attorney's husband, Pam," I said. "I guess white guys cheat, too, huh?"

"You're just saying that because I'm trying to keep my girl's head straight."

"No," I said, "I'm saying it because it's the truth! You're sleeping with a married man! You try so hard to make it seem as if it's the man's fault you're always getting hurt, but it's not! It's you! At some point you have to take responsibility for the men you attract, Pam! By now, you should know the signs and the routines, but you ignore them because you keep getting caught up in the fantasy of having a perfect man! There is no perfect man! Once you realize that, you'll be better off. The whole world would be better off!"

"The dead has arisen!" Mike said, sarcastically mocking a line from *The Color Purple* movie.

"You're right," I said to Pam. "I was wrong. I made poor decisions and I hurt my wife. But I don't blame anyone but me. I made those decisions and I have to deal with the consequences. And until you stop blaming black men for the pain you've suffered and take responsibility for the choices you've made in selecting bad men, you're going to always be bitter and angry. And you're going to try to make the people around you bitter and angry. And why? There are plenty of good men out there. You eliminate half of them because they're not lawyers, or doctors, or professional athletes. You keep setting yourself up for failure.

"You can forget that fantasy man. He only exists in your mind. And where you may judge Alicia and me because of our situation, we're going to get past this, and we're going to be happy. And you're still going to be bitter and angry. You're going to remain miserable because you're always looking for your perfect man."

"Wow!" Darsha said.

"See!" Wanda said. "That's why that niggah is my shrink!"

"Wanda," Valerie said, pointing at Susan.

"Sorry, Susan," Wanda said and kissed her on the cheek.

"Whatever, girl!" Susan said.

"So, did you know that Chris was married, Alicia?" Pam asked, now very embarrassed.

"You know, if I had known I would have told you, girl."

"Did you know, Mike?" Pam asked.

"Yup!" Mike said.

"Well, why didn't you tell me?"

"Pam. Pam. Pam," Mike said sarcastically. "You practically spat on black men and said you didn't give a damn! But I'm supposed to give a damn when you're being spat on by a white man? I'm sorry."

"So, I guess I'm the butt of everybody's joke now, huh?"

"I'm not joking with you, Pam," I said. "I care about you. But what good is it for you to use all of your energy on anger? Stop judging men so harshly, and men will stop judging you so harshly. Believe me, when you become understanding of men and other men's situations, men will be more understanding of you and treat you the way you want to be treated. But if you want love, you have to give love."

"Pam," Wanda said, "every last one of us has been hurt by a man. And every last one of us done hurt a man! You just got too much damn pride! Let that shit go! That's life! You hurt and you get hurt! Now move the hell on!"

"I miss this!" Tazzy said.

"I don't!" Valerie joked.

"Wanda, did you see your girl up there?" Darsha asked, changing the subject.

"What girl?" Wanda asked.

"The crazy chick from Johnny's office."

"What crazy chick?"

"The big chick!"

"Kimberly?" Wanda asked.

"I guess," Darsha said, "the one who chased us out of Johnny's office."

"Kimberly's here?" I asked.

"I think that's her," Darsha said. "It can't be two of them walking around here."

"I'm gonna go talk to her," Wanda said, heading for the stairs. Before Anise's murder, Wanda and Kimberly had become good friends. Wanda had taken Kimberly to lunch and had her hair styled. Although Wanda was quite generous and kind to Kimberly, she refused to accept any attention for it. She made me promise to keep her relationship with Kimberly a secret. At first I thought she was ashamed, but I truly believe she was just being modest.

"Me too," I said, following Wanda. "Alicia, you coming? Our guests are probably wondering where we are."

"I'll be up there in a minute, Johnny," Alicia said. "There's no telling when me and my girls will be together again."

"Come on, Cynt, let's go," Mike said, taking Cynthia's hand. "You don't need to be around all of this masochistic women's movement."

"Masochistic women's movement?" Valerie said. "What the hell?"

"You ain't got to worry about that, Valerie!" Wanda said. "You ain't no damn woman!"

"Keep on, Wanda!" Valerie said. "You gon' make me whoop yo' ass yet."

"Come on, Wanda," I said, pushing her up the stairs.

Wanda and I went upstairs to look for Kimberly. We found her playing with the children.

"Aw," Wanda said, "bless her retarded little heart."

"Stop it!" I said.

"Okay." Wanda laughed. "You know I'm just playing."

"Kimberly," I said, tapping her on the shoulder.

"Hey, Dr. Forrester. How are you?"

"I'm fine, how are you?"

"I'm doing good," Kimberly said.

"Hi," Wanda said.

"Hi!" Kimberly said excitedly. "You're my friend!"

"Yes," Wanda said, "I'm your friend. How you been?"

"I've been a bad girl."

"What did you do?" Wanda asked.

"I saw her hurt my friend and I ran away. I didn't help my friend and she hurt her. She hurt real, real bad."

"Who hurt her real, real bad?" Wanda asked.

I was just as curious as Wanda at that point, so I didn't stop her interrogation. As a matter of fact, I asked Kimberly to follow us into an unoccupied room.

"Now what lady are you talking about?"

"The lady who hurt my friend."

"I know it was the lady who hurt your friend," Wanda said, "but who was it? What did she look like? Describe her?"

"I don't remember," Kimberly said.

"Come on now, Kim," Wanda said, becoming anxious, "what did she look like?"

"I don't remember!" Kimberly said very nervously.

"Was she big? Was she little? Was she tall? Was she short?" Wanda asked.

"There she is," Wanda said, pointing behind us.

"Where?" I asked, turning around and looking behind me.

"Where?" Wanda shouted. "Where she at?"

"That way!" Kimberly said.

There were people walking back and forth past the door so we didn't know exactly who Kimberly was pointing toward.

"We'll be back!" I said, grabbing Wanda's arm.

We walked around my house looking at every woman suspiciously, but the fact remained that we didn't know who we were looking for, or what she looked like.

"Damn!" Wanda said as we met back in the room with Kimberly. "Did you see anybody strange?"

"No," I said.

"Sweetie," Wanda said, "Can you describe the woman you just saw?"

"I don't remember," Kimberly said withdrawing again.

"Okay," Wanda said. "Okay, sweetheart."

Wanda and I left Kimberly alone and walked out of the room.

"I don't know how you do it," Wanda said.

"Do what?" I asked.

"Be patient like that with Kimberly."

"It's nothing to me, not even a second thought."

"Well, God was right when He said He was going to protect the young and the foolish, 'cause I was about to stick my foot in Kim's ass!"

"Would you shut up?" I laughed out loud.

"I'm just playing!" Wanda said. "I still get my free sessions, right?"

"Yeah, but you're going to get them from Rosemary."

"Your secretary?" Wanda asked. "She weird herself."

"You'll be fine."

"If I come out of that office crazy, I'm suing!"

"Cut it out! You're already crazy!" I said while walking out of the room. "I better make my rounds."

"Okay," Wanda said.

"Keep an eye on Kimberly for me."

"I got you!" Wanda said.

I continued to walk around and greet guests. As I spoke to each woman, I thought to myself that maybe she was the woman who killed Anise.

"I can't thank you all enough for everything you've done for me," I said.

"You're welcome," Ms. Hattley said.

"We're just glad we were able to prove what we knew all along," Ms. Carroll said, "that you were an innocent man."

"I have to admit it!" Stacey said. "I was being selfish. I couldn't afford to lose my best friend and confidant, now could I?"

"No," I said, wondering how far Stacey would go to keep her one and only friend from going to prison. I walked on and met Betty and David.

"Nice party, Dr. Forrester," Betty said.

"Thank you, Betty," I said. "How are you doing tonight, David?"

"Great," David said. "Enjoying myself."

"Good."

"You know I can't thank you enough for getting up there on that stand," Betty said.

"Oh, come on now, Betty, you would have done the same thing for me."

"You think?" Betty asked.

Again, my mind began to wander. I was curious to know why she would ask that question. I know it was far-fetched, but maybe she knew something about Anise's murder. My mind became so suspicious that I wondered if she was the woman who killed Anise. She may have known about my affair with one of my patients and thought that, if my affair became public, I would have my license revoked. That would ruin any chance for her to have custody of her child. I was the only chance she had. Think about it, how far would you go to be with your child?

I continued on and then stopped and talked to Veronica and Tim. Veronica was feeling much better. Her health had been completely restored. Her weight was back to a consistent one hundred twenty-five-pounds. I was proud of her recovery and I let her know. "Oh my! Look at you!"

"Fabulous, huh?" Tim said.

"Oh, stop!" Veronica said.

"Seriously, you are stunning!" I said. "Absolutely stunning!"

"Thank you," Veronica said. "I couldn't have made it through without you. I can't thank you enough."

"I don't know what to say, I was just doing my job."

"No," Tim said, "before my wife came into your office she had all but given up on beating that dreaded disease."

"You gave me a sense of confidence to fight," Veronica said. "I told Tim one day that you were the key to my survival. You were the answer to my prayers."

Veronica laughed, but I didn't. I remembered the day she was taken to the hospital. It was the same day Anise was murdered.

I thought about the injuries she sustained that day which put her in the hospital. Maybe those bruises weren't the result of the accident. Maybe those bruises were the result of a fight with Anise.

Of course that doesn't explain the death of the bodyguard. She was way too weak to battle a man of that size, even on her best day. However, he was shot in the back of the hotel. She could have lured him away from Anise's room, shot him, and then went upstairs and killed Anise. Or maybe I was just reaching for straws.

There were two people alive who knew who killed Anise, Kimberly and the murderer. Unfortunately, the murderer wouldn't tell, and Kimberly couldn't tell. But whoever the murderer was, she was walking around in my house, pretending to be my friend after making me spend nearly a year in prison.

"Hey you," Alicia said. "Ready to escort this beautiful maiden around the castle?"

"It would be my pleasure," I said.

"Then what are we waiting for?" Alicia said, placing her arm in mine.

"There's something strange about tonight," I said.

"What?" Alicia asked.

"Kimberly told Wanda and me that the woman she saw hurting Anise was in this house. But I could never get her and the woman in the same room for her to pick her out. And she doesn't seem to be able to describe her."

"Oh, okay," Alicia said.

"I need to speak to her anyway before she leaves. I have to make sure she has some type of understanding of her inheritance from Anise's will. Come with me."

"Uh, you go ahead, baby," Alicia said nervously.

I immediately thought about Alicia's refusal to come upstairs with me while she was in the basement once Kimberly's name was mentioned. If I didn't know better, I would have thought Alicia was avoiding being around Kimberly.

"Alicia? Is there something you want to tell me?"

"Uh," Alicia said, "no, no baby."

"What's going on?"

"I," Alicia said. "I..."

As Alicia was beginning to speak a strange woman I had never seen before walked up to us and shook my hand. "Are you Dr. Johnson Forrester?"

"Yes, I am."

"My name is Seneca Rogers."

"Have we met?"

"No, we haven't," Seneca said. "I don't know if you killed that bitch or not, but if you did, wives all across this country owe you a huge thanks. And instead of putting you on trial, they should have been throwing you a party."

"I don't think anybody deserves to suffer what Anise suffered, ma'am."

"You would if she was sleeping with your husband," Seneca said. "That bitch used my husband to start her career. She took his career, his money, and then she took his mind! So as far as I'm concerned, she's better off where she is. Dead!"

Seneca turned around and walked away.

"What was that all about?" I asked.

"I don't know," Alicia said. "But she was mad!"

"Scary," I said. "Let's find Kimberly."

"No, you go honey," Alicia said. "That's your patient and she'll probably feel comfortable talking to you alone."

"Okay. But don't go far."

"I won't," Alicia said.

Again, Alicia refused to be in the same room with Kimberly. I found Kimberly and Wanda and we went to my basement for privacy. Wanda had no idea why I called her in there. Before she could begin with her jokes, I made it perfectly clear that this was a very serious matter. Although Wanda had a rough exterior and a street mentality, she had a heart of gold. If you treated her right, she would do anything for you. That's why I wanted her to be Kimberly's legal guardian.

I had Wanda sit across from me and then I asked Kimberly to sit in another chair on the other side of the room so that she wouldn't be a distraction. Her coherency came and went depending on the day. This was one of those days when she wasn't in tune with reality. She sat in the chair and played with a doll. She was having fun and could have cared less about the discussion Wanda and I were having.

"I suppose you're wondering why I called you in here, Wanda?"

"Yup."

"Well, as you know, Kimberly has some issues that require assistance when it comes to making decisions. Right now, if she doesn't find someone to act as her legal guardian until she is capable of functioning on her own, she is going to be put in an asylum."

"And you're telling me that because?" Wanda said.

"Because I was wondering if you would consider acting as her legal guardian until she is better."

"Johnny," Wanda said, "why can't she stay with you? Yo' house four times bigger than mine."

"I would like nothing more, but there are certain legal stipulations that prohibit me from acting as anything other than her doctor. And I had a hard enough time convincing Alicia to take in Shante."

"I can't take her around my kids!" Wanda said.

"Wanda," I said, "I've been around your kids, and if anybody's in danger, it's Kimberly. "

"Good point!" Wanda laughed. "But that's a huge responsibility and I don't really even know her."

"I understand if you can't. It's a difficult situation and it's not your responsibility. And she doesn't need to live with you. She only needs to have someone to legally make decisions for her that she is mentally incompetent of making on her own."

"What's gon' happen if I don't be her guardian?"

"They will lock her away and that will set her back years," I said. "I guess that's that. You were my last hope."

"Damn," Wanda said, looking over at Kimberly.

"Actually, you were *her* last hope."

"Damn! Damn! Damn!" Wanda said. "Okay! Shit! I'll do it! I have to convince my husband but I'm sure he'll let me do it. But if she go Lizzie Borden on us, it's gon' be on your conscience!"

"She wouldn't hurt a fly."

"I know," Wanda said. "Bless her insane little heart. Look at her over there probably somewhere on Mars."

"Wanda! That has to stop! No more retarded jokes."

"She can't hear me," Wanda said.

"Still, no more retarded jokes."

"Alright, I can't have no fun!" Wanda folded her arms.

"Whatever," I said. "Now, I have some more information for you that I think you will find extremely enjoyable."

"What?" Wanda said, trying not to be sarcastic.

"Well," I said, smiling and pulling out Anise's will. "Once you have become Kimberly's legal guardian, you will be responsible for maintaining her inheritance until she is capable of making her own decisions."

"What inheritance?" Wanda sat upright.

"Kimberly Mathis is also the half-sister of Anise Lawrence. Anise left Kimberly seventy-five percent of her net worth."

"Who the hell is Anise?"

"I'm sorry, you know her as Gizelle."

"Gizelle?" Wanda said, becoming excited. "Rich, dead Gizelle?"

"One and the same."

"Now, of course it doesn't matter," Wanda said. "But how much is seventy-five percent?"

"It's," I said, looking down at the numbers, "roughly eighteen million dollars."

"WHAT?" Wanda screamed.

"Now, it won't be your money, Wanda," I said. "You'll just have to make sure her bills are paid and her health is fine and everything is functioning normally. Think you can handle that?"

"Eighteen million dollars!" Wanda shouted, clutching at her heart.

"Yes." I chuckled. "Eighteen million dollars."

"Oh, I'm 'bout to have a heart attack!"

"Remember, it's not your money, Wanda. It's Kimberly's."

"I don't care whose money it is, just to be associated with eighteen million dollars is enough to give me a heart attack."

"Neither you nor Kimberly will have access to all of the money at once. She will be allotted a certain amount per month."

"I don't care!" Wanda shouted. "Eighteen million dollars! Where the contract at? Where do I need to sign?"

"What about your husband? Don't you need to talk to him?"

"Hell nawl!" Wanda said. "For eighteen million dollars, I'll get rid of him and get me another one!"

"Wanda."

"I know! I know! It ain't my money!"

"Anise's attorneys will meet with us in a couple of days and we can get everything signed, sealed and delivered."

"Lord, have mercy!" Wanda said while rubbing her forehead. "Eighteen million dollars."

Beep! Beep! Beep!

"Excuse me," I said, looking down at my cell phone.

I had received a new text message. I looked at the number and it was restricted. I opened the message and it read, *I'm sorry you paid for my crime. I need to talk to you. When you are alone, I will come back.*

I looked over at Kimberly and she was looking at me. I watched as she slowly slid her cell phone into her pocket. I opened my mouth to speak to her but then decided to remain silent.

"Well, that's about it, Wanda," I said. "We will go over the specifics with Anise's attorneys and that should do it."

"Eighteen million dollars," Wanda repeated.

"I have to take care of some business, Wanda, can you and Kimberly excuse me, please?"

"Oh, sure," Wanda said, taking Kimberly by the arm. "Come on, baby girl."

As Wanda and Kimberly were going up the stairs, Kimberly looked back at me and nodded. I went to my desk and sat down. I stared at the steps waiting for someone to walk down. But no one did. I began to think the text message was a prank. Only I wasn't laughing. I was coming to the realization that, no matter how much I learned about women, I would never know enough. But there is one thing I know for certain.

The admission of ignorance *is* the beginning of wisdom. Some say that this hypothesis does not hold true in certain scenarios. But after traveling three hundred and sixty degrees to discover the nature of a woman, the result of my professional and personal analysis of that theory is this: it is precise and exact.

There are over six billion people in the world and we are separated by only a mere six degrees. In the grander scheme of life, six degrees out of three hundred and sixty degrees can be construed as minuscule. But each journey begins with a solitary degree, or a solitary step. It all depends on those whom you meet along the way. Each person that you meet connects the three hundred and sixty-degree circle from your origination to your destination. Case in point, the journey to find one's self can be a pilgrimage around the world or a walk from the backyard to the basement.

To arrive at my destination, I suffered pain, shame, love, and joy. Along the way, each woman that I met provided the connection to the next woman to lead me through my journey. It should not be surprising that my discovery *of* the nature of a man would ultimately be my discovery *from* the nature of a woman.

After a while, I realized no one was going to walk down those stairs. I had again misjudged the nature of a woman based on my unreliable instincts. I sat back and rocked in my chair a few times, and then I stood to go upstairs. All of a sudden, the door slowly opened and I saw a woman walk down the stairs. Finally she came into view. It made no sense at all, but then again, it made absolutely sense.

ABOUT THE AUTHOR

Born in Saginaw, Michigan as the seventeenth of eighteen children to Henry and Orabell Stephens, Sylvester Stephens was introduced to the arts by his elder siblings. His desire for writing was developed not by the literature of Shakespeare, or the poetry of Robert Frost, but by the ever melodic, soulful voices of the sound of Motown. The lyrics that emanated from the phonograph or record player, as it was called, created images of stories in his mind.

Sylvester later attended Jackson State University in Jackson, Mississippi where he honed his craft for literature. While attending college, Sylvester became a member of the largest international fraternity in the world, the Free and Accepted Masons, Prince Hall Affiliated.

Sylvester has taught creative writing courses for the Young Voices United Youth Program and has raised literacy awareness with poetry contests and book fairs in inner city schools.

Sylvester's first novel, *Our Time Has Come* was released in October, 2004. *The Office Girls*, published by Strebor Books in January, 2008, was his second novel.

Sylvester has also written the screenplays to *The Office Girls*, *The Road to Redemption* and *Our Time Has Come!*

Sylvester's sensational stage plays include *Our Time Has Come*, *The Nature of a Woman*, *Max*, *The Office Girls*, *My Little Secret*, and *Every Knee Shall Bow*.

IF YOU ENJOYED "THE NATURE OF A WOMAN,"
FIND OUT WHERE IT ALL STARTED WITH

The Office girls

BY SYLVESTER STEPHENS
AVAILABLE FROM STREBOR BOOKS

A topsy-turvy ride through corporate America, where the male is the minority and must face a comedic blend of sex discrimination and harassment which threatens his sanity.

Michael Forrester, a floundering author, has been reduced to writing articles for a local newspaper under a pseudonym. When the newspaper runs an article he finds offensive to African-American men, he writes a rebuttal, which offends so many women it gets him fired. Michael then sets out to write a book that proves corporate women are just as scandalous, competitive, and insensitive as their male counterparts.

But when he manipulates events to get hired into an office that is staffed by all women, events quickly spiral out of control. As romances sprout like weeds and Michael finds himself fighting for the women he works alongside, rather than against them, the question is whether he will be able to focus on his work, keep his flings a secret, and achieve the success he has always dreamed of.

In turns hilarious, sobering, and eye-opening, *The Office Girls* tells the story of every woman who works in the corporate world and the challenges she faces on a daily basis.